John Esten Cooke

Beatrice Hallam

A novel

John Esten Cooke

Beatrice Hallam
A novel

ISBN/EAN: 9783337000462

Printed in Europe, USA, Canada, Australia, Japan

Cover: Foto ©Andreas Hilbeck / pixelio.de

More available books at **www.hansebooks.com**

A Novel.

BY JOHN ESTEN COOKE,

AUTHOR OF

"SURRY OF EAGLES NEST," "MOHUN," "HILT
TO HILT," ETC., ETC.

NEW YORK:

G. W. Dillingham, Publisher,

SUCCESSOR TO G. W. CARLETON & CO.

MDCCCXCII.

BEATRICE HALLAM.

PROLOGUE

THE memories of men are full of old romances: but they will not speak—our skalds. King Arthur lies still wounded grievously, in the far island valley of Avilyon: Lord Odin in the misty death realm: Balder the Beautiful, sought long by great Hermoder, lives beyond Hela's portals, and will bless his people some day when he comes. But when? King Arthur ever *is to* come: Odin will one day wind his horn and clash his wild barbaric cymbals through the Nordland pines as he returns, but not in our generation: Balder will rise from sleep and shine again the white sun god on his world. But always these things will be: Arthur and the rest are meanwhile sleeping.

Romance is history: the illustration may be lame—the truth is melancholy. Because the men whose memories hold this history will not speak, it dies away with them: the great past goes deeper and deeper into mist: becomes finally a dying strain of music, and is no more remembered forever.

Thinking these thoughts I have thought it well to set down here some incidents which took place on Virginia soil and in which an ancestor of my family had no small part to write my family romance in a single word, and also, though following a connecting thread, a leading idea, to speak briefly of the period to which these memories, as I may call them, do attach.

That period was very picturesque: illustrated and adorned, as it surely was, by such figures as one seldom sees now on the earth. Often in my evening reveries, assisted by the partial gloom resulting from the struggles of the darkness and the dying firelight, I endeavor, and not wholly without success, to summon from their sleep these stalwart cavaliers, and tender, graceful dames of the far past. They rise before me and glide onward—manly faces, with clear eyes and lofty brows, and firm lips covered with the knightly fringe : soft, tender faces, with bright eyes and gracious smiles and winning gestures ; all the life and splendor of the past again becomes incarnate ! How plain the embroidered doublet, and the sword-belt, and the powdered hair, and hat adorned with its wide floating feather ! How real are the ruffled breasts and hands, the long-flapped waistcoats, and the buckled shoes ! And then the fairer forms : they come as plainly with their looped-back gowns all glittering with gold and silver flowers, and on their heads great masses of curls with pearls interwoven ! See the gracious smiles and musical movement—all the graces which made those dead dames so attractive to the outward eye—as their pure faithful natures made them priceless to the eyes of the heart.

CHAPTER I.

AN INTERIOR WITH PORTRAITS.

On a splendid October afternoon, in the year of our Lord 1763, two persons who will appear frequently in this history were seated in the great dining-room of Effingham Hall.

But let us first say a few words of this old mansion. Effingham Hall was a stately edifice not far from Williamsburg, which, as every body knows, was at that period the capital city of the colony of Virginia. The hall was constructed of elegant brick brought over from England : and from the great portico in front of the building a beautiful rolling country of hills and valleys, field and forest, spread itself pleasantly before the eye, bounded far off along the circling belt of woods by the bright waters of the noble river.

Entering the large hall of the old house, you had before you, walls covered with deers' antlers, fishing-rods, and guns : portraits of cavaliers, and dames and children : even carefully painted pictures of celebrated race-horses, on whose speed and bottom many thousands of pounds had been staked as lost and won in their day and generation.

On one side of the hall a broad staircase with oaken balustrade led to the numerous apartments above : and on the opposite side, a door gave entrance into the great dining room.

The dining-room was decorated with great elegance :— the carved oak wainscot extending above the mantelpiece in an unbroken expanse of fruits and flowers, hideous laughing faces, and long foamy surges to the cornice. The furniture was in the Louis Quatorze style, which the reader is familiar with, from its reproduction in our own day ; and the chairs were the same low-seated affairs, with high carved backs, which are now seen. There were Chelsea figures, and a sideboard full of plate, and a Japan cabinet, and a Kidderminster carpet, and huge andirons. On the andirons crackled a few twigs lost in the great country fireplace.

On the wall hung a dozen pictures of gay gallants, brave warriors, and dames, whose eyes outshone their diamonds :— and more than one ancestor looked grimly down, clad in cuirass and armlets, and holding in his mailed hand the sword which had done bloody service in its time. The lady portraits, as an invariable rule, were decorated with sunset clouds of yellow lace—the bright locks were powdered, and many little black patches set off the dazzling fairness of the rounded chins. Lapdogs nestled on the satin laps : and not one of the gay dames but seemed to be smiling, with her head bent sidewise fascinatingly on the courtly or warlike figures ranged with them in a long glittering line.

These portraits are worth looking up to, but those which we promised the reader are real.

In one of the carved chairs, if any thing more uncomfortable than all the rest, sits, or rather lounges, a young man of about twenty-five. He is very richly clad, and in a costume which would be apt to attract a large share of attention in our own day, when dress seems to have become a mere covering, and the prosaic tendencies of the age are to despise every thing but what ministers to actual material pleasure.

The gentleman before us lives fortunately one hundred years before our day : and suffers from an opposite tendency in costume. His head is covered with a long flowing peruke, heavy with powder, and the drop curls hang down on his cheeks ambrosially : his cheeks are delicately rouged, and two patches, arranged with matchless art, complete the distinguished tout ensemble of the handsome face.   At breast, a cloud of lace reposes on the rich embroidery of his figured satin waistcoat, reaching to his knees :—this lace is *voint de Venise* and white, that fashion having come in just one month since.   The sleeves of his rich doublet are turned back to his elbows, and are as large as a bushel—the opening being filled up, however, with long ruffles, which reach down over the delicate jewelled hand.   He wears silk stockings of spotless white, and his feet are cased in slippers of Spanish leather, adorned with diamond buckles.   Add velvet garters below the knee :—a little muff of leopard-skin reposing near at hand upon a chair—not omitting a snuff-box peeping from the pocket, and Mr. Champ Effingham, just from Oxford and his grand tour, is before you with his various surroundings.

He is reading the work which some time since attained to such extreme popularity, Mr. Joseph Addison's serial, "The Spectator,"—collected now for its great merits, into bound volumes.   Mr. Effingham reads with a languid air, just as he sits, and turns over the leaves with an ivory paper cutter, which he brought from Venice with the plate glass yonder on the sideboard near the silver baskets and pitchers.   This languor is too perfect to be wholly affected, and when he yawns, as he does frequently, Mr. Effingham applies himself to that task very earnestly.

In one of these paroxysms of weariness the volume slips from his hand to the floor.

"My book," he says to a negro boy, who has just brought in some dishes.   The boy hastens respectfully to obey—crossing the whole width of the room for that purpose.   Mr. Effingham then continues reading.

Now for the other occupant of the apartment.   She sits near the open window, looking out upon the lawn and breathing the pure delicious air of October as she works.   She is clad in the usual child's costume of the period (she is only eleven or twelve), namely, a sort of half coat, half frock, reaching scarcely below the knees; an embroidered undervest; scarlet silk stockings with golden clocks, and little rosetted shoes with high red heels.   Her hair is unpowdered, and hangs in curls upon her neck and bare shoulders. ·Her little fingers are busily at work upon a piece of embroidery which represents or is to represent a white water dog upon an intensely emerald back-ground, and she addresses herself to this occupation with a business air which is irresistibly amusing, and no less pleasant to behold. There is about the child, in her movements, attitude, expression, every thing, a freshness and innocence which is only possessed by children. This is Miss Kate Effingham, whose parents died in her infancy, for which reason the little sunbeam was taken by the squire, her father's brother.

Kate seems delighted with the progress she has made in delineating Carlo, as she calls him, and pauses a moment to survey her brilliant handiwork. She then opens her ivory decorated work-box to select another shade of silk, holding it on her lap by the low-silled open window.

But disastrous event! Just as she had found what she wanted, just as she had procured the exact shade for Carlo's ears, just as she closed the pretty box, full of all manner of little elegant instruments of needle-work—she heard an impatient exclamation of weariness and disdain, something fluttered through the air, and this something striking the handsome box delicately balanced on Kate's knees, precipitated it, with its whole contents, through the window to the lawn beneath.

The explanation of this sudden event is, that Mr. Effingham has become tired of the "Spectator," hurled it sidewise from him without looking; and thus the volume has, after its habit, produced a decided sensation, throwing the work-box upon the lawn, and Kate into utter despair.

CHAPTER II.

A SERIES OF CATASTROPHES, ENDING IN A FAMILY TABLEAU.

KATE, spite of her great age and near approach to womanhood, is almost ready to cry:

"Oh cousin Champ!" she says, ' how could you!"

Mr. Effingham yawns.

" Did you speak to me, Katy ? " he says languidly.

" Yes ! "

" Why, what's the matter ? "

" You've ruined my work-box ! "

" I ! "

" Yes, you knocked it out of the window with your book —and I think it was not kind," Kate says, pouting, and leaning out of the window to gaze at the prostrate work-box.

Mr. Effingham sees the catastrophe at a glance, and apparently smitten with remorse, tries to ascertain the extent of the injury. But the morning seems an unlucky one for him. As he places his heel upon the carpet, he unfortunately treads with his whole weight upon the long silky ear of his sister's favorite lapdog Orange, who is about the size of the fruit from which he takes his name.

Orange utters a yell sufficiently loud to arouse from their sleep the seven champions of Christendom.

Drawn by his successive yells, a lady appears at the door and enters the apartment hurriedly.

Miss Alethea, only sister of Mr. Effingham, is a lady of about thirty, with a clear complexion, serene eyes, her hair trained back into a tower ; and with an extremely stately and dignified expression. She looks like the president of a benevolent society, and the very sight of her erect head, the very rustle of her black silk dress has been known to strike terror into evil-doers.

" Who has hurt Orange ? " she says, severely ; " here, poor fellow !—some one has hurt him ! "

Orange yells much louder, seeing his defender.

" What in the world is the matter with him, Champ ? " she says ; " please answer me ! "

Mr. Effingham regales his nostrils with a pinch of snuff, and replies indifferently :

" Probably Orange has an indigestion, or perhaps he is uttering those horrible sounds because I stepped upon his ear."

" Stepped on his ear ! "

Mr. Effingham nods serenely.

" Really, you are too careless ! " Miss Alethea exclaims, and her black silk rustling, she goes to Orange and takes him in her arms.

But in brushing by Mr. Effingham her ample sleeve chances to strike that gentleman's snuff-box, and the contents of the useful article are discharged over little Kate, who coughing, sneezing, crying and laughing, perfects the scene.

"See what you have done, Alethea!" says Mr. Effingham, reproachfully, and yawning as he speaks; "you have thrown my snuff upon Kate."

And turning to the child:

"Never mind, Kate!" he says, "it's excellent snuff. It won't hurt you—now don't—"

With such observations Mr. Effingham is quieting the child, when another addition is made to the company.

This is in the person of a young gentleman of thirteen or fourteen—Master Willie Effingham, Mr. Champ's brother, and a devoted admirer of Kate.

Will, seeing his sweetheart in tears, bustles up, upon his little rosetted shoes, flirting his little round-skirted coat, and fiercely demands of the company at large:

"Who made Kate cry!"

"Oh, the snuff! the snuff!" says Kate, crying and laughing.

"Whose snuff!" says Will, indignantly.

"Mine," replies Mr. Effingham; "there are no excuses to be made; arrange the terms of the combat."

"For shame, Champ!" says Miss Alethea, with stately dignity; "you jest at Willie, but I think his behavior very honorable."

"Ah!" you are an advocate of duelling, then, my dear madam?" drawls Mr. Effingham.

"No, I am not; but your snuff made Kate cry."

"Deign to recall the slight circumstance that your sleeve discharged it from my hand."

"Never mind, I think Will right."

Will raises his head proudly.

"Kate is his favorite and playmate—"

"As Orange is yours," says Mr. Effingham, languidly, the lapdog having uttered an expiring howl. "Well, well, don't let us argue; I am ready to make the amende to my little Kate—we are all dear to each other—so here, is my lace handkerchief, *ma mignonette*, to wipe away the snuff—"

Kate laughs.

' And here's a kiss, to make friends for the snuff and the work box."

Kate wrung her hands, and says, laughing and pouting·
" Oh my box! my box !"

" Your box !" says Will, who has been looking daggers at Mr. Effingham for kissing the child.

" Yes! my poor box !"

" Never mind, Katy," says Mr. Effingham, smiling as he passes his hand caressingly over the little head ; " I unfortunately broke it, but you shall have one twice as handsome ; I saw one in Williamsburg yesterday, which I thought of getting for Clare Lee—but you shall have it."

" Oh, thankee!" cries Kate, " but I oughtn't to take cousin Clare's, you know ! And there's papa! he's got my box !"

Kate springs forward to meet the squire—the head of the house—who enters at the door.

The squire is a gentleman of fifty-five or sixty, with an open frank face, clear, honest eyes, and his carriage is bold, free, and somewhat pompous.   He is clad much more simply than his eldest son, his coat having upon it not a particle of embroidery, and his long plain waistcoat buttoning up to the chin : below which a white cravat and an indication only of frill are visible.   His limbs are cased in thick, strong and comfortable cloth, and woollen, and he wears boots, very large and serviceable, to which strong spurs are attached. His broad, fine brow, full of intelligence and grace, is covered by an old cocked hat, which, having lost the loops which held it in the three-cornered shape, is now rolled up upon each side ; and his manner in walking, speaking, arguing, reading, is much after the description of his costume—plain, straightforward, and though somewhat pompous, destitute of finery and ornament.   He is the head of a princely establishment, he has thousands of acres, and hundreds of negroes, he is a justice, and has sat often in the House of Burgesses : he is rich, a dignitary, every body knows it,—why should he strive to ape elegancies, and trouble himself about the impression he produces?   He is simple and plain, as he conceives, because he is a great proprietor and can afford to wear rough clothes, and talk plainly.

His pomposity is not obtrusive, and it is tempered with

to much good breeding and benevolence that it does not detract from the pleasant impression produced by his honest face. As he enters now that face is brown and red with exercise upon his plantation—and he comes in with cheerful smiles; his rotund person, and long queue gathered by a ribbon smiling no less than his eyes.

In his hand is the unfortunate work-box, which has not, however, sustained any injury.

" Here 'tis, puss ! " says the squire, " nothing hurt—I picked up the scissors and the vest : and the grass was as soft as a cushion."

With which words the worthy squire sits down and wipes his brow.

" Oh, thank'ee, papa," says Kate—this is the child's name for him :—and she runs and takes his hat, and then climbs on his lap, and laughingly explains how cousin Champ hadn't meant to throw the box out—" because you know me and cousin Champ are great favorites of each other's : and I am his pet."

Having achieved this speech, which she utters with a rush of laughter in her voice, Kate hugs her box, and returns to Carlo.

" Well, Champ," says the planter, " whither go you this afternoon—any where ? "

" I believe not," says Mr. Effingham.

" Still enamored of your ease, you jolly dog ! "

" The Epicurean philosophy is greatly to my taste," says Mr. Effingham, " riding wearies me."

" Every thing does."

" Ah ?"

" Yes, sir : you are the finest fine gentleman in the Colony."

This half compliment produces no effect upon Mr. Effingham, who yawns.

" Why not go and see Clare Lee ?—Clary's the most bewitching little creature in the world," says the squire, unfolding a copy of the " Virginia Gazette," which he draws from his pocket.

" Clare Lee ? " says Mr. Effingham.

" Yes, sir : she's a little beauty."

" Well, so she is."

" And as good as an angel."

" Hazardous, that, sir."

" No, sir ! " exclaims the squire, " it is true ! Zounds ! she's too good for any mortal man."

" Consequently, as I am a mortal man—I draw the inference," says Mr. Effingham.

" Well, she's too good for you, sir : you had better go and see her : it may improve you."

Mr. Effingham relents.

" I think that is very desirable, sir," he says, " and on my word, I'll go. Please ring that bell."

The squire without protest takes up the small silver bell and rings it. Mr. Effingham orders his horse—descends soon in boots and riding gloves, and mounting, sets forth towards the abode of the angel—Miss Clare Lee.

CHAPTER III.

SOMETHING LIKE AN ADVENTURE.

LEAVING the group which we have seen assemble in the drawing-room of Effingham Hall, let us follow the worthy whose misdeeds in connection with the work-box and lapdog caused the dramatic assemblage.

Mr. Effingham, elegantly clad in a riding costume, perfect in its appointment, and mounted on a splendid courser which he had appropriated from his father's stud, took his way through the fresh woods towards Riverhead, the residence of Mr. Lee and his two daughters, Henrietta and Clare. But Mr. Effingham was much too sensible a gentleman to bore himself, as we say to-day, with the fine scenery of October—the fair blue skies, with their snowy clouds floating on like ships towards the clear horizon—the variegated woods full of singing birds—the streams dancing in the sun—and all the myriad attractions of an autumn afternoon. His taste had been shaped in London, and the glare of lights,

the noise of revelry, and gay encounter of bright wits and
beauty, had long since deprived him of the faculty of admiring
such an insipid thing as simple nature.   There was little
affectation about the worthy gentleman in reality: he was
really and truly worn out.   Accustomed for some length of
time to every species of dissipation, his character had been
seriously injured—his freshness was gone, and he sought
now for nothing so much as *emotions.*   We shall see if he
was fortunate in his search.

At times, as he went along, Mr. Effingham indulged in a
sort of silent, well-bred laughter, at the scene he had just
witnessed at the Hall.

"What a farce the world is," he said, philosophically,
"we all run after something—one has his literary ambition,
another political aspiration: this young lady wishes to marry
a lord: that young gentleman's highest hope in life is, that
his comedy may not be damned for its want of freedom—the
polite word now I understand.   It's all weariness: I really
begin to think that little Katy and Alethea, with their embroidery and lapdogs, are the most sensible after all.   Embroidery and lapdogs cost less, and——"

Mr. Effingham drew up suddenly—so suddenly, that his
horse rose on his haunches, and tossed his head aloft.

The meaning of this movement was simply that he saw
before him in the centre of the road he was following, a lady,
who apparently awaited his approach.

The lady was mounted upon a tall white horse, which
stood perfectly quiet in the middle of the road, and seemed
to be docility itself, though the fiery eyes contradicted this
first impression.   Rather would one acquainted with the singular character of horses have said that this animal was
subdued by the gentle hand of his rider, and so laid aside
from pure affection, all his waywardness.

This rider was a young girl about eighteen, and of rare
and extraordinary beauty.   Her hair—so much as was visible beneath her hood—seemed to be dark chestnut, and her
complexion was dazzling.   The eyes were large, full, and
dark—instinct with fire and softness, feminine modesty, and
collected firmness—the firmness, however, predominating.
But the lips were different.   They were the lips of a child—
soft, guileless, tender, confiding: they were purity and in

2

nocence itself, and seemed to say, that however much the
brain might become hard and worldly, the heart of this young
woman never could be other than the tender and delicately
sensitive heart of a child.

She was clad in a riding-dress of pearl color—and from
the uniformity of this tint, it seemed to be a favorite with her.
The hood was of silk, and the delicately-gloved hand held a
little ivory-handled riding whip, which now dangled at her
side.   The other gloved hand supported her cheek; and in
this position the unknown lady calmly awaited Mr. Effingham's approach still nearer, though he was already nearly
touching her.

Mr. Effingham took off his hat and bowed with elegant
courtesy.   The lady returned this inclination by a graceful
movement of her head.

"Would you be kind enough to point out the road to the
town of Williamsburg, sir ? " she said, in a calm and clear
voice.

"With great pleasure, madam," replied Mr. Effingham,
"you have lost your way ! "

"Yes, sir, very strangely, and as evening drew on, was
afraid of being benighted."

"You have but to follow this road until you reach
Effingham Hall, madam," he said—"the house in the distance yonder : then turn to the left, and you are in the
highway to town."

"Thanks, sir," the young girl said, with another calm
inclination of her head : and she touched her horse with
the whip.

"But cannot I accompany you ? " asked Mr. Effingham,
whose curiosity was greatly aroused, and found his eyes, he
knew not why, riveted to the rare beauty of his companion's
face, "do you not need me as a guide ? "

"Indeed, I think not, sir," she said, with the same calmness, your direction is very plain, and I am accustomed to
ride by myself."

"But really," began Mr. Effingham, somewhat piqued,
"I know it is intrusive—I know I have not the honor——"

She interrupted him with her immovable calmness.

"You would say you do not know me, and that your offer
is intrusive, I believe sir. I do not consider it so—it is very

kind : but I am not a fearful girl, and need not trouble you at all."

And she bowed.

" One moment, madam," said Mr. Effingham; " I am real ly dying with curiosity to know you. 'Tis very rude to say so, of course—but I am acquainted with every lady in the neighborhood, and I do not recall any former occasion upon which I had the pleasure—"

" It is very easily explained, sir," the young girl said.

" Madam—?"

" I do not live in the neighborhood—"

" Ah ?—no ?"

" And I am not a lady, sir : does not that explain it ?"

Mr. Effingham scarcely believed his ears : these astound-ing words were uttered with such perfect calmness that there was no possible room to suppose that they were meant for a jest. What then ? He could not speak : he only looked at her.

" You are surprised, sir," the young girl said, quite simply and gravely.

" Upon my word, madam—never have I—really—"

" Your surprise will not last long, sir."

" How, madam ?"

" Do you ever visit the town of Williamsburg ?"

" Frequently."

" Well, sir, I think you will see me again. Now I must continue my way, having returned you my very sincere thanks for your kindness."

With which words—words uttered in that wondrous voice of immovable calmness—the young girl again inclined her sumptuous head, touched her white horse with the whip, and slowly rode out of sight.

Mr. Effingham remained for several moments motionless, in the middle of the road, gazing with wide and astonished eyes after the beautiful equestrian. He was endeavoring by a tremendous mental exertion to solve the astounding problem of her identity. Vain was all his pondering—noth-ing came of all his thought, his knit brows, his lip gnawed ferociously, as he mused. Mr. Effingham was confident that he knew, at least by sight, every young lady at Williamsburg, and within a circuit of twenty miles, but this face was wholly unknown to him.   He had certainly never seen her before, and then the strange fact of her riding out alone : her self-possession : " she was accustomed to ride alone "—" she was not a lady "—" they should probably meet again "—what in the name of Fate, was tho meaning of all this ?

"May the fiend seize me, if the days of wandering knights and forlorn damsels, haunted castles and giants have not returned !" exclaimed Mr. Effingham, emphatically. And having thus disburdened his mind, he rode on—but still his mind dwelt on tho strange lady, and her more singular words.

Not a lady !" what could she mean ? was there ever since the days of the Sphinx so complete a puzzle !   In face, person, dress, and carriage she was every inch a lady—why then utter that astounding observation, enunciate that start-ling intelligence ? who could she be, however ? Mr. Effing-ham ran over in his mind, the whole of his friends and ac-quaintances, and could recollect no one whose face bore the slightest resemblance to that of the unknown lady.   He gave up in despair, finally, and struck his spurs into the noble ani-mal he rode, with unusual vigor.   The horse started forward, and in half an hour he had reached Riverhead.

------•------

CHAPTER IV.

THE ROSE AND THE VIOLET.

Two young ladies were walking upon the smooth-shaven lawn, which stretched unbroken save by a few noble oaks and clumps of shrubbery, from the fine old mansion to the wood-land on each side and the enclosure in front.

One of the ladies was tall and brilliant : her superb figure undulating with every movement would have graced a palace, and her bright eyes and merry lips were full of life and fire. She was clad with extreme richness, and the fine silks and velvets which she wore shone brilliantly in the clear October

sunlight as she moved. This sheen of silk seemed her appropriate accompaniment, and the diamond necklace which
she wore was not observed. Her eyes and brilliant expression threw the silk and velvet and all jewels in the back-
ground. She looked the incarnation of aristocracy, using
that term in its colloquial sense, and seemed to brim with
mirth and merry witticisms from a pure sentiment of life
and superiority to every one.

Her companion was smaller in stature, and plainly
younger—apparently about nineteen. Her figure was more
delicate, her beauty more pensive and aerial. The squire's
criticism, or abandonment of all criticism, did not seem at
all extravagant. A profusion of golden hair, blue eyes full
of deep tenderness and instinct with a species of quiet happy
pensiveness—these, added to a complexion as fair as a lily
and as transparent as a fresh stream, made up a countenance
of exquisite beauty.

The first lady was Miss Henrietta Lee :—the second was
her sister, Miss Clare Lee, between whom and Mr. Effingham a sort of undeveloped courtship existed.

Mr. Effingham approached the ladies, trailing the feather
of his hat upon the grass.

"Ah! Mr. Effingham!" cried Henrietta, with a merry
laugh, "and as weary-looking as ever!"

"Still jesting, Miss Henrietta—or cousin Henrietta, as
you agree I may in future call you; have I presumed, and
may I address you by that pleasant name?"

"Certainly you may," said the laughing girl, "though I
believe the cousinship is rather distant."

"To my regret."

"Your regret?—truly?'

"In sober truth," replied Mr. Effingham, languidly twirling his cocked hat: "near cousins, you know, have many
agreeable privileges. Have they not, Miss Clare?"

Clare turned her soft, frank eyes on the young man and
smiled.

"That is enough," continued Mr. Effingham, "when a
lady smiles she always means yes."

"A hasty conclusion!" said Henrietta, "many a gay
cavalier on his knees before a lady has been laughed at."

"True, true: though I am most happy to say that I

have never had the bad fortune to verify the truth of your observation."

And smoothing gently the ruffles at his breast, Mr. Effingham yawned. Henrietta burst into laughter, and her brilliant eyes flashed mischievously.

Mr. Effingham looked round in apparent astonishment.

"If I may be permitted to inquire, Miss Henrietta, or cousin Henrietta, as I shall beg leave henceforth to call you ——"

"Oh, certainly!"

"What were you laughing at, pray?"

"Shall I tell you?'

"If you please."

"At you, then!"

"At me?"

"At you."

"I am glad to find my company so agreeably entertaining: true, I am in unusually excellent spirits."

"Spirits! you? Why you yawned most portentously this moment!"

"All habit—a bad habit, I confess: and to prove that I am not weary, I have an adventure to relate."

"An adventure?"

"Yes."

And Mr. Effingham, in an elegant, *petit maitre* manner, narrated his adventure, as he was pleased to call it, with the unknown horsewoman.

"Who could it have been?" said Clare.

"Who, indeed!" echoed Henrietta.

"Upon my soul, I don't know. Some wandering queen, or fairy, I suppose—this Virginia is the land of romance and magic. I think it very fortunate that she did not bid me dismount, seat myself behind her, and go off thus to fairyland with her. In which case," continued Mr. Effingham, gallantly, "I should not have experienced the happiness of gazing at your pleasant and beautiful countenances, cousins Henrietta and Clare."

"You are too kind!" laughed Henrietta.

"And not very sincere," said Clare, smiling.

"Not sincere?"

And Mr. Effingham's glance dwelt for a moment almost

tenderly on the face of Clare, who looked like a pure angel, in the bright crimson light of sunset.

" If you thought us so pleasant you would come oftener," she said, with a flitting blush.

" My poor society would only weary you, I fear," he said, ostensibly addressing both of the sisters, but looking at Clare, " I am a poor visitor."

Clare turned away and pulled a rose.

" It is not so far," she murmured, refusing plainly to accept the excuse, and speaking in so low a tone that Henrietta, who had taken some steps to meet her approaching father, did not hear the words.

" And if I came ? " whispered Mr. Effingham.

Clare turned away to hide her confusion.

" Could I hope, dear cousin Clare—dearest Clare !—"

Mr. Effingham was getting on. But Henrietta and Mr Lee approached.

" That you could—could— "

" Good evening, Champ," said Mr. Lee, a fine portly old gentleman, coming up arm in arm with Henrietta, " glad to see you."

Mr. Effingham bowed, and Clare bent down to examine, with profound curiosity, the rosebud which she held in her little hand.

" The evening was so fine, that I thought I could not spend it more agreeably than in a ride to Riverhead, sir," said Mr. Effingham.

" Delightful !—these August days are excellent for the corn ; what news ? "

" Nothing, sir—I have not seen the ' Gazette.' "

" Oh, the ' Gazette' never contains any intelligence: sometimes, it is true, we hear what is going on in Parliament, but it never condescends to afford us any news from Virginia. The tobacco on the south side may be all gone to the devil for any thing you read in the ' Gazette.' Here it is—an abominable sheet ! Ah ! I see we are to have a the atrical performance in Williamsburg next week," added the old gentleman, glancing over the paper, " Mr. Hallam and his ' Virginia Company of Comedians '—very politic, that addition of ' Virginia !'—are to perform *The Merchant of Venice*, by permission of his worship the Mayor, at the Old Theatre near the Capitol, he announces. Truly we are improving : really becoming civilized, in this barbarous *terra incognita.*

Mr. Effingham winced; he had more than once expressed a similar opinion of Virginia in good faith—not ironically—and the old gentleman's words seemed directed at himself. A moment's reflection, however, persuaded him that this could not be the case; he had not visited Riverhead a dozen times since his return from Oxford and London—and on those occasions had never touched upon the subject of Virginia and its dreadful deficiencies.

" A play ?" he said, " that is really good news :—but the ' Merchant of Venice' is not one of my acquaintances."

" Ah, you young men are wrong in giving up Will Shakespeare for the Steeles, Addisons, and Vanbrughs. Mr. Addison's essays are very pleasant and entertaining reading, and sure, there never was a finer gentleman than Sir Roger ;—but in the drama, Will Shakespeare distances him all to nothing."

" Let us go to see the play, papa," said Henrietta.

" Oh, yes," said Clare.

The old gentleman tenderly smoothed the bright golden hair.

" Certainly, if you wish it," he said.

" And may I request permission to accompany the party, ladies ?" said Mr. Effingham, languidly.

" How modest !" said Henrietta, laughing; " certainly you may go, sir. You will tell us when to hiss or applaud, you know, as you are just from London !"

" What a quick tongue she has !" said Mr. Lee, fondly; " well, we will all go, and see what the ' Virginia Company of Comedians' is like : not much, I fear."

" Oh, we'll have a delightful time," cried Clare, glancing at Mr. Effingham softly and frankly.

That young gentleman's languor melted like snow in the sunshine, and as he placed the little hand upon his arm to lead its owner in to supper, he pressed it tenderly, and whispered :

" I know I shall, for you will be with me, dearest Clare: —don't be offended, for you know—"

The whisper of the leaves around them, drowned the end of the sentence, but the red sunset lighting up Clare's soft warm cheek might very well have spared its crimson !

CHAPTER V.

POLITICS AND COURTSHIP.

" WE cannot rationally doubt it, sir," said the squire, admir
ing the excellent glass of claret which he held between hi
eye and the window; " there must be classes, scales of re
finement, culture and authority : to state the proposition
proves it."

The squire uttered these oracular words at his dinner-
table on the day after Mr. Champ Effingham's visit to Riverhead. That gentleman was seated in a lounging attitude,
ever and anon moistening his lips with a glass of wine. In
one corner of the room Miss Alethea prosecuted some darling household work, her favorite Orange lying comfortably
coiled up in her lap : in another, Master Willie and little
Kate were having a true-love quarrel as to the proper shade of
silk to be used on Carlo's nose in the famous embroidery.
But we have omitted in this catalogue of personages a gentleman sitting at the table on the squire's right hand, and
whom we now beg leave to briefly introduce to the reader
as Mr. Tag, the parson of the parish. The parson was a
rosy, puffy-looking individual of some fifty years, and in
his person, carriage, and tone of voice betrayed a mingled
effrontery and awkwardness : having formerly served as a
common soldier, then lived by his wits, as an adventurer,
he had finally, perforce of the influence of a noble patron
for whom he had performed some secret service, been presented to a benefice in the colony of Virginia. We cannot
dwell on the worthy gentleman's character, and can only
add here that he was a regular visitor at Effingham Hall
about dinner time, and that he had no religious scruples
against taking a hand at tictac or other games of chance,
any more than he was opposed to the good old English
divertisement of fox-hunting.

To the squire's oracular dogma laying down the laws of so
cial organization, the parson replied between two gulps of
claret :

" Certainly — oh certainly."

"The men of education and lineage not only *must* always rule," continues his host, "but ought to; to trust the reins of power in the hands of common men, who have comparatively no stake in the community, no property, no family, is absurd—a doctrine too monstrous to require refutation."

The parson shook his head.

"I very much fear, squire, that these good old sentiments are becoming obsolete. We men of position and rank in society, born in high social station, will have to yield, I fear.— They are seriously talking, I understand, of giving every man in the colony a vote."

"Every man a vote! who speaks of it? who broaches such an absurdity?"

"A parcel of hair-brained young men, who will yet get themselves into trouble. As a minister of the Established Church, I hold it my duty to warn them, and after that have no further concern with them. I have pointed them out to the authorities, and I now call your worship's attention to the subject."

"Who are they?"

"First and foremost, a young man called Waters—son of the fisherman on the river there near Williamsburg. He had the audacity to intrude upon a conversation I was holding with some gentlemen of my parish in town a day or two since, and he uttered opinions over and above what I have called to your attention, which will bring him to the gallows if he does not beware."

"Other opinions?"

"He spoke of the *oppressions* of the Home Government, said that Virginians would not always be slaves, and actually broached a plan for thoroughly educating the lower classes."

"A statesman in short clothes," said the squire, with a sneer — "the wine stays with you, sir—a colonial *patriot!* faugh! Educate the lower classes! *Educate* my indented servant, and the common tradesman and farmer, and have the knave talking to me of the 'rights of men,' and all the wretched stuff and foolery of Utopian castle-builders! you are right, sir, that young man must be watched. Good heavens! how has the Home Government oppressed us? I grant you, there are some laws I would have altered—and others refused us, passed — but is this oppression? Damn my blood !" added the squire, with great indignation, " I now feel the truth of Will Shakespeare's words, that 'the age is grown so picked, the toe of the peasant comes near the heel of the courtier and galls his kibe,' or to that effect. The direct consequence of these fooleries is to abolish our rank—follow these doctrines, and where will be our gentlemen ?"

" Where, indeed ?"

" Even the very parsons will go to the devil," here in terposed Mr. Champ Effingham, with an evident desire to yawn.

The squire greeted this sally of his son with a laugh.

" You are irreverent, young sir," the parson said, making an effort to look dignified.

" I irreverent ! " replied Mr. Effingham, coolly ; " by no means, most reverend sir. I think my respect for you is sufficiently shown by attending church punctually every Sunday, and respectably going to sleep under the effect of your admirable homilies."

" You jest at my homilies——"

" Oh, no."

" But you should understand, young man, that a minister of the Church of England is not a public haranguer——"

" Precisely."

" And dishonors his high place and position by appealing to the passions and feelings of his hearers instead of giving them good wholesome doctrine."

And Parson Tag drew himself up, with a hauteur which badly assorted with his puffy face and figure.

" You are right," replied Mr. Effingham, with languid indifference ; " nothing is so disagreeable as these appeals to the feelings which you speak of, most reverend sir. How could you bend your excellent mind to ombre and tictac after such performances ; or, exhausted by such unnecessary exertion as a ' rousing appeal' demands, join in the delightful pursuit of a grey fox on the following Monday ? "

The squire laughed again, at the crestfallen parson, and said :

" Come, no tongue-fencing at the dinner-table ; we have wandered from the subject which we commenced with."

" What was the subject ? " asked Mr. Effingham, lan guidly.

" What ! was all the parson's eloquence thrown away on you ? "

" Perfectly ; I was not listening, with the exception of a moment, when you closed your address."

" We were speaking of classes, and the necessity which every gentleman is under to preserve his rank."

" I suppose it's true ; but I never busy myself with these matters."

" You should, sir ; the estate of Effingham falls to you as eldest son."

" I trust, respected sir, that I shall worthily comport myself in that station in life to which it hath pleased Heaven to call me," drawled Mr. Effingham.

" Never jest with the forms of the Established Church, sir," said his father, with some asperity ; for however willing the squire was to applaud a jest at the parson's expense, one directed at the church itself was a very different matter. " I hold every thing connected with the Liturgy of the Holy Church as sacred."

Mr. Effingham assented, with a careless inclination of his head.

" This spirit of free speaking and thinking is worse than the other," continued the planter ; " those abominable New Lights ! "

" Wretched, misguided fools," chimed in the parson, whose equanimity several glasses of wine had restored by this time perfectly.

" I cordially hate and despise them," said the planter, " and consider it my duty to do so. I hope the representa- tive of my family will share my sentiments."

This observation being directed at Mr. Effingham, that gentleman replied indifferently :

" Of course—of course."

" Champ," said the old planter, " you are really becom- ing worse than ever. Where will your indifference to every thing end, I should like much to know ? You seem to have no aim in life, no thought of advancement, no opinions, even."

" True, sir ; that is a pretty fair statement of the truth. This subject of rank and classes, gentlemen and commoners, advancement, ambition, and all that, never troubles me."

"Sunt quos curriculo pulverem Olympicum,
   Collegisse juvat metaque fervidis
   Evitata rotis,"

or something of that sort. It's Horace, I believe, and the scanning strikes me as correct. I mean, respected sir, that I am not ambitious, and have no very fervid desire to get dusty in the arena, or race-course, I should more properly say—dust soils the ruffles so abominably."

The squire always ended by laughing at his son's *peti maitre* airs, though he had sagacity enough to perceive that there was little real affectation in the young gentleman's weariness and indifference. He argued, however, that this would disappear in time, and knowing that any argument would be useless on the present occasion, turned the conversation by taking wine with the parson.

Let us see what the youthful members of the company were saying now. Human nature, under all guises, and in every possible degree of development, is worthy of attention. Master Will, who had been making assiduous love to Kate, engaged now on Carlo's nose, caught Mr. Effingham's Latin, and betook himself to a *sotto voce* criticism on the speaker.

"Just listen to brother Champ, how learned he is I He's just from Oxford, and thinks that Latin mighty fine——to be kissing you the other day !" added this young scion of the house of Effingham, thus betraying the disinterested and impartial character of his criticism.

"Why, I didn't care—I like to kiss cousin Champ," says Kate, with a coquettish little twinkle of the eye, "he's always so nice, you know."

"Nice ! he nice ? "

"Why, yes."

"He aint I"

"That's your gallantry : to contradict a lady," says Kate, with the air of a duchess.

"I'm nicer than he is," says Will, eluding like a skilful debater the charge of want of gallantry. "I don't stuff my nose full of snuff and sneeze all the powder off my hair."

"Ha I ha I" laughs Kate.

"What are you laughing at ? '

"You hav'n't any powder I"

"Never mind : I mean to."

"When ?"

"Never mind !"

"Why you'd look ridiculous, Willie."

"Ridiculous! me ridiculous! Hav'n't I high-heeled shoes—"

"So have I—I'm a girl."

"And silk stockings."

So have I, sir."

' And ruffles, and sword, and all.'

"Oh, what a fine cavalier."

Master Will looks mortified.

"Now, Willie," says Kate, "don't pout, for you know I was only jesting."

"Give me a kiss, then."

"A young lady kiss a gentleman ? Indeed ! "

The flattering word "gentleman" completely restores Master Will's good humor: and essaying to conquer a "salute," as they said in those honest courteous old times, Kate's needle pricks his finger, which circumstance causes the youthful cavalier to utter a shrill cry of pain.

"What's the matter, Will ?" asks the squire, breaking off in the middle of a sentence addressed to the parson.

"Nothing much," says Mr. Champ Effingham, who has watched the assault of his younger brother with philosophic interest, "merely an illustration of the truth of my views."

"Your views—what views ?"

"Will was ambitious to 'collect the Olympic dust '—in other words to kiss Katy, and the needle ran into his finger. So much for ambition. Moral: never meddle with the ladies."

Master Will listens to this languidly-uttered speech with many indications of dissatisfaction—uttering more than one expressive "humph!" that little monosyllable which conveys so much. At Mr. Effingham's "moral," however, he boiled over.

"Never meddle with ladies, indeed!" he said, "that's pretty, coming from you, brother Champ, when old June from Riverhead says he saw you yesterday courting cousin Clare!"—old June having, indeed, retailed to Cato that evening, in Master Will's hearing, the fact that he "spec they'd be a marridgin *somewheres* 'fore long 'sidering how Mas' Champ Efnum and Mis' Clary was agwyin' on!"

The squire burst into a hearty laugh, and rallied Mr. Effingham without mercy. That gentleman, though for a moment disconcerted, quickly regained his nonchalance, and raising his glass languidly, said with a delightful drawl, an exaggeration of his usual languor:

"Of course it's all true, sir; but why laugh at me for following your respectable advice?"

"Clare's much too good for you, Champ," said Miss Alethea, taking a pin from her mouth and affixing therewith some indescribable garment to her knee, the better to set to work on it.

"Ah!" said Mr. Effingham, indifferently, "well, I think so too."

"A thousand times," said Master Will.

"Come, Will, recollect Champ is your elder brother,' said the old planter, laughing merrily.

"Brother Champ laughed at me," said Master Will.

"True, I did, and am justly punished—but correct the word, Will: say I philosophized upon the result of your assault to steal the kiss. I never laugh."

"There's no harm in my kissing Kate," says Master Will, with great dignity.

"None—none!"

"Because we are engaged," adds Will, with the air of an emperor.

Kate suddenly fires up at these words, and exclaims indignantly:

"My goodness! aint you ashamed, Willie?"

"Not engaged!" cries Will.

"No—never," says Kate, with a charming little pout "and if we were, do you think I would acknowledge it, and have the servants talking about me like cousin Clare?"

At which speech the whole company burst into laughter and a smile is even observed to wander over Mr. Effingham's face.

"I see," says that gentleman, "that Miss Clare is given to me by universal consent:—I forgive you, Katy—"

"Oh, cousin Champ, I didn't mean—" commences Kate, remorsefully.

" No matter," concludes Mr. Effingham, yawning, " I have
only to observe that I am willing to take Miss Clare or any
other agreeable young lady for my wedded wife:—and now,
as I feel drowsy, I beg leave of you, parson, and you, respected sir, to excuse me; I am going to take a nap."

With which words Mr. Effingham saunters through the
door, and slowly ascends the broad stairs to his chamber.
Miss Alethea continues to sew: the children to play: the
parson and his host to converse over their wine.

CHAPTER VI.

HOW THEY WENT TO THE PLAY.

THE reader will recollect that Mr. Lee had promised his
daughters to go with them to Williamsburg, to witness the
performance of the "Merchant of Venice" by those newly-
arrived Virginia Comedians, of whom every one was talking.
Mr. Champ Effingham had asked permission to be one of the
party, it will be remembered, and that permission had been
granted by Miss Henrietta with the merry speech we have
recorded.

So on the appointed day, Mr. Effingham, in his most becoming riding suit, and mounted on his handsomest courser,
made his appearance at Riverhead.

The young ladies came down to him, already dressed for
their excursion to town—as Williamsburg was called, just
as they called London "the Town" in England—and Miss
Henrietta commenced immediately her accustomed amusement of bantering their visitor. She was radiant in a dress
of surpassing elegance—flowered satin, yellow lace, jewels,
powdered hair, pearl pendants, and rich furbelows—and the
bright beauty of her laughing face well assorted with her
flashing and glittering costume. As for Clare, her dress
was much more subdued, just as her manner was more quiet,
than that of her sister. But Mr. Effingham, gazing at her
quietly, with little care for Miss Henrietta's sky-rockets,

thought he had never seen a more enchantingly beautiful face; so soft and tender was it, with the bright hair gathered back from the temples, and strewed all over with its pearly powder; so warm and red were the girlish lips; so clear and mild the large melting eyes. Mr. Effingham began to think seriously of having in future a distinct aim in life—to make his own this fairy creature, who had thus moved his worn-out heart, making him feel once more some of the light and joy and enthusiasm of his boyhood—that time passed from him, it really seemed, long ages ago.

Clare did not return his gaze, but busied herself in turning over the leaves of a new book from England, with an affectation of interest which was the merest failure.

Really all my wit is thrown away upon Mr. Effingham," said Henrietta suddenly, with a beautiful pout; "he has not done me the honor to listen, I believe—my last question waiting a reply from him."

Mr. Effingham waked up, so to speak, and turned round.

"What did you say, my dear cousin?" he asked indifferently.

"I say that my cousin, Mr. Effingham, is the most affected personage I have ever known."

"I affected! You have made that charge once before. But what was your question?"

"I asked where you procured that ridiculous little muff there on the settee, which you threw down so carelessly on entering."

"In London," said Mr. Effingham, concisely.

"And are the London gallants such apers of the ladies as to wear them?"

"I don't know; they are used."

"And you imitate them?"

"I imitate nobody, my dear cousin Henrietta; it is too troublesome. I do not wear a coat, or powder my hair, or use ruffles from a desire to imitate any one."

"I don't think you do; for I never saw such preposterous ruffles in my life."

"Eh?" said Mr. Effingham, with languid indifference.

"Or such red cheeks."

"What of them?"

"They are as rosy as a girl's."

" Your own are more so, and I think cousin Clare's more so still," returned Mr. Effingham; "but let us dismiss the subject of ruffles and roses, and come to the play. Do you anticipate much pleasure ? "

" Oh, it will be delightful ! " exclaimed Miss Henrietta, always ready to run off upon any subject which afforded her an opportunity to pour out her spirits and gayety.

" And you, cousin Clare—do you think these Virginia Comedians, as they call themselves, will afford you a very pleasant entertainment ? "

" Oh, yes—I'm sure I shall be pleased,—you know I have never seen a play."

" But read a plenty ? "

" Oh yes : and I like the ' Merchant of Venice ' very much. The character of *Portia* is so delicate and noble."

" Quite true—an excellent criticism : better than anything in Congreve, I think, though I should hesitate to advance such an opinion in London."

" Who will act Portia ? "

" I don't know : but can tell you without much difficulty. Here is a play-bill which I sent to town for yesterday."

And Mr. Effingham drew daintily from his coat pocket a small roughly-printed handbill, which he spread out before the eyes of Clare.

" ' Virginia Company of Comedians,' " he read, " ' by permission of his worship the Mayor—in the Old Theatre near the Capitol, Thursday evening—a tragedy called " The Merchant of Venice," by Mr. William Shakespeare—boxes seven shillings sixpence—vivat Rex et Regina—' here it is : —' *Shylock*, Mr. Pugsby—*Portia*, Miss Beatrice Hallam : ' The part of Portia is to be performed by Miss Beatrice Hallam—I have never seen or heard of her."

" Which means," said Henrietta, laughing, " that Miss Beatrice cannot be very well worth going to see, as Mr. Champ Effingham, just from London, and conversant with all the celebrities there, has never heard of her existence."

" My dear cousin Henrietta," said Mr. Effingham, languidly, " you really seem to sit in judgment on my wearisome conversation. I do not profess to know any thing about celebrities : true, I very frequently lounged into the theatres in London, but I assure you, took very little interest in the plays .

or performers. Life itself is enough of a comedy for me, and
I want nothing more. I know nothing of Miss Hallam—
she may be a new witch of Endor, or as beautiful as Cleopatra, queen of Egypt, for all that I know. That I have
not heard of her proves nothing—the best actors and actresses are often treated with neglect and indifference."

"Well," said Clare, smiling, "we shall soon see for ourselves, for there is papa coming, all ready dressed to go, and
I hear the wheels of the chariot."

Mr. Effingham took up his muff.

"Oh," cried Henrietta, "how do you carry that funny
little thing while riding?—it's smaller than mine."

"I swing it on my arm," replied Mr. Effingham, indifferently.

"Let me relieve you of it—all the girls will then be
admiring my new London muff."

"No, thank you. I will not trouble you."

"Oh, here is papa," said Clare. Mr. Lee entered.

"Good morning, Champ," he said, in his strong, hearty
voice, "how is your good father? have you dined? Yes?
Then let us get on to town. We have no time to lose, as the
play commences, I am informed, at seven."

With which words the worthy gentleman led the way to
the door, where the large chariot, with its four pawing horses
and liveried coachman, awaited them. Mr. Effingham assisted the ladies in with great elegance and gallantry. After
performing this social duty, he made a slight bow, and was
going toward his horse.

"Come, take a place in the chariot," said Mr. Lee.

"Oh, yes," cried the lively Henrietta, "don't go prancing
along out there, where I can't get at you to tease you.
There's room enough for a dozen in here."

"No, no, my horse would get impatient."

Mr. Effingham was waiting for Clare to invite him to
enter, and no one who looked at his face, and witnessed his
tell-tale gaze could doubt it. Clare stole a glance at him,
and said, with a slight blush,

"There's plenty of room."

Mr. Effingham took two steps toward the chariot.

"But my horse," he said.

Mr. Lee called to a servant, and ordered him to take the

animal to the stable.   Mr. Effingham then yielded—he only
wanted the excuse, indeed—and entering the chariot, was
about to sit down by the old gentleman, opposite the young
girls.

"Ah ! take care !" cried Mr. Lee, with a hearty and sudden
laugh, " my glasses are on the seat ! "

Henrietta laughed too, and said, moving near to her side
of the carriage, and making room,

" Come ! you may ride between us—mayn't he, Clary ?
there's plenty of room for a bodkin."

Mr. Effingham plainly had no objection, and, as before, in
the matter of riding within or without, waited for Clare's
manifesto on the subject.   This time he would have been satisfied with a simple glance granting him permission—so very
reasonable was this gentleman at bottom—but unfortunately
Clare did not invite him, either with her lips or eyes.   The
consequence was that Mr. Effingham refused Henrietta's invitation, with a graceful wave of his muff-ornamented arm,
and the glasses of the old gentleman having been transferred
from the seat to his nose, gently subsided into the softly-
cushioned space left free for him, smoothing his ruffles, and
arranging delicately the drop-curls of his powdered peruke.

The chariot rolled on, then, with dignified slowness, toward " Town "—that is to say, the imperial metropolis of
Virginia, then, and now, known as Williamsburg.

CHAPTER VII.

THE OLD THEATRE NEAR THE CAPITOL.

THE " old Theatre near the Capitol," discoursed of in the
manifesto issued by Mr. Manager Hallam, was so far *old*,
that the walls were well-browned by time, and the shutters
to the windows of a pleasant neutral tint between rust and
dust color.   The building had no doubt been used for the
present purpose in bygone times, before the days of the
." Virginia Gazette," which is our authority for many of the

facts here stated, and in relation to the "Virginia Company of Comedians"—but of the former companies of "players," as my lord Hamlet calls them, and their successes or misfortunes, printed words tell us nothing, as far as the researches of the present Chronicle extend. That there had been such companies before, however, we repeat, there is some reason to believe; else why that addition "old" applied to the "Theatre near the Capitol." The question is submitted to the future social historians of the Old Dominion.

Within, the play-house presented a somewhat more attractive appearance. There was "box," "pit," and "gallery," as in our own day; and the relative prices were arranged in much the same manner. The common mortals—gentlemen and ladies—were forced to occupy the boxes raised slightly above the level of the stage, and hemmed in by velvet-cushioned railings,—in front, a flower-decorated panel, extending all around the house,—and for this position were moreover compelled to pay an admission fee of seven shillings and sixpence. The demigods—so to speak—occupied a more eligible position in the "pit," from which they could procure a highly excellent view of the actors' feet and ankles, just on a level with their noses: to conciliate the demigods, this superior advantage had been offered, and the price for them was, further still, reduced to five shillings. But "the gods" in truth were the real favorites of the manager. To attract them, he arranged the high upper "gallery"—and left it untouched, unincumbered by railing or velvet cushions, or any other device: all was free space, and liberal as the air: there were no troublesome seats for "the gods," and three shillings and nine pence was all that the managers would demand. The honor of their presence was enough.

From the boxes a stairway led down to the stage, and some rude scenes, visible at the edges of the green curtain, completed the outline.

When Mr. Lee and his daughters entered the box which had been reserved for them, next to the stage, the house was nearly full, and the neatness of the edifice was lost sight of in the sea of brilliant ladies' faces, and strong forms of cavaliers, which extended—like a line of glistening foam—

around the semicircle of the boxes. The pit was occupied
by well-dressed men of the lower class, as the times had it,
and from the gallery proceeded hoarse murmurs and the un-
forgotten slang of London.

Many smiles and bows were interchanged between the
parties in the different boxes; and the young gallants, following the fashion of the day, gathered at each end of the
stage, and often walked across, to exchange some polite
speech with the smiling dames in the boxes nearest.

Mr. Champ Effingham was, upon the whole, much the
most notable fop present; and his elegant, languid, *petit
maitre* air, as he strolled across the stage, attracted many
remarks, not invariably favorable. It was observed, however, that when the Virginia-bred youths, with honest plainness, called him "ridiculous," the young ladies, their companions, took Mr. Effingham's part, and defended him with
great enthusiasm. Only when they returned home, Mr.
Effingham was more unmercifully criticised than he would
otherwise have been.

A little bell rang, and the orchestra, represented by three
or four foreign-looking gentlemen, bearded and moustached,
entered with trumpet and violin. The trumpets made the
roof shake, indifferently, in honor of the *Prince of Morocco*,
or *King Richard*, or any other worthy whose entrance was
marked in the play-book "with a flourish." But before the
orchestra ravished the ears of every one, the manager came
forward, in the costume of *Bassanio*, and made a low bow.
Mr. Hallam was a fat little man, of fifty or fifty-five, with a
rubicund and somewhat sensual face, and he expressed
extraordinary delight at meeting so many of the "noble
aristocracy of the great and noble colony of Virginia,"
assembled to witness his very humble representation. It
would be the chief end and sole ambition of his life, he said,
to please the gentry, who so kindly patronized their servants
—himself and his associates—and then the smiling worthy
concluded by bowing lower than before. Much applause
from the pit and gallery, and murmurs of approbation from
the well-bred boxes, greeted this address, and, the orchestra
having struck up, the curtain slowly rolled aloft. The young
gallants scattered to the corners of the stage—seating themselves on stools or chairs, or standing, and the "Merchant

of Venice" commenced. *Bassanio* having assumed a dignified and lofty port, criticised *Gratiano* with courteous and
lordly wit : his friend *Antonio* offered him his fortune with
grand magnanimity, in a loud singing voice, worthy the
utmost commendation, and the first act proceeded on its way
in triumph.

CHAPTER VIII

IN THE SQUIRE'S BOX.

THE first act ended without the appearance of *Portia* or
Nerissa ; the scene in which they hold their confidential—
though public and explanatory—interview having been omitted. The audience seemed to be much pleased, and the
actors received a grateful guerdon of applause.

In the box opposite that one occupied by Mr. Lee and
his daughters, sat the squire, Will, and Kate, and—*proh
pudor !*—no less a personage than Parson Tag. Let us not
criticise the worthy parson's appearance in a play-house, too
severely, however. Those times were not our times, nor
those men, the men of to-day. If parsons drank deep then,
and hunted Reynard, and not unwillingly took a hand at
cards,—and they did all this and more—why should they
not also go and see the " good old English drama ? " Certain are we, that when the squire proposed to the parson a
visit to town, for the purpose of witnessing the performance
of the " Merchant of Venice,"—that worthy made no sort
of objection :—though it must be said, in justice to him, also,
that he expressed some fears of finding his time thrown away.
He now sat on the front seat beside the squire, with solemn
gravity, and rubicund nose, surveying from his respectable
position the agitated pit. Miss Alethea had remained at
home : but, beside the squire, Will and Kate were exchanging criticisms on the splendid novelty they had just witnessed. They remembered it for years afterwards—this, their
beautiful, glittering, glorious, magical first play !

" Not so bad as you predicted—eh, parson ?" said the squire. " I don't think that fellow *Antonio* acts so badly.'

" Very well—very well," replied the parson, who was in the habit of echoing the squire's opinions.

" And the audience seem delighted. Look at that scamp of a son of mine, strutting up to friend Loe's box, and smoothing those enormous ruffles like a turkey-cock."

"Harmless devices of youth, sir."

" Yes, and innocent, at least : he'll reform in time, sir, I tell you."

" Beyond all doubt."

" There's good in Champ."

" A most amiable young man."

" Who abused your homilies," laughed the squire.

" Oh ! that is forgotten, my respected friend—a mere youthful jest—the words of a thoughtless youth."

The parson was evidently in a most Christian state of mind, and had plainly left his usual severity at home. The fact was, that the worthy man felt no little complaisance at being seen the honored companion of " one of the aris-tocracy," as Mr. Hallam would have said, in that public place. It flattered him—he thought he heard the gallery say to the pit, " Who is that fine-looking gentleman in Squire Effingham's box ?"—and the pit audibly replied, " That is the Reverend Mr. Tag, the distinguished clergyman."

The parson was, therefore, in a forgiving state of mind, and at that moment would not have refused to agree with the squire if that gentleman had stated his opinion that Mr. Effingham's natural genius and moral purity were sub-lime.

Suddenly, however, the parson's face clouded over, and catching hold of the squire's arm, he said :

" There, sir ! look there ! That is the young man I spoke of, Charles Waters—below us ! "

" What of him ? "

" Have you forgotten, sir ?"·

" Perfectly," said the good-humored squire. " Oh, yes ! now I recollect, the young man who—"

" Has been propagating those treasonable opinions, sir— one of the lower classes turned statesman, as you very eloquently observed ! What business has he to be there ?—

the gallery is his place, among the servants and laborers.
I wonder he is not in the boxes, by us gentlemen!"

The squire followed the indignant finger of the parson,
and saw beneath them in the pit a young man clad in gray
cloth, and gazing with a thoughtful and fixed look upon
the curtain. Plainly, however, he was unconscious of thus
staring out of countenance the poor curtain—his own
thoughts, it was evident, pre-occupied his mind. He was apparently twenty-two or three, and his countenance was full
of truth and nobility:—the hair short, chestnut-colored and
unpowdered—the eyes large and clear,—the mouth firm, but
somewhat sorrowful. Altogether, the face of this young
man would have attracted much attention from close observers of character; and it was not without its effect on the
generous mind of the squire.

"You may say what you please of young Waters, parson," he said, "but he's no fool; you may see that in his
countenance."

"I fear he is much more knave than fool, honored sir,"
said his companion.

"If what you said of him is true, he's both," said the
bluff squire, suddenly recollecting the young man's alleged
opinions on education, "but let him go—we came here to
be amused—and I shall not talk politics. Come, let us question the juveniles here. How did you like the play, Kate,
was it pretty?"

Kate clapped her hands, and said:

"Oh, lovely, papa!"

"And you, Will?"

"Pretty good," said Master Will, endeavoring to smooth
his modest ruffles after the manner of his brother Champ,
whom he secretly admired and venerated as the model of a
gentleman and cavalier. "I think it's pretty well, sir—but
not up to my anticipations—hum!"

"My goodness, Willie!" cried Kate, in the midst of the
squire's laughter at this magniloquent speech, "you just said
to me a minute ago that you were delighted."

"I said so to satisfy you," said Master Will, grandly.

"To satisfy me, indeed!"

"Yes. I never argue with women."

The squire seemed much delighted with this speech, and

3

endeavoring to command his risible muscles, asked Kate
" what she had to reply to that ? "

" He says he never argues with women ! " answered Kate,
pouting and shaking her little fresh-looking head up and
down, " never mind ! I'll catch him at it before long. Never
argues with women ! " adds Kate, " as if he was not arguing
with me all the time 'most ! "

" Let us dismiss the subject," says Will, gently caressing
his upper lip as Mr. Champ was doing opposite, " if that's
the way you're going on when we are married, I'll have a
time of it."

" I won't marry you ! " says Kate, " to be quarrelling all
the time—"

" I quarrel ! "

" Yes ! " pouts Kate, wiping her eyes.

" Well, I won't any more," says Will, descending from his
heroics, and endeavoring to make friends ; " don't cry, Kate.
You know how devoted I am to you—"

" I won't be friends ! "

" Now, Kate ! "

" You needn't be squeezing my hand."

" I'll get you the silk for Carlo's foot."

" Will you ? "

' Yes, from cousin Clare."

" To-morrow ? "

" This very night."

"Then," says Kate, smiling, " I won't quarrel : and you
musn't."

" I ? never ! "

" How pretty Carlo will be ! "

" Lovely—and we're engaged ? "

" Oh, yes ! " says Kate, absorbed in the imaginary con-
templation of Carlo's foot, " but hush ! Willie, they are going on with the play, and you musn't be making love to me,
you know, where every body can hear you ! "

" Never ! " says Will, with Roman dignity and firmness.

The audience utter a prolonged " Sh-h-h-h ! " and the
curtain rises.

CHAPTER IX,

IN MR. LEE'S BOX.

LET us return for a moment to the box occupied by Mr. Lee and his daughters. At the end of the first act Mr. Effingham left his companions, with whom he had been interchanging remarks during the performance, to the great disgust of the pit, and sauntered to the side of Miss Clare Lee, who sat nearest the stage. Clare was radiant with pleasure : she had never seen a play before, and it was therefore as much of a novelty to her as to little Kate. Never had she looked more beautiful, with her bright eyes and soft rosy cheeks— and this fact probably occurred to Mr. Effingham : for his gaze betrayed unmistakable admiration. No one, however, would have discovered it from his manner, which was as full of languor as ever.

"How does my fair cousin relish the performance ?" he asked.

"Oh! I was never more pleased with any thing," said Clare, "and how do you like it?"

"Tolerably : but I never had a very great relish for these things—"

"Because, to wit, life itself is a comedy," said Henrietta, laughing.

"Yes," said Mr. Effingham, "and a very brilliant one it would be, if all the world were Miss Henriettas. I hope, my dear cousin, that compliment is sufficiently broad."

"Thank you, sir—I know how to take your fine speeches : don't think they deceive me."

"There! you have it, Champ," said Mr. Lee, who turned round to greet a neighbor who had just entered.

"I'm rather a poor hand at compliments," replied Mr. Effingham, "but really it is hard to do you the injustice, my fair cousin, of withholding them. Come! no reply, for I see cousin Clare is going to say something more flattering than what you are about to utter."

Clare laughed, and said, blushing slightly :

"Oh, no! I was going to say only that *Shylock* really frightened me."

"It was very well done, much like Shuter at Castle Garden," said Mr. Effingham, "how did you like it, cousin Henrietta? Come, your criticism."

"Oh, what could you expect from a mere country girl like me? Besides, there is Mr. Hamilton, my devoted admirer, coming to speak to me."

Mr. Hamilton, the fox-hunter, entered and took his seat, and Henrietta was now engaged in a laughing and animated conversation.

"How I envy them," said Mr. Effingham, applying to his nostrils, with a listless air, a delicate pinch of snuff, "they are so gay."

"Why are you not gay, cousin Champ?" said Clare, in a timid voice, "you have no reason to be sad."

"No—I do not say I have any reason. But I am out of sorts."

"Why are you?"

Mr. Effingham leaning over the velvet cushion, and speaking in a tone audible to no one besides himself and Clare, replied:

"I am out of sorts, because I am rusting."

"Rusting!"

"Yes, more than rusting. I take interest in scarcely any thing—I am wearied to death with every thing—what is life worth? Here are some hundreds of persons, and they all seem delighted with this play, which tires me to death I take no interest in it. Shylock and Antonio strut and spout without amusing me—I am already weary, and every body else seems to be impatient for the reappearance of those wonders. Why are they so much amused? For my part, I am sick of all this, and only stay," Mr. Effingham added, lowering his voice, "because *you* stay. The nearest approach to happiness I make, is in your presence."

Clare blushed this time in earnest, and yet, gathering self-possession, looked into Mr. Effingham's face and smiled.

"How beautiful you are!" he said with profound earnestness.

"Oh," said Clare, the color of a peony, "you are jesting with me."

"I am not jesting."

"Well, don't say any thing to make me feel so again—I feel as if my face was as red as fire."

There was so much childlike frankness in the tone with which these words were uttered, that Mr. Effingham felt his heart leaving him, and going quickly into the possession of the owner of the red cheeks. Yet strange to say, he felt no pain, but rather pleasure.

"I really believe I am growing less tired of the play, and all," he said to himself, with a smile : then added aloud:

"I really think you could charm away my misanthropy and melancholy, if you desired, cousin."

"How, pray ?"

"By smiling at me."

Clare smiled :

"There," she said, "be merry, then. Indeed, cousin, you could become gay again, if you chose. Do not determine to find fault with every thing—and think every thing wearisome. Seek novelty : you say that all here seem to take pleasure in the play, while you do not. They are pleased because it is new to them.—I have never seen a play, and I am highly pleased. If you have been often to theatres, there is nothing strange in your thinking this poor one excellent —though it seems beautiful to me. But you will find novelty and interest in other things. Try it, now, and see if my philosophy is not true."

The softness and earnestness in the tender voice of the young girl, and the interest in himself betrayed by her tone, was so plain that Mr. Effingham felt his languid heart beat.

"I know but one means," he said.

"What is that ?"

"To have a companion."

"A companion ?"

His meaning suddenly flashed upon her, and she turned away her head.

"To have the philosopher always near me" said Mr. Effingham, imprisoning in his own the hand which rested on the railing.

The head was turned further away.

"Clare !—dearest Clare !" he whispered, ' if you take such a tender interest in my welfare—why not—"

"Sh—h—h—h!" came in a long murmur from the au
dience.

"True," muttered Mr. Effingham, turning away, "how
ridiculous, here in the theatre!"

Suddenly his eyes fell upon one of the actresses, and he
almost uttered an exclamation. It was the unknown lady
of the wood.

CHAPTER X.

ACTRESS AND GENTLEMAN.

THE unknown lady was no gentle Virginia maiden, no "lady,'
as she had said, with perfect calmness, at their meeting in the
wood—only one of the company of Comedians. Her singular
expression when she uttered the words, "I think you will see
me again," occurred to the young man, and he wondered that
this easy solution of the riddle had not occurred to him at once.

What was her name? Mr. Effingham drew forth his
bill, and saw opposite the name of Portia, *Miss Beatrice
Hallam.*

"Ah, yes," he said, carelessly, "the same we were spe·
culating upon, this morning. Let us see how Portia looks,
and what change the foot-lights work in her face."

He sat down in the corner of the stage upon a wicker
chair, and scanned Portia critically. Her costume was
faultless. It consisted of a gown and underskirt of fawn-
colored silk, trimmed with silver, and a single band of gold
encircled each wrist, clearly relieved against the white,
finely-rounded arm. Her hair, which was a beautiful chestnut, had been carried back from the temples and powdered,
after the fashion of the time, and around her beautiful,
swan-like neck, the young woman wore a necklace of pearls
of rare brilliance. Thus the costume of the character defied
criticism, and Mr. Effingham passed cn to the face and
figure. These we have already described. The countenance
of Beatrice Hallam wore the same simple, yet firm and
collected expression, which Mr. Effingham had observed in

their first interview, and her figure had the same indefinable grace and beauty. Every movement which she made might have suited a royal palace, and in her large brilliant eyes Mr. Effingham in vain sought the least trace of confusion. She surveyed the audience, while the Prince of Morocco was uttering his speech, with perfect simplicity, but her eyes not for a single moment rested on the young men collected at the corners of the stage. For her they seemed to have no existence, and she turned to the Prince again. That gentleman having uttered his prescribed number of lines, Portia advanced graciously toward him, and addressed him. Her carelessness was gone; she no longer displayed either indifference or coldness. She was the actress, with her rôle to sustain. She commenced in a voice of noble and queen-like courtesy, a voice of pure music, and clear utterance, so to speak, such as few lips possess the power of giving forth. Every word rang and told; there was no hurry, no slurring, no hesitation; it was not an actress delivering a set speech, but the noble Portia doing the honors of her beautiful palace of Belmont. The scene ended with great applause—the young woman had evidently produced a most favorable impression on the audience. But she seemed wholly unconscious of this compliment, and made her exit quite calmly.

A buzz ran through the theatre: the audience were discussing the merits of Portia. On the stage, too, she was the subject of many comments; and this continued until Lancelot made his appearance and went through his speech. Then Portia's reappearance with the Prince was greeted with great applause.

Mr. Effingham leaned forward and touched the young woman's sleeve.

"Come," he said, with easy carelessness, and scarcely moderating his voice, "come, fair Portia, while that tiresome fellow is making his speech, talk to me a little. We are old acquaintances—and you are indebted to me for directing you home."

"Yes, sir," said Beatrice, turning her head slightly, "but pardon me—I have my part to attend to."

"I don't care."

"Excuse me, sir—but I do."

"Really, madam, you are very stiff for an actress. Is it so very unusual a thing to ask a moment's conversation?"

"I know that it is the fashion in London and elsewhere, sir, but I dislike it. It destroys my conception of the character," she said, calmly.

Mr. Effingham laughed.

"Come.here and talk to me," he said, "did you not say we should meet again?"

"Yes, sir. And I also said that I was not a lady."

"Well—what is the meaning of that addition?"

"It means, sir, that being an actress, I am not at liberty to amuse myself here as I might were I a lady in a drawing-room. Pardon me, sir," she added calmly, "I am neglecting what I have engaged to do, play Portia."

And the young woman quietly disengaging her sleeve from Mr. Effingham's fingers, moved away to another portion of the stage.

"Here is a pretty affair," said Mr. Effingham to himself, as he fell back, languidly, into the chair, from which, however, he had not deigned to rise wholly when addressing the young actress, "what are things coming to when an actress treats a gentleman in this manner. I really believe the girl thinks I am not good enough for her: 'Pardon me, sir!' was there ever such insufferable prudery and affectation! No doubt she wishes to catch me, and commences with this piquant piece of acting. Or perhaps," added the elegant young gentleman, smoothing his frill, "she fell in love with me the other day, when we met, and is afraid she will betray herself. Not talk when I desire to talk with her, indeed—and yonder all those people have seen her cavalier treatment of me, and are laughing at me. Fortunately I am proof against their jeers—come, come, let us see if Miss Portia will treat me as badly next time."

Portia entered next with the Prince of Arragon, and while that gentleman was addressing the caskets, Mr. Effingham again applied himself to the task of forcing the young woman to converse with him.

"Why did you treat me so, just now?" he said, with abrupt carelessness.

"How, sir?"

"You refused to talk to me."

"I had my part to perform."

"That is no excuse."

"Besides, sir," added the young woman, surveying Mr. Effingham with an indifferent glance, "I know you only very slightly."

"Know me only slightly," cried Mr. Effingham, affecting surprise.

"A chance meeting is very slight acquaintance, sir; but I offer this as no apology for refusing to do what I am now doing—converse with you on the stage."

"Really, one would say you were a queen speaking to a subject, instead of an actress—"

"Honored with the attentions of a gentleman, you would add, sir," she interrupted, quite calmly.

"As you please."

"Pray, speak to me no more, sir—I forget my part. And the audience are looking at you."

"Let them."

"I see some angry faces," said the young woman, looking at Charles Waters, "they do not understand the fashions of London, sir."

"What care I."

"Please release my sleeve, sir—that is my line."

The gallery uttered a prolonged hiss as Portia disengaged her arm. Mr. Effingham turned round disdainfully, and looked up to the gallery from which the hiss came. This glance of haughty defiance might have provoked another exhibition of the same sort, but Portia at that moment commenced her speech.

Thereafter the young woman came no more near Mr. Effingham, and treated that gentleman's moody glances with supreme disregard. What was going on in Mr. Effingham's mind, and why did he lose some of his careless listlessness when, clasping her beautiful hands, the lovely girl, raising her eyes to heaven, like one of the old Italian pictures, uttered that sublime discourse on the "quality of mercy"? and how did it happen that, when she sobbed, almost, in that tender, magical voice,—

"But mercy is *above* this sceptered sway,
It is enthroned in the *hearts* of kings—
It is an attribute of God himself!"—

how did it chance that Mr. Effingham led the enthusiastic applause, and absolutely rose erect in the excess of his enthusiasm ?

As she passed him in going out, he made her a low bow, and said, " Pardon me ! you are a great actress ! " A single glance, and a calm movement of the head, were the only reply to this speech ; and with this Mr. Effingham was compelled to remain content.

He returned to the side of Clare, thoughtful and preoccupied.

" What were they hissing for ? " asked Clare, from whom the scene we have related had been concealed by the projection of the wall, and the group of young men. Indeed, scarcely any portion of the audience had witnessed it, the gallery excepted, which overlooked the whole stage from its great height.

" Some folly which deserved hissing, probably," returned Mr. Effingham, wondering at his own words as he spoke ; " but here are the actors again."

The play proceeded, and ended amid universal applause. Mr. Hallam led out Portia, in response to uproarious calls, and thanked the audience for their kindness to his daughter. Beatrice received all the applause with her habitual calmness ; and, inclining her head slightly, disappeared.

Mr. Effingham's eyes dwelt upon her to the last, and even Clare spoke to him in vain.

" Bah ! she's a mere scheming jade ! " he said, at last, disdainfully, and almost aloud ; " come, cousin Clare, the chariot is ready at the door. Take my arm."

And so the audience separated, rolling, well pleased, to their homes. But why did Mr. Effingham preserve such inexplicable silence in the chariot ? Why did Henrietta tell him that the performance must have made him sleepy ? Why did he push his horse angrily as he galloped back from Riverhead to Effingham Hall ? Was he thinking of that strange Portia ?

CHAPTER XI.

MR. EFFINGHAM CRITICISES THE COMEDY, BETRAYING GREAT CONSISTENCY.

THAT night Mr. Effingham paced his room for more than an hour in moody thought, troubled and out of humor, it seemed, at something which had recently occurred. He kicked out of his way every obstacle, and betrayed other unmistakable evidences of ill-humor. At last, this annoyed state of mind took to itself words and he muttered:

"An actress, forsooth, to so treat a gentleman! making him the laughing-stock of every body by her insolent airs of superiority! As if it were not a high compliment for me to address her at all—a common *Comedienne!* One would really say that it was presumption in me to speak to one so much my superior. 'Pardon me, sir—I have my part to attend to!' and then those stupid country bumpkins around me tittering! Let 'em! I thank heaven that their mirth does not affect me—how insolent it was! And that hiss from the knaves in the gallery. Presume to hiss a gen tleman! And who caused all this? By heaven! she shall repent her insulting hauteur. Who is this woman who conducts herself in such a manner toward a gentleman? Some low woman, the daughter of that vulgar fellow Hallam: no lady, a common actress! Suppose she did act well, and I don't mean to say or think she is not a superior artist. Common justice requires me to acknowledge her genius. But what of that? Her attitude in the trial scene was fine!" continued Mr. Effingham, thoughtfully, forgetting for a moment his indignation, and returning in thought to the theatre. "How tender and noble her countenance! what music in her voice! Never have I seen such purity and truth upon the stage. By heaven! she's no common actress! and I had to tell her so as she went out! But how did she receive my high compliment," he said, returning to his grievances, "how did that respectful address, 'You are a great actress,' affect her? She looked at me as carelessly and indifferently as if I had said 'good morning,' and inclined her head with the coldness of a princess

speaking to her subject. Damn my blood!" said Mr. Effing
ham, with unusual vehemence, "I'll make her repent it, and
she shall suffer for causing me this annoyance. It is ridiculous, pitiable, silly: I, Mr. Champ Effingham, of Effingham Hall, to annoy myself about a common actress—to be
treated with contemptuous indifference by a woman of her
grade!"

And Mr. Champ Effingham, of Effingham Hall, sent an
unfortunate cricket which stood in his path, flying across the
room. The cricket struck against a table which supported a
tall silver candlestick, and all came down with a crash. The
incident served the purpose of a partial vent to the young
man's irritation, and after some more growling and impreca-
tions he went to bed.

He made his appearance at the breakfast-table on the
next morning two hours after the squire had left it, and
received a remonstrance from Miss Alethea on his late
rising, with great indifference. Entering the library thereafter, he found the squire, who had just returned, reading
the "Virginia Gazette."

"Good morning, Champ, lazy as usual, I see," said the
squire, good-humoredly; "but you were late returning from
Riverhead, which is a good excuse. How did you like the
play? we have not met, you know, since."

"I was charmed with it," said Mr. Effingham, "all but
Portia acted their parts excellently, I thought."

"All but *Portia*!"

Mr. Effingham nodded.

"Why," continued the squire, "I thought her acting
excellent."

"Poor, sir—poor—very."

"What fault did you find—come, Mr. London critic?"

"It was overacted."

"How?"

"It took up too much room in the piece."

"Why Portia is a chief character in the play."

"Yes—but not the only one."

"You are very critical."

"I always was."

"And what other fault did you find? Was Miss Hallam
ugly?"

" No—not ugly, exactly—but dreadfully affected and stiff."

" I do not agree with you."

" You liked her, then ? "

" Exceedingly," said the honest squire; " I thought her a young woman of rare beauty—'

" Bah ! "

" And great talents."

" Well," said Mr. Effingham, " tastes proverbially differ. I thought her abominable."

" Were you not speaking to her at one time ?"

" Speaking to Portia ?"

" Yes. I could not see very well through the group around her, but thought I saw her speaking to you."

" She did speak to me."

" Do you know her ?"

" At least she says we are not acquainted."

" Here's a mystery !"

" Not at all. I met her some days since riding out. She had lost her way, and I directed her to Williamsburg."

" I hope you treated her with courtesy."

" As courteously as a subject could a queen, and got snubbed last night for my pains," said Mr. Effingham, with a bad affectation of indifference.

The squire laughed, which caused Mr. Effingham to frown.

" Most insulting treatment," he said.

" Come, come—your ideas are too English and not sufficiently Virginian," said the squire. " This young woman is not degraded by her profession; and though not exactly a lady, is worthy of respect if she conducts herself properly. For my part, I was vastly pleased with her, and I believe every one but yourself who witnessed her acting thought as I did."

" Well, sir," said Mr. Effingham, " I am sorry to find we disagree. In my eyes, her acting, costume, voice, and general style were inappropriate, stilted, and in bad taste."

" You are offended at her refusal to converse with you," laughed the squire, " and so are a prejudiced witness. Hey !" he added, looking through the window, " there's the parson come over to dine."

Mr. Effingham was glad to be thus relieved from the dilemma into which he had fallen, and he greeted the parson with a bow, due to him as deliverer.

"A fine morning, squire," said Parson Tag; "how does your worship find yourself after the late sitting last night?"

"Quite fresh—sit down. How did you like the acting?" Every body is asking that question now."

"Well, well," said the parson, dubiously. "It was tolerably good, but much of it was overdone—overdone, sir, much overdone."

"What part? But excuse me for a moment. I have a word to say to Alethea, and must have your horse taken: you will stay to dinner?"

"No, I think not. I have an engagement—but perhaps —well, I suppose—"

The squire, well accustomed to this formula, was already out of the room, and the first thing he did was to order the parson's animal to be led away, as he would spend the remaining portion of the day at the Hall.

"You said the play was overdone, I believe?" said Mr. Effingham, lounging in an easy chair, and drawling out his words. "What part, please inform me, reverend sir?—I repeat my respected governor's question."

"All was overdone—especially the part of that young woman, the daughter of the manager."

"Miss Hallam?"

"Yes, young sir."

"Who acted *Portia?*"

"Precisely. I never saw a greater failure—it was wretched."

"What do you know of acting?" said Mr. Effingham, with indignant disdain, which expression did not escape Mr. Tag.

"You are somewhat abrupt, sir," he said; "but, nevertheless, I will answer you. In my former worldly days, I frequented playhouses much, and have thus some knowledge of them."

"And you think *Portia's* part was overdone?"

"Yes."

"And wretched?"

" Exactly."

" And a failure ? "

" Perfect."

" Then, reverend sir," said Mr. Effingham, with insulting carelessness, " I beg leave to inform you, that you know nothing about acting. I have never seen a more beautiful rendering of the character. Miss Hallam—whom I highly esteem, sir, and should be sorry to hear any one insult !—is an artist of rare genius ! Her conception and execution are alike uncommon and admirable. If there are persons who are ignorant of what acting exacts, and who do not know when it is of a superior order, so much the worse for them ! I repeat, sir, that any competent critic would have approved unconditionally of Miss Hallam's acting last night in the part of Portia, and I feel some surprise at hearing from you a criticism such as you have uttered. The acting of this young lady—and she is a lady in every sense of the word; for do not think that I am of the prejudiced way of thinking which the gentlemen so-called of this colony take pride in— Miss Hallam's acting is of an order superior to any I have ever witnessed. Her costume, style, voice, and whole rendering were worthy of the first comedians of the English stage. And permit me to say, that your former drilling in theatrical criticism, which you have alluded to, must have been very slight and incomplete, if, after attending the performance with which every one was delighted last night, you failed to perceive that this young girl of eighteen—she is not more, sir—is destined to take a rank inferior to no artist who now adorns with her genius or decorates with her beauty and accomplishments that department of art, the histrionic profession ! "

Mr. Tag was fairly overwhelmed. His feelings, while this storm of words was being poured out on his devoted head, might have been compared to those of a man whose eyes are dazzled and his ears deafened by lightning and thunders issuing from a cloudless sky. He could muster no reply—words failed him. He essayed once or twice to muster some appropriate indignation, but failed lamentably. The worthy gentleman was accustomed to bully—as we now say—others, not to be bullied; and Mr. Effingham having " stolen his art," that art now failed him.

" Yes, sir," continued the animated and consistent cri
tic, " I shall make it my business to call upon Miss Hallam,
and assure her of my high appreciation and admiration of
her brilliant genius.   I know what acting is, sir !—and when
we, the gentlemen of Virginia, are so fortunate as to secure
a great *comédienne*, it becomes us to offer her the tribute of
our applause ! Miss Hallam deserves it—for I again repeat,
that in style, dress, voice, and conception, she is far before
any actress with whom, in my various experience, I have
been thrown in contact."

" Why, Champ !" cried the voice of the squire, at the
door, " you are the most consistent of critics, and the most
impartial of admirers !   You praise and abuse in the same
breath."

Mr. Effingham betrayed some slight embarrassment, upon
finding that his enthusiastic tribute to Miss Hallam had
thus been overheard, by one to whom he had spoken of her
so disparagingly.   But this soon disappeared, and the versa-
tile young gentleman replied with great coolness.

" All chivalry, sir—pure chivalry.   I thought it my
duty to espouse Miss Hallam's cause, when she was attacked by so rough a tilter as the reverend gentleman here. Was
I wrong, and would you not have done the same ? "

This was very adroit in Mr. Effingham, as it diverted attention from himself to the views of the parson.

" The parson attack Portia !" said the squire ; " how
so ? "

" I did nothing of the sort, your worship," said the
crest-fallen parson, " I only expressed some dissatisfaction
with a portion of her acting :—for which crime, Mr. Effingham has been for some minutes pouring out upon my head
the vials of wrath."

" Well, let us say no more," returned Mr. Effingham,
subsiding into indifference again ; " I'm tired of the subject,
and will no longer afflict your reverence.   Bring me some
Jamaica," he added, to a servant who was passing through
the hall : then to the parson, " we'll bury all differences in
a flagon," he said, " I'm as thirsty as a fish."

The parson brightened up, and, when he had emptied a
fair cup of excellent Jamaica, was ready to forgive Mr. Effingham and all the world—even think well of *Portia*.   In

due time, that is to say, about noon, dinner was announced
and discussed honestly by all, except Mr. Effingham. That
gentleman soon rose and ordered his horse, announcing his
intention of riding to Williamsburg, where he would probably spend the night.

"Don't sit up for me, Alethea," he added, with a yawn.

"Indeed, I won't," Miss Alethea replied.

Mr. Effingham nodded indifferently, and sauntered from
the room.

CHAPTER XII.

THE OLD RALEIGH TAVERN.

THE "Raleigh Tavern" in Williamsburg had been selected for a residence by Mr. Hallam and his company of
comedians, chiefly on the ground that there was no other
hostelry of any size in the good city at the period : and before the Raleigh Mr. Effingham drew rein. A negro took
his horse, and, entering the broad doorway, the young man
found himself opposite to the manager himself.

"Give me some Jamaica," he said to the portly landlord, who bowed low to his well-known and richly-clad guest,
"and you, Mr. Hallam, come here and empty a cup with
me. I came to see Madam *Portia*. Where is she at the
present moment? I wish to pay her my respects."

So far from displaying any ill-humor at these cavalier
words, the red-faced manager bowed as low as the landlor l,
and expressed his perfect willingness to drink with Mr.
Effingham ; which, judging from his voice and appearance,
he had performed in company with himself a number of
times already. He marched up, accordingly, to the sideboard—in those simple times the bottles were set out freely
without any obstructing "bar"—and pouring out an abundant supply of the heady rum, swallowed it at a gulp. Mr.
Effingham drank his own more leisurely, talking about the
performance on the preceding night.

"A fine house, sir ! a most enlightened and intellectual

audience, such as I expected to find in this noble colony,"
said Mr. Hallam.

"What receipts?" asked Mr. Effingham.

"Nearly a hundred pounds, sir; as much as the great
Congreve's ' Love for Love ' ever brought me."

"I should have thought the amount larger,—cursed
dust! I believe it has strangled me!"

"I saw you, sir, 'and your honorable party."

"The devil you did! that's strange, for Shylock natu
rally took up your whole attention."

"Shylock was too drunk," said Hallam, quite naturally
" there he is, in the corner, now."

"Let him stay there, then. You have not answered my
question."

"Your question?"

"I asked where *Portia* was."

"Oh, Beatrice! she is somewhere about."

"I met and directed her on her way to town the other
day.—Send up, and say that Mr. Effingham wishes to see
her."

"Certainly, sir."

A messenger was dispatched to Miss Hallam's room,
and in a moment returned with the reply, that she was busy
studying her part.

"She can see you, though," said Hallam, laughing;
" follow me, sir."

Mr. Effingham followed the fat manager, and a flight of
stairs brought them to a door, which Hallam knocked at,
and a voice bidding him come in, he threw it open. It
afforded entrance to a small, neat room, the simple ornaments
of which were in perfect taste; the window of this room was
open, and at it sat the young girl, whom we have seen twice
before; once, in the bright autumn woods, and again on
the stage, in the character of Portia. Beatrice was clad
in a handsome morning dress of dove color, and her fine
hair was secured behind her statue-like head by a bow of
scarlet riband. She leaned one hand upon her book,—the
other supported her fair brow, and her classic profile was
clearly defined against the rich fall forest, visible through
the window.

At the noise made by the opening door she raised her

eyes, and for a moment gazed in silence upon the intruders Then apparently resigning herself to her fate, she closed the book and rose.

"I told the servant to say that I was engaged upon my part, father," she said, calmly, to Hallam. "I shall be badly prepared if I am interrupted, sir."

"Oh, plenty of time—and with your genius, child, you can do any thing. She is as quick as lightning, Mr. Effingham," added the manager, discussing the young girl's talents in her hearing without a thought of any indelicacy in such a proceeding, "and when she catches hold of a rôle it's done."

Beatrice was silent.

"Come, now, talk with Mr. Effingham for a quarter of an hour, since he is an acquaintance," continued the manager, smiling, "in that time you will lose nothing." And passing through the door, he descended into the lower part of the tavern.

For a moment the two personages thus left alone surveyed each other in silence. Before Mr. Effingham's bold and careless glance, Beatrice's eyes did not lower for an instant.

"Well, Mr. Effingham," she said, at length, quite calmly, "what would you have?"

"Simply, a little conversation with you, my charming Beatrice," said Mr. Effingham, carelessly.

"I am busy, sir, very. I act Juliet to-night, and am now studying."

"Oh, you can give me a few moments—"

"Well, sir," she said, sitting down and pointing to a chair.

"Especially," continued her visitor, "as you refused to say any thing to me last night."

"That is a reproach, sir?"

"Yes."

"It is unjust, as you know."

"Now, see the difference of opinion," said Mr. Effingham, smoothing his ruffles, daintily, "I think that nothing could be more just. I reproach you justly, because you have nothing but prudery to allege as an excuse for your refusal."

" I told you, sir, then, as I now do, that conversation on the stage destroys my conception of the character I am representing."

" Bah ! all theory."

The young girl seemed to be somewhat irritated by the disdainful expression of Mr. Effingham's voice.

" Mr. Effingham," she said, " be pleased not to treat me like your servant. I am no common attaché of the stage, sir, such as you have met with, doubtless, in London frequently. I say this, sir, in no spirit of self-approval, but because it is true."

" Why, Beatrice, you are really about to bowstring me, or put me to some horrible death, I believe."

" See, sir," said the young girl, with noble calmness, " we are very nearly perfect strangers, and you address me as ' Beatrice,' as familiarly as my own father."

" May the devil take it—you quarrel with a mere habit."

" Mr. Effingham," said the young woman, rising, and speaking in a tone of perfect calmness, " I quarrel neither with you nor any one; above all, I do not presume to criticise your habits, except when those habits, as in the present instance, concern myself."

" Bah !" repeated Mr. Effingham, with a laugh, " how, pray ?"

" You seem to think, sir, that it is my place to be thankful when you address me intimately, and familiarly, as you have done."

" What harm is there ?"

" That question is an insult, sir !"

" May the devil take me, but you are fruitful in imaginary offences, and insults offered you."

" No, sir—I do not exercise my imagination at all. Your tone to me is disagreeable."

" There it is again—you are really going to bite me, I believe. Let us leave the subject, and discuss last night's performance. Your acting was really not bad."

The proud lip of the young woman moved slightly.

" Ah ! ah !" said Mr. Effingham, laughing, " I see what you mean by that scornful look. I am a poor critic, you would say."

" I say nothing, sir

"I have no taste, you would say: though I beg you to observe, that inasmuch as I have praised your acting, that is a false step in you."

Beatrice repressed her rising anger, and bowed coldly.

Mr. Effingham received this exhibition of hauteur with careless nonchalance, and picking up the volume which the young girl had laid down on his entrance, said:

"You act Juliet to-night?"

"I do, sir."

"I shall come."

Beatrice made no reply.

"I beg, now," continued Mr. Effingham, arranging one of his ambrosial drop-curls daintily upon his cheek, "I beg you will not put any of that ferocious feeling you now exhibit into Juliet. The character is essentially tender and poetical, and ranting would kill it."

"I never rant, sir," said Beatrice, apparently resigning herself to the presence of her insulting visitor, and speaking in a tone of utter coldness.

"That's right," replied Mr. Effingham, indifferently; "be subdued, quiet, but intense, and all that. Juliet is deeply in love with Romeo, recollect, and love does not express itself by tirade. Do you think it suits you? Come, answer me."

"I have played it before, sir."

"That is no answer."

"Please leave me to study my part, sir—time is passing."

"Not before giving my views, Beatrice. I don't think you will act Juliet well. It requires a tender, loving nature; and you are minus the heart, it is plain; and you will butcher the part."

"Thanks for your compliment, sir."

"Oh! I never compliment, or any thing of the sort."

'I am losing time, sir."

"Conversing with me, you mean?"

"Yes, sir."

"The conversation, then, is very distasteful to you, my charming Beatrice?"

"Yes, sir!" she said.

"You hate me, perhaps?"

The young girl made no reply.

"Or, perhaps, your ladyship despises me?" added Mr. Effingham, betraying some irritation.

"I do neither, sir—you are indifferent to me."

These words were uttered with so much coldness, that Mr. Effingham's *amour propre* was deeply wounded. He began to get angry.

"You are really a very amiable young lady," he said. 'Here I ride all the way from the country for the sole purpose of seeing you."

"And insulting me, sir, add."

"And you receive me," continued Mr. Effingham, taking no notice of the interruption, "as if I were a common clodhopper, instead of a gentleman, paying you a friendly visit."

'Your friendly visits do not please me, sir."

"I see they do not."

"I am an actress, sir, and not of your class."

"Bah! who speaks of classes?"

"You yourself this moment, sir!"

"You choose to misunderstand me. I said that my visit was the friendly one of a well-bred man, not the impertinent intrusion of a country bumpkin, like those knaves who hissed me in the gallery, or that clodhopper who presumed to bend his angry glances on me from the pit—Mr. Charles Waters, I know him well—the young reformer, forsooth!"

Beatrice's face flushed.

"I saw no nobler countenance, sir," she said, coldly, "among all your aristocratic friends."

"Ah! your cavalier, I perceive!" said Mr. Effingham, bitterly; "really, I shall become jealous."

"I do not know him, even, sir—your scoff is unjust."

"Your true knight, who wished to run a tilt with me for touching your arm! Perhaps he has but now left you, and before going, devoted my humble self to the infernal gods for daring to address you."

"I repeat," said Beatrice, indignantly, "that I have seen him but once, and on the occasion you allude to."

"Well, I believe you. But let such impertinent bumpkins beware how they criticise my actions in future, even by their looks."

Beatrice sat down, with a mixture of weariness and scorn on her beautiful countenance, and, taking up the book which the young man had laid down, began to study her part. This calmness seemed to enrage Mr. Effingham not a little, and he put on his cocked hat with a flirt of irritation.

"Very well," he said; "that means that you are weary of me—I am not good enough for Miss Hallam—she is too immaculate for me."

"I have my part to study, sir."

And she began to con her character in silence.

Mr. Effingham swung his short sword round angrily and without further words went hurriedly out of the room. He brushed by Mr. Hallam, who was talking with Shylock, and, mounting his horse, galloped from the town towards the Hall.

The manager's good-humored greeting as he passed had been completely disregarded; and thinking rightly that something had happened to cause this abrupt departure, he went up to his daughter's room.

"Why did the young man go so abruptly, my, child?" he said.

"Because I would not return him my thanks for visiting me," said Beatrice, bitterly.

"Oh," said the manager, laughing, "you are too prudish, Beatrice. You should not complain of these visits, which are customary, and not strange, when you are acquainted—as you are with Mr. Effingham, he says. Your aim in life, as you say you hate the stage so much, should be to marry well—and I much misunderstand this young fellow, if he would not marry you in the face of the world, if he fancied."

"I do not wish to marry him, or any one like him!" said Beatrice, her face flushing, and her beautiful eyes filling with angry tears.

"You are mad!—he is, the landlord tells me, of one of the best and wealthiest families in the colony."

"And because he is," said Beatrice, wiping her eyes, "he thinks he has the right to intrude upon me, and speak in any tone he chooses. Father!" she added, passionately, "I am sick of this eternal persecution —in London—here —every where. I shall go mad if I remain upon the stage,

exposed to this class of persons all my life—my head is hot
and burning now, my eyes feel like fire—oh! I wish I was
dead!"

Passionate tears followed these words, and Beatrice
covered her face with her hands, bending down and sobbing.
The good-hearted old fellow, who really had his daughter's
good at heart in all things, betrayed some feeling at this ex-
plosion of grief; and betook himself to soothing the young
girl, with gentle words, and caresses, and assurances of his
own unchangeable love.

"Come, come," he said, much affected, "I can't bear to
see you so much moved. Don't think too hardly of this young
man. He is thoughtless, perhaps, but does not mean any
offence. There now!" he said, caressing her disorderd hair,
"don't cry, Beatrice. You shall forget all this to-morrow,
when, as there will be no performance, we can go and have
the sail upon James River, which you said you would like
so much—will you go?"

"Yes, sir," said Beatrice, growing calmer, "oh yes! I
want to get away from all this tormenting excitement, and
breathe the fresh river air. I am happiest in the woods, or
on the water. I won't cry any more, sir, and don't fear I
will not act my part well. I don't like acting, and at times
I feel a weariness and disgust which I cannot subdue : but
I will not let any of my bad feelings interfere with your
wishes. Indeed, I'll act very well, sir."

"And don't be too angry at the young man—he meant
nothing, I know."

"I have forgotten him, sir," said the young girl, with
noble calmness.

"A mere thoughtless youth, who admires you highly—I
saw that well, when you were speaking in the trial scene last
night. Now I will leave you. Good-bye."

"Good-bye, father—kiss me, before you go."

And Mr. Manager Hallam having retired, the young girl
growing gradually calm, again applied herself once more to
the study of her part.

CHAPTER XIII.

A LOVER, FOX-HUNTER, AND PARSON.

OUT of Williamsburg—into the forest—through the forest—
and so into the open highway sped Mr. Effingham, as if an
avenging Nemesis were behind him, and nothing but the
headlong speed he was pushing his noble bay to, could preserve him from the clutches of the pursuer. He made
furious gestures, uttered more furious words. The ordinary
languor and nonchalance of this gentleman seemed to have
passed from him wholly, and a fiery, passionate man, taken
the *petit maitre's* place.

Going at this headlong speed, he very nearly ran over, before he was aware of their proximity, a party of gentlemen
of his acquaintance, who were riding leisurely toward the
bachelor establishment of Mr. Hamilton, visible a few hundred yards ahead. Mr. Hamilton rode in front of the
glittering cortège, and became aware of Mr. Effingham's
presence, by having his horse nearly driven from beneath
him.

" What, the devil ! " cried jolly Jack Hamilton.

" It's Effingham, racing for life ! " rose in chorus, from
the laughing horsemen

" The devil, Champ ! what's the matter ? " asked Hamilton, " have you made a bet that you will ride over us, horse,
foot and dragoons ? "

" Excuse me," said Mr. Effingham, regaining a portion
of his habitual calmness, " but the fact is, Hamilton, I am
angry enough to gallop to the devil, whom you have twice
apostrophized so emphatically."

" What's the matter ? "

" I am mad."

" Intellectually, or do you mean that you are merely out
of temper ? "

" Both, I believe."

" Then, come and sleep with me, and have a fox-hunt
with us in the morning."

" No."

4

" Come, now."

" I cannot."

" Well, at least, let us have the cause of your fury."

Mr. Effingham hesitated, but at last, overcome with rage, said :

" That young actress has been assuming her airs towards me, and has made me as you find me. There it is ! I confess I am out of temper."

" What a confession it is ! " cried Hamilton, laughing " I thought you never suffered yourself to be ruffled."

" I seldom do."

" And she offended you ? "

" Snubbed me—nothing less. It is really humiliating."

And Mr. Effingham looked as if he believed what he said : his face was flushed, and he looked gloomy.

" How was it ? " asked the company.

" Why, just thus. I went to pay her a visit, and complimented her performance in Portia, highly. What reply did I receive, sir ? " said Mr. Effingham, indignantly, " why, an insult ! ' Please leave me—I must study my part !' that was her reply. And when I declined to avail myself of the privilege, she went on studying, as calmly as if I was not present."

" A perfect she-dragon, by George ! " said Hamilton, " but really, that was bad treatment."

" Abominable ! " said the chorus.

" She could not have treated a country clown more harshly," added Hamilton ; " how could she be guilty of such rudeness. She don't look like it—I thought her very lady-like."

" All acting ! " said Mr. Effingham.

" Plainly."

" She shall repent it," blurted out Mr. Effingham, " the insulting girl ! I never saw greater rudeness and hauteur. A mere London commedienne of no talents, and bringing her stilted affectations to the colony."

" Come, my dear Effingham, don't be angry. Here we are at the Trap—my respectable bachelor residence : come in, and cool off in some Jamaica "

" No, thank you—I must get on. I am bad company. '

And, leaving the fox-hunters, Mr. Effingham rode on toward the Hall. A quarter of a mile from the house he

met Parson Tag, jogging on his cob from the Hall home
ward, with broad-brimmed hat, and knees and elbows painfully angular.

"Good evening, sir," said the parson, "you return soon:
the dews of evening are scarce falling."

"I thought you were at the Hall, sir, for the evening."

"Why so?"

"Because I was absent," said Mr. Effingham coldly.
"We quarrel, I believe, always, and I thought you would remain, as I was away."

Mr. Effingham's irritation and ill-humor must plead his
excuse for this irreverent speech.

"The quarrelling is on your side, not on mine, sir," said
the parson, endeavoring to be dignified; "I am a man of
peace."

"Carrying out which character, you this morning attacked
Miss Hallam, sir!"

"Really, you seem to have espoused that young lady's
cause against all comers," said the indignant parson. "Take
care, young sir; as the parson of your parish, it is my duty
to warn you against the snares of Satan. This Jezebel will
be your ruin."

"Be pleased to speak respectfully of Miss Hallam, sir,"
said Mr. Effingham, threateningly, "when you address me
on the subject of her character. Though not her knight, I
hold myself ready to 'espouse her cause,' as you say, sir,
even against the 'parson of my parish!'"

"Here's a pretty mess," returned the pompous gentleman,
descending to the vulgate: "you threaten me, forsooth!"

"No, sir: I acknowledge the folly of my words. You
wear no sword, and are not responsible for thus slandering
my friends—yes, my friends, sir! I say again, that Miss Hallam is one of my friends, and a young lady who has thus far
conducted herself with immaculate propriety. Now, go sir,
and laugh at me. I value your derision as I value your
praise—as nothing."

And Mr. Effingham rode on as furiously as before, with
out reflecting for an instant on the strange inconsistency of
his conduct. Might not a small modicum of self-knowledge
have explained to him the truth of the matter? But he was
blinded by those dazzling eyes, and saw no inconsistency in
his words.

CHAPTER XIV.

HOW MR. EFFINGHAM STAINED HIS RUFFLES WITH BLOOD.

TEN minutes' ride brought him to Effingham Hall, and, throwing his bridle to a negro who ran forward to take it, he entered the hall. Supper was soon served, and Mr. Effingham was plied with questions as to his abrupt return, and moody state of mind. These questions were received with very little good-humor by the young man, who was in a furious ill-humor, and he was soon left to himself. The squire was not present, having some writing to do in the library, whither a cup of chocolate was sent him.

After supper Mr. Effingham sat down moodily, resting his feet on the huge grim-headed andirons, which shone brightly in the cheerful light thrown out by some blazing splinters, for the October evenings were becoming chilly. Miss Alethea, who sat sewing busily, after pouring out tea, endeavored in vain to extract a word from him.

Little Kate, who sat in the corner near Mr. Effingham, on her own little cricket, paused in the midst of her work—Carlo was going on bravely now—to ask cousin Champ what made him feel bad, and was he sick? The child was Mr. Effingham's favorite, and he was always ready to play with her; but on the present occasion he replied that he was not sick, and did not wish to be annoyed.

Kate looked much hurt, and Master Willie, who was pouring over a wonderful book of travels at the table, manifested some disapprobation, on hearing his future wife thus rudely addressed.

"You are not mad with me, cousin Champ?" said little Kate, piteously.

"No—no! I am angry with nobody," said Mr. Effingham, with some impatience, but more softly than before.

Kate, encouraged by these words, laid Carlo down, and pouring some perfume from a bottle into her hand, stole up to Mr. Effingham, and said:

"Oh, I know you've got a headache, cousin Champ! Let me put this on your forehead."

He would have refused, but the little face was so tender, and the small hand so soft, that he could not.

"I have no headache, Katy," he said, "I am only annoyed—no, I believe I am not even annoyed."

And rising abruptly, he said to a servant:

"Order my horse!"

The negro hastened out.

"Why, where in the world can you be going at this
hour?" said Miss Alethea, writing busily.

Mr. Effingham either did not hear this question, or deign
ed to take no notice of it: a circumstance which caused
Miss Alethea to toss her head, and preserve a dignified
silence.

"Well! my horse?" he said, as the servant re-entered.

"Be round directly, sir,—I told Dick to be quick."

Kate stole up and took his hand.

"Cousin Champ," she said, "it is getting cold. Won't
you wear my white comfort? I'll bring it in a minute."

"No, no! I don't need it."

Kate tip-toed, and whispered in his ear:

"I won't like cousin Clare, if she treats you badly."

"Foolish child! for heaven's sake let me alone!"

Then, seeing that the little face looked hurt and mortified, he added gloomily:

"I am not treated badly by any one, Kate: you attach
too much importance to my moods. There: I had no intention of hurting your feelings, and I am not going to see anybody in particular."

"Did anybody ever!" said Miss Alethea, raising her
hands. "Apologise to a child, when *my* questions are met
with insult."

Mr. Effingham treated this apostrophe to the unknown
personage, who finds himself called upon to express his sentiments on such astounding occasions, with profound disregard, and went out into the night. A servant held his
horse, and he vaulted into the saddle, and set forward at a
gallop—toward Williamsburg.

"That woman will be my fate!" he muttered, between
his clenched teeth; and with a reckless laugh, "I see the
abyss before me, and the mocking glances of the world are
plain to me. I, a gentleman, to trouble myself about an
actress! I suppose I will end by offering her my hand, and
then comes the storm! Married to an actress!—for, by

heaven, if I wish to do so, I will do so in spite of fire and
tempest! They'll laugh when they read of my wedding—
I see them now, leering and smiling, and giggling: the well-
bred gentlemen wondering how I could throw myself away
so,—the eligible young ladies intensely indignant, at—what?
why, at the loss of a visitor and prospective husband. They
would scout the idea, truly! but I defy them to deny it—a
score of them. Marry an actress!—I am stamped with
degradation for ever by it. Well, I'm not fool enough for
that, quite yet; but every bound of this horse is a step in my
fate. Let it be!"

And digging his spurs into the animal's sides, he fled on
through the darkness like the wild huntsman; as furious
and fast. The lights of the town soon rose on his sight,
and clattering to the "Raleigh," he gave his horse in charge
of an ostler, and repaired without brushing the dust from
his clothes, or wiping the perspiration from his brow, to the
theatre.

The play had commenced nearly an hour before, and it
was with great difficulty that the young man—pushing by a
number of ladies, his acquaintances—could reach the stage,
upon which some dozen or more gentlemen were standing or
seated. In the middle box, his excellency, the Governor,
and his household, glittered in silk, embroidery and gold.

Just as he reached the stage, Juliet made her appearance in the garden. Beatrice was the very impersonation
of the poet's conception—so tender, yet passionate; bold,
yet fearful, were her looks and tones, her gestures, and whole
rendering of the part. Her dewy eyes burned with a steady
and yet changeable flame; were now veiled with thought,
then radiant with passionate love, and like two moons, new
risen, swayed the quick currents of the blood. The audience
greeted her with enthusiastic applause, and Mr. Effingham
saw that the favorable impression she had made on the previous night had now been much heightened.

In truth, nothing could be more splendid than her countenance, as she hastened to meet the nurse, bringing her news
of her lover: and Mr. Effingham, spite of his agitation and
gloom, could not help hanging on her words and glances,
drinking in the music of her rare and wonderful voice with
greedy ears. A bitter smile distorted his features, how-

ever; for with every burst of applause—and no opportunity
was allowed by the audience to escape them—he felt more
and more how insignificant he was to this young girl, applauded, caressed, overwhelmed with the intoxicating praise
lavished on her from a thousand hands—the incense ascend-
ing in her honor there before him.

"What does she care for me!" he said, bitterly; "every
body praises her—all are delighted—those fools, there, ar
devouring her with their eyes, and think her an angel of
genius and beauty from the skies. I tear my heart in vain.'

And with passionate anger Mr. Effingham grasped his
breast, and dug his nails into the flesh, until they were
stained with blood. The rich lace ruffle, rumpled and torn,
revealed in its crimson stain the excess of his rage.

He made no reply to the laughing words addressed to
him by his companions, and taking up a position almost
behind the scenes, arrested Beatrice in her passage as she
went out.

"You do not see me!" he said, abruptly.

"Good evening, sir," said Beatrice, calmly; "I was absorbed in my part."

And she endeavored to pass on.

"Stop," said Mr. Effingham, with a sneering laugh, "you
are really too much in a hurry."

"I must look at my next speech, sir—I should have
known it but for your interruption this morning."

"You hate me—do you not?" he said, clasping her arm.

"No, sir—please release me."

"Ah! you have merely contempt for me, madam."

"Mr. Effingham," said Beatrice, raising her head with
cold dignity, "I despise no one. Your words are probably
ironical, as you ask me, an actress, if I despise you, a
wealthy gentleman; but I reply to you as if you were in
earnest. Now, sir, I must go."

"Not until I have told you that you are a heartless and
unfeeling woman—a nature of stone—a cold and unimpress-
ible automaton!"

The young girl looked strangely at him.

"You have despised the honestly-offered courtesy of a
man against whom you know nothing. Stop, madam! You
have tormented me: yes, tormented me'—the humiliating

truth will out!—-tormented me by your coldness and contempt—destroyed my tempor ;—since seeing you I am
another man, and a worse one. Look, my ruffle is rumpled
and bloody—*your* nails tore my flesh ! "

" Oh, sir ! " cried the young girl, starting back in horror,
" how could you——"

" A mere scratch, madam," said Mr. Effingham, bitterly,
" and I used a mere figure of speech in saying that your
hand inflicted it. You only caused it ! "

"Mr. Effingham, you frighten me. I must go."

" You shall hear me."

" I must go, sir ; listen, the audience are becoming impatient. Release my sleeve, sir," she said, coldly and
firmly, again ; and leaving him, she issued forth upon the
stage, and with a voice as firm and steady as ever—so wonderful was her self-control—continued her character. As
she passed out after the scene, Mr. Effingham in vain
attempted to address her. Failing in this, he ground his
teeth, and clutching a second time the unfortunate lace at
his bosom, tore it into shreds. He turned, and almost
rushed from the theatre. As he brushed through the box,
he heard a little cry of astonishment, and a soft voice full of
surprise said, " Mr. Effingham ! " He turned, and his eyes
met those of Clare, fixed on him with trouble and astonishment.

He bowed, said hurriedly something about regretting the
necessity of his departure, and left the theatre just as the
audience greeted the re-entrance of Beatrice with a burst of
applause. He hastened to the " Raleigh," mounted his
horse, and fled out into the dark night like a phantom, full
of rage and despair, that joyous applause still ringing in
his ears.

CHAPTER XV.

THE SAIL-BOAT "NANCY."

" HAVE you never, O friend, who now readest these unworthy lines, abandoned for a time your city life, with its noise
and bustle, and eternal striving, and locking up with your

ledgers, or your lawbooks, all thoughts of business, gone
into that bright lowland, which the James flows proudly
through, a band of silver wavering across a field of emerald?
Have you never sought a sensation finer, emotions fresher,
than city triumphs and delights—and, leaving for a time
your absorbing cares and aspirations, trusted yourself to the
current, like a bark, which takes no prescribed course, stops
at no stated place, but suffers the wind and the stream to
bear it whithersoever they will, well knowing that the wind
cannot waft it, the tide cannot bear it, where the blue sky
will not arch above, the fresh, waving woods will not mirror
their tall trunks and fine foliage in the serene surface?
Have you never sailed along that majestic river, with its
sentinel pines, and wood-embowered mansions, and bright
ripples breaking into foam, when the west wind, blowing
freshly, strikes against the tide, surging for ever from the
sea? Go, on an October day, when the white clouds are
shattered by the breezes of the Atlantic—those breezes still
redolent with the perfumes of the tropics,—and telling of
their long travel over lands of unimagined beauty and un-
dreamed-of splendor—go on one of those clear, sunny days
of the early autumn, when the waters ripple like molten silver agitated by the breath of the Deity; when trees are
crimson, and blue, and golden, like the myriad silken
banners which erewhile flouted the deep heaven before
Tamerlane; when the wave laps upon the shore, and silences
the whisper of the pines with its monotonous and dreamy
music; where the water-fowl sleep upon the surge, or extend
their broad wings above the glittering foam, to strike the
quick-darting prey their keen eyes have descried;—go on
some day when the white sail of some sea-bound bark bellies
in the wind, and her prow cuts the silver, dashing into foam
the bright sunlit waters; or when glorying in the fine season, and in his momadic, careless lot, the fisherman spreads
his small lateen sail, and feels his bark bound beneath him
like a sea-gull tossed upon the waves—when, trusting to Providence to guide his course, he drops the paddle he has been
plying, carelessly, and with closed eyes, dreams in the broad
sunlight of the past and future. Go, on one of these days, and
gliding over the swaying billows of the great stream, see if
there is not yet some fresh delight in this our human life—

a poetry and romance unstifled in the heart! On such a
day did Beatrice Hallam leave the town of Williamsburg,
with her father, and bend her steps toward the stream."

Thus far, the author of the MS., in that rhetorical and
enthusiastic style which every where characterizes his works.
Let us descend from the heights of apostrophe and declama-
tion to the prose of simple narrative.

Beatrice had received the assurance of her father, that
she should spend a day upon the waters, with a delight
which may readily be imagined. She was a pure child of
the wilderness, in spite of the eternal claims which an arti-
ficial civilization, an inexorable convention, laid to her time
and thoughts. She rejoiced in the forest, and on the hills:
—we have seen her riding out fearlessly to drink in the
fresh splendor of the autumn—now she anticipated a delightful day upon the river. Mr. Effingham would not be there,
with his insulting advances, his intolerable drawl, his irritating airs of superiority and patronage. She would have the
whole day to herself. She had no performance to neglect
—no rehearsal to go to. She was free for the day wholly.

Beatrice was an excellent rider, and she chose this mode
of reaching the river, in preference to the light calash,
which the manager suggested. The good-humored old fellow yielded at once, and mounting a stout cob, instead of
installing his corpulent person in the comfortable vehicle,
they set forth—the young girl riding her favorite white
horse. They reached the bank of the stream without incident, and found the boatman, to whom a message had been
sent on the night before, ready to receive them. He gathered up his fishing lines with the ease of a practised hand,
placed in the pocket of his peajacket the inseparable black
flask of rum, and led the way to his little vessel. It was
one of those light and airy barks, which obey the hand of
the helmsman, as the body of the seabird runs with the
movement of the wings, or turns obedient to the red, webbed
feet; and soon it was gliding over the water, borne onward
by a fresh wind, which filled the small triangular sail, toward
the fishing ground.

Beatrice, with clasped hands and dancing eyes, drank in
the splendor of the beautiful day. Her cheeks filled with
blood, her parted lips assumed an inexpressible softness and

delight—she was free as the bright water, and rejoiced like
an Indian once more in his native wilds !—never had she
looked more beautiful. more fascinating. She laughed, ran
on with childlike merriment in her voice and eyes ; dipped
her fingers with affected shivering in the foam before the
prow, and startled the wild sea-gulls with her cries and
laughter. She was a child again, and the manager said as
much to her.

"Oh !" cried the young girl, her whole countenance
radiant with joy and pleasure, " you can't think, father, how
happy I feel out here on the water !" I'm nothing but a
child, you know, and I always shall be. Look at that bird
with the white wings ; how he darts over the waves !"

The manager smiled.

"It's a shame to keep you where there are any houses,
child," he said, " you are never half as happy as this—in
London, or any where."

"I can't be, sir."

"Why ?"

"Oh, I feel so cramped where people are. They stare
at me, and make me feel badly ; and often when I pass, I
hear them say who I am, and laugh."

"That's because you act well."

"Oh, don't talk about acting now, father, please. I don't
want to think of it. I'm so happy ! Look at the pretty
foam !"

"Yes—you love the water."

"Oh, dearly ! you didn't know how I spent the evenings
on the ocean, while you were playing ombre with Captain
Fellowes."

"Commander of the merchant-vessel 'Charming Sally,'"
laughed the manager ; " but how about your evenings ?"

"Oh, I used to go and lean over the—what are they
called ?"

"Bulwarks."

"Yes, the bulwarks. I used to lean over, and look at
the foam, and the great fish tumbling about in the moonlight
for hours. It was delightful !"

The fresh face lit up with a childlike delight, as the
young girl spoke.

"Very romantic," said Mr. Hallam, smiling.

" Oh, I'm not romantic, sir, I'm the most matter-of-fact person in the world, but I couldn't help liking the foam."

" You are right—but we old fellows like tictac better than moonlight thinking."

" Yes—I used to think : I recollect I did think."

" What of ? "

" Of the beautiful land we were coming to—Virginia : the *Virgin Land*, they called it. How pretty that sounds I "

" Yes."

" A fresh, bright land, where the wind was always blowing, the trees always full of leaves and flowers, and no cold winter to chill one."

" A young poet I "

" No, no, father—I must have been born in the south, though. Oh, tell me where I was born. You never told me."

The manager looked somewhat embarrassed, and replied, after a moment's silence : " We were at Malta, then, I believe. But how did you find Virginia in reality ? "

The young girl's face assumed a sorrowful expression, and she replied : " Not very different from England, sir ; but it is pretty, the forest and all, and this river. Oh ! " she cried suddenly, " look at that bird carrying off the fish in his talons—stop, sir, stop ! "

Mr. Hallam laughed heartily. " What would they say if they heard *Juliet* calling after a sea-bird so. Mr. Effingham would not believe the account."

" Oh, father I " said Beatrice, returning to her sorrowful expression, " do not talk to me of playing to-day, I feel so happy now, sir ; and don't speak of that wild young man ; I shall get angry, and then be sorry, and cry—and you know, father, that would spoil our day. Don't speak of Mr. Effingham ; he looked at me so, last night, with his eyes on fire, and his frill crumpled and torn—I thought it was stained with blood."

" With blood I "

" He became angry with me for not attending to him on the stage, in the last act, and clutched his breast with his nails. Oh, don't speak of him," she added, growing gloomy, " I do not like that man."

" Well, well," said the manager, " don't think too hard

of him; he is young, and means nothing. I wish you to
marry well, much as I will lose in you; and you may find
a mate in Virginia. There, don't look so distressed."

"I don't want to marry!" said Beatrice, her face
clouded over.

"You don't like playing?"

"Oh, no! but I have you, father, and I don't wish to
part from you. I can'bear all."

"There now, dear, don't lose your bright smiles, and
spoil the day. We will talk no more of these matters.
Sink the theatre!" added the manager good-humoredly,
"we came out to fish."

"At the ground, squire," said the boatman. "Go it.
I'll keep the craft straight."

And soon the bright fish were being drawn up from the
water in numbers which would have afforded delight to
Isaac Walton, much as that worthy gentleman dwelt upon
brook-sides and art in snaring the solitary trout. They
spent the greater part of the morning thus, and Beatrice
forgot her gloom completely.

About noon the wind began to grow fresher, and large
clouds rolled themselves up from the western horizon, and
spread their dark curtain over the sun. The boatman
looked at them with an experienced eye, then turning to the
manager, said: "Look here, squire; seems to me we're
goin' to have a storm. Them clouds look like it; and hear
the wind!"

In fact the forest on each side of the river began to toss
its boughs and roll aloft that wild, surging sound which the
wind wakes up in its passage through tall trees. The pines
waved in the chill blast, and roared like great organs; and
in addition to these threatening sounds, the waves began to
roll higher, tossing the little bark like a nutshell, and
sprinkling the white lateen sail with snowy foam.

"I believe you are right, and we had better get to
shore."

"We're a mile from the cabin, squire, but this west
wind will carry us down like a flash. Must I tie the sail?"

"Oh, let's wait a little, father." cried Beatrice, with
animated looks and bright eyes, "the wind is so grand.
Oh, don't tie the sail yet!"

"The wind'll tear it to tatters if it keeps crackin' it so miss," said the boatman; "but I'm willin', for I'm goin' to do all I'm wanted to do. I ain't goin' to deny your pretty face any thing."

With which words the honest boatman laid down tranquilly in the stern of the bark, and—first taking a pull at his black flask—applied himself to the task of keeping the craft before the wind. Mr. Hallam had yielded to this arrangement, but was plainly desirous of returning immediately. He opened his mouth to say as much, but Beatrice interrupted him before he could speak.

"Oh, listen, father!" she cried, starting up and steadying herself by clinging to the slight mast; "listen to the woods! The wind roars through them like the cannon we heard at Dover! How sublime it sounds! And look at the waves; they are beginning to grow black, I believe, and they toss us about like a cork! Oh, how the wind sobs and rolls along! It makes me so happy!"

"Take care, miss!" said the boatman; "that mast is unsteady."

"Oh, don't be afraid for me."

"Come, let us get to shore at once," said Mr. Hallam, becoming really alarmed.

"That's easy, sir," said the boatman; "with the sail up the wind'll carry us down in a jiffy. Don't be afraid of upsetting. The Nancy never served me such a trick, and won't now, though there *is* a wind, squire; it's coming worse, too, but there's no danger."

And he caught the rope, which the wind was cracking as a man cracks a whip, and, with a vigorous hand, secured it to the gunwale. The effect was instantaneous. The little bark, which before had merely danced about on the waves, now shot down the stream like lightning, cleaving the waves which struck it, and shipping clouds of foam.

Beatrice hailed this accession of speed with delight. Her ardent and impressible nature rejoiced in the hurlyburly of the wind, the speed of the bark, the foam of the high waves wetting her at every instant.

"Oh, it's delightful, father!" she cried. "I could shout for joy! Look at that little boat, there, with the man in it so quiet and easy—it jumps about like a dry leaf!"

The boat, indeed, which the young girl was looking at, did seem to be of no more strength than a leaf. It was a frail little canoe, scarcely large enough it seemed to hold a child, and beautifully built. The sides were painted with great taste, and the prow ran up in a curving point, which dashed aside the foaming water like a steel blade. In the stern of the canoe a young man was seated, holding in his hand a paddle, with which he both propelled and guided the skiff on its path toward the shore. The young man seemed to be no stranger to such storms as the present, and, without paying any attention to the foam which broke over him, looked intently at the sail-boat.

"Oh, how it darts!" cried Beatrice; "look, the wind struck it then, and it jumped out of the water!"

"Take care, miss!" cried the boatman; "if she veers you'll fall overboard!"

"Take care, my daughter!" echoed Mr. Hallam; "there is a tremendous gust of wind coming right down. Get down!"

"Steady!" cried the boatman; "this is a roarer; take care of the mast, miss! Sit down!"

It was too late. Beatrice made a movement to obey, but before she had regained her seat, and while she yet clung to the mast, the frail pole bent beneath the powerful blast, the sail almost doubled up, and the spar snapping like a reed, precipitated the young girl into the stream. A huge wave bore her ten feet from the bark in an instant, and, passing over her, swallowed the fair form in its gloomy depths. The fat manager was struck motionless with horror, and the boatman, dropping his paddle, leaped into the stream. But another saviour was before him. The young man in the skiff had approached within a stone's throw of the sail-boat, when the gust struck her, and his canoe was darting directly across the wake of the bark when the mast snapped. At the same moment he seemed to have recognized the young woman—and, uttering an exclamation which was drowned in the shrill blast, threw himself into the waves, and catching her half-submerged form as she rose, struck out with the ease of a practised swimmer.

Beatrice was a dead weight on his arm, and he soon felt that exhaustion which the strongest swimmer experiences, struck every moment in the face by surges strong enough to ingulf a giant. The boatman, swimming with the wind and foam blinding him, could not come to his assistance— the two forms struggled with the devouring waves in vain —a huge billow passed over the young man's head, and he sank, clasping to his heart the chill form of the girl. As he rose for the last time, one of those providences which watch over us, giving the lie to chance, was the means of his salvation. His shoulder struck against the boat, which had been swept to the spot by the wind; and, as he caught its gunwale, he felt the body of the young girl weigh less upon him. He was taken into the sail-boat, he knew not how— he saw a woman whom he had saved lying lifeless before him—a rude boatman chafing her temples—a corpulent man weeping and still grasping a billet of wood with which he had plunged into the waves—and then he fell exhausted, overcome.

The first words which he heard when he came to himself, were:

"Well, squire, she's all right now: only a little wetting. Here we are at neighbour Waters', and that's his son, that saved the young woman."

* * *

CHAPTER XVI.

SEQUEL TO THE ADVENTURE.

THE fat manager did not know whether to laugh or weep. She was saved! that was all he was conscious of; and he scarcely knew how he got on shore. Beatrice, who had by this time revived wholly, though she still shivered with cold and terror, was borne to dry land by the strong boatman; and the rest following, the whole party was safe from the storm, which raged more furiously still, at thus being forced to give up its prey.

Before them rose a rough but comfortable cottage, which from its bluff, overlooked the river up and down for miles. A walk of ten minutes brought them to the door, and within a cheerful fire was burning, apparently made necessary by the high and exposed situation of the house. The boatman

deposited, we may almost say, the young girl on a comfortable chair. She had been supported from the landing between the honest fellow and her father—the young man
walking in silence before.

After thus getting rid of his charge, the boatman turned
to greet the owner of the mansion, saying:

" Well, neighbour Waters, here's a mess!—the young
lady's been overboard and nigh gone."

The host was an old man of sixty-five or more: in every
thing about him, the simplicity of his nature was manifest.
His open features were almost constantly lit up by a cheerful smile, and his eyes were full of kindness and good-humor.
He was clad as the humbler class were almost universally at
that day—in a broad-skirted coat of drab cloth, with plain
cuffs, but turned back after the fashion of the time: his
stockings were of wool, and his waistcoat was of plain serge,
with large pockets, and reaching almost to the knees. On
his feet he wore heavy, thick-soled shoes; and his gray hair,
gathered in a club behind, was free from powder.

To the boatman's address, he replied, cheerily:

" Overboard! how so, neighbor Townes? and in your
craft? I never hearn tell of such a thing happenin' to you
before. The pretty bird! we must see how to fix her. Sit
down, sir: sit down—your daughter, I reckon. Well, well,
this is a bad day to be on the water. How does the young
lady feel now?"

Beatrice had profited by the cheering blaze, and replied
quietly, though with a slight shiver:

" I am a great deal better than I was, sir: I owe you
many thanks for your kindness,"

" No kindness in the world," said the old man, " I'm
poor and simple, but you're heartily welcome."

" Poor and simple as you say you are, neighbor," here
broke in the boatman, " there ain't a squire about here equal
to you: and I've been knowin' you this thirty years: and
Charley," here he looked at the young man, who had taken
his seat in silence, " Charley is a chip of the old block. Ef
it hadn't been for him, the young lady'd a been at Davy
Jones' locker by now."

" Why, did Charley?"

" Yes, he did so, neighbor; he saved the young 'ooman.

As for me, I'm most nigh 'shamed to say it, but the wind and foam blinded me."

" Well, well—it's what Charley ought 'a done, and there's an end on it. Now we'll see to a room for you, miss," he said to Beatrice ; " you musn't move to-day. I don't know you, but you're welcome to any thing old John Waters owns."

"You are very kind, Mr. Waters," said the fat manager, who had been looking around him, " but we had better get back to town. Our horses are down at your house, friend," he added, to the boatman ; " couldn't you bring 'em here ? "

"Easiest thing in life. Jest give me time to swallow a drop ; and that puts me in mind, won't you take somethin' yourself, 'squire, and the young lady ? Neighbor Waters drinks nothing but water—he don't."

Mr. Manager Hallam received this proposal with extreme satisfaction, and no doubt reflecting that it was just " what the great Congreve " would have done—a favorite authority with him—emptied nearly half a pint. Beatrice, however, refused the rum, with a shake of her head.

" Now, I'll take Sam, neighbor," said the boatman, "and jog down. There's Lanky onhitchin' him. 'Seems to me the sooner I am back the better."

" Yes, yes ; and there's a pistole," said Mr. Hallam.

The boatman received the money doubtfully, hesitated, then pocketed it ; finally, mounting Sam, a rough-looking cart-horse, harness and all, clattered off through the whirling leaves of the forest toward his cabin.

" But you ain't goin' to take the young lady away so soon," said old John Waters ; " she'll catch the agy, friend. We'll have a room for her—the little place up there—fixed in no time. Lanky's just come from town, and will make a blazing fire."

" I think we had better get back," said Hallam, uneasily ; " eh, daughter ? "

" Yes, sir ; I feel quite strong now, and would like to ride. I never can thank you, sir, and—and your son, enough for what you have done. He saved my life."

" Oh," laughed the old fisherman, " that's his place— you're a weak little thing, and couldn't be expected to take keer of yourself—not a strong woman, either ; only a little easy-livin' lady."

" Oh no, sir," said Beatrice, with her lip twitching, " I am only an actress."

" An actress!—what's that ? Oh—"

" My name is Beatrice Hallam," said the young girl, regaining her calmness.

" Well! did any one ever !" said the old man, " the young lady that played !—I heard all about you, the other day, and made Charley go to see the playin': and he said a heap in your favor. Charley, you know," said the old fellow, with a smile, " aint much given to these things—and I 'most fear he hurts his health over his books—look through the door, there what a parcel ! He works hard, too, in the field, and helps me with the seine, but he's been studyin' too much lately I told him so : and says I, ' Charley, you'd better go to town and take some rest : go and see the players.' At first he wouldn't hear of it ; but he went, and praised you a heap, I can tell you, Miss ; though I'm bound to say he didn't say much in favor of young Squire Effin'ham."

Beatrice flushed to her forehead, and stole a glance at the young man. He rose, and seeming to banish with an effort the thoughts which preoccupied his mind, said, in a grave and serious voice :

" I confess, Miss Hallam, that your acting was faultless, as far as I could judge of it ; and my father has not misunderstood my opinion of Mr. Effingham's very unworthy conduct toward yourself. But let us dismiss all these matters —you must be greatly fatigued, and not much disposed to listen to conversation. We are very poor, here, as you see, but can give you, and you also, Mr. Hallam, shelter for the night. Remain."

Beatrice gazed a moment furtively at the noble and thoughtful face, allowed the last sound of the clear voice to die away, then replied :

" We had better return, sir—indeed, we should not refuse your kindness, I know : but—"

" Yes, we must return : you have not dried your own clothes even, sir," said the manager, " and we are under sufficient obligation for one day. You saved my daughter's life, sir—God reward you."

" I did nothing but what I should have done, Mr. Hallam. My father has told you that it was my simple duty,

and there was little risk. Had there been real risk, I trust
I should still have done my duty."

"I know you would, Charley," said the old man proudly, "you'd throw your life away for a child: and I rather
think Mr. Effingham would a had a hard time, if you had
met after the play!"

"Come—come, father," said the young man, gravely, "do
not repeat my follies. I have repented it. Harsh words do
no good."

"If what you said was true, he deserved 'em and more,"
said old Waters: "you can't deny it!"

"Well, yes! he deserved harsh comment! you are
right!" said the young man, his face flushing, "for he insulted and annoyed a woman. We cannot go far wrong in
saying that the man who annoys a woman or a child, must
have a bad heart, and ungenerous and narrow soul!"

The young man's voice, ordinarily grave and simple,
changed, as he uttered these words: and his flushed face
positively overawed the fat manager, who, feeling his own
character of *pater familias* indirectly called in question, was
about to speak, and ask Beatrice the particulars of Mr.
Effingham's conduct. His tone was so firm and proud—his
eye so clear and full of disdain—his attitude so erect and
noble, as he uttered these words, that the wide apartment,
with its fishing-nets, and rough chairs and tables, seemed to
grow brilliant and imposing—mind penetrating matter, and
transforming it to its own likeness.

Beatrice Hallam felt her face fill with blood, her heart
throb: for the first time in her life she had found the nature
which heaven had moulded in the form of her own, and when
the young man, apparently regretting his excitement, mo-
mentary as it was, returned in silence to his seat, her lus-
trous glances, brilliant as light itself, but dimmed by a haze
of emotion, followed him, and could not withdraw themselves
from him.

A few moments afterwards, the boatman returned with
the horses, and the manager, who began to feel some embarrassment, rose to go.

"We've treated you very bad considerin'," said the old
man, "but the fire here was about the best thing for you, I
thought, after the wettin'. Lanky's makin' the fire now for

the young lady: but 'sides that, we had in the way o' clothes nothin' much better 'n a peajacket to offer her, and you said the rum was the best thing for *you* after the wettin'."

"All I wanted—all I wanted, sir," said the manager, with a good-humored laugh.

"And I am nearly quite dry now, sir," said Beatrice, with a timid smile; "I shall never forget your kindness to me, Mr. Waters."

And she pressed with her small fingers the huge, hearty hand of the old fisherman, and then held out the same little hand to his son, who pressed it with a sensation at his heart which he could not understand.

"Strange!" he said, as they turned away, "I seem to have met this young girl in some other world—well, well, the common fancy!'

And following Beatrice to the door, he assisted her to mount—which operation was somewhat embarrassed by the long riding dress, brought with the horses from the boat-man's cabin—after which the guests set forward toward Williamsburg.

"Waters—Waters? I seem to have heard that name before, father," said Beatrice, "and really seem to have known Mr. Charles."

"It's a very common name," replied the manager, "and we often find these resemblances. How the evening has cleared off. I don't think any rain has fallen; the storm must have passed off to the southward."

Whether Mr. Manager Hallam wished to turn the conversation or not, remains a mystery: but if such was his design, it succeeded perfectly, and Beatrice began to talk about the adventures through which they had passed. Soon the houses of the town came in sight, and they passed along, and drew up before the " Raleigh."

Beatrice changed her wet garments, and felt no bad effects from her accident beyond a slight chill. One would have said that the warmth at her heart vivified her person, and defied the chilly waters of the river. All that evening, while the fat manager was relating the adventures of the day, she sat studying, apparently; but merely her dreamy eyes were fixed upon the page.

Of what was she thinking, and why that flush upon the tender face, that light in the veiled eyes?

CHAPTER XVII.

MR. EFFINGHAM MAKES A FRIENDLY CALL.

On the next morning, just as Beatrice was binding up her hair before the single mirror of her small sitting-room, she heard a knock at the door, and answering, "Come in," she saw through the open door Mr. Champ Effingham, who entered the apartment with a smile.

"Ah, good morning, charming Miss Beatrice!" he said, with a pleased air, too elaborate indeed not to be somewhat affected; "how is your ladyship to-day?"

Beatrice uttered a sigh of despair, with which no little irritation was commingled. She, however, remembered the wish her father had expressed, that she should not receive her visitor harshly, and this consideration silenced the haughty reply which rose to her lips, though it could not subdue the flash in her proud, brilliant eye.

"I am very well, sir," she said.

"For which reason," replied Mr. Effingham, playing with his ruffle, and sitting down languidly, "you receive me very ill."

"No, sir; my reception is neither the one nor the other; but you have no right to expect a very friendly reception."

"Why not friendly?"

"Can you ask, sir!"

"Certainly."

"I have nothing to reply, then, sir."

"Ah, ah!" said Mr. Effingham, first smoothing the feather in his cocked hat, then negligently playing with the bright hilt of his short sword; "ah, you are thinking about my naughty behavior in the theatre the other evening."

"I have forgotten all, sir," she said calmly.

"Well, well, I have come to-day to ask your ladyship to pardon these various exhibitions of ill-humor. My unfortunate ruffle, which you, no doubt, observed, had suffered somewhat in the *melée*, proved to me the next morning that I must have been rather violent. The fact is, I was in a bad humor—out of temper—a most mortifying acknowledgment for a star of fashion and nonchalance like myself, but still true."

Beatrice made no reply.

"Granted! I *was* out of sorts—nervous, in a bad humor; but, this morning, I am in a delightful state of mind. I feel as if I could embrace the whole world, yourself included with the most fraternal and enthusiastic regard. Am I not in an enviable state of mind? But this is nothing to you. Ah! you take very little interest in my welfare, I am really afraid, and have not forgiven, as such a lovely saint should, what I have been guilty of. Come, my charming Miss Beatrice, exert your amiability, and pardon all."

Beatrice, with her quick eye, easily discerned the painful emotion beneath this raillery—the fire concealed beneath the ashes. For a moment she hesitated, then said:

"I am not revengeful or unforgiving, sir, and the painful ordeal you subjected me to in the theatre is already forgotten. Now, sir, I must go to rehearsal."

"Bah! don't be in a hurry, Beatrice, and, above all, don't *pity* me; I am not a man to be pitied; and, as to rehearsal, that can wait a little, while we have a short conversation. You have a charming voice, and this morning I am really wearied to death. Come, amuse me."

"I have no time to converse, sir; I must leave you."

"Come, come: don't be so unamiable—you may go directly!"

Beatrice sat down, with a sigh of resignation, instead of leaving the room, as she felt tempted to do. Her father's wish made her patient.

"Where were you yesterday?"

"We went to the river, sir, for a sail."

"To the James?"

"Yes, sir."

"Why did you not send me word?"

"Send you word—why, sir?"

"Why, my new sailboat is just launched, and we might have had a delightful day in her."

"We had a very good one."

"Any adventures?"

"I fell into the river, sir."

"The devil! And how did you get to land?"

"A gentleman rescued me."

" A gentleman—who, in heaven's name?

Beatrice felt her face flush, half with embarassment—half with anger, at this persevering cross-examination. For a moment she hesitated; but her frank and fearless nature made her reply almost instantly,

" Mr. Charles Waters, sir."

" Charles Waters!" cried Mr. Effingham, with a sudden pallor, and a flash of the eye, which revealed the volcano beneath his affected carelessness.

" Mr. Charles Waters," said Beatrice, calmly and firmly, " to him I am indebted for my existence, at this moment."

A flush of hatred passed over Mr. Effingham's brow, and he said, with a sneer:

" Ah, your cavalier! I had forgotten, Madam."

Beatrice felt her heart throb with anger, and a scornful answer arose to her lips : but she repressed these evidences of feeling, and said coldly :

" Mr. Effingham, I will not exchange another word with you, if I am to be insulted thus. Mr. Waters is, as you well know, almost a perfect stranger to me, and I am nothing to him :" with which the lip trembled: " he saved my life yesterday, at the peril of his own, and I owe to him deep gratitude. For this reason, sir, you will understand that I am not the proper sympathizer with your dissatisfaction. Now, sir, I must go."

Mr. Effingham made a powerful effort over himself, and burst into a laugh which was painful to hear.

" Well, well," he said, in a voice which he in vain endeavored to render careless and easy, " we won't quarrel about the Chevalier Waters. I'm sure I am very much obliged to him for restoring to the community so charming an actress; though, as I always had a partiality for heroism, especially being heroic myself, when nothing was to be lost by it, I regret that the present grand effort was not made by myself. Come! don't burn me with your eyes."

" I must go, sir."

" Without pardoning my naughty treatment of you in the theatre? Wasn't it horrible?"

" Yes, sir!" said Beatrice, flushing; " it was unmanly."

" Striking coincidence of opinion, at least. Yes, it was dreadful ; and do you know what occurred when I was mak-

lng my exit, right of centre?—that is the phrase, I believe
—why, I very nearly ran over a young lady with whom I
am dead in love."

Beatrice looked at the young man with a strange expression. Had she met with a real life actor superior to herself?

"Just so," continued Mr. Effingham, bursting into laughter; "my *chère amie*, you know—one of the most beautiful,
highborn, and wealthy young girls in the colony; pretty,
fair hair, blue eyes, and all that—just opposed to your style.
Did you see her?"

"No, sir," said Beatrice.

"Well, you might have done so. I'm certain she saw
you, and possibly had a view of the attack upon my ruffles,
when I accidentally scratched myself, you know. In going
out, I placed my foot upon her dress, and nearly tore a furbelow away. What horrible awkwardness! I shall never
forgive myself."

"Your tone is bitter, sir."

"Bitter? Not at all! I am ready to laugh now, reflecting on the melodrama. After the affair of the furbelow,
the hero made his exit—myself, that is to say—and then I
rode quietly away, accomplishing the first ten miles in fifteen
minutes, I believe."

"Mr. Effingham, you seem to me to be laboring under
some bitter emotion; you shock me. If you love a lady, do
not, sir, do not abandon her for me. I know not what I say,
sir,—I only know that you banish all sunshine from my life.
I have not enough to spare, sir. For heaven's sake, leave me."

"You are right," said Mr. Effingham, losing his forced
gayety, "I am carried away by my infatuation—I love you."

"Sir! you must not—"

"Bah!" he said, gloomily; "don't let us mince matters."

"I must go, sir."

"Not before giving me one word not altogether harsh."

"I must go, sir—"

"Beatrice Hallam, you are the most bitter and unreasonable of women. You choose to despise me, because I
seek you; you are not only unreasonable, you are a woman
without heart!"

Beatrice suppressed her emotion, and said:

5

" No, sir ; that is unjust. I am not a woman without
heart—I have feelings, deep feelings.'

" I have never discovered them."

" You do not know me, sir."

" Ah, you mistake, madam ; I know you well."

" For heaven's sake, go, sir."

" I prefer remaining."

" I must then leave you, sir."

Mr. Effingham rose with a threatening gesture; but,
collecting himself, sat down again.

" Ah, madam," he said, with gloomy bitterness; " you
are very prudish: you hate me—Mr. Charles Waters takes
you in his arms—I cannot approach you."

" Sir ! " said Beatrice, indignantly, " I avoid you, because I feel that you are not a proper companion for me. No,
sir ! I am not prudish—I am no silly girl. My life has
been hard and changeable—my fate adverse. I have embraced the profession of the stage from necessity. My father
was an actor. I am an actress because I am his daughter.
As an actress, I know that I am exposed to a thousand
temptations, and a thousand insults. I know very well that
we are considered the bond slaves of the public, especially
of the aristocratic portion. But I will not accept the questionable attentions of yourself, or any other young gentleman, who is trained to look upon me, and upon persons
of my profession as infinitely beneath him—as so many
slaves. No, sir ! I have chosen to go and exhibit myself
in public, that the bread I eat may be honestly procured.
After the theatre, I am a woman, and I will not have my
name tossed from mouth to mouth unworthily—remember,
sir."

The young girl looked so lovely at that moment—her
beautiful eyes flashed such vivid lightning—her rosy face
was so eloquent with indignation, that Mr. Effingham found
words fail him—lost in, overwhelmed as he was by, her
splendid and fiery beauty.

" You are a strange actress," he said at length, in a low,
deep-toned voice, " and certainly unlike any other I have
ever seen. Yes, I have seen many actresses, in France,
Italy, England, every where, and I find in you nothing like
them. Well : you say you are no common comedienne, and

you see that I agree with you. You hint that I would be
apt to abuse any friendship you granted me—I do not say
you are wrong there. There is some truth in your views, and
I find no fault with you. But, at least, I should not scoff
at you :—I might bless you, or only mention your name with
a curse upon my lip—but I do not think I could do aught
else. For you are not indifferent to me. You smile : you
think I am very inconsistent. But when I say that I can
never treat your name as that of an indifferent woman, I
mean this : I mean that from our first meeting in the forest,
near the Hall yonder, your image has dwelt in my mind and
heart—or if not quite in my heart, to be frank, at least in
my memory. At the theatre we met again, and I treated
you as gentlemen are accustomed to treat actresses; for I
laughed at my feelings. You received that treatment as became you—you are a noble girl—and I went away cursing
and loving you almost. I spent a bad night after the play,
and worse since—I came here to-day to jeer at you. In
place of further jeering, I bow to you, and offer you respect
and admiration, if not love, and ask your friendship in
return."

Beatrice betrayed some feeling at these earnest words,
and no longer looked at the young man so disdainfully.

"I have listened to you, sir," she said, "and I request
you to pardon any harshness in what I have but now said.
But, let me here say, what you will feel to be true, and no
less true than unchangeable—that there can be nothing in
common between us. You cannot be my friend—visiting
and talking unreservedly with me as friends may—without
causing a scandal in the Colony :—a scandal which will be
as injurious to yourself as to me. Now, sir, you had better
leave me. We may meet again—indeed, I have it not in
my power to refuse to meet you—in the theatre. This is
not an invitation, for I say again, there cannot and must not
be any thing in common between an actress, like myself, and
Mr. Effingham. Good evening, sir."

Mr. Effingham stood looking at the young woman in
silence, with an expression upon his countenance which she
could not understand   At last he said, with a pale lip, and
very abruptly :

"Are you acting ?"

" No, sir ! " said the young girl, indignantly.

" Then you are a prodigy of truth and nobleness," he said, with a lightning-like glance. " Come, come, let me throw aside all this sophistry with which I am trying to deceive myself. I love you ! " he said, gloomily.

The young girl drew back.

' You shall love me in return ! " he said.

And there was so much haughtiness in his tone that her cheek flushed.

" You are consistent, sir," she said ; " just now, your regard for me was slight, you said—at least, I thought so."

" As you please—I do not know whether I love you or not, and am sure I love another. But what I do know is, that there is something about you, which tears me from all else toward you, my beautiful diabolical syren ! "

" Mr. Effingham, you really seem to have grown mad : let our interview end here."

" I am mad, and it is you who have driven me crazy. Beatrice ! mine is a family of fiery traits—we love or hate strongly, and do nothing by halves. I am not unlike my ancestors. Look at me ! I am a *petit maître*—exhausting my life in idleness and ease. Why ? Because I need some great passion. Now I have opened my breast to you, and I add, that you will be my passion."

" Mr. Effingham, dismiss all thought of me. I am an actress, sir—an actress : my associates are players, those who are now waiting for me yonder, sir—no other persons : a barrier is raised between me and the world, by my profession. For the hundredth time, I say we can have nothing in common. Even now your presence is causing discussion in the room below, and rude lips jeer me. Oh, sir ! leave me, for heaven's sake ! If you have any regard for me, go, and end this trying interview ! "

He gazed at her for a moment in silence, and then, putting his hat on, left the room, full of gloomy rage, but with a sneering lip   Ten minutes afterwards he left the town.

CHAPTER XVIII.

THE MAN IN THE RED CLOAK.

JUST as Mr. Champ Effingham left Williamsburg, by the western road—his splendid animal careering at full gallop in obedience to his rider's spur—a young man entered the town from the south on foot, and directed his steps toward the Raleigh Tavern. He soon reached the long platform in front of the inn, and entered the ordinary.

He was about to address some question to the portly landlord, when turning his eyes to the opposite side of the room, he saw seated in one of the large leathern chairs, a man whose face seemed to excite some slumbering thought in his mind, for he passed his hand over his brow, and seemed to question his memory. This man, who was reading the last issue of the "Virginia Gazette" with some interest, seemed to be verging on thirty, and did not appear to be above the rank of what then were called yeomen. His crisp hair was curled up beneath the ears, outwardly: his mouth had in it a world of character, though it was rather stern : and his forehead, very broad and high, was tanned and freckled. He was clad in coarse leather breeches, leggings, a long fustian waistcoat, and coat of shaggy cloth, without a particle of ornament, then almost universal in the costume of gentlemen. Over his shoulders was hung loosely an old red cloak, and his slouch hat lay by him on the rude pine table.

The new comer took in all these details with a single glance, and was about to turn away, when, raising his eyes, the stranger saw him looking at him.

He rose, and extended a hard, brown hand, saying .

" Ah, sir I good-day, I believe we are acquaintances, though I fear you have forgotten me."

" No sir," said the new comer, " I recognized you at once."

" Because you found me an agitator of ideas, like yourself on our last meeting—which I believe was also our first. You will recollect we met some days since near the Capitol, when Parson Tag took politely from your hand the ' Gazette,' you had just purchased 'to look at it,' he said: in return for which courtesy you gave him some original ideas."

"I did not obtrude them," said his companion, calmly "he questioned me, and I replied."

"Yes, and he treated your crudities, as he called them, with well-bred contempt, when he found an opportunity to turn his back on you."

"I was not offended, sir. He had a perfect right to turn to those gentlemen who bowed to him."

"Offended! I should say that would be a loss of time with a parson, not to mention the deadly sin." As he uttered these words, a grim curl of the lip betrayed the irony of the speaker.

"The fact is," he added, "you gave him, as I said, some original views on the subject of education; and he did not seem to relish them from a gentleman clad, like yourself, in drab and fustian."

"Well, well, sir," said the other, "perhaps he was right. Men of my class are not generally worth listening to on matters of policy, as I feel I am not—he is a cultivated scholar."

"Bah!" said the man in the red cloak, good-humoredly, "mind is mind, sir, and it matters little whether the frame be covered with fustian or cut velvet, the head with a gold-laced hat or a slouch, like mine there; the man, weak or strong, remains."

His companion felt again the strange influence of that voice, at once careless and earnest, laughing and grave; a singular sympathy seemed to have already sprung up between these two men, spite of their acquaintance of yesterday.

"Now," said the stranger, wrapping his old cloak about his shoulders, "I find in you a thinking man—you scarcely reflect about classes and dresses, I venture to say. You have walked far this morning?" he added.

"Yes, that is, some miles," replied the young man somewhat at a loss to understand this abrupt question.

"You are dusty."

"Yes; the sand is dry."

"Well, did you think of that dust as you came along?'

"I believe not, my thoughts were elsewhere."

" Good, that is what I mean. The squire riding in his coach has his book, or takes his nap; you can't read or nap walking—the consequence? why you must think."

The young man sat down to rest; that coarse yet musical voice drew him in spite of himself.

" It remains to tell me what you were thinking of as you came along, friend," added the stranger; " come, let us talk unreservedly. Let us clash our minds together, and see if some sparks do not spring forth. What were you thinking of?"

" Well, I can tell you easily," said his companion; " I was reflecting upon the system of education we spoke of some days since."

" Oh, I recollect. Your free school ideas?"

" Yes."

" Broached to the parson?"

" Yes."

" They were striking, I confess, but wholly out of the question."

" Out of the question?"

" Certainly; is it possible that a man of your clearness of head—let us speak like friends, and as roughly and honestly as we can—is it possible that you could for a moment be in favor of such a doctrine as you stated, that the men of property should put their hands into their pockets to take out money for people they know nothing of, to support free schools; to give a premium for idleness? That, I think, is what you said they were bound to do, the other day."

" Well, sir," said the young man, looking at his interlocutor with some surprise, " I am still of that opinion."

" It is Utopian!"

" Utopian?"

" Yes, as impossible as it is unjust," said the stranger.

" You are then of the past, instead of the future," said his companion, with noble simplicity, " I am sorry that I misunderstood you so completely."

" Of the future? Oh, yes, I understand you. Well, I did take your part, as was natural: "—the speaker pronounced this word, *nat'ral,* " but my only end was to draw out the parson. Do not think that, on that account, I a am reformer, as you are, sir."

"Yes, sir: had I the power to make my words felt I would be a reformer."

"Take care, reform is often merely change: and change for the worse. You would reform, what?"

"Nearly every thing; but originate more."

"Ah, we return to the question of education."

"A paramount question."

"Your darling Utopia—above all the rest."

"My thought always—yes."

Nothing was ever more visionary," said the man in the red cloak, "excuse my plainness: but I do not even see any necessity for such a system, leaving the possibility of founding it entirely out of the question."

"No necessity, sir!"

"There is very little popular ignorance in Virginia—"

"Very little!" interrupted the other with animated looks, "you deceive yourself! It is immense! From the indented servant who drives his master's coach, to the yeoman who toils with the sweat running from his brow, all is ignorance, darkness and gloom. The children grow up like wild beasts, the animal cultivated in place of the soul—the man is but the larger child— as ignorant and more dangerous."

"Dangerous, did you say?"

"Yes, dangerous! dangerous as a wild animal is dangerous to approach: dangerous as a marsh is to tread upon! This mind, which holds so much of richness and God-given, inherent capability of improvement, is a mere morass; tread on it, it will ingulf you!—a morass covered with poisonous flowers, festering with decayed vegetation, lit up only by dancing fires—a dance of death! But, clear this morass:— drain it, expose it to light, and it will fecundate. Light, light is what it wants, what it cries for despairingly; and no answer is vouchsafed to it."

"You wish government to answer it, eh?"

"Yes, I would have government to change the animal into a human being, the wolf into a civilized man."

"Now you make us all wolves," said the man in the red cloak, "how are men animals, sir?"

"Why, who that has opened the records of the world, for an instant even, could controvert it! The normal condition

is animal—the spirit is there, God be thanked! but it flick-
ers, glimmers, burns faintly in the poisonous miasma. Still
environed by a thousand foes it lives on. Encourage it never so little and it flames aloft in clear heavenly radiance!
what a noble field for those who love the race, and have the
power to benefit these souls steeped in gloom. For this
poor feeble existence is a soul—it will never die!—the re-
sponsibility of leaving that soul to struggle alone and unaid-
ed against its foes seems to me dreadful, sir! It seems to
me that God will some day ask of those men who had the
power and did not use it, what he asked of Cain: 'Where is
thy brother?' If they have not struck the blow themselves,
they have allowed the better part of men to be overcome
within them, and this spiritual murder will lie at their doors.
That better part moans and mutters its inarticulate despair,
the very life-blood arrested in the veins by this nightmare of
ignorance and darkness, which, squatting upon its breast,
makes it writhe and groan and toss, in the deep darkness.
The more I reflect upon this thing, the more dreadful does it
seem to me. There are thousands who have never known
the means of salvation—pagans in this Virginia of to-day.
Christ has wept tears of blood for them in vain: his hands
were not pierced for them, they never heard of him—mere
heathen men—there within a stone's throw of us. Is it not
dreadful?"

The thinker carried away by his excitement, had risen
from his seat, and now stood erect before the man in the red
cloak, who seemed to regard him with that philosophic interest which a naturalist takes in a new species of animal.

"Well, well," he said, "there is much truth in your
views, but they do not convince me Governments, my
friend, are rather selfish, it seems to me; and though we
common people here discussing them, pride ourselves upon
our fine and noble views, I fancy we should act much after
the same fashion were we in power. Good policy would keep
us from testing these elevated ideas.

"No, never!" said his companion; "I cannot agree
with you. Rather is it a most false and narrow policy to
trample thus on the low."

"Why, pray?" said the stranger, who seemed to have
no end beyond making the other talk.

"Because ignorance is the most fatal of all curses to rulers. The ignorant soul is the prey of demagogues and false leaders—it is a sea which any wind will lash into foam. The little history which I have read has been read in vain, if it has not shown me that an ignorant and uncultivated people are the most dangerous of all. You see the great mass every day, and do not look at it from your elevation—you are ruler! Well, sir, some day, that great ocean will be agitated by some popular grievance, it will rise in its might—as strong as it is ignorant—and, with its world of fury, it will burst your vain dykes, and bury you and your government for ever."

The stranger looked at the speaker with the same curious expression.

"You have thought much upon this subject, sir," he said.

"Yes," said the other, "often and deeply. I must have wearied you, and I shall now permit you to return to your paper, sir. Free schools—the form in which I would have this vast evil attacked—are not, to all, the absorbing subject of thought which they are to myself."

"Oh, no; you have given me thoughts. I have listened with attention," said the stranger; "I do not live in Williamsburg, and am thankful for the time and society you give me. I am one of the people myself, and, though I have a smattering of Latin, and some reading, feel, in my own person, the truth of many of your remarks."

"I did not mean, believe me—"

"Come, come, don't let us interchange any compliments," said the stranger, with a laugh; "we understand each other—there is something like sympathy between us."

"Yes, from our first meeting I have felt it."

"You are more of a student than myself, doubtless,' said the stranger; "I recognize in you the patient worker. For myself, I am very indolent, and would rather play the violin, or hunt, or fish, than study."

"But you think—reflect."

"Yes," said the stranger, "much."

And his wandering, careless eye became steadfast, and full of steady strength. There was wonderful clearness in it, and that proud and lofty glance peculiar to men born to lead and rule, did not escape the attention of his companion.

It was the eye of the eagle looking down from the clouds upon men and things, the past and present; old things and new; the glance of fire, which, rejecting petty details, and piercing the heaviest mist, caught the central idea, the living fact, then turned to renew itself at the great source of light. The thinker felt that the stranger was greater than he seemed, greater than he even knew himself. He felt that this ungainly man, clad so rudely, and speaking with such clownish accent, was a born leader of men—a thinker of new thoughts.

"Yes," the stranger added, "I reflect much, and my conclusions would, perhaps, astound the parsons more than your own ideas have done, sir. At a more opportune moment, I hope to interchange thoughts with you upon some of the vital questions which affect this age and country now. I recognize in you a spirit which sympathizes with my own —a nature like my own—for I am a man of the people. You shall give me your ideas—I will give you my own. Who knows that from this collision of thought fire may not dart. You do not know me by name or condition, sir; I know as little of yourself: still, mind speaks to mind, and recognizes its co-worker. And if, in future, occasions shall arise, whic' require bold hearts and hands, I shall come to you, and claim your aid, without fear of refusal, as without dread of the result."

With which words the man in the red cloak put on his old slouch hat, made an awkward bow, and with a gait, which was half stride, half shamble, went out of the Raleigh, and disappeared. Charles Waters stood, for some moments, looking thoughtfully after him: then, arousing himself, turned to the landlord, and asked for Miss Hallam. The landlord pointed through the door: the young girl was just going up stairs, having returned from rehearsal, and her visitor followed her.

CHAPTER XIX.

BEATRICE AND HER SECOND VISITOR.

He knocked at the door which he saw close behind her, and, being bid to come in, opened it and entered. The young girl was standing in front of the window, which was open, and did not seem to be in a very amiable mood. Her brow was knit, and her firmly closed lips appeared to indicate the expectation on the part of their mistress, of an unwelcome visitor.

No sooner had she caught sight of the young man, however, than this expression of annoyance and ill-humor vanished like magic: and, running forward, with the abandon and fresh grace of a child, she held out her hands, saying:

"Oh, I am very glad to see you!"

Her beautiful face was, at that moment, lit up with such joy, the eyes were so bright and happy looking, the parted lips radiant with a smile of such tenderness and child-like simplicity, that her companion stood, for a full minute, looking at her in silent surprise. She had taken his hand, and pressed it so warmly that, spite of himself, spite of the preoccupation, caused by the interview which he had just passed, he felt his heart throb with a new and delightful emotion.

"Oh!" said Beatrice, "this is very kind to come and see us: have I kept you waiting?"

"No, madam," he said, "and I am very happy to find you so well. You are right in supposing that my visit was to you and your father. We were all desirous of knowing whether you had suffered any bad effects from your accident."

"I am very well, sir, I believe," replied Beatrice, becoming more calm, "and I only have a slight cough which will go off, I am sure: sit down, sir."

He was on the point of saying that he only called to ask the simple question to which she had just replied: but, in spite of himself, he was swayed by the bright, tender glance of the young girl, and sat down.

"I am afraid I interrupt you," he said, "you are busy."

"Oh no, sir: I have just returned from—from rehearsal. You know I am an actress, sir," she added, with a slight blush; but, at once calling her pride to her assistance this blush disappeared, and she said calmly, "I have to play to-night."

He saw the blush, and perfectly well understood it.

"You said, 'I am an actress,' with some hesitation," he replied. "I do not find in that fact any thing that you should be ashamed of. It is an honest and worthy employment, when it is pursued worthily, as you pursue it, Miss Hallam."

"All do not think so, sir."

"At least, I do; and do not expect to find in me the mode of thinking which characterizes the wealthier classes of the day. Nothing is derogatory which is undertaken in a pure and elevated spirit—which is honest. It would take much to persuade me that the ' player,' to use the phrase of Shakspeare, who labors honestly and nobly in his vocation, should not rank above the idle gentleman, who consumes merely, without producing any thing. I do not say this in a fault-finding or bitter spirit : it seems simply true to me; and thus I cannot understand why you should hesitate to avow your profession."

"I do not, sir," said Beatrice softly; "but spite of my-self, I am affected by the popular opinion of my class, and find all my pride necessary to combat it. Oh yes, sir l it is unjust—indeed it is l " added the young girl, earnestly; "and though I do not like acting, and dread the approach of every night, I cannot think the gentlemen are right in despising us ! "

"I am sure they do not think so of you," he said; "and though Mr. Effingham has behaved toward you in a manner most unworthy of an honorable man, I cannot think he meant a deliberate insult to a young girl. That were too base," he added, with the latent flash of the eye which characterized him.

"Ah, sir l " said Beatrice, with the same cloud upon her face, which had warned the manager upon the river, " do not let us speak of Mr. Effingham—he does not treat me as a gentleman should treat all persons, however much beneath him. I feel that I am not beneath him, and I can forget the suffering he causes me. Come l I won't talk of him any more. I see your face becoming gloomy, and your anger rising. Do let us leave all this, and not talk about it any more."

"Well, madam, you teach me a lofty lesson. If I am indignant, I had the right to be; but there is something greater than anger, that is forgiveness. Let this young man, then, be no longer the subject of our thoughts; he is beneath you far enough—I say it with no scoffing, much less to flatter—far enough for you to pardon him."

The face of the young girl flushed with feeling, and her eyes filled.

"Oh! how different from the other," she murmured, turning away; "these words are a balm to me: they make me happy, though I do not deserve his opinion."

And looking at him with happy eyes, bathed in their tender mist, she said softly:

"You are very kind to me, sir; you must have a noble nature to speak thus to a poor young girl like myself."

Never had he seen a more winning countenance—so much purity and simple truth in human eyes. He began to look at her more closely, surveying in turn the noble brow, the soft, melting eyes, the tender, childlike mouth, the maidenly attitude, so full of modesty and grace. She had just called herself a poor girl, and he found himself looking upon her as a princess.

"I am a poor man, too," he said, "much poorer than yourself. You have many things which I have not. How grateful must the applause your genius excites sound to you! I have no such pleasure," he said with a smile at his own sophistry.

"Ah! but you have liberty."

"Have not you?"

"No—that is, I mean not your liberty."

"What is mine?"

"Oh!" cried Beatrice; "you have the forest, the river, and the clouds. Don't smile at me, sir; when I think of them, I am a child again, and forget all my worry and every thing."

"And you love the woods?"

"Oh, dearly!"

"And the water."

"More still."

"Strange that your career has not made these simple things distasteful," he said, regarding her with more and more attention.

"Never could any thing make me dislike them," said Beatrice, with a lovely rose-color in her beautiful cheek "I must have been born in the country—I never heard from father, and I only recollect London—for it makes me happy to get away among the leaves and flowers. I like autumn

especially, and, I believe, I could listen to the woods sighing
in the wind for whole days.   I have often thought the great
trees were men with grand souls, sheltering all that come
beneath them, and raising their heads to heaven without
fearing the lightning or storms! "

He had not taken his eyes from the animated face.

"And then on the river," added Beatrice, with a happy
light in her eyes, "on the water I feel freer than ever.   I
feel like dancing sometimes, and father was laughing at m
for calling after the waterfowl the other day—when you
saved me, you know," she said, with a look which went to his
heart.   He made a movement with his hand.

"I love the water," she said, "and the clouds and waves,
and all—the sunlight makes me deeply joyful.   I could
never have felt it again," she added in a subdued voice, "but
for you—and who knows—who knows—"

The impulsive young girl passing, as was her wont, from
excitement to quiet, from joy to melancholy, paused, hanging
down her head.

"Who knows—you would say ?" he asked, taking the
little hand which hung at her side, with scarcely a consciousness of doing so.

"I am not fit to die," said Beatrice, with tears in her
eyes, and turning away.   There was a silence more eloquent
than any words.   Her hand remained in his, and neither
spoke, but once their glances met, and then were withdrawn.

"God alone knows who is prepared for that voyage to
eternity," her companion said at length, in a grave, serious
voice, releasing her hand as he spoke; "we are mere instruments—as I was—in his hand: mere wood and metal, which
cannot see or know any thing—which are wielded by the
right hand of the Deity.   But I am trespassing on your
time, Miss Hallam, and must go."

"Oh no, sir—no."

"Do not rate my service to you too highly," he said,
taking no notice of this interruption, and rising; "if you sustain no inconvenience, I need not say I shall be most happy
—as I am happy to have been near you when you fell; any
debt you owed me has been more than repaid by the pleasure
I have felt in this friendly conversation, and now I must go
I fear that I have trespassed too much upon your time."

"Oh no—please sit down: I am not busy" said Bea-

trice, with all the simplicity of a child, "you know I have
been to rehearsal."

"You play to-night?"

"Yes, sir: but will you do me a great favor?"

"Is it very great?" he said, gazing with a soft smile
upon the tender face. Beatrice caught the expression, and
her own countenance became so radiant and winning, so full
of happiness and tender feeling, that he felt his breast heave.
' What is the favor?" he added.

"To promise me not to come," said Beatrice.

"To see you?"

"Yes, sir."

"At the theatre?"

"To-night—yes, sir: I would rather you would not
come, to-night or ever."

"Tell me why: we are friends, are we not—enough for
that?"

"Oh, you please me more than I can tell you, by saying
that," said Beatrice; "indeed I wish you to have no worse
one than myself. But I cannot tell you why I do not wish
to see you ever at the theatre. I hope you will not come to
see me."

"Well, I will not," he said with a softness which was
uncommon with him, "at least to-night, but I may come and
see you here again?"

"Oh, will you?"

"Indeed—if you will permit me."

"Oh, always—I so love to hear you talk."

Beatrice seemed to be carried away by her feelings, and
afterwards blamed herself severely for acting in so childlike
a manner. Her companion said, as he exchanged a pressure
of the hand at parting,

"I will certainly come as often as I can—you have no
better friend than myself, believe me."

And with these simple and sincere words, he took his
departure, thinking of the bright, fresh face, which seemed
to have risen for the first time, like a harvest moon, upon
his sight. As for Beatrice, she sat still for half an hour,
with her head bent down, pensively, and her eyes veiled with
their long lashes. At the end of that time she raised her
face, and said, with deep tenderness, and eyes that swam in
happy tears, "He is so good and noble!"

CHAPTER XX.

THE EXPLOSION : SCENE, EFFINGHAM HALL.

' WHEN an individual of violent temperament adopts a manner of ease and unconcern, sedulously avoiding every thing
calculated to arouse his latent passion, the effect, after a
series of years, is undoubtedly beneficial.   The character
takes the color of its nutriment in a great degree ; and if it
is nourished upon strong emotions, and critical sensations,
will become more and more violent :—if upon quiet pleasures, and moderate delights, the result will be just the re-
verse.   Still, there is this to be observed in such cases.   The
mind of man is not unlike a river ;—it may be directed into
a new channel, but scarcely arrested wholly in its course.
Build a dam of convention across it—bid it curb its waves,
arrest its current, and it will sweep all before it.   The higher
you build the obstruction, the more violent the rush of the
waters, when once they have broken loose.   This was the result with my respected ancestor, Mr. Champ Effingham.
True, he declared often and believed, that he needed strong
emotion—novelty—passion, for his existence ; but this was
a mistake.   His passions were naturally strong enough, and
emotion was dangerous to himself and others.   The quiet
life of his native country had allowed these passions to sleep
for a long time, and he fancied that he had none.   He was,
as I have already declared, very greatly mistaken.

" The first view of young Miss Hallam had stirred up a
hurly-burly in his breast ; not because she was so much
more beautiful than Miss Clare Lee, for whom, as the reader
of these pages has perceived, my respected ancestor had
begun to have something more than a friendly regard :—
not that she was one of those fiery phenomena, who, like
Cleopatra or Aspasia, dazzle the eyes, and set the brain and
heart on fire.   The effect produced upon Mr. Effingham by
the young woman was attributable to the novelty and
freshness of her character, and the state of his own mind,
ripe for some great passion, and dissatisfied with the tranquil affection of the little beauty at Riverhead.   Miss Hallam's reception of his advances had blown the vague and

dubious spark into a blaze—her favorable smiles would in all probability have extinguished it at once: and no one who has read the human heart attentively, more especially that strange chapter dedicated to *love*, will fail to understand this simple fact.   Love, I am convinced, is a mere thing of the imagination at first: the heart seeks something new and strange—something to ponder upon and treasure up, and spend its passionate yearnings upon: tranquil, quiet, unostentatious affection succeeds, and this is love indeed, but the storm precedes the calm.

"These few words will explain what I mean when I add that Mr. Effingham was not, properly speaking, in love with Miss Hallam.   He experienced for her a violent, passionate emotion, which had ripened in a few days to full size and vigor, and though many persons may say—if, indeed many read these pages—that his love was ' love at first sight,' and genuine, still I must be permitted to doubt it; and I hope to show conclusively, before ending this narrative, that those views I have stated are correct.   I am convinced that it was a sort of infatuation, like that of the drunkard for the draught of fire: if he comes near it, he seizes and swallows it.   Miss Hallam declined being swallowed; if I may be permitted to make a very poor witticism; she was offended, and I think very justly, at the manner in which Mr. Effingham uniformly addressed her, and she did not take the trouble to conceal her feelings.   She showed him plainly that she did not desire him to visit her, and the consequence was a vast increase of Mr. Effingham's passion.   We have seen how inconsistently this violent emotion led him to speak and behave:—now praising, then scoffing at the object of his passion: at one time almost cursing her, as he said, then blessing her, and declaring that she was a noble, highsouled girl.   The last interview he had with Miss Hallam, at which the reader has been present, was the capstone to all these passionate interviews; and the state of Mr. Effingham's mind may very correctly be inferred from his mingled mockery and earnestness, sincerity and sarcasm in Miss Hallam's presence.   After leaving her he left Williamsburg—just when Mr. Waters entered it as we know—and launched himself, like a flash of lightning, toward the Hall, overwhelmed with rage and despair."

Thus far the writer of the MS., to whom we shall recur whenever his narrative commentary on the events of this narrative elucidates the posture of affairs, or the emotions of the various personages.

Mr. Champ Effingham soon reached Effingham Hall, and, throwing his bridle loose, hurried to his room. He did not make his appearance again that day, sending word in reply to the various messages dispatched to him, that he was unwell, and wished to be left in quiet. The result of two replies of this description to Miss Alethea's messenger, was the desired quiet. The young gentleman made his appearance on the next morning, at the breakfast-table, after the squire's departure to ride over his farm, looking very much out of sorts. The sallow rings beneath his eyes were darker than ever, and he seemed to have spent a bad night, if indeed he had slept at all before morning. Miss Alethea declared her opinion, that he had not slumbered: and asked an explanation of the stamping and striding over her head —the noise of flying chairs, and rattling swords, hurled apparently for amusement on the floor. She worded these questions in such a manner, that the impression left upon all minds, was to the effect that Mr. Champ Effingham was a naughty boy, who had been behaving badly, and deserved a scolding.

The reader will no doubt imagine, without any explanation upon our part, the manner in which Mr. Effingham received these observations. He looked at Miss Alethea, as a mastiff does at a lapdog who is worrying him, and went on with his breakfast. Miss Alethea was a lady of excellent sense, and did not meddle with him any more during the whole day. Mr. Effingham spent the day in gloomy thought —varying this monotonous amusement, by hurling from his path every thing which stood in his way. Orange, Miss Alethea's lapdog, chanced to obstruct his steps, as he was passing through the hall, and this unfortunate scion of a royal race, found himself kicked twenty feet across the passage, into the embraces of an astonished tortoise-shell cat, his inveterate enemy. Orange was so completely astounded, and overawed by this summary treatment on the enemy's part, that he did not utter so much as a single whine. He was cowed.

Mr. Effingham spent several days in this manner, scarcely eating any thing, but sitting long after dinner, drinking claret. The squire could extract nothing from him; and soon little Kate, his favorite, was repulsed, to her sorrow and mortification. The child prayed earnestly that night for cousin Champ, and could not get her geography the next day for sorrowing about him. As for Master Will, that young gentleman preserved a rigid silence, and a respectful distance from the irate Achilles, whose sombre mood he regarded with astonishment and awe. He saw with dumb astonishment that Mr. Effingham's hair had remained unpowdered for a whole week, and that his ruffle was torn regularly every evening.

One morning, Mr. Effingham was observed to sit with his head bent down for more than an hour, in gloomy thought; at the end of that time, he rose and ordered his horse. Mounting, he directed his way, with a strange expression on his lips, toward Riverhead. At the stream, which ran across the road, a quarter of a mile from the house, his new cocked-hat, with its magnificent feather, blew off into the water, and was all muddied and draggled; and when, after picking it up, he again mounted, he found that his horse had by some means become suddenly lame.

"Well," he said, bitterly, "fate is against my seeing her. I will not go." And returning to the Hall, he shut himself up in his room, and did not issue forth again until evening. It was the seventh day after the interview with Beatrice Hallam; but it brought him no rest from his harassing and gloomy thoughts. He was growing reckless; burnt up by his complicated emotions, he began to regard things in a mysterious and fateful light. Was this young woman to be his curse, appointed by Heaven to ruin him here in this world, for some dreadful sin he had committed? He felt no penitence, shrank not, but with the same mocking, reckless smile, entered the supper-room, where Miss Alethea was preparing chocolate. He sat down in moody silence, but was not long left to himself.

"Champ!" said Miss Alethea, as she finished the arrangement of the table to her satisfaction, "you really must have something on your mind."

No reply.

" What has made you so moody for several days ?   I
never saw you more disagreeable."

The same silence.

" Have you addressed Clare Lee and been discarded ? "

Mr. Effingham's face flushed, and he turned with an
irritated look toward Miss Alethea, which that lady understood perfectly.

" Oh, well, sir ! " she said.   " If you are going to eat
me, I will not presume to speak.   I should like to know
what there was so insulting in my question ? " she added,
oblivious of her intention not to address the young man further, on any consideration.

" It is no insult," said Mr. Effingham, gloomily, " and
I have not seen Miss Clare Lee for a moment since the play,
more than a week ago.   But I do not desire to have my
affairs meddled with."

" Indeed ! " replied Miss Alethea, indignant at the tone
of the young man, " perhaps they are better not meddled
with, they may not bear examination.   I believe that that
young play-girl has something to do with the matter ; and
Clare told me the other day, that some gentleman had told
her that you had met him in a distracted state of mind,
galloping from town.   You had better take care, they are
already talking about you."

Mr. Effingham's rage on hearing this intelligence, may
be better conceived than described.   Clare Lee to know of
his infatuation ! to hear of his acquaintance with Beatrice
Hallam ! to be told of his violent, infatuated conduct ! And
that impudent fellow who had dared to meddle with his
affairs !   Mr. Effingham ground his teeth, and grasped his
sword-hilt with ominous meaning.   This, then, was what he
was coming to be ; the gossip of the country side.   Clare
Lee, even, was one of the laughers, and pitied him, no doubt,
if she did not despise him.   Pity or contempt !   Mr. Effingham's lip curled, and his brow contracted ; then his face
resumed its gloomy look again, and he said : " Woe to those
who busy themselves with me.   Who spoke of me to Miss
Clare Lee ?   Come, tell me, madam."

Miss Alethea, though somewhat awed by his manner, replied, that she did not consider herself called upon to cross-
examine Clare.   The fact was bad enough.

" What fact ?" Mr. Effingham said, rudely.

" That you, my brother, sir," replied Miss Alethea, bri·
dling up, "should make yourself the talk of every one :—in
love with a common actress ! "

" Madam ! " said Mr. Effingham, with a flash of the eye

" You may scowl upon me as much as you choose, sir,"
said Miss Alethea, now thoroughly aroused, " but I say it is
disgraceful."

Mr. Effingham bit his lip until it bled.

" Yes, disgraceful ! " continued Miss Alethea, " for you
to be making yourself ridiculous—and not only yourself, but
me and all—by your infatuation for this woman, who would
not be permitted to enter a respectable house. Yes, sir !
you imagine because you have been to Europe, that you are
at liberty to do just as you choose, and to act without refer-
ence to any one's pleasure but your own. Don't think to
awe me, Champ, for you cannot. I say it's a shame—a
burning shame ! and you ought to be ashamed to treat Clare
so. You know it will break her heart, but this has no
weight with you. I don't mean to submit to your scowling
and growling, though," added Miss Alethea, " I can tell
you, sir."

Mr. Effingham rose and said to a servant who was going
out—

" Pack my portmanteau, and order my horse."

And without further words he left the room, and was
seen by that lady no more. She half regretted her vehemence, for she was a woman of excellent heart at bottom,
but her strong religious feelings, made her intolerant of conduct like that attributed to Mr. Effingham ; and the result
of an argument held with her conscience, was, that she had
not said a word too much.

Those words had put the capstone upon Mr. Effingham's
feelings, and he went to his room, pale, and with a sneer upon
his lip, which boded no good. Thenceforth he was perfectly
reckless.

CHAPTER XXI.

CHAMP EFFINGHAM, ESQ., COMEDIAN.

ON the next morning Mr. Champ Effingham made his ap-
peaiance in Williamsburg, accompanied by a mounted servant, and the two horsemen drew up before the door of the
Raleigh Tavern. The portly landlord came forth, cap in
hand, to welcome him.

"Well, Master Biniface," said Mr. Effingham, with elegant pleasantry, "is the room my servant engaged—No. 6—
ready?"

"Yes, sir—quite ready, sir."

"Carry up my portmanteau," said Mr. Effingham to the
negro, who had brought that article behind him, "and then
return. Answer no foolish questions asked you do not
hear."

"No, Massa Champ," said Tom, with the grin of intelligence peculiar to his race, "not by no means, sir."

"And tell no lies either: if you do, I'll amputate your
ears."

Having given this caution, and made this unmistakable
promise, which the negro received with a broader grin, as he
turned away, Mr. Effingham lounged into the ordinary.

"Where's Hallam?" he asked, sitting down carelessly.

"He's out somewhere, sir—at the theatre, I should say:
but this is nearly his rum hour," laughed the landlord.

"Bring me a cup," said Mr. Effingham; "or no, I'll
have some claret."

The landlord hastened to bring the wine, and placed the
bottle at Mr. Effingham's elbow.

"A cracker!"

The cracker was brought with the same respectful rapidity, or rather a basket of those edibles, placed generally at
hand, then as now, to refresh the company. Mr. Effingham
then betook himself to the agreeable employment of sipping
his claret, one leg being thrown carelessly over the arm of
his leather-bottomed chair: and when tired of this monotony,
he varied it by dipping a cracker in his wine-glass, and
throwing his leg over the other arm. The young gentleman

was more than usually splendid : his coat of crimson cut velvet, was ornamented with a mass of the richest embroidery, and had chased gold buttons :—his waistcoat was of yellow silk, with flowers worked in silver thread, and his new cocked hat, just from London, was resplendent with its sweeping feather.   At his side dangled the finest of his short swords, and, altogether, Mr. Champ Effingham seemed, to judge from his "outward accoutrement," the very pet of fortune.   His manner was not unsuited to his dress : it was, if possible, more nonchalant and indifferent than ever ; but any one who would have taken the trouble to scan the handsome face closely, would have perceived a dark shadow under the eyes, which betokened sleepless nights, and a reckless, mocking expression upon the lips, very much at variance with the *petit maître* airs assumed by the young gentleman.

Half an hour passed, and Mr. Effingham was visibly becoming very impatient, when the entrance of the manager caused him to lay down the " stupid gazette " he had been reading and maligning for the last fifteen minutes.

" Ah ! there you are at last, Hallam," he said, " what the devil kept you so long ? "

The fat manager received this address with great good-humor, and replied, that they had been getting up a play of the " great Congreve " for that night's performance.

" You had better let Congreve alone, and stick to Shakespeare," said Mr. Effingham, " he won't take here among these barbarous Virginians.   But come here, and drink some claret with me—I'm tired of it myself: bring me some rum ! "

The rum came, and Mr. Manager Hallam sat down.

" Good ? " said Mr. Effingham.

" Very excellent indeed, sir," said Hallam, smacking his lips.

" Well, now, let us come to the matter I am thinking about.   Hallam, I am going to join the company."

" The company, sir ! "

" Yes—*your* company : what, the devil !   Is there any thing so astounding in that ? "

" Really, sir—really now—you take me quite aback ! *You* join the company ? "

" Yes !   The ' Virginia Company of Comedians.'   Is

there any thing strange in a Virginian belonging to that excellent association of his Majesty's, or his Excellency's
players ? "

"Upon my word, sir," said the manager, laboring under
great astonishment, "never in my life—"

"Why, what surprises you ? "

"That a gentleman of your wealth and standing should
join us."

"Curse my wealth and standing! That is not your
look out."

"But it is yours, sir," said the manager, with a troubled
look, "if you knew about these things—your family, sir—
really a most extraordinary proposal—"

"Come, no humbug! Let us look at the matter. I am
a gentleman, you say, and I have a family to affect. That
is a mistake—any thing I do will not affect my family : and
if it does, I am a free man. Now, on the other side—I
rather flatter myself your house would be filled, when Champ
Effingham, Esq., was announced in some thrilling and overwhelming part. What do you say to that? Drink there!
give me another cup."

"You would really play, sir ? " said the manager, surveying his position with a hurried glance, " you would really appear ? "

"Bah! you don't know me. Of course I would : and
the fact would *appear* to you too, in adding up your receipts. I needn't tell you that when a gentleman takes to
the stage, something more is due him than what your common fellow gets—'a beggarly account of empty benches.' "

Hallam hesitated ; evidently troubled.

"I would, you know, sir, be more than pleased—it would
make my fortune, sir—I feel, sir, that I ought not to hesitate—"

"Bah! don't hesitate, then. Can't you understand
that I would make a better *Romeo*, a better any thing, acting with Beatrice, than that stupid fellow Pugsby ? "

A light dawned on the muddy brain of Mr. Manager
Hallam. Here was the exciting cause : Beatrice was the
engine which had produced this extraordinary convulsion in
the heart of Mr. Effingham. And with the thought in his
mind, the course he ought to pursue became plainer. One

6

of the darling projects of Mr. Manager Hallam was to marry his accomplished and beautiful daughter to some wealthy and high-born youth:—once married, Beatrice would, of course, abandon the stage: that was the loss to him—but the advantages of such connection would vastly outweigh this. The manager was growing old, and getting tired of his nomadic, restless life; tossed from inn to inn, from country to country: and he wished to settle down. Now, if Beatrice married, of course, her husband would not separate the daughter from the father :—the consequence? "I would live in clover all the rest of my life, in a fine house, with plenty to drink, tictac every night, and nothing to do but eat, drink, and sleep," he said to himself. To eat, drink, and sleep was the height of this worthy gentleman's ambition, and he had already conceived the intention of performing those agreeable ceremonies, for the rest of his days, at Effingham Hall, if that were possible in the nature of things.

The reader will now be able to understand the effect produced upon the worthy manager by the mention of Beatrice's name. That explained all. Mr. Effingham was desperately enamored of her—his family no doubt scoffed at the connection—he came to join the company—time would do the rest; and, once married, a few dramatic scenes of father's weeping and relenting—daughter-in-law kneeling in tears—son promising to be immaculate in future, would make all well again. He trusted to his theatrical experience to arrange these little matters, and already dreamed of ending his days tranquilly, in what he seemed to consider the place of happiness—in "clover."

So, when Mr. Effingham had repeated his disdainful question, "Would he not make a better companion for Beatrice, in every thing, than that stupid fellow, Pugsby?" Mr. Manager Hallam melted from his doubtful state of mind into increasing conviction, and said, that "He really felt—hum—he must certainly acknowledge—hum—Pugsby was certainly not what he had been; and, if Mr. Effingham was bent on joining them, he did not feel himself at liberty to refuse his most flattering proposal. As the great Congreve had said to him, on one occasion, such common players as himself could not feel too much flattered when gentlemen condescended to associate with them on terms of equality; and nothing was more reasonable. He could not refuse Mr. Effingham, whom he was proud to call his friend; he had many such distinguished friends; among the most so, the great Congreve. Therefore, if Mr. Effingham was still of the same mind, he would be most proud, most flattered to have him. He would find them a plain, honest set; and the only drawback was on the delicate subject of his remuneration. For, as to salary, he feared——"

"Curse the salary!" said Mr. Effingham, with disdainful carelessness—he had listened to the above tirade with perfect indifference—"I don't want your money, Hallam. You don't think that I would join your set for a few pistoles, do you? No, sir! I have quite sufficient; but what I want is excitement, novelty,. jovial society. I'm sick of the well-bred insipidity of good society, and the 'repose' they consider the *summum bonum* and great desideratum of human existence. I'm done with it—tired of it. I am going to pick out a piece to act this very day. Go, and put 'Champ Effingham, Esq.,' on your roll of comedians."

And Champ Effingham, Esq., rising from his seat, went out, and stood at the door of the Raleigh, yawning and frowning, and scowling on such members of that insipid good society as passed in their coaches. He did not take the trouble to return the nods of the gentlemen, or the smiles of the ladies. He felt perfectly reckless, and cared, at that moment, for no human being on earth. Yes, there was one whom he loved and hated, blessed and cursed; and she passed him, coming from the theatre, with a quick step, and an averted face. Why, else, did the frown become deeper, and the glance of the eye grow more gloomy and reckless?

Beatrice hurried up to her room, and Mr. Effingham re-entered, and began again to converse again with the manager, over a second bottle of claret.

CHAPTER XXII.

THE DOOR OF THE "GAZETTE" OFFICE.

AFTER his interview with Beatrice, Charles Waters returned homeward, lost in thought. Was he pondering again upon his system of education, or upon any of his novel political ideas, such as Parson Tag had "called to the attention" of the squire, for their absurd and treasonable character? Was he admiring the beautiful autumn woods, all yellow, and gold, and crimson, through which the fresh fall breezes laughed and sang, from the far surging ocean? None of these things occupied his thoughts; ideas of national politics were as far from his mind as the forest, which his dreamy eye took no note of.

He was thinking of that young girl he had just left; so womanly, yet childlike; so beautiful and attractive in the richness of her great loveliness; yet so like a girl who has never thought to bind up the careless waves of her hair. What an anomaly was here! And was there not food for thought? He had seen her on the stage, and, spite of his total ignorance of what acting was, felt perfectly convinced that she was a great genius; and now this splendid woman, whose magical voice had interpreted every change and phase of passion, glancing from the highest to the lowest tones, with lightning-like rapidity and marvellous ease; whose attitudes were so grand, whose very walk rivetted the attention, and hushed the crowd; this great interpreter of the greatest of human intellects, with whose name the whole colony was ringing, had thrown aside in his presence all this intellect and strength, to take his hand, and laugh merrily, and talk with rapture of the fresh beauty of the river and the forest, and, like a child, plead for another visit from him! Was the scene real or imaginary?

He passed over the whole distance between Williamsburg and his home in a dream, and all that day, and for more than a week thereafter, was plainly busy with some problem that he could not explain to his satisfaction. He would go and work in the field; and, before he knew it, find himself leaning on his spade and murmuring, "Could she

have acted all this?" He pored over his books hour after
hour, and found he had made no progress; for her image
rose in all its fresh and tender beauty between him and the
page. Then he became conscious of his preoccupation, and
determined to banish it. She was nothing to him—he had
other ends in life, and other duties than idle visits. This
young woman was, no doubt, very original and striking in
every point of view, and he felt a strange sympathy with
her—a strange sensation of having seen and known her elsewhere, perhaps in another world—but that was nothing to
him. Realities were his food, not fancies—henceforth he
would drive from his mind this fit of dreaming.

And he succeeded. This young man had a mind of rare
vigor and resolution; he had trained his mind like a courser
to obey the bridle, and now he found the effect of this mental
discipline. By degrees the young girl's image no longer
made his eye brighter, his lip wreath into a tender smile;
he returned to his grave, patient labor, and his thoughts on
the great questions which absorbed him.

On the day after Mr. Effingham's instalment at the
Raleigh, Charles Waters visited Williamsburg again. His
business was to procure some little articles for his father
who seldom went to the town—Lanky, the lad we have seen
on the day of the river adventure, attending to the sale of
fish and other things which old Waters sent to market.
Having dispatched his errand, he went to the office of the
" Virginia Gazette " to purchase a copy.

As he was coming out with the paper in his had, he felt
a touch upon his arm, and turning round, perceived his friend
with the red cloak, who had come for the same purpose, it
seemed, as he had a copy of the Gazette under his arm.

" We are well met, friend," said the man in the red cloak,
"and at a place which is not extraordinary. We might
have expected to find each other here."

" How so?" asked Charles Waters, gravely extending
his hand, but betraying evident pleasure at the meeting.

" Why," replied his companion, " we are both thinkers."

" Yes, but—"

" And as thinkers must have food for thought," added
the man in the red cloak, " we both decided, some moments
since, to come and purchase the 'Gazette.' Is it not so?"

" With me—yes."

"Something new is as much your passion, or I greatly mistake, as it is my own. What is new in facts, what is new in ideas ? "

"You will search long in this paper for the latter novelty,' said the other; " there is generally, however, a good budget of news from Norfolk, York, and—when a vessel arrives— from England."

"Good ! That is what we want more than comments on facts. Give me the food—I can myself digest it. I beg leave to decline taking any writer's opinion on the eternal legislation in Parliament on Virginia affairs—the said opinion being invariably favorable to government. I ask for the new act of Parliament—I will light my pipe with the commentary."

"Still the two things might be combined in a gazette."

" Yes, when thought is free."

" It will be, some day."

"Well, I think so, too," said the man in the red cloak. " I hope I shall live to see the day when the public journal will be the great speaker of the time—though I could never express my own ideas with a pen; it freezes me—I dream sometimes of this mingled chronicle and essay you mention · a great daily volume, containing intelligence from every quarter of the world, news upon every subject, comment free from partisan falsehood ; and this great organ of thought I sometimes think will, in future, be scattered over the land like the leaves of that autumn forest yonder. When the time comes, mankind will take a great stride onward."

" I scarcely hope to live so long," said his companion.

" Why ? The new era comes slowly, but still comes."

" This paper I hold in my hand is a bad commencement of your grand dream, liberty ! Yes, liberty will come—but will it be in our day ? "

" What do you mean by liberty ? " said the stranger, bending his keen eye on his companion; "are men fit for such a thing ? "

" Yes."

" Let us see, now—but here we are at the Raleigh Tavern, accompany me to my room, and we will talk ; or if not talk, I will play you a tune on the violin, and before you go show you something I have written."

Charles Waters willingly complied, and, passing Beatrice's door, which he merely glanced at, they entered the apartment of the stranger. It was, like most rooms in Virginia taverns, of considerable extent, and of a rather bare appearance. In one corner, a neat bed covered with a white counterpane, stood, with its tall, slender posts; and the rest of the furniture consisted of a rude oaken table and some leather-bottomed chairs. On the table lay a violin and bow, and beneath it an open book. The fire-place had two square stones in place of andirons, and these stones now supported an armful of twigs, which were crackling and blazing pleasantly. The day was not cold, but the stranger seemed to be one of those men who rightly consider a cheerful blaze always pleasant, and he sat down before it, resting his rudely-shod feet on the iron fender. His companion sat down opposite, and for a moment there was silence. It was first broken by the man in the red cloak, who said:

"We are now separated from the outer world; this inn is our castle, and before I amuse you, as my guest, by playing the violin, let us have a few words upon the subject we were speaking of but now."

———◆———

CHAPTER XXIII.

A THINKER OF THE YEAR OF GRACE, 1768.

CHARLES Waters sat down, and resting his elbow on the table, leaned his head upon his hand; he seemed to be thinking; but scarcely upon the subject they had adverted to, if one might have formed any opinion from the compression of the lips and the troubled expression of the eyes. The man in the red cloak, whose keen eye nothing seemed to escape, observed this expression, and determined to try the effect of music. The reader will have already perceived, that one of the peculiarities of this strange man, was great curiosity as to the working of the human heart, and the means of affecting men through their feelings. He took up the violin, which was an old battered instrument of little value, but not without much sweetness of tone, and drew the bow across the strings.

"What shall I play?" he said. His companion raised his head at the sound of the stranger's voice, and looked at him inquiringly.

The man in the red cloak repeated his question with a slight smile.

"Any thing," said the other, relapsing into reverie again; he was subject to these fits of thinking, and the stranger seemed to understand the fact; for he commenced playing without taking any notice of his auditor's preoccupation and indifference. His bowing was firm and strong, and playing evidently from his ear wholly, he executed a minuet with great delicacy and force. His whole soul seemed to be absorbed in the grand floating strain, which, with its crescendos and cadences, sweeping onward in full flood, or dying like sinking winds, filled the whole chamber with a gush of harmony. But still his eye was fixed curiously upon his companion, and he noted with great care every change of expression in the lips, the brow, and the eyes veiled with their long dusky lashes. He finished with a vigorous flourish, and Charles Waters raised his head.

"Do you like it?" asked his companion.

"Yes; you are a fine player, sir," he said indifferently.

"Perhaps you would prefer a Virginia reel?"

"No, I prefer the other, which is a minuet, I believe."

"Yes; but listen to this."

And, first tuning a rebellious string, the stranger struck up, with a vigorous and masculine movement of the elbow, one of those merry and enlivening tunes, which seem to fill the air with joy and mirth. His fingers played upon the strings like lightning, the bow rose, and fell, and darted backward and forward; and, throwing his whole heart into the piece, the stranger seemed to imagine himself in the midst of some scene of festivity and laughter, to be surrounded by a crowd of bright forms and merriest faces, running through the dance, and moving in obedience to his magical bow. He wound up with a tumultuous, deafening roar, his eyes flashing, his crisp hair seeming to move with the music:—and then, stopping suddenly, laid down the instrument. Charles Waters raised his head, waked, so to speak, by the silence.

"You play excellently well, sir," he said; "but I am so wholly ignorant of music, that my praise, doubtless, is of little value."

This seemed to afford the stranger much satisfaction: he evidently prided himself upon his proficiency on the instrument.

"It is a very enviable accomplishment," his companion added, "for it affords you the means of easily contributing to harmless enjoyment. Music is a great educator, too. Dancing is one of the most healthful and innocent of pastimes, I am convinced; and the violin is, I believe, the best instrument to dance to."

"Yes—yes: none other is comparable to it, and I confess I do feel satisfaction in knowing that I perform tolerably on this great instrument. There is but one other superior to it."

"What is that?"

"The human voice."

"Yes—yes, I understand."

"That is, after all, the great master-instrument, constructed by the Deity. The violin is merry and joyous, or mournful and sombre, but the voice is all this, and all else, in a degree ten thousand times more powerful. To move, to agitate, to sway, to bend; what is like it. Ah! my Livy, there, upon the table, gives me the words; but who shall fill my ear with the magical voices, dead and silent? Who shall 'speak the speech,' as Virginius did, when fronting the tyrant Appius, he plunged the dagger into his child? Would I had been there!" added the stranger, with one of those brilliant flashes which seemed, at times, to convert his eyes into flame. But before his companion could reply, this expression had disappeared, and the man in the red cloak took up the open volume of Livy, and, turning over the leaves, carelessly, seemed to have forgotten Virginius and his misfortune, in a moment.

"After all," he said, with one of his adroit turns, and apparently desiring to make the other talk, "after all, I don't know whether Appius was so much worse than other despots: and men have in all ages required to be ruled strongly, and often tyrannically. Despots are disagreeable, but necessary."

Waters looked at his companion with astonishment: he thought he must be jesting: but there was not the least indication of any such thing: his countenance—that index of the mind, ordinarily—betrayed nothing of the sort. Apparently the stranger had spoken these words in perfect good faith.

"Could I have understood you, sir," said the thinker, "and did you really mean that men required despotic rulers?'

"Yes: certainly."

"This, from *you?*"

"Come, come—you may have taken up a wrong impression in regard to my opinions; let us not break into exclamations, companion; rather let us sift opinions and compare ideas.   Is it not undeniable that men in all ages have been weak and faltering, preferring rather the bad and false to the great and good? and if this is true, does it not follow that despots are a necessity of the world's being?"

"Ah!" said his companion, "but that is not true—it is false, permit me to say honestly, and with no desire to offend you—"

"Not at all—not at all: go on."

"I deny your maxim totally, sir—it is not true."

"Have not the records of the world proved it? Are they not darkened every where by deeds which prove the truth of the Bible, saying, that mankind are prone to deceit and desperately wicked?—have not the annals of all lands and governments shown conclusively, that truth and grandeur and purity have ever attracted to themselves envy and hatred, malice, and all uncharitableness?   Come! let me hear you deny that men are radically hateful, false, unworthy of trust, as they are of respect: come, let me hear you deny that they are swine before whom it is the merest boyish folly to throw that brilliant pearl called liberty.   You cannot deny the truth of this view:—men have always been radically false and unworthy."

"I do deny it, sir," said Waters, his brow flushing and his eyes suddenly growing brilliant with the fires of enthusiasm.   "Never was any philosophy so weak, so wholly based on sand!   It is a dreadful, an awful philosophy, that which scoffs at and seeks to overthrow all that is pure and worthy in our fellow-men—all that is brilliant and imposing for its

truth and beauty in the annals of the race! I cannot believe
that you speak seriously, for I have seen that in your eyes
and your spoken words which is opposed to this terrible philosophy utterly. No, sir! men are not by nature destitute
of truth and love, nobility and purity—the annals of the
world show how untrue it is. Go back as far as you may,
penetrate the gloom which wraps the overthrown columns of
the Syrian desert, the Egyptian plains, and you will find in
the midst of crime and falsehood the light of heaven; among
those monsters whom God, for His own wise purposes, sent
upon the earth, flowers of majesty and honor; in the moral
desert those oases of verdure and pure limpid waters, which
prove that beneath this burning sand the eternal springs
exist, the germ remains. No; I do not deny that men have
in all ages fallen and sinned—yes, they have hated and
despised, blasphemed and cursed, dyed their right arms in
blood, and revelled in the foul, the false, the unnatural.
None can dispute it. I acknowledge it. But what is equally
true is this—that every where the instincts of humanity,
planted by God in it, have revolted against this abnormal
state; love has effaced hatred, justice the spirit of wrong;
heaven has opened and the abyss has closed!

"Go into this Golgotha of nations, this Jehosaphat of
extinct generations, and question those dry bones which once
supported living frames such as our own here now. They
will make you but one reply—a reply which embraces
the history of humanity—'I sinned, I repented; I was
human, I endeavored to grow divine.' Look at Greece,
Rome, Modern Europe—embrace at a glance the whole surface of three distinct civilizations, three diverse ages, from
horizon to horizon, from their dawning in the East, fresh,
rosy, and pure, to their sad and sorrowful decline—sorrowful
and sad because the soul ever doubted—ever was afraid to
hope for the new dawn! In Greece, art overthrowing rudeness, beauty driving away deformity—the good and beautiful passionately yearned for by all classes of men—eternally
sought! The childlike and poetical nature filling the streams
with naiads, the woods with dryads, the mountains with the
oreads and the graces—every where the false, which is the
deformed, overthrown to make way for the true, which is the
beautiful Arcadian temples glittering in the forests, altars

of white marble crowning the blue mountains.   Phidias and
Apelles, famous in all countries for their incarnations of
grace and beauty, rather than their incarnation of the Gre-
cian idea!   And not in sculpture and painting only did the
true and beautiful conquer the false and deformed.   In literature, Sophocles and Euripides purified the heart by pity
and terror—Aristophanes lashed with his satire the unworthy and despicable—Homer embodied in his heroes grace
and strength, as in Achilles—nobility and tenderness, as in
Hector—in Ulysses, the dignity of suffering and misfortune.
Socrates taught immortality — Plato penetrated the mists
of prejudice and ignorance with that glance of lightning
given him by God.   Every where mind overcame matter,
the moral conquered the brutal; and such was the force of
their teachings, the vitality of their dogmas, that all the
nations of the world turned their eyes to Greece as toward
the dawn of civilization.

"The cry, 'Great Pan is dead!' was only heard when the
Roman Colossus had strangled in his arms this nascent civilization, this pure ray of the dawn.   Pan had taught men hus-
bandry, and tranquil country happiness, and that wars should
be no more.   When he died, that cry told the nations that
the glory of Greece had disappeared, and with it the only
civilization which surpassed the ripe majesty of Rome.   But
that civilization was not altogether lost; Juvenal was greater
than Aristophanes, as Cato and Cicero rose in moral height
above the statesmen of Athens.   You know well the history
of that empire, stretching its vast roads through every land,
and drawing to the great centre, the imperial city, towards
which those vast highways converged the silks, and gold, and
pearls of every land—the captives of all nations.

"I know that you would say that human depravity cul-
minated in those emperors—and that they had fit subjects.
Yes; God had given that race dominion, permitted it to
conquer every land, and then cursed it with rottenness and
decay.   Men felt the divine curse, and shook their clenched
hands at the gods in impotent wrath.   See how every thing
reveals the despair which fell upon the men of Rome; see
how the race, blind, staggering, rioting in an eternal orgy,
still knew their foulness, gnashing their teeth with rage at
their own depravity; see how every thing became venal—

female honor, the arms of men, the suffrages of the legions.
The commander who could glut the revelling multitude with
the greatest shows was emperor—Messalina was queen. The
race was staggering, despairing; they saw the night coming,
and the lurid glare of burning cities lighting on their way
to Rome those 'hammers of God,' Alaric and Genseric.
They felt that the impending fate was the just punishment
of the unspeakable corruption reigning in the land, and they
sought to drown conscience in those moral stimulants which
now horrify the world.   They clamored for wild beast shows;
they rolled on the seats of the Amphitheatre in convulsive
laughter, when the slave was torn to pieces in the arena by
the lion or tiger; they intoxicated themselves with blood
to drown despair, and, drunk with horror, staggered and fell
into the welcome grave dug for them by war, or pestilence,
or famine.

"Then, on this worn-out world—this chaos of darkness
and corruption, rose the sun of Christianity, blessing and
healing. God took pity on the race, and would not overwhelm it with a new deluge; and men cast off their foulness,
abjured their heathen gods, and and knelt like children at
the foot of the cross.

"But I weary you, sir. Every where the annals of the
world show the god-given instincts of the race, leading then
to seek the true and beautiful—to embrace love in place of
hatred. See how the northern nations worshipped their hero
souls, as the Anglo-Saxons almost did their brave King Ar
thur.   They still yearn for them, and say they will return to
bless the nations.   The precursor of the returning god is still
looked for in the northern solitudes by the rude islanders—and
Arthur, the middle age believed, would come again, his sword
excalibur turned to the shepherd's crook, and with him peace,
love, and happiness. Look at all nations. In France, see how
the convulsions of a thousand years have proved the yearnings of the race for something better, truer, nobler than
their effete royalty, their nobility, exhausted by Duguesclin
and Bayard. See England, grand and piteous spectacle!—
heart of the modern world, as she was the torch, whose light
glared on the crumbling props of old imperial Rome—the
star of the new era. See England, groaning through all her
history with the fatal incubus of a privileged class, sucking

up all offices of profit or distinction; a king, whose person is
sacred—who can do no wrong. Seo her still seeking for the
true, the pure, the just; see those men of England plunging into
war and blood to find the jewel—beheading the king in the
name of justice—embracing puritanism, because it clad itself
in the robes of truth and purity—returning to their king,
when puritanism became bigotry—love, hatred—justice, a
scoff—and only to find in that son of the man they had be-
headed a worse curse than any yet ! For Charles II cursed
the rising generation with corruption, unbelief, despair; no
longer levying tonnage like his father—only destroying the
honor of families; no longer holding down the nation with
a rod of iron—only inaugurating that horrible comedy of the
Restoration, which made all that is good contemptible—the
honor of men, the fidelity of wives, the faith of humanity in
God.   The poor, struggling nation bargained for liberty and
toleration—they received bigotry and licentiousness.   Yes,
yes, sir I this is the truth of that great revolution, and the
English people therein embodied the history of humanity in
all ages, every where.   Yes, yes! if any thing is true, this
is true—that men are not false and hateful, black from the
cradle, foul from their first breath ! On this conviction
alone do I base my hopes for the future of the race—in
Europe, America, every where.   That this land we live in
will prove mankind able to think, to act, to rule, above all,
to love, I have a conviction which nothing can deprive me of.
The old world totters ; she is diseased, and though this dis-
ease may demand two hundred years to eat its way to the
heart, yet it will finally attack the vital part, and all will
crumble into dust.   The new world lies bathed in the fresh
light of the new age : here will the heart of man vindicate
its purity; here the tiger will lie down, the serpent no
longer hiss; here, I feel that God will accomplish the political regeneration of humanity, proving the eternal truth
of these poor words I have uttered I "

The thinker paused, and leaning his brows on his hand,
seemed to be buried in thought. The stranger was also
silent, either from conviction or in order that he might marshal his thoughts for the struggle of intellects.   But if
this last were the reason of his silence, he was deomed to disappointment.

His companion rose and said:

" I.fear I have wearied you, sir, and fear still more that you will think it discourteous in me to leave you, after thus taking up our whole interview in talking myself. But I have just recalled a business engagement at this hour—the clock has just struck."

" Well, well," said the man in the red cloak, who did not seem greatly put out by these words, " I cannot think hard of that. Your ideas, sir, have found in me an atten- tive listener, and if I led you to suppose that I believed nothing good could come out of human nature, I miscon- veyed my meaning. Let us part, then, for the present—we shall meet again, as my stay here will be prolonged for a week or two longer, and I count upon seeing you again. I do not fear a disappointment. We shall come together often in the future, I feel a conviction."

His companion bowed his head in token of willingness and assent, and looking at the door, said :

" Your room is No. 7, is it not ? "

" Yes—that one opposite is occupied by a young gentle- man from the neighborhood; and that one next to me by the young actress, Beatrice Hallam, I believe. Mr. Effingham' seems to be her very good friend."

" Effingham ! " exclaimed his companion.

" Yes, he has been an inmate of this tavern for two or three days—don't mistake and enter his room for mine."

Charles Waters could only bow his head : and turning away from the man in the red cloak, he went in silence down the stairs. The house seemed to stifle him ; and when he reached the open air he seemed suddenly to revive, for his face was suffused with blood.

CHAPTER XXIV.

WARLIKE PROCLAMATION FROM THE SQUIRE.

JUST as Charles Waters left the door of the inn, and while the stranger was still looking after him, with a curious ex- pression upon his finely-moulded lips, the door of No. 7

opened, and Mr. Champ Effingham issued from it. The young gentleman, who had just been refreshing himself with a cup of chocolate, served to him in bed—was clad with his usual elegance and richness, and for a moment his eye dwelt on the coarsely-dressed stranger, who stood with the knob of the door in his hand, gazing, as we have said, after Charles Waters. The man in the red cloak surveyed him with great calmness, and some curiosity. An imaginative spectator might have fancied them the representatives of the old world and the new—the past and the future—the court and the backwoods. Mr. Effingham looked every inch the gentleman and courtier. The drop curls of his powdered peruke reposed ambrosially on his clear pale cheek, his lace ruffles at bosom and wrist were of spotless purity, his surcoat of cut velvet, with its chased gold buttons, just lifted up the point of his richly ornamented sword, and his waistcoat, silk stockings, cocked-hat, and jewelled hands, completed the vivid and perfect contrast between himself and the rude-looking, coarsely clad stranger. Plainly the court and the wilds, Europe and America—stood face to face.

The man in the red cloak having apparently satisfied his curiosity, made a slight and very awkward bow, which Mr. Effingham returned with negligent carelessness, and then re-entered his chamber, with a smile on his grim features. Mr. Effingham descended.

The reader will recollect that he had been at the tavern now for some days :—the manager had regularly enrolled him as a member of the " Virginia Company of Comedians," and availing himself of the privileges of his membership, Mr. Effingham had met Beatrice daily, in the theatre, in the tavern, every where. He was no longer a chance visitor, an occasional torment to be borne with, and endured patiently, in consideration of his going away soon ; he was now her shadow, and in the young girl's own words, he " drove away all the sunshine from her life." At rehearsal she had seen daily his reckless and mocking smile, glittering and gloomy, follow her every movement—at the inn, when he condescended to appear at the common table, she had been transfixed by his burning glances—in all places and at all times he had obtruded himself with his ironical and yet sombre smile ; a smile which seemed to say audibly, " You defied me, scorned me, thought yourself more than a match for me and I have foiled you and conquered you, by superior will and reckless carelessness."

Whether Mr. Manager Hallam was conscious of Beatrice's unhappiness—of Mr. Effingham's treatment of his daughter—we are not able to say. At least, he took no notice of it, and was always ready to echo the young man's jests, and drink with him as long, and as deeply as he desired.

"At the Hall the storm was rising, and ere long it was destined to fall upon the devoted head of Mr. Effingham. Miss Alethea had deeply regretted her violence, and earnestly prayed for him, and that he might return to them again. She saw too late that her injudicious words had driven him away, and this she confessed to her father, with tears; but that bluff gentleman had pish'd and pshaw'd, and told her that she was too soft-hearted, and that she was not to blame —he would see to the matter! The rest of the household soon found out the dreadful fact that Mr. Champ Effingham had abandoned his home for the young actress, and the very negroes, following the wont of Africans in all years, discussed and commented on " Master Champ's " wild conduct. Will reflected upon the matter, with a dreadful feeling of alarm, and fear, and admiration, for the rebel—and Kate sorrowed in quiet, wiping her eyes frequently, as she bent over Carlo, and sometimes getting up from the table, and hurrying out, with no imaginable cause for going away, unless she had tears to hide. She loved Mr. Champ Effingham dearly— much more fondly, I am compelled to add, than my respected ancestor deserved—and wept for him, and every night and morning joined her hands together and asked God to bless him, wetting the pillow all the time with her tears. As 1 have said, this was by no means the spirit of the squire: he was indignant, he felt outraged, he knew now all about the matter, and felt excessive dissatisfaction at Mr. Effingham's conduct, as he called it. It never occurred to him that his own youthful career had been by no means immaculate, and without regard to Mr. Champ's peculiarities of mental organization, he determined to bring the rebel to subjection."

Thus far, the MS. from which these events were drawn; the extract may serve to explain the appearance of a mounted servant at the door of the Raleigh, where Mr. Effingham descended, after his meeting with the stranger. It was Tom, who, with many smiles, presented to his master a missive directed, in a large, firm hand:

"To Mr. Champ Effingham, at the Raleigh Tavern Williamsburg."

Mr. Effingham frowned, tore open the letter, and read it, with a flush upon his brow, which froze the smiles of the shining African. Having gone through it, he crumpled it furiously in his hand, scowled upon the negro, hesitated, in evident doubt as to what course he should pursue, then bidding the servant wait, hurried to his room.

The letter was in these words:

"Effingham Hall, Thursday Forenoon.

"MY DEAR CHAMP—I have heard of your conduct, sir, and have no intention of being made the laughing-stock of my neighbors, as the father of a fool. No, sir! I decline being advised and pitied, and talked about and to by the country on your account. I know why you have left the Hall, sir, and taken up your residence in town. Alethea has told me how you insulted her, and flouted her well-meant advice, and because she entreated you, as your sister, not to go near that young woman again, tossed from her, and fell into your present courses. I tell you again, sir, that I will not endure your conduct. I won't have the parson condoling, and shaking his head, and sighing, and, when he comes in the Litany to pray for deliverance from all inordinate and sinful affections—from all the deceits of the world, the flesh, and the devil—have him looking at the Hall pew, and groaning, until every body understands his meaning. No, sir! If you make yourself a fool about that common actress, you shall not drag us into it. And Clare Lee! have you no regard for her feelings? Damn my blood, sir! I am ashamed of you. Come away directly. If you are guilty of any thing unworthy toward that young woman, I will strike your name from the family Bible, and never look upon your face again. Remember, sir; and you won't be fool enough to marry her, I hope. Try it, sir, and see the consequence. Pah! a common actress for my daughter— the wife of the representative of the house of Effingham, after my death. 'Sdeah, sir! it is intolerable, abominable; and I command you to return at once, and never look upon

that young woman again. For shame, sir. Am I, at my
age, to be made a laughing-stock of, to be jeered at by the
common people, at the county court, as the father of the
young man that played the fool with the actress? No, sir.
Leave that place, and come and do what you are expected to
do, called on to do—take Clare Lee to the Governor's ball.
I inclose your invitation. Leave that woman and her artful
seductions. Reflect, sir, and do your duty to Clare, like a
gentleman. If it is necessary, I repeat, sir, I command you
to return, and never see that girl again.

" EFFINGHAM."

Mr. Champ Effingham read this letter with those mani-
festations of wrath and indignation which we have described,
and as we have said, hurried to his apartment, bidding the
servant wait.

Once by himself, he tore his unfortunate frill furiously,
and shook his clenched fist at the representation of himself
in the mirror.

"Dictation! I am a child!" he said. "I am to be
whipped in, like a hound, because I choose to come and
spend a few days in town here, and to be ordered about, as
if I were a negro. I am, forsooth, to come back to the Hall,
and humbly beg Alethea's pardon, for leaving her so abruptly, and hear the servants tittering behind me, and go,
like a milk-and-water girl, to escort Miss Clare Lee to the
Governor's ball! Curse me, if I will submit to be lashed
into obedience, like a dog, and Miss Clare Lee may find
some other escort. I will go to that ball with Beatrice Hallam, and I will act next week."

With which words, he sat down and wrote :

"I have received your letter, sir, and decline returning
to Effingham Hall, or being dictated to. I have passed my
majority, and am my own master. No one on earth shall
make a slave of me.   I have the honor to be,

" CHAMP EFFINGHAM."

Mr. Effingham read this note over, folded it, sealed it
deliberately, stamping the wax with his coat of arms, and
summoning a servant, ordered him to deliver it to the negro
at the door. Then rising, with a mocking laugh, he went
toward Beatrice's room.

CHAPTER XXV.

MR. EFFINGHAM REQUESTS THAT HE MAY HAVE THE PLEASURE OF ESCORTING MISS HALLAM TO THE BALL.

MR. EFFINGHAM knocked at the door of the young girl's apartment, but being in doubt whether he heard her voice, was about to retire. He decided, however, after a moment's reflection, to enter, and opening the door, which yielded to his push, found himself in presence of Beatrice. She was sitting at the window, and leaned her head upon her hand, which lay upon the sill. She did not move when Mr. Effingham entered, and a second glance proved to him that she was asleep.

For a moment, Mr. Effingham gazed at the beautiful head bent down, the forehead moist with the dews of sleep, the small hand hanging down, from which the volume of Shakspeare, she had been reading, had fallen to the floor. None of these things escaped him, and for a moment he paused, silent, motionless, his eyes becoming softer, his brow less gloomy. Then the shadow returned ; thought, like a hound, again struck the trail, for a moment lost, and the eye of the young man assumed its habitual fire, his lips their curl of scornful and gloomy listlessness.

Beatrice stirred in her sleep and awoke ; it might have been supposed that the glittering eye fixed on her face, had not permitted the sleeper to continue insensible to the presence of the visitor. She opened her eyes and sat up, placing her hand, with an instinctive movement, on her disordered hair.

Mr. Effingham approached her. " I knocked," he said, negligently, " but was uncertain whether you answered or not, so I entered. How is Miss Beatrice to-day ? "

" I am not well, sir," she said, resigning herself to her fate.

" Not well ? "

" I am worn out, sir."

" Worn out ? "

" Yes, sir ; the exceedingly late hours I have kept lately, have injured me."

" All imaginary ; you are accustomed to them."

Beatrice made no reply to these words, which Mr. Effingham uttered with careless indifference as he sat down.

" Have you been to the theatre, this morning ?" he added.

" Yes, sir."

" Rehearsal ? "

" Yes, sir."

" Well, that wore you out. That fellow, Pugsby, is
enough to put any one to sleep, he's so somniferous."

" He did not come."

" And so after rehearsal, you came here ? "

" Yes, sir."

" And went to sleep ? "

" I tried to study, but could not."

" True; there is your Shakspeare on the floor."

Mr. Effingham picked the volume up with a yawn, and
politely restored it to the young girl.

" By the by," he said, " when shall we appear together ? "

" I don't know, sir."

" Come, now; wouldn't you prefer me as your vis-à-vis
in acting to Pugsby ? "

" It is perfectly indifferent to me whom I play with, sir."

" Amiable, at least ! But we are going to play together
soon."

" Are we, sir ? "

" Yes, madam, the duchess ! By heaven, you must
have been born in a court, or you never could have caught
the imperial air so perfectly ! ' Are we, sir ? ' " continued
Mr. Effingham, mimicking the frigid tones of the young
girl's voice; " the devil ! you carry acting into private
life ! "

" No, sir; I am not sufficiently fond of it."

" You hate it ? "

" I do not like playing."

" You would prefer quiet domestic happiness, eh ? "

" Yes, sir."

" Then, marry me," said Mr. Effingham, with perfect
coolness, " I have half ruined myself for you."

Beatrice looked at him fixedly.

" Your great pleasure in life is to scoff at me, Mr. Effingham," she said, calmly.

"No, by heaven! There's my hand. Take it. I am just in the mood to-day to follow any whim which seizes me."

Beatrice was silent.

"You won't accept me, then?" said Mr. Effingham. "Well, that is wrong in you. Effingham Hall yonder comes to me, and you might indulge your dreams of rank and station to any extent, as we are of tolerably good family."

"I have no such dreams, sir."

"Well, then, your dreams of domestic happiness, but now discoursed of."

Beatrice was again silent; and Mr. Effingham burst into a harsh laugh.

"Ah, ah!" he said, "you don't reply, but I know very well what the expression of your ladyship's face signifies. You mean, Madam Beatrice, that you would have very little domestic happiness as the wife of reprobate Mr. Champ Effingham! Hey? Come, now, let us chat like tender friends, as we are. Is not that your thought?"

"I do not think we should be happy together, sir?"

"Why?"

"We are not congenial."

"Bah! we were cut out for each other."

"No, sir; indeed we were not."

"We were! Come, now, I'll prove it. We are both hypocritical——"

"Sir!"

"Both exceedingly worldly and unamiable——"

"Mr. Effingham!"

"And we love each other devotedly. Could better matches be found?"

"You are in a bitter humor this morning, sir," said Beatrice.

"I? Not in the least, as I believe I have replied to similar charges on previous occasions. I never was in more charming spirits. I have just had a little correspondence which raised my spirits amazingly. Just fancy my respected father writing me word that if I did not give you up, never see you again, the paternal malediction would descend. Think of it."

"Oh, sir!—did your father write that about me?" said Beatrice, suddenly losing her frigid indifference.

" Yes."

" Advising you to come away from this place ? "

" Advising ? not in the least !—commanding me."

" Oh, sir ! then obey that command ! Recollect he is
your father ! Remember that you will cause yourself to be
talked about, and I shall be the cause of all this !—I shall
be the means of distressing your father ! Oh, sir, abandon
me; leave the company which you have so rashly united
yourself to; do not cause me the misery of standing between
father and son ! Be reconciled, sir ! Oh, do not stay here,
sir ! "

Beatrice had risen, in the excess of her emotion, and
stood before the young man now pleading for mercy—mercy
for himself ! Her eyes were full of earnestness and emotion, her words impassioned and tearful, her hands clasped
before her in an attitude of what seemed irresistible entreaty.

Mr. Effingham leaned back, and looked at her with a
mocking smile.

" You are really exceedingly handsome," he said, " and
upon my word the gentlemen, and even the ladies of the
colony, might show some cause for not liking you, and thinking it very naughty in me to come near you. Talk about
me !—you think my infatuation for you *will* make me talked
about ! My dear Miss Beatrice, don't be hypocritical. You
know well that I am at present the most interesting topic of
conversation in the colony of Virginia. I fancy I can hear the
tittering—the delightful gossip about my unworthy self, every
where—here, in the upper country, south side, every where.
Didn't you see how they stared at me, night after night, in
the theatre ? And some of the moral and irreproachable
young ladies would no longer return my bows, if their respected parents would permit them to quarrel with so illus-
trious a nobleman as myself. Talked about ? Bah ! let us
be easy, madam; we are both the scoff of Virginia ! "

" But your family, sir," cried Beatrice, " much as you
affect to despise general opinion—"

" My family will not care much for me—a little worry,
and when the matter ends in some diabolical way, some an
noyance : that is all ! Come, don't talk of my family—or
of any of these matters. Let us speak of acting."

" Oh, sir ! I am sick. You have made me feel so badly
by what you have said."

Mr. Effingham's laugh was the perfection of recklessness and scorn.

"Bah!" he said, "let us talk of business matters. I am going to act Benedick soon, and you shall play the part of your namesake. Can you act it?"

"Yes, sir—but I do not wish to again," said Beatrice, sitting down, overcome with emotion.

"You must not have a voice in the matter—it suits me, madam, and with all possible respect, I shall make my *debût* in 'Much Ado about Nothing.' What an exceedingly apposite piece to appear in! It will be a practical epigram upon public sentiment—the very title!"

"Will you really act, sir?"

"Yes: that will I! nothing can prevent me."

"Then I am the most unhappy of created beings," said Beatrice, tearfully. "Oh! to be the occasion of this altercation between father and son!"

"That is all arranged: and all will go on well now. We will have a delightful time at the ball."

"What ball, sir?"

"Have you not heard? Why, the Governor's. I am going to take you. You will then have an opportunity of seeing all the gentry of this noble colony."

Beatrice looked at the young man with astonished eyes.

"You would escort me, then, sir?" she asked coldly.

"Certainly."

"You must not, sir."

"I will."

"Oh, no, I will not go! I cannot go, sir—I am not invited, sir."

"Pshaw! I am, and of course I can bring any lady I fancy."

"Mr. Effingham!" said Beatrice, wildly, "I am not a lady! I will not accompany you, and be the occasion of a new and more distressing sorrow to your family. No, no, sir—I will not!" and the young girl's face flushed.

"Well—here's my respected friend and manager :—good morning, Hallam," he added carelessly, as that gentleman entered, smiling and rosy; "here, I have been talking to Madam Beatrice about the ball."

"At the Governor's, sir?"

"Yes."

"He wants me to go, father, and I must not," said Beatrice, covering her face.

Hallam stared; and his incredulous glance asked the young man if he really thought of such a thing. This meaning was so plain, that Mr. Effingham burst into laughter, and said:

"Yes, Hallam! I am going to escort Madam to the ball, and be her most devoted cavalier. Now talk to her about it, and remove her scruples—I must go and take a look at the streets of this great town."

And bowing, he went out.

The scene which ensued between the manager and his daughter is not one of those which we take pleasure in describing. Art cannot compass all things. Hallam saw the means of attaching the young man to Beatrice for ever by this ball, for his appearance there with her would be regarded as his public defiance of all the powers of society: and this social prejudice, he felt convinced, was all which prevented Mr. Effingham from marrying Beatrice. It was necessary thus to overcome her scruples, and he did overcome them. Beatrice, at the end of an hour of passionate pleading, fell back, weak, nerveless, overcome. She had consented to go to the ball.

———

CHAPTER XXVI.

IN WHICH A PISTOL FIGURES.

MR. EFFINGHAM passed the whole of the day succeeding this interview in a state of mind more easily imagined than described. The reader will not have failed to perceive that his reckless, and scornful indifference, his mocking laughter, were but the mask which concealed a profound emotion of pain and depression. Proud, headstrong, and passionate, he had nevertheless experienced a sinking of the heart even in the midst of his violent passion, on reading the bluff gentleman's letter—and ill-advised as that letter undoubtedly was, he already bitterly regretted the tone of his reply. The consequence of these conflicting emotions was frightful:—he tossed about, gesticulated, astounded the members of the Virginia

7

company of Comedians by replying to the simplest observations with insult, and betrayed every indication of a mind ill at ease, and charged with

> "that perilous stuff
> Which weighs upon the heart."

His brow was gloomy, his eye fiery, his walk hasty and by starts. So the day passed, and the morning of the next.

In the afternoon he went to his apartment, and sitting down, leaned his head gloomily on his hand. Where would all this end? That abyss he had imagined to be awaiting him, after the first interview he had passed through with the young woman, now seemed to open visibly before him. He had left his home—defied his friends—abandoned all that made life tranquil and happy—for what, for whom? For a woman who scorned him, and did not take the trouble to conceal that scorn; for a beautiful demon, who met all his advances with indifference or disdain, and, strong in her weakness, defied him with looks and words. If he had abandoned all that happy life for some angel of love and purity, whose heart was a treasure grand enough to console him for all the blasts of obloquy or the winds of scorn, there might have existed some reason which would have calmed him. But no! she hated him—scorned him—could not bear his presence!

He rose, and with clenched hands stood looking at his sneering and unhappy visage in the mirror over the fireplace. There he stood, young, handsome, graceful; clad in the costume appertaining to his rank of gentleman; the brow untanned by sun or wind, the hand white and jewelled, not brown, and hard and knotty with rude toil; every thing in the image reflected from the mirror betrayed the enviable position in the world which the young man sustained. The plain gold ring upon his finger was the gift of Clare years ago, when they were sweethearts; the beautiful cravat he wore, with its gold and silver flowers, was worked by the child at the Hall; the diamond pin in his bosom was a birthday present from his father—lastly, the snuff-box peeping from his waistcoat pocket had been given him by Lord Botetourt when he had admired it one day in England.

All this flashed through the young man's mind; and then, with a mental effort as rapid and comprehensive, he

surveyed his future. What would that future be? Young,
high-born, wealthy, heir to the estate of Effingham and representative of that stately house, all honors and pleasures
were open to him, did he but sit down and wait quietly. No
exertion was necessary—the future was assured. Would
that be his future? Would he go on in life surrounded by
friends and tender relatives—gladdened by the smiles of
true-souled companions, the tender love of gentle woman—
and so passing his early youth, arrive at a middle age of influence and honor; his old age finally to come to him, bright
with all that makes it fair and attractive—"as honor, love,
obedience, troops of friends?" Would he keep up the
honors of his ancient house—be a worthy representative of
his honorable name; would he find in that gentle girl whom
every one loved, the companion of his joys and sorrows, the
light illuminating his existence to its close?

Was this his future, he asked himself, with a bitter curl
of the distorted lip—could this be his destiny in life? No!
that was not for him; he had made his election—thrown
away the goblet of limpid and healthful water, to grasp the
bowl foaming with its fiery and poisonous draught. The
Circe had taken him captive—he was no longer human; no
longer had any power over his will; felt that he would not,
if he could, abandon the shore upon which he had cast himself away. No! that bright and happy future was not for
him—he had forfeited it. Effingham Hall was closed to
him—Clare despised or pitied him—friends had deserted
him—he had stopped at the Siren isles, and never would
sail forth again for ever. The name of Effingham would
die if he had to uphold it—he would be stricken from the
annals of his house—nothing remaining of his name and
life but a sad and shameful recollection!

Again he gazed steadily at his sneering and unhappy
image in the mirror—upon his pale cheeks, fallen away so
quickly, upon his bloodshot eyes, his colorless, mocking lips,
and the point to which his thoughts had carried him, was
reflected in his visage so faithfully that a groan issued from
his inmost heart. Then his eye fell upon a pistol, lying on
the table, and he took it up and gazed gloomily at it:—a
harsher, more mocking smile, wreathed his proud lip, and,
cocking the weapon, he murmured the first words of the
soliloquy in Hamlet.

" Yes," he said, " I know, now, what my lord Hamlet meant, when he asked that question of his soul:

> ' Whether 'tis nobler in the mind to suffer
> The stings and arrows of outrageous fortune,
> Or to take arms against a sea of troubles,
> And by opposing end them ! ' "

Then, looking with gloomy curiosity upon the murderous instrument, he said, with a sigh which resembled a groan: " Yes, now I understand those words:

> " —*To die ! to sleep !*
> *No more !*—and by a sleep to say we end
> The heartache and the thousand natural shocks
> That flesh is heir to ! ' Tis a consummation
> Devoutly to be wished !
> For who would bear the whips and scorns of time,
> The oppressor's wrong, the proud man's contumely,
> The pangs of despised love ! ' "

There he stopped, with an expression painfully affecting ; and, sitting down, he covered his face with his hand, and was silent for a time.   Then, the hand was taken away, and the head rose again—and on the lips the same mocking smile played with terrible meaning. He looked again at the pistol, and, with a sneer, placed the muzzle to his forehead.

" It is plain that I am a comedian," he said, bitterly ; "I go for authority to plays ! Well, now, if I were to play the tragedy to the end—imitate the Moor ! Is it not easy ? This little instrument ends all, at once ! "—and his finger touched the trigger.

Suddenly a tap at the door startled him, and hastily un-cocking the pistol, he thrust it into his bosom, and said, harshly and gloomily, " Come in ! "

The door opened softly, a light step was heard, and little Kate Effingham entered the apartment.   Kate, smiling and fond ; her fair hair falling on her shoulders in long girlish curls ; a tender, loving light in her mild, soft blue eyes ; the little hands stretched out to greet him ; her face, and form, and smile, and very dress redolent of home, and that happiness which the weary heart but now looked back upon, as the wrecked mariner clinging to the floating mast, about to be ingulfed in the dark waves, launches a last thought back to the sunshine and pure joy of his far inland home !

CHAPTER XXVII.

HOW MR. EFFINGHAM'S ROOM AT THE RALEIGH TAVERN WAS ILLUMINATED.

In a moment the child was in his arms, clasped to his heart. The fresh, bright-eyed little face—though now those eyes were bathed in dews of happiness—lay on his bosom, and two hot tears from the dry, weary eyes of the young man, rolled down, and fell upon the child's hand. For some minutes no word was uttered. Kate spoke first, and said, earnestly :

" Oh! I'm so glad to see you, cousin Champ—indeed, indeed, I am."

" And I am as glad to see you, Katy," he said, turning away ; but no longer with that painful expression of mockery ; " you came in like a sunbeam! I was so gloomy."

And again the poor, weary eyes were bathed in moisture, and the man's tears mingled with the child's.

" Come," he said, at length, " how is it possible you are here ?"

And as he spoke, the young man caressed fondly the bright locks of the little head.

" Oh!" said Kate; " I just came by myself. I was so sorry, cousin Champ, when you went away, and have been crying about it often since—I couldn't help it. For you know you have always been so good to me. I couldn't help loving you dearly, and crying when you left us. Then papa got angry, and told cousin Alethea you had not done right; and then, when the parson came, he abused you, and papa quarrelled with him, and he's going away. Papa said no one should abuse you, and that you were not half as much to blame as they chose to say; and then went away to the library, and didn't come back to tea."

" But, Katy," said Mr. Effingham, turning away, " this does not explain how you—"

" Oh! I am coming to that at once, cousin Champ. You know I love you dearly—and I couldn't bear to think you were here all by yourself, and not happy. So as cousin

Alethea was coming to town in the chariot, me and Willie thought we'd come, too, and cousin Alethea said we might."

"Is Alethea in town?"

"Yes, cousin Champ; she's down at the store, buying a cake mould, and Willie was looking for a now whip. So I just slipped out and ran up here, and asked if you were here, of a gentleman—though I don't know if he is a real gentleman—wearing such a funny red cloak. He laughed, and was very good, and said you had just gone up to 'number 6,' and I came up, and saw the figure on your door, and tapped."

"Heaven sent you, Katy," said Mr. Effingham, pressing his tremulous lips to the child's forehead. "God knows what might have happened," he added, in a murmur.

"What did you say, cousin Champ?"

"Nothing, dear."

"What is this hard thing under your lace?" said the child, whose arm had struck against the concealed weapon.

"Nothing, nothing!" he said, hastily. And rising suddenly, he went to the open window, and hurled the pistol to the distance of fifty feet. Then returning, after seeing it fall into a pile of rubbish in the yard of the tavern, he took the child in his arms again, and leaned his weary head upon her shoulder.

"You don't seem to me well, cousin Champ," said Kate, tenderly, and endeavoring with the tact of a grown woman, to come to the subject which she wished to reach, without offending Mr. Effingham. "I don't think you are well, indeed I don't, and they can't take very good care of you in this place. I don't like it—it don't seem clean and nice. And then I'm sure you haven't got any body who can bathe your forehead as nicely as I can. Please come and go back with us, cousin," added the child, earnestly. "You can't think how happy it would make me, and all—indeed I would cry for joy."

"I can't make you cry, dear," said Mr. Effingham, with a fond look.

"Well, then, I'll laugh."

"I can't go now."

"But you are sick."

"No, no."

" Indeed—indeed, you're not well."

" Perfectly, dear Katy—but I am as glad to see you as if I wanted you to bathe my forehead."

" You don't seem to think that, cousin," said Kate, sighing, and looking wistfully at him, " or you would not leave us so long."

" Why, I have not been here a week."

" That's a long time—a long, long time indeed ! "

Mr. Effingham softly smoothed the bright head.

" I was much longer away, when I went to England,' he said, " and you did not write me a word to return, dear. You did send me enough of love, however."

" Yes, but I love you more now :—you didn't take much notice of me when I was a little chicken, running about the Hall—and then, and then, cousin—"

" What ? "

" You know, you *had* to go England — "

" You mean — "

" Yes, dear cousin Champ," said Kate, with a tremulous but earnest voice, " I mean that you needn't have come here. Don't be angry with me, please."

" Angry with you ! "

" For I love you so much. I don't think you ought to stay here now, indeed, you would be better at the Hall. Come now," she said, with an earnest pleading look, which made the little face inexpressibly lovely, " go back with me ! won't you ? Oh ! I'll be so good if you'll go back ; and so will Willie—for I will make him. Think how happy we would be, dear cousin Champ—indeed we can't be happy at all, while you are away. I can't."

And the little head drooped, the fair curls falling down, and veiling the child's cheeks. Mr. Effingham was silent, but he unconsciously clasped the small ·hand lying on his own more tightly, as if some invisible and hostile force were pulling him the other way, and in the child lay his only hope of resistance.

" You can't think how your being away has made me feel—indeed, you can't," continued the child, in a low voice, and glancing at his face with wistful, dewy eyes; " you know I never liked any body I loved to go away, and after papa, I love you better than any body in the world. Ever since you went, and papa got angry, I have felt as if I was going to fall sick—I was so sorry! Papa didn't look like he was well either, and sometimes I think I saw cousin Alethea looking sorry. When Tom was packing up your portmanteau, I thought you were going away, and put in it — "

" Did you put that Bible—"

" Yes, cousin Champ—for I knew you would like to read out of my little Bible."

Mr. Effingham rose, and going to his dressing-table, took the small volume from his portmanteau.

" Here Katy," he said, turning aside his head as he spoke, " I have not time to read it now."

" Oh, but keep it!"

" No—I don't wish to."

" Not when I ask you to, cousin Champ?"

" No—no—not now," said Mr. Effingham, with a shadow on his face.

Kate looked inexpressibly hurt, and two tears which she could not restrain, rolled down her cheeks. Mr. Effingham strode up and down the apartment—passed his hand wearily over his forehead, gazed wistfully at the child, and the book she held, and then away from her again. He stopped finally before the window, and looked out. Then he felt a little hand, warm and soft, take his own; and turning round, the child was again in his arms, pressed to his heart.

" Katy," he said, with a troubled voice, " I cannot keep your Bible now—I have not time to read it—and some one coming in here might take it."

Mr. Effingham's face clouded. The thought had occurred to him that some one of the rude, jeering actors might touch it—and at that moment he felt as if he would preserve it from such profanity at the hazard of his life.

" Keep it, dear," he added, tenderly, " I will read it if I ever—when, I mean, I come back to the Hall. Now, don't ask me to take it back any more, Katy—indeed, I cannot."

The child put the volume into the pocket of her frock, with an expression of quiet, uncomplaining sorrow, which was very touching.

" I'll promise to read it every day, when I get back, dear," said Mr. Effingham, " now don't feel badly."

" Oh ! if you would only come back," she said, hiding
her head in his bosom, and crying, " Oh ! cousin Champ !
if you would only come back ! Oh, please do—please leave
this place, and don't be angry with papa any more.   They
said you came—to see—to see—a—lady, cousin Champ
You know you've seen her now, and if she is good, and I
know you would not like her if she was bad—if she is good
she wouldn't have you to distress us to come and see her !
Oh, where is she ?   I'll go and tell her myself, if you'll let
me, how much we want you to come back to us, and I know
you will not think I am presuming.   Now, do let me go :—
I'm sure she will not be angry with a little child like me—
where is she, cousin Champ ? "

Mr. Effingham held the child upon his lap, overcome
with gloomy and yet hopeful thoughts.   She looked into his
face, and saw the troubled expression.

" Oh, come—come ! " she said, in an earnest, pleading
voice, " indeed you are not well.   Oh, cousin Champ, you
will not refuse me—your pet—please come—now cousin
Champ—we'll all go back so nicely in the chariot—and—
won't you ? "

He looked at her for some minutes in silence, and said :

" Katy, do you believe in guardian angels ? "

" I don't know—if you mean—"

" Then, do you believe in angels ? "

" Yes ! oh, yes ! "

" And in heaven ? "

" Yes : mamma is in heaven, and papa," she said.

" What do you think it is like ? " he continued, gazing
on the tender face, " a great city of pearls, and diamonds,
and gold ?   Come, don't be surprised at my speaking so
abruptly.   Do you think there is really a heaven, and
angels ? "

" Oh, yes, cousin Champ—and I'm sure it is not made
of gold and diamonds—I mean I don't think it is.   I think
it's a place where we all love each other more than we can
on earth—and God, too."

" Can we love more than we do on earth ? " he said,
thoughtfully.

" Oh, yes—I believe we can—and then we will not have
any thing in heaven to make us sorry.   We won't be sick,

and grieved, and all, but be happy, and love God for ever
and ever."

Mr. Effingham made no reply; he only murmured to himself.

"Angels are good—like little children before they get
bad," added Kate, earnestly; "there's a verse about ' the
Kingdom of Heaven,' and it's being filled with good people,
like little children.. Must I show it to you?"

" No, no—I believe not," said Mr. Effingham, "I don't
know that reading the Bible would do me any good. I be
lieve what that verse says already, dear," he added, looking
with moist eyes at the child, "and I meant that when I
asked you about heaven; 'Suffer little children to come
unto me and forbid them not—for of such is the kingdom of
heaven.' Is not that the verse? I knew it was. Well, I
wish I had died at your age."

"Oh!" said Kate, in a low voice, "I am not good
enough—I'm very bad."

"You are heavenly in comparison with me."

"Oh, cousin Champ!"

"I am—well, well," he said, suddenly checking himself:
and he murmured, "Why should I deprive myself of this
child's heart."

"Indeed, indeed, you are not well," said Kate, gazing
with a long, sad look, on the troubled and gloomy face, "and
I think something has grieved you."

"No, no—"

"Let me read a little to you, please—I know you'll
like—"

"No, no; I'm not fit to hear reading now, dear," he
said, but more softly, and with less decision in his tone.

Kate noted this change, with that marvellous quickness
of children, and said:

"Oh, yes; let me read you just a little about heaven.
When I read it, I never feel sorry afterwards; and, if I am
sick, it makes me feel almost well and happy. Sometimes I
think about my being a little child, without any father or
mother—any real father, I mean, though papa is my father
—and I feel like crying; but I read a little in my Bible,
and think that papa and mamma are in heaven, and that, if
I am good, I'll go to heaven, too; and, then, I feel as if it

wasn't much matter whether I felt sick and badly or not, so I kept myself good; for I will see them in heaven, if I obey God."

The weary and storm-tossed soul listened to these simple words, and felt a strange emotion at his heart, as if that heart had been frozen, and was slowly melting.

" For you know," Kate went on, earnestly, " this world is not a good place, and we can't be very happy here, though some things are very sweet and pleasant. We have to suffer a great deal here, and we must get mighty tired. But we ought not to complain when we have heaven to think of, where all will be happiness and joy... We feel wrong towards people very often, at least I do, and people behave badly to us, and make us suffer; but we ought to bear all this, when we think of living and loving dearly in heaven, for ever and for ever. Oh! let me read what St. John says about loving each other and God: I always loved to read what he says."

And, without waiting for a reply, the child opened her little Bible, and read, in a low, subdued, earnest voice, some verses, which the young man listened to in silence. Kate closed the book, and leaning her head on his shoulder, said :

" That sounds to me so sweet, that it makes me happy."

" Yes, yes," murmured Mr. Effingham, covering his eyes

" Do you like to hear me read ? " she asked, wistfully.

" Yes," he murmured again.

" Then," said Kate, with an expression of entreaty, which lit up her tender little face, like a light from heaven, and putting her arm round his neck as she spoke—" then come and go back! Oh, please come and go back, and I'll read to you whenever you want to hear me ; and, oh ! we'll be so happy, cousin Champ ! I can't be happy while you are here, and I think that you are not well, may be, and haven't any body to do little things for you. Don't stay in this place, and be all by yourself. I'm sure cousin Alethea's sorry if she said any thing to make you angry ; indeed, I know she is for she said to papa that she ought not to have said something to you. Papa is dreadfully distressed at your going away, and, indeed—indeed—" (here the child's voice faltered) " I shall be so unhappy—so—so—Oh, cousin Champ, do come and go with me ! Oh, please don't stay ! You can't find any body to love you as much as we do, and till you come back the Hall will look dark to me."

The little arm around his neck drew him toward the door; the beseeching voice went to his heart, and melted all his pride, and hardness, and stubborn coldness; the half jest he had uttered about his guardian angel, seemed to become a heavenly reality—to be there in the person of that child, entreating him to go away with her.

"Oh, come!" cried Kate, clinging closer and closer to him, and turning her moist, tender eyes upon his own; "come with me, cousin Champ—come back with us—oh! you are coming. I knew you would. You wouldn't refuse me, I know."

And she placed one hand on the door to open it.

Before she could touch the knob the door opened, and a servant appeared on the threshold.

"A gentleman to see you, sir; ask him up, sir?" he said, bowing.

Mr. Effingham hesitated, and was silent. It might have been imagined that he feared to leave the child—to go beyond the reach of her voice, the brightness of her eyes.

"Well, well," he said, after a moment's silence, "whoever it is I will see him. Stay here, dear—wait till I come back—I will return directly. Say I will be down immediately," he added, to the servant.

Then stooping, and pressing his lips to the child's forehead, he said, tenderly and softly:

"Stay till I return, Katy; I will soon send this gentleman off, whoever he may be. I cannot lose you so soon, and I think, before you go—if I do not go with you—you may read me some more."

Kate looked inexpressibly delighted, and this expression of joy seemed to touch and please Mr. Effingham extremely. He threw a last fond glance on the child, and saying again that he would be back in a moment, went out and closed the door. Kate sat down overcome with joy and pride: her smile seemed to illuminate the whole apartment, dimming the very radiance of the sunlight.

Ten minutes passed thus, when suddenly a knock at the door made her heart throb; and rising quickly to her feet, she said, before she was aware of it, "Come in!"

CHAPTER XXVIII.

ENTER SHYLOCK, AND HIS SHADOW.

THE door opened, and two men made their appearance. We say *men :* it would be sacrificing too much to courtesy to call them gentlemen ; for neither in their dress, features, nor expression, was there any thing whatsoever remotely entitling them to that distinction. He who came first was that worthy who had acted Shylock on the opening night, at the theatre near the capitol ; and the reader may possibly recollect Mr. Manager Hallam's criticism of his performance, delivered in the presence of the worthy himself, on the next morning, at the Raleigh. His present state was not materially an improvement upon his condition that night, and having dined not very long before, his spirits were naturally in an elevated and generous condition. When Mr. Pugsby had emptied his pint of rum or his bottle of port—a delicacy which he did not usually indulge in, however—he felt at peace with all the world, and ready to embrace the whole of mankind. His companion was a lean, cadaverous gentleman, whose favorite characters were " Shallow," " Slender " the apothecary in " Romeo and Juliet,"—he had been assisting Mr. Pugsby in emptying his last bottle.

Kate beheld the entrance of these worthies with great alarm ; though her womanly little air of dignity did not desert her. Perhaps it was rather distaste than alarm which she felt, child as she was, for certainly no contrast could have been imagined less to the advantage of the stage worthies. Kate, clad in her rich and tasteful little costume of silk and velvet—with her bright eyes and rosy face, looked like a flower, a picture, something beautiful, rich and rare, to be approached with reverence, and regarded with love and admiration :—she seemed out of place in the rough apartment, as some masterpiece of Titian, framed in gold, would look hung up in a wide garret, with a ceiling of dirty rafters. She had the beauty and tenderness of childhood : purity and gentleness enveloped her like a cloud. None of these things appertained to the worthies who now entered, inasmuch as

they were extremely rough and common specimens of human
ity, with bloated faces, and unsteady gait, and sleepy-look-
ing eyes, which rolled, and winked, and leered, as authentic
tradition relates of the ancient worthy Silenus.

Shylock hesitated for a moment on the threshold, and
exhibited a species of inane surprise, at finding a child, instead of his brother-comedian, Mr. Effingham, in the apartment.

"Hum!" said Shylock, by way of signifying that he
was about to speak.   This expressive monosyllable was
echoed by Shallow, who, to save himself the trouble of
thinking, generally repeated or coincided in, the observations
of his friend.

"Stand and unfold thyself," continued Shylock, striking
an attitude, and facetiously pretending to consider Kate a
ghost.

"Unfold—yes, unfold," echoed Shallow, stretching out
his cadaverous hand as his friend did.

"Be thou a spirit of health or goblin damned? thou
comest in such a questionable shape, I'll speak to thee!"
continued Shylock, "hey? come, speak!"

Kate felt as if she should sink into the floor, and was so
frightened that she could scarcely restrain her tears or command her voice.

"Come, come, pretty damsel!" exclaimed Shylock, with
some impatience, and descending into prose, "come, why
don't you answer?   Who are you?   Why are you here,
instead of that jolly minion of the moon, that lad of metal,
hight Childe Effingham?"

"Oh, sir!" said Kate, with a trembling voice, and re-
treating as the leering tragedian approached her, "Oh, sir,
I am—Mr. Effingham—I mean, he is just gone, sir."

"That is no answer."

"No answer," echoed Shallow.

"A subterfuge."

"Perfect."

"And subterfuges are a deadly sin," said Shylock, whose
words unconsciously flowed into a metrical shape.

"An awful sin," said Shallow.

"So now perpend, young damsel," continued Shylock,
approaching the child, who shrank back, "either thou diest

presently, or do'st relate to me the marvel strange, why thou
art here—all armed in complete—no, thou hast no steel!
Speak! what art thou? And if thou do'st conceal the least
small thing—" Shylock drew out the knife which he was
accustomed to whet upon his shoe, when Antonio was to be
sacrificed, and flourished it with deadly meaning. Kate
shrank further back and turned pale.

"Oh, sir, you frighten me!" she said.

"I'll eat thee whole ere the leviathan hath swum a
league—"

Kate fell into a chair.

"Come," said Shylock, putting up his knife, "I'll be
merciful, if I am a Hebrew vile, and thou, fair lass, a Christian."

"We'll be merciful," said Shallow.

"Therefore, unfold—unfold, I say!" continued Shylock,
"art thou base, common, and popular; or, high and mighty,
like Prince Hal?—discourse. Whence art thou?"

Kate murmured, with a throbbing heart: "From the
Hall, sir."

"What is thy name?"

"Catherine, sir!"

"Well, Catherine, listen: thou shalt go below, and bid
the tapster draw a measure of rum, which thou shalt bring
to us. We are noble gentlemen, come hither to see Prince
Hal, that noble bully. Do'st thou understand?"

"Oh, sir, I cannot! I don't know—"

"Do'st thou reply?"

"Oh, sir, don't come near me, I do not like you!"

"Not like me? Well, I will be calm! Go bid them
draw the ale; do'st hear, thou varlet vile?"

Kate's indignation began to conquer her fear, and, child
as she was, in the midst of such persons, her face flushed
with anger, at the word *vile*. "I can't go, sir," she said.

"Cannot! sayest thou? Why, 'cannot'?"

"I do not know any body here, sir," she replied;
"please let me pass out."

"Never! thou shalt pass over my dead body, rather."

"And mine," said Shallow.

"Oh, I must pass!" cried Kate, endeavoring to leave
the room.

"Stand back! ill met by moonlight, proud Titania.
But thou shalt not go hence."

"I must, sir!" said Kate, endeavoring to pass again, and
nearly crying from fear and indignation.

"By heaven, thou diest!" And uttering these words,
Shylock moved with unsteady gait to shut the door. But
Kate was too quick for the worthy, and ran through, brushing against him as she passed. Shylock made a grasp at
her, and caught the ribbon of her little hat, tearing the
covering from her head. The next moment he would have
reached her and brought her back by main force, but just
as she was about to fall upon her knees, in despair, the door
opposite opened, and a young woman, evidently attracted by
the noise, appeared upon the threshold.

"What is this?" she said.

"Oh, ma'am! that man won't let me go!" cried Kate,
"he has frightened me nearly to death. Oh, don't let him
take me from you!" And clinging to the dress of Beatrice,
she shrunk from the infuriated Shylock. Beatrice, with a
single word and a look, closed the door in the face of that
worthy, and she and the child were alone together.

———◆———

CHAPTER XXIX.

KATE AND BEATRICE.

For a moment the young girl and the child were silent;
Beatrice knew not what to think of the scene, and Kate was
indulging in a hearty cry. At last she dried her eyes, and
stopped sobbing by degrees, and looking at Beatrice, said:
"Oh, ma'am, I'm so thankful that you saved me from that
horrid man!"

"How did he come to annoy you, my child?" said
Beatrice, looking affectionately at the sweet little face.

"Oh, he came in, and—and because I wouldn't go and
get him something—for I couldn't, you know. Oh, he
frightened me so!" and Kate began to sob again.

Beatrice wiped the child's eyes and got her a glass of
water, all the time soothing her with kind words.

"Don't speak if it makes you cry," she said, softly.

"Oh, I am not frightened, now!"

"You are quite safe here."

"Am I quite?"

"Yes, that rude man will not presume to come into this room, and were he to do so, I would send him from it with a single word."

And Beatrice, with a disdainful motion of her hand, seemed to wish to dismiss so insignificant a subject. Kate looked at her attentively, for the first time, and said;

"Do you know him? I think you are too pretty and good to know that rude man."

Beatrice turned away.

"I am sorry that I am obliged to know him," she said in a low tone, "but how did you come to be pursued by him? It was disgraceful!" added Beatrice, with a generous flash of her proud, brilliant eye.

"I was waiting a minute for cousin, who had gone down to see a gentleman. He left me in his room, and I was so frightened when those rude men came in. I am not used to such people, you know;—papa don't have any visitors like them, and the gentlemen that come to the Hall are always kind to me. Oh, he drew out such an ugly sharp knife, and threatened to kill me!" added Kate, very nearly beginning to cry again. Beatrice looked at her attentively: some recollection seemed to be struggling in her mind.

"Strange!" she said, "I seem to have seen this child before—somewhere—where was it?"

And she pressed her forehead, and seemed to be buried in thought. Kate looked at her, and said, timidly:

"I am afraid ma'am, that you were busy when I came in."

"Yes, I was my child—but that is nothing."

"Were you sewing? what a pretty handkerchief!"

And remembering the scene she had just passed through, Kate used the embroidered handkerchief she had taken up to admire, for the purpose of drying a rebellious tear.

"I was not sewing," said Beatrice, with a look of weariness, "I was studying. But you have not told me, my child, how you came to be in the Raleigh."

"Oh, cousin Alethea, and Willie, and me, came to town and—"

" Then you do not live here: but I forget—you spoke of the Hall, and there are no halls here."

" Oh, no: a hall is a house in the country."

" And you came to see your cousin—a gentleman who wears a red cloak—?"

" Oh, no! he's not my cousin—"

" Ah!" said Beatrice, her eyes suddenly dazzled with a rapid lightning-like thought, " your cousin—what is his name —the Hall—?"

" Cousin Champ is his name, and we all live at Effingham Hall. My name is Catherine Effingham—but papa is not my father."

Beatrice sat down, murmuring.

" Effingham!—Effingham—always Effingham! Yes— at the theatre!"

Kate misunderstood these half-audible words, and said.

" Did you ask if Effingham was our name, ma'am? Yes; and I know papa will be mighty thankful to you and cousin Champ too. He's a dear good fellow, and I love him dearly."

Beatrice remained silent, and turned away her face in order that the child might not see the painful and gloomy expression which dimmed the eyes, and took the tender smile from the lips.

" And you were in yon—in Mr. Effingham's room—were you, my child?" she murmured, at last.

" Yes; and cousin Champ had just gone down to see a gentleman. He told me to wait till he came back."

" Is he fond of you?" asked Beatrice, why she scarcely knew.

" I know he is!" exclaimed Kate, with a bright smile shining through her moist eyes.

" And you love him?"

" Oh, dearly! he is so kind and good!"

They were almost the very words which had escaped from the lips of Beatrice after her interview with Charles; and the recollection of that interview now came to efface the bitter expression which followed little Kate's words. The bitter smile only glanced, then flew away.

" Did your father bring you to town, my child?" she asked, pressing her hand upon her heart to still its throbbing.

" Oh, no!" said Kate, " papa is not pleased with cousin

Champ." Then regretting this speech, she added—" that is—I mean, ma'am—cousin Champ went away from the Hall, and hasn't been back."

Beatrice could not look at the child.

" And is he angry ? " she said.

" Who ?—papa ? "

" Yes," murmured Beatrice.

" No, I don't think papa is much angry; but he don't like cousin Champ to be here."

" Why ? " said Beatrice, in a low voice, and like a despairing soldier turning the weapon in the wound.

" He came to see some lady here, and papa and cousin Alethea do not like—"

" No, no—not a lady—"

There the young girl stopped, overcome, panting, avoiding the child's look, her head drooping, her forehead burning.

" I don't know who it is," said Kate, " but I think cousin Alethea said it was that young actress we saw act in the ' Merchant of Venice.' "

" Do you not recollect her ? " murmured Beatrice.

" Who—Miss Hallam ? Oh, yes ! She wore a lovely fawn-colored silk, and was very pretty."

" I did not know I was so completely changed," said the young girl, turning away and smiling painfully. Then she said aloud :

" And so Mr. Effingham—your cousin—came to see the actress, and his family are displeased ? "

" Yes, ma'am, we all want dear cousin Champ to come back. I don't think he ought to come here to see an actress She is not good enough for him, and oughtn't to distress us.

" Oh, it is an unjust punishment !—it is unjust ! " murmured Beatrice, with tears in her eyes : but Kate neither saw the tears nor heard these bitter words.

" I came to tell cousin Champ to-day he was too good for her—but I didn't like to," continued Kate, not observing the change in the countenance of Beatrice ; " we read some in the Bible, though, and cousin Champ 'most promised to go back with me—"

" Did he ! "

" Yes, ma'am."

" Oh, take him back ! "

Kate was somewhat surprised at these vehement words, but said:

"I think he is going with us. I don't think he would leave us, all who love him so, for a common playing girl."

"Oh, it is unjust—it is unjust!" repeated Beatrice, in an inaudible voice. "I have not deserved it!"

"She's very pretty—for I believe it is Miss Hallam," continued Kate, "but she is not good enough to marry cousin Champ, you know."

Beatrice rose wildly, and said, with passionate tears in her eyes:

"She would not marry him!—she does not wish to! I am that actress! I am Beatrice Hallam! He has made my life miserable and wretched; he follows me, persecutes me, and will not leave me! Oh, I am not to blame—I am not! I do not deserve so much unjust blame—no, no! It is cruel in you to make me suffer so!—oh, it is cruel!"

And hiding her face in her hands, the young girl trembled and shook with passionate sobs. Kate was so much startled and alarmed by these passionate words that she stood for a moment motionless with surprise and astonishment. Then her tender little heart overcame every thing, and running up to the beautiful girl who had been so kind to her, she took her hand, and, sobbing, said:

"Don't cry!—please, don't cry!—I didn't mean to be so rude—indeed, I am ashamed and sorry—oh! please don't cry!"

And Kate herself cried, as if her heart would break. Beatrice suffered the little hand to imprison her own, and slowly raised her head again—her eyes full of tears.

"Pardon me, my child," she said, with noble dignity and calmness, "I did not mean to blame you—I could not help speaking abruptly and shedding some tears—for indeed I am not to blame. My lot is very unhappy, for I cannot even ask a little child like you to love me."

And her humid eyes dwelt with great softness and tenderness on Kate's fresh little countenance, over which large tears were chasing each other.

"I am glad I was near to save you from that rude man," continued Beatrice, rising, "and that is my only reward—my own feelings. I ask no other—"

Kate would have fallen into the tender arms, for very weakness and emotion.

"No," said Beatrice, gently repulsing her, "I am an actress.   Come !"

And she went toward the door.   At the same moment it opened violently, and Mr. Effingham stood before them.

CHAPTER XXX.

SHOWING TO WHAT USE A LOAF OF BREAD MAY BE PUT.

THE young man entered grasping his sword—which he had drawn half from the scabbard.

"Ah !" he said, with a deep sigh of relief : then turning upon Beatrice, he said : "I have to thank you, madam, for robbing me of my visitor !"

And his haughty eye flashed, as he put his arm round Kate, and drew her away.   Beatrice made no reply—but Kate cried out.

"Oh! cousin Champ! Don't speak so to her ! She was so good to me."

"Good to you, Kate ! What do you mean ? "

"Those horrid men !   Oh, they frightened me so !"

Mr. Effingham looked from one to the other, to ask an explanation.

"What men ?" he said.

"The men that came into your room."

"Men in my room !   Who ? "

"I don't know, indeed, cousin Champ, but they behaved very badly to me."

"Behaved badly to you !" said Mr. Effingham, his brow flushing with haughty fire.

"Oh, it was nothing," said the child, becoming alarmed at the storm she had aroused, "they only frightened me a little !"

Suddenly Mr. Effingham looked at the child's hair still disordered and rumpled—for the worthy Shylock, in pulling away her hat, had naturally dragged the well-brushed hair from its place.   Mr. Effingham observed this at a glance, and said, with a flashing eye :

" Where is your hat, Kate ? "

Beatrice rose.

" I can tell you what has taken place in a moment, sir,'
she said, calmly; " it is nothing more than happens almost
every day—only disgraceful, you know, sir. Mr. Pugsby
annoyed your young relative, and the child came to my apartment for refuge. I gave it to her, that is all; and now,
sir— "

Mr. Effingham did not wait to hear the end of the sentence. His eye burned fiercely, and hurrying out with the
child, he said, hastily :

" Come, Katy, let us go to the carriage : I must put
you in : I can't go to-day to the Hall. Ah, when you are
once safe, we 'll have a settlement— "

" But my hat, cousin Champ ? " said Kate. Mr. Effingham's teeth ground audibly, but before he could make a
reply, a voice behind him, loud and familiar, said :

" Here's your beauty's hat—where the devil are you
going— "

It was Shylock, who came along the passage behind, and
turning, Mr. Effingham saw the child's hat in his hand. A
flash as of lightning blazed from the young man's eye, and
to abandon Kate's hand, throw himself upon the leering
worthy, clutch him by the throat, and hurl him headlong
from the landing-place to the bottom of the stairs, was
the agreeable employment of a single moment. But this
did not satisfy Mr. Effingham's rage; and motioning the
child to remain behind, he sprung down the steps, and ar-
riving at the bottom just as Shylock, in a violent rage, rose
up, he shouted wrathfully :

" Draw, you dog ! draw ! you wear a sword ! Damn my
blood, I 'll have your heart's blood !'

And drawing his sword, the young man would have plunged it into Shylock's breast, had not the jolly host thrown himself between the combatants and received the thrust in a huge
loaf of bread he was lugging into his larder. This incident
so far delayed further employment of the weapon, which had
completely passed through it to the hilt. The crowd then
parted the infuriated combatants, and this consummation was
one for which Shylock seemed devoutly grateful. Having
only frightened the child for fun, as that worthy said, after-

wards, Mr. Effingham's sudden attack upon him had taken
him completely by surprise : and his blood had scarcely
time to rise.   So it was they were parted, and Shylock, muttering curses and threats of vengeance, retreated to his apartment.   Mr. Effingham, with insulting disdain, called after him
that he should have an opportunity to right his wrongs at
the sword's point, though he might be excused from match-
ing himself against such a cowardly villain ; and so this little
interlude ended.

Kate, sobbing and agitated, had put on her little hat,
and now, with Mr. Effingham's hand in her own, left the
inn.   At the threshold they ran against Master Will, who,
breathless, his face flushed, his mouth open, was running to
ask if any one at the Raleigh had seen Kate.

" Here I am, Willie," said the child ; " I'm not crying,
you know—only laughing."

And Kate, after this abortive effort to show that nothing
had happened, burst into a passion of tears.   Mr. Effingham,
with a short and curt greeting to Will, went on to the place
where the carriage stood, and placed the child in it.   Miss
Alethea had felt much less anxiety about Kate than Will,
and was still making her purchases.   Will ran in to tell her
that Kate was found.

Mr. Effingham was going away in silence, after pressing
the child's hand, when, sobbing, she said :

" Oh, won't you kiss me ? you are not angry with me,
cousin Champ ! "

And tears choked the tender, distressed voice—deep
sighs shook the little frame of the child.   Mr. Effingham
went over toward her, but, suddenly resuming his erect
attitude, said, gloomily :

" No, no, Katy ; I cannot kiss you.   No ; do not think
of me in future ; and never come near the Raleigh again
Have you your Bible ? "

" I believe so," sobbed Kate.

" Good," he said, in the same quiet, gloomy voice ; " I
will love you dearly as long as I live, but I can see you no
more.   Good-bye," and, turning away, he muttered,

" The die is cast ! "

CHAPTER XXXI.

WHAT MR. EFFINGHAM MEANT WHEN HE SAID THAT THE DIE WAS CAST.

LET us now endeavor to explain why Mr. Effingham acted so strangely toward the child, refusing to kiss her at parting, and exhibiting that singular solicitude about her Bible's safety, in the little pocket. The explanation of these matters will be found in that interview with the nameless gentleman, whom Mr. Effingham left Kate to go and see.

When the young man descended, he saw, seated in the ordinary, waiting for him, his friend, Jack Hamilton, the fox-hunter. A family tradition, supported by the family Bible, averred that this gentleman's name had originally been John, but this was not generally credited, so completely had the sobriquet by which he was almost universally addressed, come to be regarded as the name given to him by his sponsors in baptism. The face which Mr. Hamilton rejoiced in, was, perhaps, remotely responsible for this alteration in his patronymic; and it seemed almost impossible to feel that he should be addressed by any other name than a nickname. He was a hearty, laughing, honest-looking fellow, with frank, open eyes; a nose, which seemed to be everlastingly engaged in snuffing up the odors of broils and roasts, or critically testing wines; a voice, which greeted all, high and low, with nearly equal friendliness, cordiality, and heartiness. Mr. Hamilton was richly clad, but down his velvet pantaloons ran a long red stain, the blood of a fox he had followed to the death on the preceding day.

Mr. Effingham greeted him with unusual cordiality, and his languid, indifferent, *petit maître* manner seemed to have entirely disappeared—at least, this was the observation made by his friend.

"You were busy, were you not?" said Hamilton; "any friends?"

"No, no; I'm very glad to see you, my dear fellow."

"Well, that's understood, or, it would be understood," said honest Jack Hamilton, ' if my visit was a mere dropping-in, as I passed by, to use the new slang which is becoming fashionable; but I came to say something to you, Champ. Come, let's take a stroll."

"I would—but—really—"

And Mr. Effingham thought of Kate.

"Oh, you need not fear being detained any time, scarcely. Come, we cannot talk here."

And, putting his arm through Mr. Effingham's, the fox-hunter led him away.

"Well, well," said the young man to himself, "Katy can amuse herself for a few minutes, until I return; and I must know what brings Hamilton to see me. He evidently has something on his mind."

They strolled out into the square, in the centre of the town, and found themselves thus insulated from the ears, if not from the eyes, of the community. Hamilton stopped, and said :

"I came to talk about this ball, Champ."

"What? at the Governor's?"

"Yes."

"Well, my dear fellow?"

"These actors, here, and the people at the tavern, are saying—"

"That I am going to it?"

"Yes."

"With Beatrice Hallam?"

"Yes."

"Well, they had the right to say so I announced my intention to do so," said Mr. Effingham, in a gloomy and hesitating voice.

"The people at the tavern have been talking through the town about it," continued Hamilton, "and so it got to the gentlemen in the neighborhood, and created quite a sensation."

"It seems that every thing I do creates something of that description," said Mr. Effingham, gloomily.

"But, really, you must confess that this—"

"Deserves to create a sensation, you would say : is it not so?"

'Well, Champ, I'll be honest with you, and say that I think it does."

Mr. Effingham passed his hand thoughtfully and wearily

8

across his brow. A struggle seemed to be going on in his mind. "If I fancy going with this young woman, I will go," he said, at length.

"You have not determined, then?" said Hamilton, displaying great satisfaction at these words.

Mr. Effingham mused. "I had determined," he replied, "but I do not know now if I shall go—I think not."

"Delighted to hear it! really now, Champ, you must permit me to say that you are too good a fellow to throw yourself away upon that young girl, though I grant you she is pretty. I suppose, though, you are running after her as we run a fox, for the glorious excitement of the chase. Up and away! ride all day and night! no matter if you break your neck, you gain the excitement and glory!"

Mr. Effingham's countenance displayed still the struggle going on in his mind. Then a bright light cleared away the gloom and doubt, and his features became serene and soft once more. He had thought of Kate, and now said: "Jack, I don't think I will go. No, I will not!"

"By George, I'm delighted to hear it!"

"You're a good friend!"

"I hope so; we have run many a fox together."

"Yes, yes!"

"Don't you remember the gray rascal we ran from Cote's to the ford? what a day we had—and Tom Lane has not got over his dislocated shoulder to this day."

"Those were fine times, fine times!" said Mr. Effingham, cheerily.

"And you remember, by George!" said Hamilton, laughing heartily, "I recollect it as if it was yesterday! You remember when we swept by the Hall like a parcel of wild devils, Tom Lane came near running over your little cousin—what was her name? I think it was Kate?"

"Yes, yes!" said Mr. Effingham, with a soft smile.

"A lovely little creature, and as good as she's pretty; I saw her at the Hall the other day, when I went to see my good friend, Miss Alethea—think of a bachelor, confirmed and obdurate like myself, having lady friends!—the child took my eye mightily, and I do believe she recollected the old times before you went to England!"

"Happy times, happy times!" said Mr. Effingham

returning to his youth again, as the fox-hunter brought the
past back to him with his familiar, honest voice, his frank
eyes, and laughing reminiscences.

"Yes, they were happy enough," said Hamilton, "and
you thought so then, I know, judging from the foolish things
you were guilty of about Clare Lee. By George, she was a
perfect little angel, and is yet!"

Mr. Effingham's head drooped.

"I remember when we all used to go to gather apples.
I was a young man, then, but just as young as the youngest,
and your favorite practice was to hold up the corners of her
silk apron, until that black monkey, Joe, threw down enough
to fill it—"

Mr. Effingham smiled.

"And as the little apron slowly got full, it weighed
down more and more, and naturally you came closer to pretty
Clare; and somehow your face struck against her own, the
lower portions thereof! and—ah, Champ, my boy, you were
a wild fellow then!" And Mr. Hamilton laughed heartily.
His companion smiled, with dreamy eyes and tender lips,
thinking of his boyhood and of Clare.

"After that, you took it into your head to go to England, and came back the perfect dandy you are," continued
honest Jack Hamilton, with refreshing frankness.

"Yes, yes!" said Mr. Effingham, smiling.

"And snubbed us."

"No, no!"

"And swaggered about like a lord, and talked literature
like a wit—what a wearisome thing literature is! And you
altogether deteriorated! Come, now, deny it?"

"I'm afraid I cannot," said Mr. Effingham, thinking of
Clare.

"Still our family—we are distant kin, you know—our
family comes of too good a stock to degenerate, and I don't
think your foreign journeyings, have hurt you much. The
folks all about stand up for you, and have one eternal observation, which makes me yawn, about your 'sowing your
wild oats.' They always shake their heads when my name
is mentioned, and hint that my crop is always being put in,
and never reaped and disposed of."

"You're better than I am, Jack," said his friend quietly

" The devil! no compliments! If some folks heard that,
they would dissent most emphatically !"

" Who ? "

" All sorts of people, even down to that little chick we
were talking of, Kate. By George, sir, you should have
heard the eulogy she pronounced in your honor, on the visit
I mentioned I made to the Hall ! "

" What ! little Kate praised—"

" Yes, I should think so : the private impression of any
stranger who had heard her, would have been that her illus-
trious cousin united in his single person all the graces, attractions, and virtues of the greatest sages and heroes of modern
and ancient times. Of course such extravagance couldn't
deceive one who knew you as well as I did ! "

Mr. Effingham found himself laughing delightedly, and
murmuring, " Darling Kate ! "

" Well, now, I'm glad to see that my well-meant advice
is not needed," continued Hamilton. " You will not go to
the ball with Beatrice Hallam ? "

" No—no ; I think I shall go back to the Hall to-day."

" Good ! Take a seat in my turn-out ! I'm glad you
are not going there—for there would have come no good
from it. Those fellows are very hotbrained."

" Who ? "

" Oh, I was just thinking of what a party of fellows were
saying of it," said Hamilton, not reflecting upon his words,
or being at all conscious how injudicious they were. " They
talked so that I thought I would come and see you."

" What did they say ? " Mr. Effingham asked, with an
imperceptible clouding of the brow.

" Oh, don't mind them. They got to talking, and said
nothing but what was foolish—they said that your going
with Miss Hallam was out of the question—and I agree
with them."

" How out of the question ? "

" Why, ridiculous."

" Ridiculous ? "

" Come ! my dear fellow, don't think of them."

" But what did they say ?—who were they? " asked
Mr. Effingham, feeling his anger rise at what he regarded as
an impertinent piece of interference with his private affairs.

" I will not tell their names," said Hamilton.

" Well—their words, then."

" Their words ? "

" Yes; what did they say of my going to the ball Come, tell me, Hamilton."

" Well, as I came to tell you, I will," his friend replied thoughtlessly; " they said it was wrong."

" Wrong ! "

" Yes, and ridiculous."

" Is that all ? " asked Mr. Effingham, with a curling lip.

" No !" said Hamilton; " they got to saying after the third bottle, that they would not permit it—by George ! There it is out, fool that I am ! But when did I ever fail to make a fool of myself ! "

And conscious, too late, of his indiscretion, Mr. Jack Hamilton regarded his own conduct with profound contempt and indignation. He was not far wrong, if this were on the score of discretion: for his last words completely aroused the devil of pride and obstinate wilfulness, which had been put to sleep by those familiar reminiscences of youth and home, and Clare's tenderness—Kate's, too.

" Not permit *me* to attend the ball with Beatrice Hal lam !" said Mr. Effingham, with disdainful pride. " By heaven ! I will know who dared to say that ! "

" I will not tell you," said Jack Hamilton, stoutly. Mr. Effingham's hand grasped the hilt of his sword.

" I have been insulted ! " he said.

" None was meant."

" None meant !"

" I tell you, Champ; they had all been drinking, and did not know what they said."

" No man shall insult me, and say he was intoxicated ! I will not take such a lame excuse, Hamilton."

" Come, now—challenge me," said his friend, coolly.

" No; I shall apply to the proper parties for redress."

" Of course, I am responsible, Champ. Come, run your short sword through me, and let out the foolish mind which has made me act so childishly ! "

" Hamilton, you have acted as a real friend," said Mr. Effingham, with a frown. " I hold that no friend should hear another spoken of in such terms, without informing him of the assault upon his honor "

"What assault is there here, in the devil's name?"

"They said that my conduct was ridiculous—"

"A mere joke!"

"And they—the paladins of respectability and chivalry—they would not *permit* me to go to the Governor's ball—to escort Miss Hallam thither. By heaven! I'll make them repent it."

"Champ, you are as furious as a Spanish bull—you see red at a moment's warning! Come, moderate your anger.'

"I am not angry!" said Mr. Effingham, furiously.

"Not angry!"

"No—I am indignant, though; and I will show these excellent gentlemen that my actions or intentions are not such as concern themselves. I shall find the paladins!"

"How will you?"

"Why, I will go to that ball with Miss Hallam, and if any gentleman in the room looks sideways at her or at me, I will call him to account for it. Your bottle critics will not fail to expose themselves!"

And Mr. Effingham's lip curled with anger and scorn.

"Presume to criticise my affairs thus!" he continued, indignantly, "I am then a child who is to ask permission of these worthy gentlemen—these potent, grave, and reverend signors—if I chance to feel a wish to escort a lady to a ball! Yes, a lady, Hamilton! for by heaven! I tell you, that Beatrice Hallam is as pure and high-souled as the noblest lady in the land! I know her well, and to my cost; and I tell you that she is the pearl of honor, delicacy, and truth. You may smile, and I know well what causes your mirth. You are thinking of my wild words, that day when I met you going out of town. Well, I was angry that day, because Miss Hallam had received my familiar addresses with proper coldness—had repulsed me. She was right—and I honor her for it. If she scorns me again, I may hate her, and taunt her; but at the bottom I respect and honor her. You look at me ironically! well, say I do love her—say I am infatuated about her—better men have made fools of themselves! whether that be true or not, one thing is certain, I shall allow no *man* to make a fool of *me!*"

And Mr. Effingham put his cocked hat on with a movement which betrayed his anger and indignation: he had taken it off during this speech to wipe his brow, moist with perspiration.

For a moment Hamilton said nothing.

"Well, Champ," he replied, at length, "I repeat that I was a great fool to tell you this, and I still hope you will regard these hasty words I have reported to you—I did it in the most friendly spirit—in the light they should be regarded—as the mere idle talk of young men. Come, dismiss your anger, and go back with me. Forget what I have said, and let the matter end."

Mr. Effingham shook his head, with a frown.

"It will end otherwise," he said.

"You will not go to the ball?"

"Yes, I will."

"With Miss Hallam?"

"With Miss Hallam."

"It will be a dreadful thing for you:—you will be laughed at all over the colony."

"Let them laugh!" said Mr. Effingham, dsidainfully.

"You may even get a dozen duels on your hands."

"Oh, very well!—very well! I wish some little excitement. I have a good deal of time on my hands. I think it highly probable that some chevalier will espouse the cause of outraged society, and avenge its accumulated wrongs upon my insignificant person—if I do not give an account of the chivalrous gentleman myself!" added Mr. Effingham, with a scornful pride. Hamilton saw that he had raised a storm beyond his power to quell, and with mingled sorrow, and self-upbraiding, very unusual with him, led the way back to the tavern in silence.

"Well," he said, as they reached the door, "I have used my best efforts to persuade you to give this up, Champ: you are determined, I see, and I know it is useless to say any more. I have only to add, that as you are alone, and the enemy is numerous, I shall hold myself prepared to espouse your side in any thing which may arise of a hostile character. Good day."

And the honest fox-hunter, refusing to receive Mr. Effingham's assurances of regret, for any thing that he might have said, and declining to enter the tavern, parted from him, with a shake of the hand, full of cordiality and friendship. Mr. Effingham for a moment looked after him with friendly re-

gard, then the old gloomy expression usurped its former
place upon his visage, and he ascended to his chamber.
Kate was not there, and he hurried out to look around for
her.   He heard voices in Beatrice's room—Kate's, he
thought; and hastening to the door, opened it just as they
were issuing forth as we have seen.   What ensued thereon,
we have related.

CHAPTER XXXII.

IN WHICH PARSON TAG APPEARS AND DISAPPEARS.

" IN former pages of this true history, I had occasion to set
down a few reflections upon the feelings of my worthy ancestor, Mr. Effingham, when, having been repulsed by the
young actress, he rode back to the hall.   I come now to say
a few brief words of Mr. Charles Waters, another of the
characters whose mental development it is my duty to ad-
vert to.   Charles Waters was, as the reader will have per
ceived, by nature a student and thinker.   Unused from his
very childhood to the amusements and employments of his
associates, his character had assumed a peculiar mould.   To
strong feelings he united a cool and self-possessed intellect,
and this intellect he had trained by hard study, and long
and profound thought.   Accustomed to live thus in the past
and future, not in the present—or if at all in the present,
only so far as to examine its bearing on that future—he had
grown up without experiencing any of those sensations which
men generally become acquainted with when they are thrown
in contact with the fairer sex.   In other words, he had passed
his majority without experiencing what is universally known
by the name of love.   His character had thus become serious,
and his countenance habitually wore an expression of thoughtful quiet.   He seldom laughed, and scarcely ever joined in
the rough, jovial converse of his father's guests —the boatman
Townes and others—and though he was greatly beloved by
this class of persons, and respected also, this personal popularity was rather to be attributed to his well-known goodness and nobility of character than his social traits.   He

had visited the theatre, as we have seen, on the opening
night, in compliance with his father's request, not from any
motion of his own. His father had imagined that his cheek
was pale, his eye mournful, his health injured, by those incessant explorations into the ruins of systems and nations;
the play, he thought, would be of service to him; and he
had gone, and admired Beatrice Hallam, and felt some in·
dignation when Mr. Effingham annoyed her—and nothing
more. Then he had preserved that young woman's life, and
there is much of significance in this fact. We experience
warm regard toward those we have greatly served—a young
girl is never afterwards wholly indifferent to the man who
has preserved her life. He had felt the truth of this, and
required no urging on his father's part to go and inquire
how Miss Hallam had borne her accident. We were present at that interview, and were witnesses of the pleased
surprise he betrayed at the exhibition by Beatrice of such
fresh and virgin innocence and childlike enthusiasm. He
came away, as we have seen, thinking of her, and thereafter
for many days neglected his books, and felt at his heart the
new and strange emotion I have spoken of. Then impelled
by the desire to see again that enchanting face, hear again
the fresh voice, so pure, and loving, and musical, he had
gone to town persuading himself that business required his
attention there, and at the office of the 'Gazette' encountered his friend, who, at the conclusion of their interview,
had conveyed to him the intelligence that *number seven* was
occupied by Mr. Effingham. We have seen how his face
flushed and his breast labored as in a close atmosphere. He
had intended to visit the young girl, but business called him
away, and when he had dispatched it, the evening began to
draw on, and he was obliged to return homeward. He returned, then, with that one thought in his brain—that one
sensation in his heart. Persecuted—for this was plainly
persecution on Mr. Effingham's part—loved and followed,
for this, too, was as plain—Beatrice became more dear to
him than ever. His breast heaved, his eye flashed, his
haughty lip trembled, and he passed a sleepless night think
ing of her. Then for the first time he started at his own
feelings, and he felt his heart throb. He would be her pro·
tector from that man, who had, on the first evening of her

appearance, annoyed and insulted her; he would watch over
her, find if he really persecuted her—yes, and if necessary,
avenge her! Then he stopped, like a horse at full speed
suddenly checked by his rider. Where had his imagination
borne him—what was he dreaming of? What interest had
he in this young girl? say that he had preserved her life,
would not any courageous man have done the same? She
was grateful to him for that, there the matter ended; the
service rendered, the thanks returned, what were they further but strangers? What was he to the young actress?
The young actress! What could she be to him? She was
a bird of passage with gorgeous wings, and magical singing,
caressed, applauded, swaying all hearts—and he, what was
he? An obscure man, without name, or wealth, or birth;
his station repelled her, as her profession repelled him.

A thousand thoughts like these chased each other
through his mind during the two or three days which followed his interview with the stranger; and then, drawn as
by a magical influence—he sought Williamsburg again—he
had an object, too, as will be seen.

Thus, the writer of the MS.: Charles Waters entered
Williamsburg, and, thoughtful and absent, took his way along
the main street toward the Raleigh. Suddenly, as he walked
on rapidly, he found himself stopped by an obstruction. He
raised his head, and found himself in the presence of the man
in the red cloak. That gentleman was conversing with no
less a personage than Parson Tag; and when Charles Waters
joined them, the parson was about to pass on. He scowled
upon the homely-clad man, bowed with patronizing condescension to the stranger, and with head borne magisterially
erect, went down the street.

"There goes one of the lights of the age—one of the
pillars of the church," said the stranger, with his habitual
coolness, but smiling as he spoke, "the good Parson Tag!
The worthy gentleman is indignant to-day, having, from his
own account, just quarrelled with his wealthiest parishioner
Squire Effingham."

His companion raised his head at this name: and this
movement did not escape the stranger's keen eye.

"Yes," he added, "there seems to have been some little
private matter in the business. The squire has a son, my

neighbor at the tavern—No. 7, you know—and this son, it appears, has been making himself the subject of discussion, for presuming to experience an honest friendship for the young actress, Miss Hallam."

The stranger did not fail to note the troubled and gloomy look of his listener, as they walked on toward the Ralçigh.

"Well," he continued, "the parson took the liberty of condoling with the worthy squire on the reprobacy of his son and, thereby, excited the rage of his parishioner. High word followed—the squire declared, indignantly, that he would permit no one to insult his son in his presence—that it was a mere youthful freak on his part—and that the Christian religion made it incumbent on all men, especially parsons, to exercise a little of the spirit of forgiveness, or affect the same, if they had it not. Tolerably plain, you observe, that intimation of his excellency, the squire. The interview ended by the parson's getting enraged, and declaring he would no longer live in a parish which was cursed with so unreasonable a member—and by the squire's replying, with a bow, that his holiness should be called elsewhere, as the parish had long desired. These are pretty nearly the facts of the interview, I suppose—sifted from the rubbish—and now, it seems to be understood that the good Parson Tag goes to the Piedmont region, and a Mr. Christian—an excellent name—takes his place. 'A mere milk-and-water family visitor,' says Parson Tag. Ah, these parsons, these parsons!"

And the stranger shook his head, in a way which signified that the representatives of the established church were far from occupying a distinguished place in his regards. Charles Waters had listened to this account with a troubled expression, which did not escape the stranger. The name of Effingham evidently excited some painful emotion—and he remained silent, until they reached the Ralcigh. He inquired for Miss Hallam. She was not at the tavern, but would probably come in soon. He turned away.

He was diverted from his absorbing thought, by feeling the arm of the stranger in his own.

"Come." said his companion, "as I suppose you will wait, in view of the fact, that a lady is in the question—let us sit down here on the porch, the sun is warm and pleasant. Perhaps we may wile away a tedious moment. I leave this place to-day, and may not see you again for years."

Charles Waters sat down by the stranger.

"What a singular race these parsons are," said the man in the red cloak; "come, dismiss your meditations, companion, and listen to me. What do you think of them?"

"There are many worthy, not a few unworthy," said his companion, absently.

"True: but as they are an important element of our society, it seems to me that the proportion of the unworthy is too great."

"Yes, sir: they are a very influential class," said the other, endeavoring to banish his thoughts.

"And wealthy."

"Many I believe are."

"They love their tobacco salary—but after all we cannot complain of them. They are necessary, just as it is necessary to have a class that rules and a class which obeys."

"That is true in a very limited sense, sir."

"Why, we of the lower orders must look up to the gentlemen: fustian cannot rub against velvet. The wealthy gentleman and the poor laborer cannot associate with each other. One rolls in his chariot, the other digs in the field, and admires the grand machine rolling on with its liveried coachman, and glossy four-in-hand. The necessity of the thing is as plain as the fact, that we envy these lords of creation."

"We should not, sir."

"Pshaw!—whether we should or not, we always will envy and hate them. We are poor and obscure; they are distinguished and wealthy. Could a clearer case be made out?"

Charles Waters looked at his interlocutor with the same expression, as on a former occasion, when the stranger had said, "All men are false."

"To envy those fortunate possessors of wealth and ease, sir, is neither liberal nor true philosophy," he said. "True, there are classes, and must ever be, in some form; but the poor are not, and should not be the enemies of the rich —beyond all, they should not base such enmity upon the ground that the gifts of fortune are unequally divided. What a world we should have if that were so! We have here in Virginia all grades of wealth and rank, from that negro yonder rubbing down his horse, to Governor Fauquier in his palace. We have first, the rude ignorant servant indented for a term of years, and almost an appendage of the glebe— almost as much a slave as the negro. Then the coarse overseer, scarcely better. Then the small merchant, factor, and the yeoman, plain in manners, often very ignorant—but a step higher. Then the well-to-do farmer. Lastly, the great landed proprietors, with thousands of acres and negroes, wearing velvet and riding in chariots, as you say. Well, now sir, apply your philosophy! Let the well-to-do farmer hate the great wealthy gentleman—the common yeoman hate the farmer and the gentleman—the overseer hate all three— and the indented servant, following the example of his bet- ters, hate all four of them, where would the clashing of these complex hatreds, these inimical and bitter envyings, have their termination? No, sir," said Charles Waters, raising his noble head, and speaking in that earnest and persuasive voice, which it was hard to resist being moved and convinced by—even by its very intonation—" No, sir: believe me-- these harsh and bitter feelings retard the advance of our race, rather than forward its destiny. No sir—no! hatred is not the element of progress, as envy and uncharitableness are not the precursors of liberty!"

CHAPTER XXXIII.

HOW THE MAN IN THE RED CLOAK THREW HIS NET, AND WHAT HE CAUGHT.

THE stranger was silent for some moments, then, drawing his old red cloak around him, he said:

" Liberty! Well, that is a great word; but, unfortu- nately, it is also one of those nobly-sounding terms which fill the ears only, never conveying to the brain much more than a vague and doubtful meaning. What is liberty? True, I ask you to answer a hard question; but you have drawn it upon yourself, companion, by your anomalous and contradictory statements "

" How contradictory, sir ? " said his companion, losing his absent-mindedness, and looking earnestly at the stranger.

" Why," replied the man in the red cloak, coolly, " nothing could well be more paradoxical than your views. You agree that there are classes here, and elsewhere, separated by unreasonable distinctions, holding, as regards each other, unjust positions. You do not deny that we—we, the common people—are the mere hewers of wood and drawers of water for our masters, and, when I chance to say what is perfectly reasonable and natural, namely, that we must hate and envy these dons, why, you answer, ' No, no; envy and hatred are not the elements of progress, the forerunners of liberty.' I say, they rule us !—the wealthy gentlemen, the house of burgesses, the English parliament—why not hate and envy, and, if necessary, match ourselves force for force against them, and see if we cannot achieve this noble end you speak of—liberty ! "

" Because force—the blind force of envy and hatred, striking in the dark, and without thought—is the mere movement of the brute, who closes his eyes, and tears, without seeing, whatever comes beneath his paws. No, sir ! before we can overturn parliaments, and dictate laws, we must mould public opinion."

" Public opinion ?   What is that ? "

" It is the great unseen power which governs the world."

" Oh yes; the opinion of kings and autocrats. Now I understand."

" No, not of kings and autocrats—of common men, the masses ! The calm, just judgment, formed in silence, and without prejudice, of those men and things which figure on the great stage of life. Not the mere impulses of envy and hatred, any more than the jealousy of rank, but the cool, deliberate weighing of events and personages in the scales of eternal justice."

" Fine words. Well, then, you would not overthrow the present state of things; or, perhaps, you are well content with the social organization of this colony. We must not hate, we must not envy—all is for the best ! "

" No, sir, all is not for the best ; far from it."

" It seems to me that we are wandering in our ideas, and liable to misunderstand each other. Let us see, now—explain.

You are more or less dissatisfied with the present position of things ; but you like the gentry, the Established Church, you admire the traditions of feudalism, and revere his gracious majesty King George. Eh? Come, let us know if you do not?"

"We must have misunderstood each other, indeed, sir. I would overthrow—or, at least, materially change—all that you have mentioned."

"What, the gentry—the church—the king? Treason !'

"That cry does not daunt me, sir."

"Beware; I shall inform on you, and his majesty will send for you to come and visit his handsome residence, called the Tower."

"Let me explain, briefly, what I mean, and meant," said his companion, too gloomy to relish these pleasantries of the stranger. "You have misunderstood me wholly—you would say that I am an advocate of the present, with all its injustice, its wrong, its oppression ; and, that, because I am not willing to go and turn out proprietors of great landed estates, at the point of the bayonet ; shatter those splendid mirrors, which reflect gold, and velvet, and embroidery, with a pistol's muzzle ; organize the lower class, with bludgeons, hay-forks, cleavers, knives, and scythes, against the gentlemen, who roll in coaches, and eat from gold and silver plate—you would say, that, because these revolutionary proceedings, the offspring of envy and hatred, are not to my taste, I am an advocate of those oppressions, those bitter wrongs, inflicted on the commons by the gentry. No, sir! I am not an advocate of them; I know them too well. I have studied, as far as possible, with a calm mind, an unbiassed judgment, this vestige of feudalism which curses us, and I have found, · every where, as in the old feudal system, wrong, oppression, a haughty and unchristian pride of rank, and birth, and wealth—"

"Good, good," said the stranger, no longer interrupting his companion.

"An unjustifiable pride ! an unchristian arrogance, scorning charity, humility, all that Christ inculcated, as so much weakness !" continued the thinker, in his noble and earnest voice ; "I find it here, as I find it in the history of England, of France, of Germany, of the whole feudal world;

among the gentry of to-day, as the nobles of the middle age!
Go back to that middle age—see the great lord passing in
his splendid armor, and surcoat of cloth of gold, on his glossy charger, followed by his squires, his men-at-arms, while
the battlements of his great castle ring with trumpets, greeting his return : see the serf there in the shadow of the wall,
with the ring around his neck, with his wooden shoes, his
goatskin covering—swarthy, with his shaggy beard, his brow
covered with perspiration, as becomes the villein, his cere-
bral conformation, as he takes off his greasy cap to lout low
to his master, like the head of the wolf, the jackall, the
hyena. That serf is no longer a man—he is a wild beast,
with strong muscles and sinews like rope, who will fight well
in the field, and be cut to pieces cheerfully, while his master
reaps undying renown, covered by his proof armor of Milan
—yes, he will fight and toil, and go home and kiss his children in their mud hovel—but he is not a man : his lord is a
man—how can he be of the same race as that splendid and
haughty chevalier, honored by kings and emperors for his
deeds of chivalry, smiled on by fair ladies every where, like
the noble dame who reigns in yonder castle with him. True,
the serf has legs and arms, and his blood, strange to say, is
much the color of the great seigneur's—but they do not belong to the same race of animals. They both feel it—are
convinced of it. When my lord passes, see the back bent
down; the eyes abased, as in the presence of the God of
Day—the dog-like submission, when harsh words are uttered
by the seigneur to his animal. The serf does not dream of
there being any impropriety in all this—it is a part of the
order of things that he should be a wild beast, his lord a
splendid, noble chevalier, glittering with stars, and clad in
soft silk and velvet. He always submits : he is a part of
the glebe, the stock—like the horse, the hound, the hawk.
Does the seigneur wish some amusement for his noble
guests ?—the boor comes, and with another of his class
cudgels away in the court-yard, until he is covered with
bruises, and falls or conquers : and the noble lords and
ladies, glittering like stars in the balcony, throw *largesse* to
the knaves, who lout humbly, and go down to their proper
place—the kitchen. "There is the past, sir !—look at it!"

The stranger nodded.

" You don't like feudalism," he said.

" It makes me shudder, sir."

" How ? why it's dead !"

" No : it is alive."

" Alive, say you ?"

" To this very day and hour."

" What ? in full force ?"

" No, sir—not in full force : far from it.   But in a de gree, at least, it exists."

" Hum ! you are a metaphysician."

" No, sir, I am practical."

" You are a dreamer !"

Waters sighed.

" I thought you dreamed as I did," he said.

" Perhaps I do—who knows ? "

Waters was silent.

" Define your idea," said the stranger.   " I understand you to say—and we won't discuss the subject—that this thing we call feudalism—which has come in for so much abuse from you, still exists in a degree ?   Come ! let us see how it looks in Virginia."

" We have but the shadow—thank God, the edifice has crumbled in part : but the flanking towers remain, and that shadow still lies like gloom upon the land.   See how human thought is still warped and darkened by it—how rank and unwholesome weeds possess the earth ! "

" Root out these weeds, then—begin !   Hurl down these towers which shut out the sunlight,—your historical reading must have told you of the Jacquerie ! "

" Yes, sir ! and I have seen how that rising led to worse evils than before, for hatred was added to contempt.   No, to attack this still vigorous remnant of feudalism, something besides hammers and pickaxes are necessary ; gunpowder, even, will not blow it into atoms ! "

" What, then ? "

The winds of Heaven !   God will strike it ; he has thrown down the donjon keep, where captives gnashed their teeth and cursed and blasphemed in darkness ; he will also level with the ground what remains of the great blot upon the landscape !"

" Figures, figures !" said the stranger; " come, let us have ideas !"

" By the winds of Heaven—the breath of God—I mean those eternally progressive steps of mind, which go from doubt to certainty, from certainty to indignation, from indig-nation to revolution !"

" Very well; now we get on firm ground again. We meet and shake hands over that toast, ' Revolution !' "

" Understand me; revolution is not a slight thing. It levels many valuable things, as the hurricane and the tem-pest of rain sweeps away much more than the accumulated rubbish. Revolution, sir, is the last thing of all—the tor-nado which clears the poisonous atmosphere, cannot be loosed every day or year, for the land is strewed with ruins by it. The slow steps of public opinion must be hastened, the soil prepared for the seed, the distance made plain, the body armed—then, if it is necessary, the conflict."

" Ah, you come back to your ideas upon education, sir ?"

" Yes; I would unfetter the mind."

" Enlighten it ?"

" Yes, sir; I would teach the great mass of the people, that God made this world, not man; that wrong and oppres-sion is not the normal state of human things; I would point out all the falseness, I would point to the lash-marks on the back; I would, if necessary, pour brine into those bleeding furrows !"

" Yes, and drive to madness—to what you deprecate, mad violence !"

" No ! for minds would be enlightened, men would see—and seeing, they would wait. I would have them know when to strike; I would organize in their minds an oppo-sition, quiet, stubborn, unbending, never-sleeping; a confi-dence in time, faith in the ultimate intervention of God using them as his instruments."

" You generalize too much," said the stranger; " let us come now to Virginia, at this day and hour. Let us see what are the great abuses. Speak !"

" First, an established church, which dictates religious opinion—forces itself upon all the community, armed with the terrors of the law."

" Yes, that is just; and I promise you something will
be said soon about the twopenny-act.   Well, the church !
What else ? "

" The offspring of that feudalism I have spoken of—
aristocracy ! "

" Yes, ' power of the best;' that is, the wealthiest.
What next ? "

" Laws, without representation ! " said his companion,
compressing in these short words the great popular grievance of the age.

" Ah ! " said the stranger, with a grim smile, " there is
something in that, too.   What more ? "

" What more ? Is it not enough, sir, for the Established
Church to wring from you, whether you conform or not,
support for its ministers—to stuff itself and its tenets down
your throat ? is it not bad enough for the house of burgesses to legislate for the great landed proprietors alone,
who form the body, ignoring the very existence of the common man, who has no vote ? is any thing more needed to
make us slaves, than laws passed in the English parliament,
crushing our trade, our very lives, without representatives .
of us there in council ? "

" I confess that seems to me quite enough," said the
stranger ; " and this great, oppressive, intolerant church—
this haughty arrogance of rank—lastly, that English law-
lessness, seem to me to constitute a case of mortification—
gangrene—to be burnt out by the hot iron of revolution ! "

" No ! it has not gone far enough yet ; let us advance
step by step.   At present we coutemplate that great, intolerant, bigoted establishment with respect and awe ; we bow
to the grand chariot, doffing our caps ; we search in our
minds for what will justify that oppression of Parliament ;
we are not convinced that this great triple wrong is a wrong.
We doubt ; let us scan the matter calmly—dispassionately
investigate the nature of things ; let us educate our minds, we
common people, and with the calm, unobscured eyes of truth,
test the error.   We will not say to the parsons, ' Off with
you, you are the vermin of a rotten system, you shall not
tyrannize over us ! '   No, let us, with the Bible in our hands,
and God in our hearts, say, ' We come to try you, we come
to know whether you are false and bigoted, or true and
Christlike—' "

" Yes," said the stranger, " and those worthy gentle
men, who procured benefices by marrying the cast-off mis
tresses of lords, will, with one voice, for about the space of
two hours, cry, ' Great is Diana of the Ephesians ! We
are holy, pure, and immaculate !' What, then ?"

" Reason ! the light of education still ! flooding the whole
system, lighting up every hidden crypt ! "

" Good ! And you would apply these fine ideas to the
aristocracy, too ?"

" Yes. I would have men scan that system also ; not
strike it blindly ; I would have them come with the law of
nature in their hands, the evangel of truth and justice, and
say, ' Show us what you are. Show us if you are really
our natural and rightful superiors. Show us whether those
titles you derive from kings, are like the authority of those
kings, derived, as they say, from God, and so, just and right.
Show us if you are really superior beings, because you descend from the knights of the middle age—we inferior to
you, your born slaves, because we draw our blood from
the serf who tilled the glebe below your grandsire's castle
walls. Show us if this mysterious sentiment of awe we feel
in your presence, is direct from the Deity, planted thus in
us to make us keep our places ; or, whether it is the mere
tradition of the past, the echo of injustice, the shadow of
that monstrous oppression of the dark ages, yet lying on our
souls ? "

" Very well—and what then ?" said the stranger.
" Why, these worthy gentlemen would reply, ' Friends, the
distinction of classes is absolutely necessary ; some must
rule, others obey ; some wear fustian, others velvet ; some
must ride in coaches, and eat from gold plate, others jog along
in the dust of the highway, eat their brown bread and swill
their muddy ale. Order is heaven's first law. Come, now,
and listen to this splendid passage from Shakspeare, about
degrees in a state ; it is there, in that volume with a gilt
back in the gothic book-case—don't muddy the carpet with
your dirty brogues, or stumble over that damask chair in
reaching it. Very well. Now, listen ! Can any thing be
more just than these views ? Some must be great, others
small ; one must vote, another be denied that privilege. We
are gentlemen, you commoners. Can any thing be plainer,

than that we should have the offices and honors, live easily,
and sustain our proper rank, while you till the glebe, and
leave your interests in our hands?' That is what they would
say—what then?"

"Reason, again!" said his companion; "reason, turning
away from the dazzling pageant, stopping the ears to shut
out the rumbling of the coach and six, forgetting the past,
and questioning that great evangel of right open in their
hands—reason, which should weigh and test, and try the
whole system by the rules of a stern, inexorable logic."

"I admire your logic! and you think that it would apply to English legislation on Virginia matters?"

"Yes; I would remonstrate, petition, debate with Parliament; I would exhaust every means of testing and overthrowing this cruel and bitter wrong; I would ask for light
—ask nothing but that right should be made manifest—I
would go to the foot of the throne, and say, 'Justice, justice,
nothing but justice, as a British subject—as one laboring
under wrong!'"

The stranger's lip curled.

"Well, your system is now tolerably plain," he said.
"You would go and ask the parsons to tell you if they are
in truth, pure and immaculate—you would ask the gentry if
they really are the distinguished gentlemen they pretend to
be—you would fall at the feet of King George, and sue for
leave to argue the matter of taxation with his gracious Majesty! Very well. Now, suppose—it is a very extravagant supposition, I know, and springs, no doubt, from my
irreverent, incredulous, and obstinate prejudices—suppose, I
say, that the worthy parsons thus adjured, as to their purity,
were to tell you that they were the salt of the earth, and
that your question was an impertinence; suppose—if you can
suppose such an incredible thing—that the wealthy gentleman tells you that he is your born lord, and that he will
commit you in his quality of justice of the peace, for misde-
meanor, should you intrude upon him again with your
wretched folly; suppose his gracious Majesty were to remove your humble petition with his royal foot, bidding
you begone, and learn that when money was wanted to support his splendor, you were to sweat and pay it, and be
silent on pain of being whipped in by armed soldiers; sup-

pose these disagreeable incidents greeted your philanthropic
exertions—what then ? "

"Then, revolution ! revolution, if that revolution waded
in blood ! " cried his companion, carried away by his fiery
thoughts, and losing all his calmness and self-control ; " revolution, with God for our judge ! history for our vindication
If, after all their sufferings, all their wrongs, all the injustice
of long years, of centuries, the prayers of humanity were
thus answered—revolution ! A conflict, bitter, desperate,
unyielding, to the death ! A conflict which should root out
these foul and monstrous wrongs, or exterminate us ! A
revolution, which should attack and overwhelm for ever, or
be itself overwhelmed ! That is the hurricane I spoke of,
sir ! If God decrees it, let it come ! "

CHAPTER XXXIV.

IN WHICH BEATRICE RETURNS.

WITH head erect, brows flushed, eyes clear and fiery, lips
still agitated by the tumult of thought, the speaker was
silent. His eyes then turned toward the stranger.

A singular alteration seemed to have taken place in his
features, and the expression of grandeur and majesty which
illuminated the rugged features, usually so cold, was start-
ling.

The stranger's expression was so noble, his eye so bright
and proud, his whole manner so completely changed, that
his companion found himself gazing at him with an astonishment which he could not suppress.

"Pardon me, sir," said the man in the red cloak, in a
voice of noble courtesy, strongly in contrast with his habitual
roughness; "pardon me for the manner in which I have
seemed to sift your opinions, and provoke a collision of your
ideas with my own, in this and our former interviews. It is
one of the bad habits which I acquired in a country store,
and I find myself now its slave—since the temptation to
open and study that grand volume, human nature, wherever
I find it, has become irresistible. In your case, I have been

instructed and interested; and though I say with a frankness which you may consider rude, that I have thought most
of your thoughts before—still, sir, permit me to return you
my thanks for an honor and a pleasure."

The haughtiest nobleman in the world would not have
found in these words, uttered by the coarsely-clad stranger
on the rude tavern porch, to a man of the people like himself, any thing to cater to his laughter or amusement; for
the man in the red cloak seemed no longer to be coarsely
dressed; his pronunciation no longer appeared vicious and
incorrect; the very porch of the tavern seemed to be trans-
formed by his magical voice and look into a palace portico.

"In all your views I concur," continued the stranger,
"and your ideas are mine. God himself placed us in the
condition we both find ourselves in, that mind might speak
to mind, freely, sympathetically, with that frankness and
plainness from which Truth springs, armed, ready for the
conflict."

"Yes, sir," continued the stranger, with that high and
proud look which his companion had observed once in a
former interview. "Yes, sir! this Virginia of 1763 is in
an unhappy state! Social organization to-day, with the in-
fluences that environ it, is one of those phenomena which
occur but once in a century. On all sides murmurs, mut-
terings as of an approaching storm! Men doubtful of the
ground they walk on—new ideas dazzling them—old institu-
tions crumbling—the hand upon the wall tracing, in fiery
letters, the mysterious future—that future crammed with
storms—groaning like a womb which holds the destiny of
humanity! The heavens are dark, the ways we tread
devious and full of hidden snares. England, our tender
mother, might say, who planted them? For England, from
whose loins we sprung, has cursed us!—like a stepmother,
she has struck, with a bitter and remorseless hatred, those
who would be her children! She cursed us with this race
of Africans who are eating us up and ruining us, and some
day, in the blind convulsions of her rage, she will taunt us
bitterly for asking what we do not grant ourselves—for de-
manding freedom, when our arms are holding down a race
human as ourselves! Let her gnash her teeth in impotent
and irrational complaint!—let her complain, we will not;

for God decreed that she herself, black with crime and in
justice, should be the means of bringing hither this race,
that in the future Christianity should dawn on that vast continent of Africa—that land where the very air seems tainted
with paganism—where the very palms which wave their long
plumes on the ocean breeze seem celebrating some horrible
rite! No; this is not the head and front of the accusation
which, in the name of justice and humanity, we bring against
England. She has thrust upon us her despotic regulations.
She has contracted suffrage. She has given to Lord Cul-
peper the whole territory from the mouth of the Rappa-
hannock to the sources of the Potomac—enthroned him a
prince and king over us! She has crushed our commerce
by navigation laws which are so odious and unrighteous that
the very instruments of her tyranny shrink from enforcing
them! With a blind, remorseless hatred—a policy destitute
of reason as it is foul with injustice and wrong—she has
bound on this poor laboring brute, Virginia, burdens which
crush her, under which she staggers, groaning, and tearing
herself with rage, terror, and despair! She has made for
herself a gospel whose commandments are—'Thou shalt
steal'—'Thou shalt bear false witness against thy neighbor'—'Thou shalt have no other god but George III.' She
has gone on from wrong to wrong, from injustice to injustice,
until like those unhappy creatures whom the gods intend to
strike, she has grown mad, lost her brain, her reason, braced
herself to rush upon an obstacle which will hurl her back, as
a wave of the ocean is hurled back from the cliff of eternal
stone! Yes, sir, that empire rushes upon what will tame
her! Already she speaks of an act decreeing that a stamp
shall be placed upon every instrument written or printed of
human affairs. Journals, deeds, conveyances—pleadings in
law, bills of lading—on the marriage contract, and the bill
for the headstone—nothing to be operative without that
stamp! Well, sir, that act will make the cup filled with the
bitter and poisonous draught run over—that law will make
the infuriated animal, thrown on her knees, rise up, and
then, sir, God alone knows where things will end! You wish
to wait and let the old world pass away by virtue of its inherent decay, its immemorial rottenness—you would have
the crumbling monument of wrong fall slowly, stone by

stone, as the winds and rain descend upon it year after year!
Such will not be the event, sir! The tornado you spoke of
will bring down that godless monument, at one blow, with
a crash that will startle nations! And do not think that
this is not as legitimately God's act as the slow ruin you
advocate. That Great Being unlooses the hurricane of revolution as easily as he sends the zephyr to cool the cheek,
each in its place!—the hurricane here! You may even now
scent the odor of the storm!"

And the stranger rose with such grandeur in his visage,
such majesty in his attitude, such a clear fire in his proud
eyes, which seemed to plunge into the mysterious future, and
see with the vision of a prophet all which that future was to
bring, that his companion felt himself overwhelmed, he knew
not how, carried away in spite of himself.

" It is coming!" continued he, with indescribable grandeur in voice and countenance and attitude; " the storm which
will topple down the edifice of fraud and lies, which has so
long shamed the sunlight!—in that storm old things shall
pass away, and behold! all things shall become new. The old
world is decayed, she totters on the brink of the abyss prepared for her:—she rushes on, blindly, full of curses, and
hatred—the gulf yawns—let her foot trip, she is swallowed
up for ever!"

And the brilliant eye seemed to grow brighter still, the
voice became more clear and strong. The rude visage of the
speaker glowed as if the light of a great conflagration streamed upon it. His stature seemed almost to grow before his
companion's eyes, and become gigantic, his two hands to be
filled with thunderbolts!

" Yes, sir! yes!" he exclaimed, " the storm comes!—
the tocsin of a revolution is already being sounded! Ere
long the clash of arms will fall upon our ears, the sound of
firearms and the roar of cannon. War and storm, tempest
and hurricane, are waiting, like hounds held back by the leash,
to burst upon this land. Let it come! let the storm roar,
the lightning flash, the waves roll mountain high—God still
directs that storm, and will fight for us! Let the bloody
dogs of war be loosed, let them dye their sharp fangs in
blood, they shall not daunt us. I repeat it, sir,—let it come!

9

I, for one, will grapple with the monster, and strangle or be strangled by him! Liberty or death!".

And the man in the red cloak, with a gesture of overwhelming grandeur, stood silent, motionless, his eyes on fire, his hands clenched as though the struggle depicted by his brilliant and fiery imagination were about to begin. Charles Waters, carried away by his tremendous passion could make no reply, and they both remained silent.

The stranger wiped his brow, and drew his cloak around him: then gazing on his companion with an expression of nobility and pride, which glowed in his eyes and filled them with light, said:

"And now, sir, we must part. I go hence to day, having yesterday been retained in an important cause in Hanover county, brought by the Reverend Mr. Maury against the collector. I am for the defendant, and must prepare myself for a hard struggle. Permit me again to thank you, sir, for many hours of your company. I repeat, that you have done me a pleasure, and an honor: for I find in you a mind clear and strong, competent to test, to sift, to grasp, to wield those new ideas which will change the world. Do not dream that we will pass through the years, directly following this, without convulsions and a conflict, such as the world has never seen. Prepare yourself, put on your armor, get ready! For my part, I ask in that inevitable conflict, no better companion. These are no idle words, sir. I shall call upon you, and am well convinced, that my call will not be in vain!"

And bowing with lofty courtesy, the stranger entered the tavern. At the same moment the footfall of a horse attracted the attention of Charles Waters, and looking up, he saw Beatrice Hallam, who had stopped before the inn, mounted as usual on her tall white horse.

CHAPTER XXXV.

HOW BEATRICE PRAYED FOR STRENGTH TO RESIST HERSELF.

HE rose and went toward the young girl, walking as in a dream. Those magical accents of the stranger's voice were

still ringing in his ears—he almost thought he heard the
roar of thunder, and the crashing of the sea—the air almost
seemed alive with lightning flashes. For thunder, lightning,
and a stormy ocean, seemed to be the elements of that grand,
fiery oratory.

But he soon found this preoccupation put to rout by
something more powerful than the grandest eloquence, the
most overpowering oratory—a young girl's eyes. Slowly,
his great thoughts fled away from his mind—the fate of Virginia was forgotten—mind beat an ignominious retreat, and
the heart knew of but one object in the universe, a fresh,
bright face that smiled upon him, a mild, tender pair of
eyes, that filled with happy light when they fell upon him.
He assisted the young girl to the ground quietly:—neither
spoke, but their eyes were more eloquent than any words
could have been. On their last meeting, Beatrice had hastened forward, exclaiming, "I am very glad to see you!"
and now, when day after day, and night after night, she had
thought of him with inexpressible tenderness, and come to
feel, indeed, that her life was illuminated by a new, unimagined glory—now she did not assure him that she was glad
to see him. The human heart in 1763 was much the same
as at present, the reader will perceive.

So without speaking, she passed in and he followed her,
with no need of invitation in words: her eyes said all—and
they entered the little apartment which had witnessed so
many memorable scenes. Then for the first time Beatrice
taking off her little hat, and throwing back her beautifu.
hair, which had become loose, said :

"Oh, you have been away so long! You promised to
come often!"

How could he resist that earnest tender voice—how feel
any more sorrow or disquiet—how prevent his heart from
beating more rapidly, as these soft words sank into it.

"Indeed, I have not kept my promise," he said, with
that gentleness and softness, which at times characterized
his voice, " but fate has seemed to decree that we should not
meet."

"That was very naughty in fate!" said Beatrice, with
a winning little smile, "because we are good friends, you
know."

And the soft voice trembled with its depth of meaning.

"Indeed, I can answer for myself," he said, sitting down.

"And I do not think I need say any thing for my part," answered Beatrice; "you saved my life."

And again, the tender eyes dwelt for a moment on his face, and were cast down.

"You have not forgotten that yet?"

"No—how could I?"

"Well, well, pray do not speak of it again. Has your wetting caused you any inconvenience? I hope not."

"Only a little cough—but I have not coughed a bit to-day."

With which, as if to improve the portion still remaining, the young girl began to cough, but with no violence.

"You see I began just because I boasted," she said, smiling. "Is Mr. Waters well?"

"Yes, very well."

"He was very kind to me," said Beatrice, gratefully, "please give him my best love."

And, without being conscious of any reason for it, she blushed, and turned away. It is probable that something similar to what was passing in her mind, passed in the heart of her companion also, for his countenance brightened, and grew very tender.

"My father sent you his best regards," he said, "and I came for the purpose of bringing them. I must confess, however, that I was somewhat selfish—"

"Selfish?"

"Yes; since I promised myself the pleasure of seeing you."

"Oh," said Beatrice, "please, don't let us make any polite speeches to each other."

"But, indeed, that is not mere courtesy; it is the truth," he replied. "I had such a quiet, friendly talk, when I was here before, that I wished to keep my promise, to visit you every day."

He had paused slightly before the word "friendly," and, conscious of the reason, avoided the frank, tender eyes.

"Why did you stay away so long, then?" she said; "indeed, I have longed to see you."

These words were uttered with great simplicity, and with that childlike frankness, which was one of the young girl's most striking traits of character. One would have said that she was so innocent and truthful, that she could not school herself with forms; and such, indeed, was the case. Beatrice was no longer the actress, in his society; she was the young, girlish being we have seen shouting after the sea-gulls, and said, " Indeed, I have longed to see you," without a thought of any impropriety.

"Fate would not let me come, as I said," he replied, smiling; " but, now I have conquered destiny, and bring you, not only my father's regards, and my own good wishes, but a trinket, which, I fancy, must belong to you. The initials upon it must be those of your mother."

Beatrice rose quickly, and ran up to him.

"Oh, have you got it?" she cried.

He smiled, and taking from his pocket a small locket of gold, attached to a narrow blue ribbon, handed it to her. Beatrice took it quickly, and with an eagerness which betrayed the importance she attached to it.

"Oh, I am so glad!" she said; "I am so glad you found it!"

"It is yours, then?"

"Yes, yes!"

"You must have dropped it, on the day of your sail."

"Yes, I must have."

"It was picked up, upon the river's bank, by my father, and, from the letters B. W. upon it, he fancied that it belonged to you."

"Yes, yes; I have worn it a long time, and I believe it was my mother's. But I don't know," added the young girl, with some sadness; " I never saw my mother, I believe."

"Did your father give you the locket?"

"No, I believe not. I do not remember. I think I wore it around my neck when I was a little child; at least I have worn it as long as I could remember."

"I am glad to have been able to restore it; though the merit really belongs to my father.'

"Please say I thank him very much," said Beatrice; "indeed, it is very dear to me. I had been to look for it,"

"What! this morning?"

"Oh, yes; you know I am a great rider. So I thought I would just put on my skirt, and go to the river, where Mr. Townes lives—you know it was his boat we sailed in—and ask him if I had dropped it there, or in the boat."

"You had, then, been to the river?"

"Yes, indeed; and I had a delightful ride. Mr. Townes was very kind to me," she said, laughing, like a child, "and was good enough to praise my cheeks, and bless my eyes and, I think he said he would drag the river, or something for my locket. Oh, he praised you so!"

"Townes is an excellent and worthy man, and loves my father and myself very much, I believe."

"I will like him more than ever, hereafter; for you are my friends, you know," said Beatrice, with the most charming simplicity; "indeed, I like him very much already, for his kindness to me on the day we sailed."

"He really saved you," said her companion.

"No, no!" cried Beatrice; "indeed I owe my life to you."

He shook his head.

"I was very strong once," he said, "but have been of late devoured by a thirst for study—I was nearly exhausted when Townes came. But let us dismiss the subject. I am very glad your locket is safe."

And he gazed, with a look of great softness, upon her bright face.

"Yes, indeed, I value it highly," said Beatrice; "see how prettily 'tis chased."

He took and examined it.

"Here are the letters I observed," he said; "but they are nearly worn away. Still, as you see, they are distinct. There they are—'B. W.' The B. stands for—for—your first name, I suppose."

"My mother's name was Beatrice, I imagine. Strange," the young girl added, half to herself, "that father has never talked to me about mother."

And she sighed, and looked very thoughtful. He sat gazing on the tender, gentle face, the veiled eyes, and girlish lips; thinking he had never seen any one more beautiful—never, among those fair maidens who passed in their chariots like lovely princesses, enveloped in clouds of lace, with bright diamond-like eyes, and snowy hands hung out against the cushion of the door. The features of Beatrice were always striking for their purity and elegance, but the cloquent expression was the great charm of her face.

"I suppose it was my mother's," she added, "but I do not know what the 'W.' stands for. I'll ask father."

"Would it not be singular if it stood for Waters?" he said, smiling.

She started.

"Waters! Oh! how singular!"

"Beatrice Waters?" he added.

She did not reply.

"How strange!" she said, at length, buried in thought; "it is very strange!"

"What?" he said.

"The coincidence—Beatrice—Waters," she added, after a pause.

And her soft eyes met those of her companion, who looked at her with so much unconscious meaning, that she turned away, blushing.

"I am afraid we are not related," he said.

"I fear not," she murmured.

"Even if your mother's maiden name had been the same with my own, it would not follow that we were connected. There are many persons named Waters."

"Yes—I do not think, however, that the 'W.' stands for that."

"What then?"

"I do not know."

"It might."

"Yes," she said, with the same thoughtful look, "but I had a brother who died—he did not live with us—somewhere abroad—I never knew him—but his name was Wesley. I suppose that was my mother's name."

"Oh, you are determined that I shall not have the satisfaction of being your kinsman."

The tender face clouded.

"Would that be a satisfaction?" she said, softly.

"Ah, yes!" he muttered.

"I am an actress," said Beatrice, softly, and in a low tone, casting down her eyes as she spoke, "I had forgotten it."

And a moisture which she could not drive back made
her eyes swim, and gathered on the long dusky lashes. Those
swimming eyes went straight to his heart, an irrepressible
gush of tenderness made his brow flush, and taking the little
hand, he pressed it between his own, with a tenderness which
made Beatrice burst into tears : for his meaning could not
be misunderstood.

"Oh!" she sobbed, turning away and hiding her face
with the other hand, "you are so good and noble! I
felt it when you left me before, and more than ever now!
It is so good in you to treat a poor young girl like me so
kindly!—a poor actress, that other people look upon with
contempt! Oh! how can I ever thank you! I can only—
only bless you! and never forget you!—Oh I never—never
will forget how kind you were!"

And bending lower still, the young girl sobbed and
sighed; and then gently drawing away her hand, took from
her pocket a handkerchief, with which she attempted to dry
her eyes from which a flood of tears were gushing. That
last word which she had uttered had jarred upon his heart
strangely. "How kind you *were!*" Then she was soon
to leave him—they were to be separated—this brief glimpse
of happiness and joy was to disappear like a sift of blue between driving thunder clouds! "I will never forget how
kind you *were!*" Then, she would be lost to him! she
would pass on like a bird of the tropics, brilliant and
beautiful, attracting all eyes and hearts, but sailing far away
to other skies! He would see her no more! Her pure,
tender face would never smile on him again! those large
melting eyes would no more flood his heart with unspeakable
happiness—that voice of marvellous sweetness and earnestness, so full of joy and softness and music, would no longer
greet him—those small hands would no longer press his
own, sending the warm blood to his heart, and filling his
soul, his being, with a delicious tranquility, a pure delight!
This enchanting form now before him, would, before many
days—at most a few months—had elapsed, be to him but a
memory, a picture for the eyes of the heart! She would
leave him!—that one thought gathered into a burning focus
all the scattered rays of tenderness in his heart, and that
heart now throbbed passionately.

We have said that Charles Waters was a man of strong

passions, spite of his ordinary quietness—a quietness which sprung from self-control. Under that mild exterior he concealed a heart of powerful impulses, and he proved it on this occasion. Unable to bear the thoughts which the young girl's unconscious allusion to her departure had aroused, he yielded, giving himself up unresistingly to the flood of emotion.

" Oh l " he cried, seizing the young girl's hand and covering it with passionate kisses; " Oh, Beatrice l you wound me to the heart !—do not speak thus to me again! I cannot bear it ! No, you are not a mere actress—no l you are the pearl of purity and honor l Never wound me again with such words, for they pierce my heart l But you will have no occasion, perhaps,—you are going to leave us ! to leave me ! No l I cannot endure the thought l—for I love you passionately, devotedly l I love you with my heart and soul, and would ask no greater satisfaction than to pour out my blood for you. You think I am cold because my face is calm: undeceive yourself: few men have so much fire in them—such a dangerous and fatal temperament when aroused. No, I am not cold, and I love you, Beatrice, with a love which has grown and increased in a short time to the height of a violent passion. Oh, no l you shall not go—you must be my wife—you *must* love me at last, because I almost worship you ! "

No words can describe the brilliant expression which flushed the young girl's face, then left it pale. That flush was the evidence of an emotion of unspeakable happiness. The pallor was from the thought which darted through her brain like lightning. She saw all the future spread out before her like a sunny landscape, all the happiness within her grasp; she felt his arm approach her—and drew back with a start, a cry.

Her face was bathed in tears: her eyes swam; her lips trembled; all the nerves of the weak woman's form rebelled and shook—but the great heart remained.

" No," she said, with a passionate sob, which seemed to tear its way from her heart—" No l no l I cannot . . . l It breaks my heart to say it—God pity me !—but no, no, I cannot ! Oh, God will accept this agony I am suffering as an expiation for all sin I have committed !—no no ! do not tempt me ! my heart failed me for a moment, but is now strong— yet do not tempt me l "

And she covered her face, over which her hair fell down, and sobbed as if indeed her heart were about to break; scarcely hearing his entreaties, his prayers, his passionate assurances of love.

"I cannot be your wife," she said, at length, with more calmness; "God has not permitted me to be, and I submit! I am an actress,—do not interrupt me! for I have scarcely strength now to think or speak. I am a poor playing girl, with nothing in the wide world but my self-respect! I will not make your father blush for an unworthy daughter!—Oh let me go on!—I cannot take advantage of your noble devotion—I cannot weigh down and darken your life—for pity's sake, do not look at me so! do not! I cannot—oh, no! I cannot!—God has no pity on me—it is not my fault that I am such as I am—but I must suffer—Oh! it is a bitter suffering!"

She stopped for a moment, choked by her sobs; then went on:

"Your eye flashes! and I know well what you mean. Yes, you are noble and courageous—you would trample on this unjust prejudice—love me more for that; I know it, it is the bitterest of all—but—"

"Oh, I would die for you!—give my life, oh, how willingly, for—ah! let them dare!"

And his eye flashed, his breast heaved tumultuously.

"Why do you speak of that! Beatrice, I love you—love you so devotedly, so passionately, that I could ask no greater happiness than to dare the world's scorn for you—go down to death with you! But there is no scorn! What is there in our positions—I am poor and obscure, you are the admiration of all! They shall not deprive me of you! No, no! I cannot exist without you now—you are my soul, my life, my blood, my heart! I die without you!"

The young girl felt her heart yielding—her brain swam—overcome, exhausted, faint, she sobbed, and shook, and struggled with her rebellious heart. He saw the hesitation.

"Oh, be my own, Beatrice!" he cried, overwhelming her hand with kisses; "be my wife! the sunlight of my existence!—make my life happy—come, my Beatrice, my beautiful, noble girl!"

And opening his arms, he would have clasped her to his

heart. Overcome, powerless, another moment and his arm would have encircled her, her head lain on his bosom; but suddenly her hand fell on the locket, and she started back with a cry, and burst into an agony of tears.

"Oh, mother! give me strength, if you look down on me from heaven!" she cried, "give me strength against myself, against my own heart! Oh, I am so weak! I know what is right, and am tempted to do wrong! Mother! mother! give me strength! Oh," she continued, looking at him and sobbing violently, "do not tempt me—longer! Do not make me yield, and suffer remorse for ever while I live for this moment's weakness! I cannot be your wife! You tempt me in vain. I am—broken-hearted, but you cannot move me now! I am weak—exhausted—but—God has—heard me! I have—conquered myself!"

And falling into a chair, she fainted. Ten minutes afterwards she was stretched weak and exhausted on her couch, and Charles Waters was hurrying with a pale brow from the town.

Yes, she had conquered herself!—she had drawn back from those arms opened wide to receive her, clasp her like a poor dove beaten by storms to the true breast—her refuge. She had overcome that passionate yearning to fall upon his bosom, and—given up to love and tenderness—weep away all her unhappiness in those strong arms; she had closed her eyes to that seducing picture of such calm and lifelong happiness as his wife—she had resolutely bidden her heart lie still—she had by a sublime effort of devotion drawn back from that tranquil future to be passed with him;—but she was firm. Yes, the weak body had succumbed, the nerves given way—her strength had failed her, but not her soul.

The struggle, however, was not over. Stretched upon the little couch to which he had carried her in his arms, the conflict was renewed with her returning strength. Oh, how unhappy she was! What a poor, lonely, wretched thing she was! How heaven had cursed her when it made her destiny so miserable! How terrible that trial!—on one side love, with open arms and smiling lips, and eyes full of tenderness, saying to her, "Come, weary heart! come, poor unhappy child! here is a future of full, quiet happiness, a nature which your heart yearns for—both are yours—come!" and

on the other side, stern, inexorable duty, saying, with a
frown, " Come away !—preserve your self-respect—close your
eyes to this. Self-respect is all you have, retain your treasure!" Was it not bitter, she sobbed, was it not too much
agony for one poor heart ! and for a moment heaven seemed
black to her—truth a mere lie—her moral sense was being
deadened.

Suddenly her bare arm struck against something on the
couch ; she looked at this object and saw that it was a small
Bible. She opened it and read on the fly leaf—" Catherine
Effingham, from dear papa"—and would have closed it again,
but her good angel held her hand.

" The child dropped it when she sat here, doubtless,"
she murmured, faintly.

And her eyes fell upon the open page, where she read,
through tears :

" Come unto me all ye that labor and are heavy laden,
and I will give you rest.

" Take my yoke upon you, and learn of me : for I am
meek and lowly of heart : and ye shall find rest unto your
souls.

" For my yoke is easy and my burden is light."

As she closed the book, her eyes expanded with wonder
and solemn thought; her brow was overshadowed, then
bright; then all this passed, and clasping the volume to her
bosom, she sobbed, and prayed, and slowly grew more calm.
A voice had spoken to her which she had not heard before.

CHAPTER XXXVI.

EFFINGHAM HALL—SLUMBERS.

WHILE these events were occurring at Williamsburg—these
various and conflicting passions, writhing, bubbling, boiling,
and exploding—while the town began to thrill, and buzz, and
rouse itself, and make preparation for the meeting of the
burgesses, and the great opening day—all this while profound quiet reigned at Effingham Hall. Embowered in its
lofty oaks, which only sighed and rustled mournfully in the

sad autumn days, it seemed to sleep, looking, with its sunset illumined windows, like great eyes, on the broad woodlands and champaign, and the far river flowing solemnly to the great ocean. One might have fancied, without any violent effort of the imagination, that the great manor-house was a living thing, which mourned for something which had happened not long since. The casements rattled gloomily in the chill autumn evening, and the mourning winds, scattering the variegated leaves, sighed round the gables like an invisible host of mourners, then died away with sobs in the dim forest. The sun came up, but did not shine with cheerfulness and warmth—something seemed to have dimmed his light, and the rainy mist drooped long above the fields before his struggling beams could pierce and overthrow it. He went down in a pomp of golden clouds, indeed : but even they looked sad—for it was like a great monarch dying on his purple couch of state, and taking with him to the far undiscovered land beyond the immense horizon, all that blessed and cheered the hearts of nations. In the long nights, the breezes of the ocean sighed, and sobbed, and murmured to each other round the antique chimneys, and a sombre desolation, uncheered by any light but the great struggling blood-red moon's, appeared to brood over the broad domain of Effingham and the thoughtful, silent Hall.

Within, there was scarcely more cheerfulness than without. The servants moved about with quiet steps and subdued voices ; for they felt that the echoes should not be aroused. The cloud on their master's brow awed them, and instinctively they spoke in whispers, and tipped in and out, and when a silver cup or salver chanced to fall, they started and held their breath, and looked round fearfully. Little was said by any member of the household ; days, it seemed, passed sometimes without a word being uttered by any one. That gloom upon the old squire's brow repelled any advances —silenced any attempts at social intercourse. The meals passed in silence, with their array of almost motionless black servants, standing behind the chairs, and moving noiselessly in obedience to signs. All countenances were clouded, and, when the old gentleman had swallowed his chocolate, or eaten something with an obvious effort, he passssed in silence to the library, and was seen no more for hours.

Miss Alethea had grown unusually good-tempered, she
did not scold, or rate the servants, or fill the house with
clatter in her housekeeping, as her wont had been: she
looked sad, and spoke little—passing her time in assiduous
sewing on household articles—a dress for Kate, or else a frill
for Willie, or maybe a neckcloth for her father. Orange
was no longer in high favor, and would come and wag his
tail, and look up wistfully, and whine, and then, finding that
no notice was taken of him, would go and lie down on the
rug, and, resting his chin upon his paws, gaze into the
singing fire, hour after hour, in silence. Willie was, he
knew not why, in low spirits; he often thought of Champ,
now, and regretted all those hasty words he had uttered
lately. His whip no longer waked the echoes of the old
portrait-decorated hall; his halloos to the fox-hounds drag
ging their heavy blocks and baying hoarsely, were never
heard now startling the silent lawn; the gallop of his pony
never sounded on the gravelled road winding through the
rich grounds up to the door. Little Kate had not had a
ride behind him now for weeks—Willie had lost his relish
for the amusement, and for all else, it seemed—he went
slowly singing about the house, in a low, melancholy tone,
and seemed to be looking for something which he could not
find.

And what of little Kate? She was, perhaps, the sad-
dest of them all. Her tender, sensitive heart had received
a wound from that which had occasioned all this gloom in
them. She loved him so dearly! as she had said, with her
simple, childish truth—they had been so happy all those days
and years before and since his return! How could she miss
his presence and not grieve? They had such quiet, smiling
talks together in the evenings, when stretched upon the sofa
with his head upon her lap she had sung for him her little
songs—"The Flowers of the Forest," "Birks of Invermay,"
or "Roslin Castle," in the clear sunny voice, instinct with so
much marvellous sweetness, he had said, one day. They had
walked together, hand in hand, far into the deep woods, and
he had never complained of the pebbles hurting his feet
through the frail Spanish leather slippers, as he had done
in her hearing to grown ladies; they had looked upon the
setting sun from the high hill westward from the Hall and

then, turning round, seen the tall windows all in flame : he
had taken such good care upon those rides that she should
sit easily, and pressed the little hand clasped round his
waist with such smiling goodness. She remembered so well
his voice, and looks, and smiles—other people said they were
affected or sarcastic smiles, but they were very bright when
they shone on her ; and now, when she no longer saw them,
she missed their light, and sat down in her little corner. and
wetted the silk of which Carlos was composed with silent
tears. After one of these quiet, uncomplaining cries, she
felt that she must see him, and she did, as we know, at the
Raleigh. She came back from that interview with a greater
weight than ever on her heart. She could not understand
those gloomy words he uttered, but she heard him say, they
could not meet again, and that he could not go back with
her—and all the way back to the Hall, the child sobbed and
shook, and hid her face, making no reply to Miss Alethea's
questions. What could have changed him so at the tavern
—so suddenly ? She knew she had half persuaded him when
he left her—and then the child shrunk and trembled, thinking of those scenes which followed. She sat down in her
corner again, and mourned, and cried, and went on with her
work, or said her lessons, with a dumb sorrow, which it was
a cruel sight to see ; at night, though, she was calmer—
having read her Bible and prayed for him.

One day the parson came to see his parishioner and con-
dole with him. He performed this parish duty by endeavoring to prove that the prodigal was not worthy to be his father's
son, and that his " conduct " could not in any manner affect
the squire : he wound up with a reiteration of his argument
proving the young man's unworthiness, and then, to his horror, saw the squire rise, and flush to his brows with passion.
High words followed—Champ should not be abused in his
father's house, the squire said, by any person in Christendom ! This was all the thanks he got, the parson said, with
indignation : and proceeding thus from irritation on both
sides, to rage, the interview had ended, as the parson had related to the stranger, Kate to her cousin. Parson Tag had
drank his last glass of port at the Hall, and before many days
had accepted a call from the Piedmont region, and so shaken
the dust of the parish from his feet for ever.

Visitors talked about the weather, when they came to
the Hall, and of the crops, the news from England, the ap
proaching speech of his excellency, Governor Fauquier, at
the opening of the House of Burgesses, and indeed of every
thing but that one subject. Mr. Effingham's doings were,
indeed, the talk of the colony, as he had said, with such disdainful indifference, but none of the colonists introduced the
subject at the Hall. One day Mr. Lee and his family dined
there, and Willie asked Clare, in the middle of a profound
silence, if she was going to the governor's ball with brother
Champ. Clare had colored, and her lip had trembled slightly,
as she had answered that she did not think of going to the
ball. Whereupon the squire had struck the table, and
sworn that he would go and take her—and he had looked so
mournful after his outburst, that Clare had said nothing.
It was half understood that she and Henrietta would go—
with the Effingham party, or accompanied by their cavaliers.

So the days passed, and Effingham Hall seemed to become more and more sad and still :—its inmates conversed
less, and a deeper quiet seemed to reign. The winds that
sobbed across the lonely autumn fields, and swayed backward
and forward all the haughty oaks, seemed only to increase
the stillness. So the Hall slept its sleep.

CHAPTER XXXVII.

WILLIAMSBURG: EXCESSIVE WAKEFULNESS.

WHILE Effingham Hall was falling asleep more and more
deeply, Williamsburg having passed through its night—that
is to say, the period of time elapsing between the adjourn-
ment and the re-assemblage of the House of Burgesses,
that galaxy of brilliant suns which periodically shone upon
it—Williamsburg woke up from its long slumber, laughing,
merry, full of activity and expectation. Already the grateful chinking of merry-faced pistoles were heard, as they rose
and fell in jovial planters' pockets, while the owner pon-
dered how to lay them out to the best advantage—already,

though the meeting of the House was three days off, the
town was filling fast; and on every hand jests and laughter,
hearty greetings, the slamming of doors, the rattle of car-
riages, the clatter of hoofs, the jingle of spurs, and the neighs
of horses, gave abundant proof that the joyous season had
arrived.   The taverns were filling rapidly, and mine host of
the Raleigh was in full activity—running, that is to say
toddling; bowing, that is to say ducking his fat head; laughing, that is to say shaking the windows, in honor of the
jolly patrons of his establishment clapping him on the back
asking about his health facetiously, and calling for his rum.
claret, and strong waters.

Whips cracked; the streets were full of sound; the men
roared over their cups; the ladies filled the stores, running
the clerks mad with orders; every thing said very plainly
that the great gala day of the middle class had come : the
class who visited the town but once a year with their wives
and daughters, and were so determined to suck joy from every
thing.

Through this laughing, jesting crowd some lordly equi-
page would pass from time to time, with its glossy four-in-
hand, its liveried coachman and small footman on the board
behind; and, through the window plainly seen, the lovely face
of some young beauty, smiling in her silk and velvet, like the
countrymen in their fustian; or else some fat, pursy squire,
with puffy cheeks, and formal look, set off by his good wife
in plain black silk and diamonds.

Young gallants, pranced by on their splendid horses; country carts toiled slowly on, laden with vegetables and drawn
by diminutive, shaggy, solemn-looking animals; a thousand
bright-faced, grinning negroes illuminating like black suns
the buzzing, restless, laughing, jovial, hearty, shouting uproar—and behold! A drum comes from the distance, quickly rolling, trumpets blare aloud and split the ears, and mounted on his car of state—a cart fixed with a platform and pulled by three mules—the great Hallam rides in state above
the tuneful throng.   The drums deafen all; the trumpets
shatter all tympana with a gush of sound, flowing from bearded lips, blowing for life; and high above the whole the noble
Shylock rears a pine sapling with a placard beauteous.

That placard says, that at the old theatre, near the cap-

:tol, and by permission of his worship the mayor of Williamsburg, the company will that night enact the tragedy of Hamlet, written by Mr. William Shakespeare. Hamlet, the prince,
by the great tragedian, Pugsby; Ophelia, by Miss Beatrice
Hallam, the delight of the noble aristocracy and the wonder
of the universal world. This information is conveyed in letters half a foot long, and with a profusion of exclamation
points.

Such is the placard, gazed on wonderingly by those barbarous country people, who had never delighted their eyes
with the sight of the great tragedian Mr. Pugsby, nor of
Miss Hallam, the delight of the whole aristocracy and the
wonder of the universal world; perhaps, indeed, had been
so sunk in barbarism as never to have done aught but *read*
the great drama written by the glorious Mr. William Shakespeare! But to-night they will go and have their ignorance
of play-acting turned into grand illumination on the subject.
Yes! they will go and see the play, the actors, and the noble
aristocracy! Their pockets are well filled—five shillings
nothing! And shouts sound louder, the great trumpet blares
more shatteringly, the drum wakes the thunder, and the splendid pageant passes onward; Hallam and Shylock proud,
and full of dignity and state. At the Raleigh—as on Gloucester-street and everywhere—life is jubilant, and men consider drinking, with every friend they recognize, a duty. And
rum and claret, port and Rhenish, flow in streams, and doors
bang, windows rattle, heavy shoes clump, merry lips laugh:
Williamsburg scents the coming banquet of mind, spread by
his excellency and the burghers—the boasted flow of reason
and the soul—and, full of joyful anticipation, empties count-
less flagons at the Raleigh, kicks its chairs, plays cards upon
its tables, and erects it into a great jolly temple—a temple
where, at most reasonable charges, as mine host avers, they
may worship Bacchus, Momus, and all the heathen gods.

CHAPTER XXXVIII.

IN WHICH THE TALK IS OF COSTUME.

LET us now descend from generalities to particular scenes,
and in order to make this descent, ascend to Mr. Effingham's
apartment in the "Raleigh." Aloof from all the bustle, confusion and laughter of the crowd, indifferent to it, or despising it, the young man sat thinking in silence, and glancing at
times with a scornful smile on the merry groups, seen through
the window, passing up and down the street. His lips wore
that same bitter weary expression we have so often noted;
his cheek was more sallow, his eyes more gloomy. He was
clad as usual in the richest and most elegant manner, but
the gayety of his toilette—the lace, the embroidery, the feather
in his cocked hat, which lay beside him on the floor—was a
mockery, contrasted thus with the moody and exhausted
face.

The young man's lips moved, and he muttered, bitterly:

"Yes, now the die is really cast! While it rattled, I
might have drawn back—now the throw has been made, it
is but to raise the box, and the future is decided for the
player—he is a beggar! Yes, I am mad; I feel that this
infatuation amounts to madness!—this girl will ruin me!
I love her, and hate her! She is an angel, and a devil!
So pure and innocent in face, with such a bitter and scornful
heart. By heaven, I'll conquer her—she shall be mine!
And yet—and yet," he murmured, looking down, "why not
draw back? There is time! And Kate! how I distressed
the tender child, who loves me so much, more than I deserve—who, perhaps, saved me! I thought a ray of sunlight fell upon me when she came. She would have persuaded me; I feel it, I know it, I could not have resisted—
dear child!" and the poor, weary eyes were softened, the
mocking smile disappeared; "thank God, she loves me still.
Why should I not go back now? But Beatrice! Aye,
those chivalric gentlemen, who would display their courage
at my expense. Ah!" he continued, smiling bitterly again,
"they will not *permit* me to act as seems proper to me. By
heaven, we shall see!"

And his reckless, dare-devil eyes flashed haughtily. At the same moment, the drums and trumpets of the cortège we have seen, attracted his attention, and he gazed through the window.   There stood the noble Shylock, on the platform, moving slowly, holding in his hand the banner, on which was inscribed the words we have seen.   The letters were enormous, and Mr. Effingham read, without difficuly, " Miss Beatrice Hallam, the delight of the noble aristocracy and the wonder of the universal world."

" Yes," he said, smiling grimly, as the procession passed slowly on ; " yes, she is the delight of the noble aristocracy !   I am one of that noble aristocracy, I believe, and she is my delight.   Ah, Madam Beatrice ! you go on now in pride and happiness, scorning me, and all who are not your abject slaves ; but wait !   You go to affect to-night, in the character of Ophelia, griefs you have never known, sufferings you can only imagine.   Some day you will suffer really, and I shall be avenged."

He was not present at that interview with Charles Waters, and had not heard those prayers, and sobs, and despairing murmurs, or he would never have uttered that bitter taunt.   For a long time he sat thinking of her, and would mutter curses and blessings in the same breath.   He had estimated justly his passion—it was not so much love as infatuation.   He did hate and love, respect and despise her ; at one moment he thought her a devil, at the next he was convinced she was an angel.   But, by degrees, these conflicting emotions settled down into a collected recklessness, so to speak—a careless, bitter, mocking unconcern, and he rose up, with a sneer.

At the same moment the door opened, and Mr. Manager Hallam made his appearance, jovial and smiling.   Mr. Effingham sat down again.

" What the devil puts you in such a good humor, Hallam ? " he said, with scornful carelessness.

" I am laughing at the people, sir."

" The people ? "

" Yes, their folly."

" What folly ? "

" At their surprise and wonder on seeing my placard."

" Yes ; that was foolish enough."

" They absolutely looked all eyes, as the grea. Congreve was accustomed to say."

" Did they ? "

" And the negroes ! "

" What of them ? "

" They looked like charcoal, with two lumps of fire in it."

" Eh ? their eyes, you mean ? "

" Yes."

" They are a facetious race."

" Oh, sir, they would make great comedians, I assure you.   Now, there was one monkey-like boy, who went along, blowing the trumpet through his hands, beating two stones together for the drum, and at times sawing his left arm for the fiddle—really, now, in a way indicating lofty talent."

" In the low comedy ? "

" Yes."

" The buffoon? ''

" Well, low comedy requires something like that.   How would a company of negro actors take here ? "

" Take ? "

" Yes, sir ; would it attract ? "

" Strongly—the attention of messieurs the justices. But come, let us estimate the receipts to-night."

" Impossible, sir."

" Come, think."

" Really can't say, sir."

" As much, think you, as on the night I perform ? " said Mr. Effingham, with his usual disdainful coolness.

" Why, really—now—I should say not, sir.   I calculate that you would draw a large crowd."

" There is but one obstacle to my acting."

" And that, sir ? "

" Miss Beatrice Hallam."

" Beatrice ! "

Mr. Effingham shrugged his shoulders.

" Yes," he said.

" How is it possible ? " began Hallam, with some indignation.

" Come, no exploding," said Mr. Effingham, with cool disdain ; " do not affect astonishment.   You know she does not wish to appear with me."

" Not wish, sir ! "

" Yes."

" Oh, you must be mistaken."

" No, I am not," said Mr. Effingham, gloomily.

" She is young, sir."

" Well, what does that mean ? "

" And diffident."

" Bah ! "

" She would prefer acting with her associates. But, throw any obstacles in the way—I would soon stop that, sir ! "

" There is a virtuous father for you ! You would command your child to do what she wishes not to do ? "

" She is full of whims, sir."

" One of which whims is a contempt for the name of Effingham ; is it not ? " said the young man, with a curling lip.

" Oh, never, sir."

" Come, now, deny—"

" She honors, and looks up to you, sir."

" She has a queer way of showing it," he said, with gloomy scorn. " What makes her hate me so ? I am really curious to know."

" On my word, sir, you astonish me, as the great Congreve used to say : Beatrice, I am sure—"

" Well, no more protests, and curse the great Congreve ! Is the agreeable Shylock still determined to eat me for kicking him down stairs ? "

" No—no. He is a reasonable fellow, and will take no more notice of the matter. I told him, sir, my opinion of his disgraceful conduct to your fair young relative, and he sincerely regrets it."

" Very well : I will take no further note of the knave. Only, on the next occasion, I shall pin him to the wall without warning, like an enormous beetle—my sword for the pin. He would be a striking object. Now, let us talk of my first appearance."

" Willingly—with pleasure, sir."

" The town is full ? "

" Yes, sir."

" And more coming ? "

" Yes : they are pouring in."

" Well, if it is now full, and they are pouring in, by the day of opening the House of Burgesses, that is in two days, they will be sleeping in the streets."

" Quite likely, sir."

" And hence it follows," continued Mr. Effingham, " that there is no danger of having a thin house to greet me."

" Oh, sir ! "

" I understand you—"

" How could—"

" Yes ! how could the fashionable Mr. Champ Effingham, of Effingham Hall, turning comedian, fail of a crowded house? You would say that ? "

" Yes, sir : it is impossible."

" Well—perhaps you are right. But I choose to wait, and I have fixed upon the day after the opening of the House, for my début. I shall appear in ' Much Ado about Nothing.' "

" As you say, sir. Well, we can easily get it up. The honor—"

" Bah : let us have no foolery ! It's no honor to either party. Now for the dress—the costume : I have none that would suit the character."

" I think I can serve you, sir—though my best military dresses are still at Yorktown, in the sea trunks. I have not needed them yet."

" A military dress—rough soldier's costume, is indispensable : you know very well that *Benedick* is just from the wars."

" Indispensable, as you say, sir."

" Have you one here ? "

" Let me see—"

And Mr. Manager Hallam, placing his fat finger upon his puffy brow, repeated :

" I think there is such a costume in my private trunk, in my room. Will you go see, sir ? "

" Yes : I'll follow."

And the two worthies went out, and closing the door, bent their way to Mr. Manager Hallam's sleeping apartment situated on the same floor.

CHAPTER XXXIX.

HOW MR. EFFINGHAM BECAME THE INSTRUMENT OF PROVIDENCE

THE apartment occupied by Mr. Manager Hallam was an odd place, and we regret that, from its want of importance to the present narrative, we cannot give a description of it. It is sufficient to say, that the bed was covered with heterogeneous costumes, of all ages and nations—the table with prompt-books and rolls of paper containing " parts "—the floor with shoes, buskins, and sandals, which had troddcn many stages in their day.

In one corner a large trunk, with heavy iron binding, and knobs, contained the manager's finer costumes. This trunk he approached, and unlocked with a key which he took from the breast-pockct of his doublet.

" Now, sir," he said, raising the lid, " I think I shall find what we want."

" Good," said Mr. Effingham, leaning over his shoulders.

The manager took out several parcels.

" Those are the fops," he said.

" Of course, they would not suit me," said Mr. Effingham, with his usual disdainful indifference.

" Oh, no, sir."

" Certainly not," said Mr. Effingham.

" These are the first class costumes—for the heroes," said the manager, unrolling another parcel.

" That would suit me as little," replied Mr. Effingham.

" Yes, sir—I mean—"

Luckily Mr. Manager Hallam was relieved from his lame apology. A servant entered, and said :

" There's a gentleman, sir—Mr. Joyce, sir—to see you—to get a private box at the theatre, sir."

Hallam rose quickly, which possibly might be owing to a slight love of money.

" Say I am coming," he replied to the servant : then turning to Mr. Effingham, he added, " just wait for me, sir—I'll be back in a minute. These business matters must be attended to."

And with these words he hurried out of the room, puffing and red in the face. Mr. Effingham had received this speech with extreme indifference, and gazed with great disdain on the half-emptied trunk : then he seemed to change his mind, and stooping down he turned over and tossed the costumes about, carelessly. Suddenly his eye fell upon one which seemed to suit perfectly his purpose. It was a dark military coat, with heavy embossed buttons, and an embroidered collar. He took it up, and said aloud :

" Well, here is what will answer my purpose, I suppose —a pretty heavy bundle ! Come, let us try it on."

Had he done so, the whole course of this narrative, thereafter, would have been different—how different no one can tell. But he changed his mind before unrolling it, and added :

" Bah ! I cannot judge !—let us go to Madam Beatrice, and ask her opinion. Doubtless she will afford me her valuable advice most willingly and sweetly. Of course she will."

And leaving the trunk open, he walked carelessly along the passage, and scarcely taking the trouble to knock, entered Beatrice's apartment.

The young girl was engaged as usual, in studying, and looked completely exhausted. Her eyes were heavy and red, her cheeks pale and thin; in her very attitude there was an indescribable air of weariness and sorrow which was painful to behold. The round shoulders drooped, the head inclined toward one side—seemed to be bent down by some ever-present grief : the bosom labored and heaved : she seemed to draw breath with difficulty. For a moment Mr. Effingham stood looking at this eloquent picture, returning her silent and cold gaze.

" Ah," he said, at length, " studying as usual, I see ! Really, madam, you will injure your health, which, as you know, is very dear to me."

There was great bitterness in these words : but Beatrice made no reply.

" You do not answer," he said, still more bitterly; " perhaps I am not worth answering, madam."

Beatrice raised her cold, heavy eyes, and looked at him fixedly.

" Mr. Effingham, I am in no humor to converse this morning," she replied, coldly

10

" With me : you never are, madam."

" With no one, sir."

" Are you sure, madam ? "

" Yes, sir."

" Perhaps your dear friend is an exception."

" What friend, sir ? "

" The Chevalier Waters," replied Mr. Effingham with a sneer.

A flush of pain and wretchedness threw a lurid glow upon the young girl's brow, and she trembled.

" Come, now, madam, get angry if you please. That is your favorite amusement when I chance to address you."

She bent down and made no reply : and this seemed to irritate her visitor more than any words.

" Really your ladyship is in a charming mood to-day," he said, with a scornful curl of the lip ; " you have chosen a new and brilliant means of insulting me."

" Mr. Effingham," said Beatrice, raising her head with cold solemnity, and speaking in a voice hoarse with sorrow, " I insult no one, sir. I have said that I was not disposed to converse to-day. I am not well, sir."

" You are always sick when I visit you," said the young man, pitilessly : his passion had changed his whole character : " you hate my very face, I believe. My presence is a discord. I have given up every thing for you, and you scorn me ! Beware, Beatrice Hallam ! God will punish you ! "

Her lip quivered, and she looked strangely at him.

" Have you come to make me more unwell than I am, sir ? " she said, pressing her hand upon her breast.

" No, madam," he said, with his former bitterness. " I came on business, strictly professional."

" What is that, sir ? "

" To ask your most respectable opinion of my costume, in the character of Benedick. Having determined to ruin myself, I wish to do it handsomely—with the best bow I have and in the most appropriate costume ! "

" Well, sir," said Beatrice, taking no notice of his terrible irony, " I listen."

And she closed her book.

" This, which I hold in my hand, madam, appears to me to be very suitable for the character of Benedick."

· I do not know, sir."

He was a gentleman, you know, madam."

" Yes, sir."

" Ruined."

" I do not remember, sir."

" Yes, ruined in the wars—like myself, by this infatuation I have for you: wounded and scarred as I am by your scorn."

" Mr. Effingham, we waste time."

" Oh, pardon me, madam, my grief and agony are nothing to you—I had forgotten."

" My own occupy my whole thoughts, sir."

" Really! then *you* have griefs too."

" Yes, sir."

" Agony perhaps."

" Overpowering agony, sir," she said, hoarsely, and with a trembling lip.   He looked at her in silence, and said, with some feeling,

" Then, you really suffer ? "

" Yes, sir."

" Deeply ? "

" Yes, sir."

" Then have some pity on my own," he said, in a voice of anguish, which was most affecting.   " I love you, you scorn me !   Do you know what that means ?   It means days and nights of agony—hours of despair, such as the bitterest foe would not inflict on his worst enemy—sleepless hours in the dim night, when the rain pours, and the winds groan, and your own groans reply.   Have you no pity, Beatrice ? "

He stopped, overcome with so many conflicting and terrible emotions, bending down his head and groaning.

" Did you only know what it is to love, and know that love can never solace your life ! " he continued, passionately ; " to see the paradise open and then close upon you ! to love madly, and feel the cold hand of fate pushing you back inexorably ! "

These broken words painted her own condition with such truth that Beatrice uttered a moan.

" I know it," she said, hoarsely.

" Then pity me ! "

" I do, sir, from my heart ! "

His face flushed.

"And nothing more?" he said, in a low tone.

"No, sir—no, no!" she said, shrinking back.

"Ah, you despise me—you hate me!"

"No, sir."

"I ruin myself for you, and you meet me with a contemptuous smile."

"I do not, sir."

"You will not love me."

"I cannot, sir!"

"You love another, perhaps, madam—already you have selected your future husband!" he said, becoming again bitter and scornful as before.

Beatrice turned pale.

"I shall never marry," she replied, in a low voice.

"I am not good enough for you, I make no doubt, madam!"

"You taunt me, sir."

"I do not—I offer you my hand!"

"I cannot accept it."

"Never?"

"Never!"

"Then we shall see," said Mr. Effingham, with that bitter and reckless laugh which at times issued from his lips, "force against force!"

Beatrice colored, and said, coldly:

"That is a defiance, sir."

"Yes—to the death."

"I despise it," she answered, with haughty coldness; then murmured, turning away, "God pardon me!"

"Ah, that is not singular; contempt for the person necessarily comprehends as much for all he can effect."

"Mr. Effingham, I am weary—I have my part to study."

"Well, madam, permit me to trespass upon your kind patience for a moment still. I came to ask of your great experience if this coat will suit my part."

"You may see at a glance, sir," she said, frigidly, "that it is moth-eaten, and unsuitable."

"Ah! I had not perceived that. Pray what shall I wear?"

"I do not know, sir."

" You act *Beatrice* in the comedy, I believe— or do some of those delightful characters your father has picked up here in the colony, and trained to murder dramas, take the part?"

"I know nothing of the matter, Mr. Effingham," she said, coldly.

"But *Beatrice* is young?"

"Yes, sir."

"Brilliant?"

"Yes, sir."

"And very scornful?"

"I believe so, sir."

"Then it will suit you admirably. Young, brilliant, and scornful! Could the description answer more perfectly! Shakespeare must have known you!"

"Mr. Effingham, your great pleasure in life seems to lie in insulting me."

"Insulting? Really you are very unreasonable, ma dam—"

"What, sir—is not—?"

" No, madam, let me say, even at the expense of politeness—for I know how ill-bred it is to interrupt you—no, it is not an insult, only the truth! It is very amusing, very laughable, but it is true—that you really *scorn* me. As to the *young* and *brilliant*, that is undeniable in your ladyship's presence."

" Mr. Effingham, I am exhausted—your voice agitates me—pray leave me, sir—"

Mr. Effingham listened to these coldly-uttered words of dismissal with an internal rage, which broke forth and displayed itself in a mocking and harsh laugh.

"Ah! you are very lofty, madam!" he said, with a sneer; "you bring your queenly airs from the stage for me! Nothing that I say, nothing that I do, provokes any thing but scorn and contempt from you! I have not sacrificed enough to you, perhaps! Do you know what trifling things—mere trifles, madam—I have left to follow your diabolical eyes! I have only forfeited the affection of my family, only lost my position in society, only struck cruelly a pure young girl's heart, who loves me! I have only left peace and happiness for agony and rage!—only abandoned love and tenderness for scorn and contempt—only given up loving faces

and caressing hands for a woman who hates me and repulses
me! These are mere trifles, madam!—they are nothing!
What is the love of Clare Lee—that is her name—to me,
compared to your overwhelming tenderness and affection?
True, we have loved each other, I may say, I think, for
years; true, we were bred together, and have always felt a
tenderness toward each other deeper than words could utter
or the eyes speak! True, her face filled with sunshine when
she saw me, as my heart overflowed with joy at her innocent
smiles! But what of that? You are all·this to me and
more! Your love is a treasure greater than her own; what
matter if her heart is broken; what if she gazes from her
father's window on the Hall which she once thought she
would enter as my wife, and sobs and moans, and feels that
henceforth life is dark to her—as I feel it is to me? *Your*
tender heart, *your* loving nature, *your* mild, angelic soul,
your overwhelming love for me will more than make me
forget her. What matters it if the poor girl dies broken-
hearted, are you not all my own?"

And overpowered by rage, and remorse, and agony, his
brow wet with perspiration, his lips trembling, all his form
shaking with the terrible war of emotions so profound and
bitter, the unhappy young man, waiting for no reply, rushed
from the room. Beatrice rose from her seat, trembling with
excitement, and bursting into tears of agony, cried:

"Oh, is this really true! Is this a horrible dream, or
not! God has cursed me! all that I approach is ruined.
Oh, can I be the cause of this dreadful suffering, which I
feel myself, in the heart of a pure, young girl? God pity
me! But no, it shall not be!" she cried; "my life is lost
and ruined—my very soul is giving way! But this stain
shall not rest upon my memory—no, no! Oh, her name!
I heard it—near his father's house—I will go there—tell
her all—God give me strength!"

And hastening out, she ordered her horse, made her pre
parations quickly, and was soon upon her way to Riverhead
galloping feverishly.

So feverish had been her emotion, that she had not observed the presence of an object, which Mr. Effingham had
dropped upon the floor of her apartment.

CHAPTER XL.

BEATRICE HALLAM AND CLARE LEE.

SHE reached Riverhead in an incredibly short space of time; and, dismounting at the gate, hastened to the door, and trembling, shuddering, followed the astonished servant into the reception-room, where she fell into a chair, exhausted, overcome, and shedding torrents of tears.

A light step startled her, and she rose, trembling, from her seat. The young girl she had asked for, stood before her.

" Did you ask for me—Clare ? " said the young girl, wonderingly.

" Oh, yes! for you ! " cried poor Beatrice, clasping her hands and sobbing: " I could not breathe until I saw you! I came to tell you that I am not the miserable creature that you think me! that I am not so abandoned as to wrong you so ! "

Suddenly Clare recognized her rival, whose features had been hidden by the partial darkness of the room. She drew back with a sudden faintness.

" Yes ! you shrink from me ! " cried Beatrice, with inexpressible anguish in her voice; " and perhaps you are not wrong—you have heard so much falsehood of me ! But you wrong me bitterly—my heart is bursting with this load of unjust scorn—I cannot bear it ! It is cruel—oh, it is unjust ! "

And she covered her face with her hands, and sobbed passionately. Clare felt as if she were about to faint; but indignation, and the bitterness of wounded love and pride sustained her. She looked at Beatrice with scorn, and shrunk from her as she approached.

" Do not—do not touch me ! " she said, alternately flushing and turning pale.

" Oh, you are cruel ! " cried Beatrice, wringing her hands; ' you are cruel and unjust ! He told me you were tender and that every body loved you—and I find you with a heart harder than stone ! You have no pity on me—you scorn

me—my very presence is loathsome to you! Oh, madam,
it is unjust!—it is a bitter and unmerited punishment! I
never could have come had I really expected this—though
what more had I the right to expect? But he told me you
were so good—that your heart was so pure—that you were
in such distress—how could I live with the thought that
you despised and scorned me!"

Clare shrunk further back and trembled. Then she had
been the topic of careless conversation between this unworthy
creature and her lover! Her name, and her love for him,
even, had been bandied in tavern purlieus with scoffs, and
rude jests, perhaps! He had said she was "so good"
—doubtless, deriding her soft, tender manner, so tame, compared with the fiery and brilliant carriage of this shameless
creature!—her "heart so pure"—no doubt contrasting de-
risively her simple truth with the scoffing boldness of this
woman! Then, to crown the whole, he had told this woman
that she, Clare, was "distressed"—that she was pining for
him!—that she envied, hated, would give life to hold the
position of that rival in his affections! This last bitter
thought put the finishing touch to Clare's agony, and she
rose.

"I can listen to no more, madam!" she said, hoarsely,
and with inexpressible anguish and indignation in her altered
voice. "You are deceived—Mr. Effingham—if you refer to
him—Mr. Effingham is nothing to me!"

And, shuddering from head to foot, she looked at Beatrice with an expression of sick and scornful aversion, which
pierced the poor girl's heart like a dagger.

"Oh, no—no! do not look at me so!" she cried, clasping her hands, and sobbing as if her heart would break; "do
not look at me so! I am not the unworthy creature you
think me! I am innocent! He sought me—has persecuted
me with attentions I abhor—he has made my life, dark
enough, God knows, already, darker still by his eternal persecution. Oh! madam, you have no right to scorn me!
You have no right—however much you may hate me! I
am innocent before God of any thing done to give you pain—
this rash young man has done all! Do you think I am his
paramour, madam? I see your cheek flush and your eyes
flash! Doubtless your maiden purity is shocked by the

very word. But we, madam, we poor actresses have to look
at and hear things coarsely, and call them by their names.
God forgive you, if you thought that of me! I am a poor,
unhappy girl, with no defence but my self-respect; but I
am innocent—innocent as a child, in thought as in deed!"

And sobbing, moaning, shedding floods of tears, Beatrice
stood before the young girl like an angel pleading for a word
of love, of charity. Her fair hair had fallen, from the violence of her emotion, her snowy arms had let the cloak covering them fall down, her face was eloquent with a sorrow and
despair which sublimated its tender beauty, and would have
touched, indeed, any but a heart of stone.

Clare's was that heart; she only saw how lovely this
young girl was; she only saw in her a triumphant rival,
darkening her life, and taking from her him she loved.
What did it concern her whether this woman was innocent
or not? And the frigid, sick, and scornful look remained.
She pointed to the door, and, unable to say more than—
"this interview—must—end!" hoarsely and almost in-
audibly.

"No, no! it shall not end," cried Beatrice, wringing her
hands, and sobbing, and speaking with passionate grief; "it
shall not end until you have heard me! I am innocent—
Oh! I am innocent—before God! your distress is not upon
my hands! He came and addressed me on the stage, the
first night I appeared in this country—I drew back and endeavored to avoid him! He came to see me the next day.
I tried to deny him any converse with me;—he staid,—he
came again and again—he has made my life wretched! I
shrink when I see his face, or hear his voice!—Ah, I am innocent of wounding you,—as God hears me, I am innocent!"

And falling on her knees, Beatrice hid her face in her
hands, and shook with passionate weeping. She seemed so
broken and overwhelmed by her sorrow, her accents were so
profoundly miserable, she resembled so much some tender
bird, wounded mortally and about to fall and die, that Clare,
with all her pride and love, and hatred and indignation,
melted. She struggled with herself, echoed the sobs of Beatrice, and then turning from her, murmured:

"Leave me—I cannot speak—I pardon you—God
will—"

There she stopped, overcome by emotion.   Beatrice raised her head.

"Oh, I have done nothing to ask pardon for !" she cried,
in a voice of bitter anguish. "God is my witness, that I have
acted as a loyal and pure woman!   I saw your scorn of me
was unjust, and it is—it is!—for I am innocent—I had no
part in inflicting this wound upon you; you have reason to
hate me—but you cannot—no ! no ! you cannot scorn me !"

"I do not," muttered poor Clare, sobbing and turning
away.

"Oh, thank you! We poor girls are not like you ladies,
protected and surrounded by every comfort, able to choose
our associates," continued Beatrice, weeping, but betraying
great feeling at these words from Clare. "God exposes us
to every persecution and temptation!   We are met with intoxicating applause upon the stage—a dangerous and fatal
thing !—and there we fancy that we are really something
more than human !   Alas ! we go out in the sunlight, and
those hands, which applauded us, repulse us; those smiles
are turned to frowns !   The commonest woman that toils in
the meanest employment, is more worthy.   Contempt is our
portion—for what are we but abandoned playing girls !   Or,
if not contempt, what is more dreadful—oh ! so dreadful,
madam, that you in your pure home here cannot imagine it.
The temptation which a strong man offers to a defenceless
girl, without a thought of that avenging God who looks down
on this world !—I will not speak of it—I shudder to think
of it !—my brain burns, and my temples throb !—God decreed
that I should fill the position I do, and I know its terrors and
its snares.   Oh, do not undervalue them, madam ! if a poor
weak girl comes from that furnace of fire, still pure in all
things, she is not fit for scorn !"

And the poor agitated breast labored and heaved, the
cheeks were bathed in tears, the childlike hands trembled
and could not arrange the hair, falling around the face so
eloquent and pure.

And Clare felt her true woman's heart moved—with that
high truth and worth which the reader will find she possessed from future pages of this narrative. She violently suppressed her sorrow and wounded love; she saw only a poor
broken-spirited girl before her—a mere child she seemed;

praying and sobbing, and entreating mercy—or rather justice, but simple justice.

"I have listened—to you—and pity—you—and do not, cannot scorn you—or—hate you—" she said, in a broken and agitated voice, shedding tears as she spoke. "If I have been—unjust—to you, I pray for your pardon! We are all weak—and—poor;—God does not permit us to scorn each other!"

And covering her face with one hand, she felt as if earth was dark for ever for her from that day—heaven only left.

Beatrice heard these words with passionate delight, and burst into an agony of tears.

"Oh, you are too good!" she cried, seizing the hand of the young girl, which hung down, and covering it with kisses; "you are too good and noble, to speak so kindly to a poor, weak child like me! Oh, God will reward you! God sent me to you, to hear these blessed words from you—to know that my existence was not wholly cursed! God had pity on me, and inspired me with the thought! Oh, say again that you will not hate or scorn me;—forget that I am a common actress, one of a proscribed and branded class— one who has cruelly wronged you, however innocently;— forget that I am so much your inferior in goodness,—forget that my life has been thrown in contact with so much that is vile! See before you, at your feet, only a poor weak girl, who prays you not to scorn her!—See in me a feeble creature, like all mortals, weak and stumbling and sinful, like all the world, but with good impulses and pure feelings like the purest! Oh, bless me again with the sound of your kind voice—I am so helpless! so broken-hearted—so overborne by agony and suffering!" she continued, strangling a passionate sob at the thought of Charles; "so wretched—ah! so miserable!—Speak to me!—one more kind word, before I leave you—Oh, for pity's sake!"

And covering the hand she held with kisses, she half rose in an agony of weeping. And that hand she held was no more drawn away. The trembling forms approached each other with a last shudder, and the two women were in each other's arms: the bitter rivals, the wronged and she who had wronged her, the actress and the lady! Sobbing upon each other's shoulders, trembling like a single agitated form, they wept in silence.

A quarter of an hour afterwards Beatrice was on her way back to Williamsburg. God had spoken: her tears were happy tears.

CHAPTER XLI.

HOW MR. EFFINGHAM RODE FORTH, AND BEFORE MIDNIGHT RE-APPEARED EN MILITAIRE.

AFTER uttering that mad, passionate speech, so crammed with bitter and scornful irony, Mr. Effingham, as we have seen, flung from the young girl's room, in an access of rage, which tore him like a vulture's talons. He had passed through many of these fiery interviews lately, and had many such pale rages, which tore his heart for a time, then slowly subsided, like a storm muttering away into the distance. On this occasion he found himself, as usual, grow somewhat calmer, when her cold and inexorable face was removed from him; and soon his bitter, reckless smile returned, and mockery replaced anger.

He went back to the manager's room, and threw the costume disdainfully into the trunk; then, scarcely conscious of what he was doing, proceeded to restore the various bundles to their places. Fate still directed him, for who knows what would have occurred if that fit of absence had not seized him, and he had left those dresses where they lay—throwing down carelessly the one he had brought back upon them? He had just slammed down the lid of the trunk violently, when Mr. Manager Hallam returned.

" Ah, sir," he said, with a smile, " you are tired of the search ; are you ? "

- " Yes."

" Well, I think there was little good in it. My military costumes are still at Yorktown."

" Are they ? " said Mr. Effingham, coldly.

" Yes, sir, as I informed you."

" Did you ? '

" Ha, ha ! don't you recollect, sir ? "

" How can I ? I have just had such a charming interview with your amiable daughter."

" Ah ! have you, sir ? " said Mr. Manager Hallam
anxiously ; for his matrimonial project never left his
thoughts.

" Yes," returned Mr. Effingham, with scornful carelessness ; " I think she is beginning to like me."

" I am sure of it, sir," said the delighted worthy.

" She seemed to brighten up, when I entered."

" Did she, indeed ? "

" Of course she did !   She seemed delighted to see me ! "

" She is the most truthful and sincere girl in the world
—a gold mine would not make her smile, if she did not
choose to," said Hallam, with real fraternal pride.

" Quite true," replied Mr. Effingham ; " she is perfectly
sincere."

" Indeed she is, sir."

" And plain-spoken."

" Oh, remarkably ! "

" And we spent half an hour delightfully."

" You are gaining on her, sir."

" You think she don't hate me, then ? "

" Oh, sir ! "

" Come, answer."

" Hate you, sir ?   Never, sir ! "

" How then ?   Does she love me ? "

This somewhat embarrassed Mr. Manager Hallam ; for
the young girl's demeanor to Mr. Effingham, when he had
observed it lately, was exceedingly far from supporting an
answer in the affirmative.   But he replied, at once :

" I think she will in time, sir."

" In time ! "

" Very soon, sir."

" Really ? "

" Yes, sir ; I have observed little things of late which
prove to me that you are acquiring her affection ; and she no
longer—"

" You are right—I understand—she no longer scorns,
and insults, and hates me—"

" Oh, sir ! "

" She no longer tells me that she will never look at me

but with hatred and aversion. In our interviews now she
smiles, and presses my hands tenderly, and seems to pity my
pale cheeks, and languid eyes—my health is dear to her—
or becoming dear—she is beginning to love me. Yes, as
you very justly say, sir, I am 'beginning to acquire her
affection' ! "

And the young man laughed, with terrible irony—a
laugh which jarred upon Manager Hallam's ears, and dis-
pelled, unpleasantly, the agreeable impression the words
were calculated to produce.

"Bah!" continued ·Mr. Effingham ; "let us leave love
matters, and come to business. You have no Benedick costume here ? "

"Really—I believe not, sir ; but—"

"Have you at Yorktown ? "

"Oh yes, sir."

"In trunks ? "

"Yes, sir."

"Where are they ? "

"Stored in the warehouse."

"Good ; then you have a complete Benedick dress at
Yorktown in trunks, stored in the warehouse ? " said Mr
Effingham, summing up with disdainful nonchalance.

"Yes, sir."

"Give me the key."

"The key, sir? "

"I am going to get the dress.

"You, sir ! "

"Certainly ; what the devil are you staring at ? '

"Why—really, sir—"

"Give me the key ! "

"Of course, sir ; here it is," said the manager, taking a
huge iron key from a drawer of the table.

"Is there but one trunk ? "

"Three, sir."

"Well, the dress—"

"Is in the green one, bound with brass hoops."

"Very well. They know me there ; and when I assure
them further that I am a member of the company, there will
be small difficulty. Order my horse," he added to a servant passing through the passage.

And the young man, without taking the trouble to say good-bye to Hallam, went out, and going along the passage, entered his own room, leaving the worthy manager in a state of stupor, staring after him.

"Well, really," said Manager Hallam, at length, "that young man is an extraordinary character. I don't know how to deal with him. He snubs me; I feel he is continually a-roasting me, and I don't know how to answer. He has such lordly airs--worse than the great Congreve. Well, he is going to act, and go to the ball with Beatrice; and then I'll have him. He is not good enough for her, I know, except that he is so rich. Effingham Hall comes to him, I understand; and that is enough."

With which Mr. Manager Hallam began to dream of the clover-enveloped life which he desired so ardently.

An hour or two afterwards Mr. Effingham issued forth, clad as before in his rich foppish costume—only that his slippers were replaced by elegant riding buskins reaching a little above the ankle and ornamented with rosettes: he seldom wore boots, then rapidly becoming the fashion among all classes. In his hand he carried an elegant gold-ornamented riding whip—and so he mounted, and, as the evening closed in stormily, set forth toward Yorktown.

Half an hour afterwards it began to rain heavily, and this circumstance distressed Mr. Manager Hallam exceedingly; without reason, however, for the theatre was crammed from pit to dome, and Beatrice had never been more completely overwhelmed with applause, or had acted with such overpowering splendor. They could not know what gave that supernatural power to the young girl's voice, that marvellous reality to the expression of her lips and eyes— but they saw the wonderful genius, and rose up with a shout that drowned the thunder rolling through the sky without.

Long before midnight the storm cleared away, and in the now silent streets the stroke of a horse's hoof was heard, and this horse stopped before the Raleigh. Mr. Effingham dismounted, and summoning the sleepy servant, gave his animal into his hands.

The horse was covered with sweat, and his mouth dropping foam.

Mr. Effingham was clad in a complete military suit—huge boots, curved heavy sword, broad belt, and Flanders hat. Mr. Manager Hallam had no such costume in his repertory, and indeed, Mr. Effingham had not visited the good town of York, at all.

———◆———

CHAPTER XLII.

WHAT MR. EFFINGHAM HAD DROPPED.

BEATRICE had reached Williamsburg just as the theatre was about to commence, and was compelled, without losing a moment, to hurry away to her painful duty. We may fancy that she felt little disposition to appear that evening: but one of the lessons of her hard life, was an unhesitating sacrifice of private feelings to her duty, and she repaired to the theatre, without even tasting a morsel. Indeed, she could not have eaten any thing—her heart was too much overcome by the thousand conflicting emotions she had experienced throughout the day; and she did not feel weak. Something sustained her, and she began her part with strange calmness. Never had she acted better, as we have seen—but those tumultuous plaudits fell upon unheeding ears: they were now painful to her—as that profession, which a cruel destiny forced her to pursue, was revolting and a cruel trial. She made her concluding bow with the same coldness which had characterized her, when, on her entrance, she had been greeted with thunders of applause; and then calmly returned to the Raleigh. She wished to be alone with her grief—to shed tears without being subjected to the wondering questions of any person:—she wished, after delighting the crowded audience, and sending them away thinking how rapturous her happiness and pride must be at such intoxicating praises—she wished to go and sob her heart into calmness, in the stillness of her chamber.

Bidding her father good night with a kiss at the door of her little room—from which another door led to her bedchamber—the young girl entered and lighted a taper. Then she observed for the first time, on the floor, that object which

Mr Effingham had dropped, when he rushed from the room, and which in the tumult of her feelings she had lost sight completely of.

It was a little frock, such as were worn by very young children; and so slight was it, that Mr. Effingham had doubtless not observed that it had escaped from the bundle which he held in his hand. Beatrice picked it up, and examined it wonderingly, completely at a loss to understand how such a thing had gotten into her room. Why does she start so—why does her cheek flush, then grow pale again? On the collar of the little frock, is written in distinct though faded letters, " Beatrice Waters ! "

Beatrice sat down, feeling too weak to stand : a sudden faintness invaded her heart, and her temples throbbed. "Beatrice Waters!—Beatrice Waters!" What did this mean ? Whence could the frock have come—who brought it thither ? Beatrice Waters ? Had Charles then guessed correctly, and did the letters " B. W.," on the locket really mean this ? She felt her mind whirl—her face flush and turn white again—some indefinable presentiment seemed to seize upon her, and the frock fell from her hand to the floor. For some minutes the young girl remained motionless— then she picked the dress up again. Suddenly she felt something in the pocket, and drew it out. It was a letter —faded and discolored, and worn at the edges. She tore it open and run her eyes eagerly over it—trembling—coloring —growing pale—breathing with difficulty. Then it fell from her hand, and pressing the other hand upon her heart, she leaned back overcome, as though she were about to faint.

The letter was in these words—words traced in faded yellow ink.

" A man about to die, calls on the only Englishman he knows in this place, to do a deed of charity. Hallam, we were friends—a long time since, in Kent, Old England, and to you I make this appeal, which you will read when I will be cold and stiff. You know we were rivals—Jane chose to marry me ! I used no underhand acts, but fought it fairly and like an honest soldier—and won her. You know it, and are too honest a man to bear me any grudge now. I married her, and we went away to foreign countries, and I be-

came a soldier of fortune—now here—now there :—it runs
in the family, for my father was covered with wounds. She
stuck to me—sharing all my trials—my suffering—as she
shared my fortunate days. She was my only hope on earth
—my blessing :—but one day God took her from me. She
died, Hallam, but she left herself behind in a little daughter
—I called her Beatrice, at the request of her mother. The
locket around the child's neck, is her mother's gift to her :
preserve it. ·Well : we travelled—I grew sick—I came to
Malta, here—I am dying. Already I feel the cold mounting
from my feet to my heart—my eyes are growing hazy, as
my hand staggers along—my last battle's come, comrade !
Take the child, and carry her to my brother John Waters,
who lives in London somewhere—find where he is, and tell
him, that Ralph Waters sends his baby to him to take care
of :—she is yonder playing on the floor while I am dying. I
ask you to do this, because you are an honest man, and because you loved Jane once. I have no money—all I had is
gone for doctor's stuff and that :—he couldn't stand up
against death ! Keep my military coat to remember me by
—it is all I have got. As you loved her who was my wife,
now up in heaven, take care of the child of an English soldier ; and God reward you.

" RALPH WATERS.

" Malta, March, 1743."

The last words were written hurriedly, and were exceedingly indistinct; as though the writer had been warned of
his approaching death by a chill hand covering his eyes,
but Beatrice ran over them like lightning, as by inspiration.

We may now understand why she leaned back faintly, dropping the letter from her nerveless hand. Here was the
mystery illuminated suddenly by a flash, which made plain
every recess, the most gloomy depths. All was as plain as
light now ! She was not Hallam's daughter !—that locket
was the gift of her dying mother—that coat in Mr. Effingham's hand the soldier's—that little frock was the garment
she had worn, a poor little baby, while her brave father,
stretched upon his couch, was struggling with the cold hand
of death, and dedicating his last moments to her own safety
and restoration.

Her powerful and vivid imagination painted the scene with lifelike reality. The brave soldier dying—the poor apartment—the trembling hand contending with the dread angel—those dim eyes—herself a little child unconscious of all this—and the glazing eyes fixed on her as she laughed and prattled—and the last sigh of the stalwart breast a prayer for her! The scene was so real that she burst into a passion of tears, and sobbed until she was completely exhausted. Oh, that dear father dying there alone!—his brow covered with the sweat of the death agony, far away from friends and home, in a foreign land! That strong frame fighting with the destroyer—that face, which dawned on her memory now like a dim dream, convulsed with pain and dread for her after fate!

How could she bear to think of this and not feel her very soul overwhelmed with an agony like that which he had suffered? And she wept and sobbed, and shook with the tempest of her feelings; and then slowly grew more calm.

Why had she not been restored to her friends. Was not that old man, whose son had saved her, her uncle—Charles her cousin? And this thought dazzled her mind, for a moment darkened by that scene of death; plain through so many misty years. Yes, yes! she had heard the boatman Townes call him "Old John Waters." Thousands in the colony had come from England to retrieve their fortunes, and this must be her uncle!

Overwhelmed with this new weight of thought—bewildered by this new light streaming upon her mind, she felt her brain for a moment totter, and pressed it with her hand. The other hand was laid on her breast, through which shot an acute pain; that hand fell upon the locket—her mother's locket—and drawing it forth, she pressed it passionately to her lips, and again burst into a flood of tears.

Her mother! her poor mother, who had loved her dear father so much, and been his good angel until she died, away from her home and friends, as he did! This was her mother's, and she pressed it convulsively to her lips, and wept herself faint and quiet. The taper died away and flickered, but she heeded it not; for that whole scene again was passing through her mind, and she was far away in the bright south—that south which she had rightly dreamed she

had been born in.   Scenes now came to her which had been
long buried in oblivion—ah ! so long; kind faces, rude bivou-
acs, the implements of war—and orange groves!   That far
dim past enveloped her with its marvellous breath, and from
it rose dear faces, tender smiles, rough, rude caresses of
great bearded faces, and the sound of trumpets.   Those
trumpets echoed faintly through the air, and died away like
an enchanting harmony—like the clear voices of gondoliers
singing the wondrous lays of Tasso, under the starry skies
of Italian nights.   The far muttering of cannon then rose
to her memory, and this, too, died away; and then rose
beautiful rosy headlands, orange trees, and waves of gold
rolling their molten fire to the great wide horizon in the
sunset.   Then her thoughts rushed backward to her after
life—the English scenes, the theatres, the rough city life,
the loud applause, the nights of study, the days of weariness
and patient grief.   Virginia rose on her last, and all she
had suffered—Mr. Effingham's persecutions, the scorn and
forgiveness of that young girl who loved him—lastly, the
love and unhappiness of Charles.   That thought made her cheek
flush, she knew not why!   Would not this change every thing
—would she not leave the stage—would they not take her
to their hearts, their long-lost child ?   Why had her father
not obeyed that dying request of her real father?   Was it
because he could not find her uncle, or because self-interest
was too strong for him—foreseeing her proficiency in his art ?
If the latter, was it not cruel in him?   If the former, did
she not owe him deepest love for his long years of tenderness
and care ?

     Then these tumultuous thoughts disappeared, and that
far dreamy land rose on her mind again—and with her eyes
closed she saw it plainly—ah, how very plainly!   She saw
again those scenes which had but now come back to her with
a reality more real than the outward world—a charm more
marvellous and grand than she dreamed possible.   Again,
those strong bearded faces shone on her and uttered tender
words—and one was far more tender than them all!   Again,
she heard those trumpets sounding like liquid gold, shattered and sprinkled in the deep blue air; again that faint
and solemn murmur of the distant cannon rolled upon her,
and spoke to her with its grand, eloquent voice, of a great

conflict and the clash of arms! She heard them now dis-
tinctly—no longer dying away farther and farther into the
dim past—but real, audible as reality, and instinct with a
heavenly harmony which wrapped her heart in ecstasy and
delight.

And then again she saw that wondrous southern land, where
the blue skies drooped down upon a marvellous horizon—
where the warm seas, covered with white-sailed ships, were
ruffled by soft winds, laden with the rich perfume of orange
trees and flowers—perfumes that set her dreaming, breezes
that soothed her agitation and anxiety, like winds from heaven. Again, the vast wide sea rolled its great liquid gold,
its billows crested with a fiery foam in the red sunset, gradually fading :—and above the whole, grand in its softness,
beautiful for its light, rose the dear father's face—smiling
upon his child!

The taper flickered and went out—she did not heed it,
dreaming of the bright southern home and of his face. She
leaned her head upon the window-sill, and dreamed and
dreamed :—sleeping, those wondrous memories clung to her,
and when the full sunlight streamed upon the tender, gentle
face, waking her, she almost thought it was her father's kiss.

CHAPTER XLIII.

FROM THE MS.

" Let us pause here a moment," says the author of the MS.,
"and observe how events march onward obedient to the
great Chief of heaven ; how personages of all ages and conditions are but blind puppets in the hands of an all-seeing,
all-wise Providence. Heaven decreed that this young woman should, in Virginia, be subjected to a persecution, more
systematic than she had ever experienced in any other land
before—and this persecution proceeded from one of that
class which social feeling then separated from her own by
barriers as striking and impassable as those existing between
the peasant and the great lord. This persecution was to be
a daily and systematic one, a trial of the temper and the

heart—a test of the young girl's patience and her strength
It was to come to her at the theatre, in the street, in her apartment—every where. It was to insult, to worry, to irritate,
to wound the subject of its enmity. It was to try the character of the young woman to the utmost, as the spur inces
santly plunged into the quivering side tests the endurance
of the noblest animal.

"Then, not satisfied with this systematic, chain-like train
of wounds and insults, Providence one day sent a child of
the same race as her arch-persecutor to her presence :—and
from that child's lips came words which wounded, mortified,
humiliated the already overburdened heart so cruelly, that
the poor heart had cried out passionately against the injustice, and the bitter, cruel, terrible wrong.

"Then, having tried the young woman with such apparent
harshness, that same Providence began to unroll the chain
of circumstance—that chain formed of such a myriad of invisible links, links which by the short-sighted are called
'small events' and 'trifles,' but which hold the universe
together. The instruments of all this persecution were to
hasten the light upon its way to brighten Beatrice's life—
and to do this, spite of themselves, not knowing what they
did. All things were to work harmoniously to that end,
nothing was to fall short, or occupy its wrong position. The
trunks containing that much-coveted costume were at York
—hence the two men were led to open that other one,
wherein the secret of a life was shut up. The only obstacle
to the revelation, was the man who knew it—he was called
away. That this secret should dawn upon the proper person
first, the coat is not unrolled—the young man goes to ask
her advice. He becomes agitated, and in his agitation drops
the child's garment—then he returns, and instead of throwing down the coat carelessly, replaces it with all the rest in
the trunk : the time has not arrived for the manager to know
that all is known. Thrown thus at her very feet, the young
girl does not see the frock, until having made her peace with
Clare, she returns to the stillness of her chamber. Then
she knows the whole, and all is clear to her. But she has
no harsh thoughts of the man she had called her father for
so long—she does not cry out in bitterness against the cruel
concealment which has made her so unhappy—which has

placed her in that position which renders acceptance of the hand of Charles impossible. Why? Because the second chain of circumstance had been unrolled also. A child had been brought to the place by the presence there of him who had persecuted her :—a coarse ruffian had frightened her :— she had fled in her terror to the young girl's room :—there she had left her Bible—that Bible which was to affect the spirit of Beatrice, as the accident—the world would call it—of the child's frock affected her life. That Bible was to make her meek, to give her strength to bear the sneers and mock- ery and reproaches she was to be subjected to in that fiery interview. That Bible was to give her strength to hold fast to the victory she had won over herself, when Charles went from her in despair—the thought of which nearly bent her resolution, broke her remaining strength.

"Those two personages, man and child, whose words had wounded her more cruelly than all else, were thus fated to become the instruments of Providence—the one to reveal her far southern birth, the other to be the direct agent of her purification—spiritual birth. There was the chain—no link of it defective—bearing up the weight of a whole life , shaped link by link by Providence, and slowly, certainly un- wound by hands which thought themselves at other work. Is there no overruling Providence?"

CHAPTER XLIV.

HOW THE GHOST OF MR. EFFINGHAM ARRIVED AT THE "RALEIGH," AND CALLED FOR SOME VINO D'ORO.

THE manuscript from which this veracious history is taken, contains many passages similar to that which we have just transcribed. The writer, indeed, seems very fond of tracing thus the secret steps of Providence—making plain the won- drous ways of that invisible Power which guides the uni- verse in its onward course—directing men and events as it rolls the great globe through the realms of space, around the central sun of Eternal Law. The reader would, how- ever, be apt to complain were we to transcribe many such

pages; for this narrative is much more a development of
events and characters than a bundle of essays. The words
which men and women utter are far more powerful interpret-
ers of what they think and feel than any mere comment on
their thoughts and feelings by an indifferent person; and,
acting upon this conviction, we shall proceed to deal again,
directly, with the personages of the history.

We have seen how Mr. Effingham, with that blind and
obstinate wilfulness, had clung to his determination to appear upon the stage, and how he had ridden forth to procure
the necessary costume. We have also seen how he returned
to the "Raleigh," a few hours afterwards, equipped in a complete military costume perfectly adapted to the character which
he designed to represent. Busy with other and more important events, we could not follow him on his night ride;
but we now proceed to show in what manner he became possessed of the costume—a costume which no less a personage
than Mr. Manager Hallam himself had declared wonderfully
appropriate, not without many exclamations and interrogatories, which were left unanswered.

Mr. Effingham, on the next morning, had just repaired
to his room, after languidly conversing at the door of the
"Raleigh" with half a dozen of the wild hangers-on of the
dramatic company, to whose society he had learned to stoop
in gracious condescension, when a singular circumstance attracted the attention of the worthies who surrounded the
door. This circumstance was the arrival of a traveller,
who, pushing his way through the crowd, halted at the door
of the "Raleigh." This event, it is perfectly plain, was not
in itself very remarkable, inasmuch as travellers were accustomed to come and go in Virginia at that period—to and
from Williamsburg and the "Raleigh"—as at present. The
observable circumstance about the foreign-looking gentleman, who now drew up and called in a loud, hearty voice for
the ostler, was that, in his outward appearance, he presented
a perfect counterpart of no less a person than Mr. Champ
Effingham. His broad, muscular shoulders were clad in a
rich velvet coat, which was stretched across them as tightly as
the skin upon a drum; his waistcoat was of embroidered silk,
and not more than three of the buttons had yielded and
given way; his vigorous limbs were moulded on a scale en-

tirely too large for the velvet knee-breeches and silk stockings, which fitted so tightly as to define every swelling muscle
with the utmost distinctness. The rosettes had burst off
from his shoes—his hands were saffron-colored, and you
only found, upon close inspection, that he wore gloves fitting
as closely as the cuticle—in one of these remarkable hands
he carried a gold-handled riding whip. As he dismounted,
the other hand arranged conveniently the hilt of a small,
highly-decorated sword, and then raised from its owner's
brows his feather-ornamented hat of the last London fashion.

The head thus bared was that of a man of about thirty
or thirty-two, whose profession was evidently arms. The
bright martial eye, black and full, could not be mistaken;
the straight form, which indeed almost bent backward, so
erect was it, plainly indicated the profession of the worthy.
The face was an excellent one, not because it was very handsome, in the ordinary acceptation of the word, but for its
frank and bold carelessness—its sunshine; in the open features mental and physical health fairly shone. The hair was
dark and somewhat grizzled; the brow broad, and darkened
by sun and wind; the eye, as we have said, black and brilliant; the nose prominent, the chin and under lip full of resolution and character. We say the chin and under lip, because the stranger wore a long and very heavy moustache,
as black as jet, under which his white teeth sparkled when
he laughed—very frequently, that is. For the traveller's
face seemed to be made for laughing—it was so bold, so
careless, he seemed to enjoy life so much that laughter more
or less loud was a necessity to him, and he reminded the
observer irresistibly of Hamlet's friend, Horatio. But a
single glance was needed to perceive that this was

> "A man that fortune's buffets and rewards
> Had ta'en with equal thanks:"

a soldier who had been tossed upon the surges of war, until
he had grown quite indifferent to storms, and, in the gloomi-
est weather, still saw the sunshine through the clouds; who,
losing once, rattled the dice again; who took the world
easily, and pushed his way, and laughed and drank, and
slept and fought. contented. endeavoring still through all to
do his soldier's duty."

11

This is a brief and hurried sketch of the martial gentle
man who, stopping at the "Raleigh" tavern that bright
morning, delivered into the hands of the astounded ostler
the bridle of his cob. Ned, the ostler, rubbed his eyes and
gazed at the stranger precisely as the worthies on the portico were doing.

"Well, well, my friend," said the traveller, in a strong,
hearty voice, "what detains you? my horse is weary."

"Yes, your honor—yes, sir—"

And Ned the ostler led away the animal, with his eyes
still fixed upon the stranger, to the serious inconvenience of
his neck, twisted until the blood covered his face.

The stranger entered the "Raleigh," politely giving the
good-day to those gentlemen who, after staring at him with
a curious look, made way for him.

Mine host stopped in the middle of a sentence, which he
was addressing to one of his numerous patrons—a crowd of
whom filled the ordinary—and the look which accompanied
this sudden silence was more eloquent than any words.
Then, suddenly recollecting himself, he bowed low, and said :

"Your honor is looking for me, the landlord?"

"Yes, *parbleu*," said the stranger; "my horse has
gone to the stable, where they will, doubtless, take good care
of him?"

"Oh yes, sir—the best ostlers, sir—"

"And now, mine host," continued the stranger, twirling
his mustache, "now a stall for me."

"A stall! oh, your honor, sir—"

"Perpend, *mon ami*—a room, I mean."

"Oh yes, sir—I understand, sir. I have an excellent
room, just given up by Farmer Williamson—number 8, sir—
just up there, sir."

And mine host pointed to the stairs.

"*Bon*," replied his guest, "and send me a bottle of wine.
I'm as thirsty as a fish."

"What will your honor have?" asked the landlord, still
riveting his eyes upon the extraordinary counterpart of Mr.
Effingham.

"*Val de Peñas*—my favorite vintage."

"I'm really afraid, sir—"

"Haven't the blood of Spain!" interrupted the stranger,

who exhibited some disappointment at mine host's apologetic grimace.

"We are just out, sir—exceedingly sorry, sir—but Mr. Williamson—"

"Well, well; give me a flask of *vino d'oro*. I must be satisfied.

Mine host made a second grimace, which was more eloquent than words.

"What! none of the *vino d'oro*!" cried the stranger, who seemed to understand perfectly well what the expressive features of the landlord indicated; "none of the bottled sunset, as one of my friends calls it! I really am afraid, mine host," continued the traveller, shaking his head, "that this hostelry of yours is not a place for an honest and Christian soldier to tarry in;—none of the wine of Lebanon?"

"Oh, sir!—the most unfortunate thing, I know—but really, now—my last bottle has just been sent up to Squire Wilton."

"I should like very much to engage in single combat against your Farmer Williamson and Squire Wilton! Most unjustifiable in them to be drinking up my favorite wines in this way!"

"We have some excellent claret, Madeira, and some Rhenish, sir, which I think your honor—"

"*Bon!* I choose the Rhenish. Send it to my room."

"Yes, sir; directly, sir. Would your honor give me your name to write in my book? I wish to keep that book, sir—for my family, sir—that they may know the distinguished gentlemen I have had the great pleasure to entertain, sir."

The stranger's mustache curled, and his white teeth shone under the black fringe.

"My name? Ah, very well," he said; "that is easy."

And raising up the hilt of his sword, the stranger carefully scanned some letters cut into the gold.

"My name is Effingham," he said. "*Parbleu*, I had forgotten it; as nothing is more troublesome to recollect than names."

And, leaving the landlord in a state of semi-stupefaction, the stranger pushed his way through the crowd, who drew back for him, and went up the stairs. The worthies who

had witnessed his arrival, also, were present at the scene be
tween the traveller and mine host; and now they crowded
round the landlord, to give vent to their astonishment. We
need not take the trouble to report their sage opinions. The
general conviction was, that Mr. Effingham had a ghost, who,
unlike himself, wore a mustache, and they waited for the reappearance of the spectre.

CHAPTER XLV.

BEATRICE REVEALS HER SECRET.

"It is not a trifling thing, when some soul, the noblest and
purest ever sent by God to bless us, is torn from us by the
hand of what seems a blind and pitiless destiny. This is,
perhaps, the hardest trial of poor, feeble human patience, and,
if the very soul succumbs, and the heart grows sour and bitter, is there any room for wonder? Under one of these
overwhelming strokes, the head bows down and faints, as the
knight of the middle age, struck by some gigantic battle-axe,
lost his firm place upon the saddle, and was hurled to earth.
All suddenly is gone—all that made life desirable—the
sunshine and the blue skies—in place of them, darkness,
despair.

"At such moments, poor humanity doubts its God;
that God who does all things for the best, but does not
deign to anticipate the future for his justification. It
is maddened. Its faith, and purity, and trust in God are
gone; and the blood lingers in the veins, frozen, yet fiery;
the eyes, by turns, glare and are glazed. Ere long this
passes, however, and, if the mercy of God is not manifest,
still the heart forces itself to believe—to trust in that mercy,
and then, with the slowly-dragging hours, some of the bitterness passes; the day is not so dark; and if the sunshine
cannot lie with such a glory on the earth again, at least we
know and feel it is not wholly gone away for ever, but is
there behind the lurid cloud, from which crashed the great
thunderbolt which struck us.

"These trite sentences may indicate, in some measure,

the feelings of Charles Waters, when, leaving Beatrice after
that interview, in which, overwhelmed by her agitatio n, she
had fainted he left Williamsburgh pale and despairing."

Thus writes the author of the MS.

For days his soul was the prey of bitter and conflicting
passions. For the first time he felt how completely she had
grown to be a portion of himself. He never knew how much
he loved her until he lost her. And now, when all the
powers of his being were subdued to an unutterable tenderness for that bright, gentle creature—when he could not
think, or read, or study, or see any thing around him, for
her ever-present image—now, when he loved her passionately, with the full force of his affluent and large nature
—now he felt an impassable barrier rise up between them—
a huge wall, more durable than adamant—more lofty than
the stars—a barrier which defied his utmost efforts, which
must separate her eternally from him. He raved and tore
his hair; he felt his heart growing sour—all those great and
noble thoughts, which were wont to tenant the palace of his
mind, like a troop of radiant angels, fled away; and if he
again attempted to gather hope or tranquillity from the pure,
veiled brows, they changed and gibbered at him like a troop
of imps, and jeered and fled away with horrible mocking
laughter !

So days passed—nights, almost sleepless : calm succeeded.

He began to feel the dignity of suffering :—he rose
grander from his despair, and saw the sunlight through the
clouds—the light of heaven. With his brow resting on his
clasped hands, the strong man prayed, and went forth in the
quiet evening, and was comforted. Nature looked on him
with her soft, luminous eyes, and the bright river, and the
autumn forest, spoke to him. He now saw what his duty
was plainly. She was immovable; he knew, he felt, that she
was lost to him : that she might passionately yearn to fall
upon his bosom, but not yield. She might love him far
more deeply than she had done—still, he felt well convinced
that she would be equal to the struggle with herself. She
could not turn his life into splendor,—be his dear wife : he
had no claim upon her, would not ask to have any. But he

could watch over her—protect her—if necessary, match his
own heart and arm against that insulting annoyer.

Yes, all was lost to him—but she had gained, at least :—
and so he returned to his labors in the field, and having
finished his work, entered the house where his old father
dreamed in the chimney corner, to prepare himself for
another visit to the town. The old man and his son exchanged a tender greeting as he passed into his small apartment, and taking off his blanket coat, he donned his usual
doublet of coarse drab. As he was putting on his hat, he
heard voices in the next room, and going thither found himself in the presence of a servant whom he had seen frequently at the "Raleigh." The servant delivered to him a note,
directed succinctly "to Mr. Charles Waters."

He opened it with a flush upon his brow, and read :

"Please come to me.   BEATRICE."

A sudden paleness chased away the crimson flush, and
the young man turned away and fell into a chair.

"Answer, sir ?" said the negro boy. He made a movement of his head, and muttered :

"I will come—say to Miss Hallam that I shall come
at once."

And again he read the simple words which had aroused
such a tumult in his heart. Her hand had rested on this
paper ; she had traced those words——she was lost to him !
Those were the thoughts which made him again breathe
heavily and close his eyes.

Telling the old man that he would return very soon, he
left the house, and took his way towards Williamsburg.
Why had she sent for him ? To rend his heart by the sight
of that paradise for ever closed to him ? To try herself, and
show him that her life was not wholly dark ? To say "you
think that I am wretched, that I suffer pain because you
suffer—see ! I am calm ?" No ! none of these thoughts
dwelt for a moment on his mind : his clouded brow plainly
rejected all of them. Suddenly, a light like the flush of
dawn broke over those gloomy eyes, and his face brightened
like a midnight sky, illuminated by some great soaring conflagration. Could it be ? Could she have sent for him to say
"my strength has failed me—I cannot resist myself—I am

too weak—my heart, my life, are yours!" Had she relented, banished that stern resolution, given herself up to what her heart called out for?—No! and the light changed to gloom again. He recollected too well that last faint cry of love and grief, of passion and despair, of weakness and strength. "You cannot move me now—I have conquered myself!" No, no!—that woman's resolution was adamant—he felt that all he loved her for was against him in the strife—her noble disinterested devotion, and strength of purpose to continue in the right!—could she have called upon him to protect her! had Mr. Effingham dared to persecute her in reality!— and with the thought his hand clenched, his breast heaved, his brows were curved into a haughty frown; his pace, already rapid, became the walk of a race-horse. He would soon know, for there was Williamsburg: he is in the streets: he passes through the noisy, laughing, bustling throng: he enters the inn: he knocks and goes into her room—she is there before him!

Beatrice rose, with such an expression of mingled anxiety and joy, that he remained for a moment without advancing, gazing at her in silence.

Beatrice broke that silence:

"Oh! this was very kind," she said, with that simplicity and tenderness, which at times made her voice pure music, "I could not have expected you so soon."

And her voice trembled slightly, as she placed her hand in his, with fond and confiding affection. A tremor passed over his frame as he took it.

"Do you need me—has any one annoyed you?" he said, coming with a bound to his absorbing thought.

"Oh no!" said Beatrice.

He breathed more freely, and sat down, passing his hand over his throbbing brow.

For a moment they both remained silent, scarcely daring to look at each other.

"You sent for me?" he murmured, with his face turned from her.

"Yes," said Beatrice, in the same low tone, "I was troubled, and unhappy—no, not unhappy—"

And her voice faltered.

"Unhappy?" he said, not feeling himself strong enough

to encounter her gaze: "what could have made you unhappy?"

The tone of these words plainly indicated that his meaning was, "*I* am the wretched and unhappy person—your
suitor for a priceless boon denied to me—*I* have a right to
feel miserable, you have not." Beatrice felt her heart throb,
and her throat fill with tears.

"I have—much—to make me—unhappy!" she said, in
a broken and faltering voice, "very much."

"Yes, yes, we all have—we are mortal," he replied, in
a low voice, "I have had much myself."

"Oh, do not speak of that," cried Beatrice, bursting into
tears, "I cannot speak if you do."

"I will not," he murmured, his large shadowy eyes
turning to her own for a moment, then averting their gaze.

"I am so weak now, that I don't think I could endure
another—such—" and the tears choked her.

He suppressed his emotion by a powerful effort, and taking her hand, said, sorrowfully:

"You shall not be agitated again by any thing I say; let
us not touch upon that subject then. Tell me frankly,
Beatrice, what you wished me to visit you for—you cannot
have a more devoted—brother!"

Beatrice looked at him, with inexpressible affection, and
murmured, "that might be nearly true."

"What?" he said.

She trembled.

"I do not think, father—Mr. Hallam—is my father,"
she said, greatly agitated.

"Not your father!" he exclaimed, raising his head
quickly.

"It is so strange!" she murmured again, half to herself.

"Not your father!"

"I am certain that—heaven has—the wildest fiction
could not"—

She stopped, overcome by agitation.

"Beatrice!" he exclaimed, rising erect, "something
strange has happened: you tremble: you send for me:
speak! What is this in my brain, my soul!—What is that
so strangely familiar in your features!—my brain struggles—"

" Charles ! I am Beatrice Waters—your Uncle Ralph's daughter ! I feel it !—Oh, heaven has removed my doubts ! —I d) not need your assurance ! You are my cousin ! "

F)r an instant, the two hearts beat fast—the two frames felt a tremor run through them.

" Yes ! heaven tells me, I am that little child !—the child of a father who died in that foreign land !—but speak ! Had you not an uncle Ralph ? "

" Yes," he murmured, looking at her as in a dream.

" Your father's name is John ! "

" Yes ! "

" You lived in Kent once ! "

" Yes ! "

" In London next ! "

" Yes ! "

" Your uncle died in—"

" In Malta, twenty years ago ! " he said, scarcely conscious of what he was saying, scarcely able to speak from agitation—wonder—an overwhelming, undreamed of delight, which paralyzed his limbs, it seemed, arresting the very blood in his veins, making a lifeless statue of him.

Beatrice was almost as much agitated as her companion, and had uttered these hurried interrogatories with a trembling voice, a heaving bosom, a brow flushing and growing pale by turns. But when his last reply came—when he said, " In Malta, twenty years ago : " then her remaining doubt became a dazzling certainty; all mists swept away, and, covering her face with her hands, she murmured :

" I am his daughter !—God directed the orphan's steps ! —I am his child ! "

Her knees bent under her, and overcome, exhausted, she would in another second have fallen upon his bosom :—when suddenly the door was thrown open, and Mr. Effingham entered the ayartment.

CHAPTER XLVI.

THE RIVALS AND THE GHOST.

THE rivals stood face to face, and surveyed each other, with glances which flashed and crossed like lightning.

They were both strong men: for one had the strength of passion, the other the strength of resolute courage, and great self-control.

How the singular interview would have commenced, it is impossible to say—for all at once, the wheezy voice of Mr. Manager Hallam was heard at the door, saying:

"Ah, Mr. Effingham! Mr. Effingham! I called after you, and you have made me lose my breath, puffing after you up the stairs. But here is metal more attractive, you would say, after the great Congreve—or, rather, the grand Shakspeare."

With which words, the voice took to itself the sem-blance of a puffy, red-faced gentleman, who entered smiling.

At sight of Charles Waters, however, the manager's face fell.

"Good morrow, sir," said Waters, calm and self-collected, spite of the various emotions he still experi-enced.

"Welcome, sir," said the manager, with some constraint. "We have a very fine day, sir—hum!"

And Mr. Manager Hallam cleared his throat.

"We do not see you so often as our friend Mr. Effing-ham," he added, for the sake of saying something.

"Which is probably attributable to the fact that I live here," replied Mr. Effingham, coldly.

There was a pause.

"You look agitated, Beatrice," continued the manager, turning to his daughter with a constraint which was very observable.

Beatrice turned away her head, and murmured,

"No, sir!"

"Are you sick?"

"Oh no, sir."

"Mr. Waters left his father well, I trust?" he continued turning to the silent man.

"Perfectly, sir," was the calm reply.

"Commend me to him when you return—I feel as if we—had met before," the manager said, with some hesita-tion.

His constraint was so plain, that Charles Waters deter-mined to remove it, by taking his departure. His presence evidently caused it; and it was not pleasant to behold. The strange and mysterious revelation made to him by Beatrice —a revelation which his mind still struggled in vain to realize—had moved him, as we need not say, profoundly; and the sight of the man who, beyond all doubt, knew and had been the chief actor in the hidden drama, then threw him into unwonted agitation. He wished for solitude and quiet to collect his scattered thoughts, and with a few common place words took his departure.

He had reached the top of the stairway, and was on the point of descending, when he felt a hand upon his shoulder.

He turned round; Mr. Effingham stood before him.

"A moment, sir !" said that gentleman, haughtily.

"Well, sir," said his opponent as coldly.

"Mr. Waters, I believe, who saved Miss Hallam's life ? "

"My name is Waters, sir."

"And mine Effingham."

His opponent inclined his head coldly.

"Ah !" said Mr. Effingham, haughtily; "you will not understand; you are a marble statue. One would really say that my name had struck upon your ears for the first time."

"No, sir; I have heard it before."

"From Miss Hallam, doubtless ? "

"Yes, sir."

"Coupled with a highly favorable opinion, I suppose ? "

"No, sir."

"Ah ! ah !—now we approach the point."

"What point, sir ? It is impossible for me to understand your meaning."

These cold words seemed to irritate Mr. Effingham more and more.

"I mean, sir," he said, "that you and Miss Beatrice Hallam have been making me the subject of criticism—you have been indulging in abusive words relating to myself."

"You are mistaken, sir."

"Ah ! indeed ! "

"Yes, sir; but as you have thrust this conversation on me, I will add, that I have at different times spoken of yourself—not abusively—for that is a species of conversation which I do not indulge in—but critically, that, sir, I confess."

"Very well, sir. It only remains for you to repeat those critical observations."

"Mr. Effingham," said his opponent, "look at my face.'

"Well, sir!"

"If you have ordinary acuteness, you must perceive that I adopt this tone of calmness by a violent effort."

"Well, sir; permit me to request that you will deign to look at me. If I spoke my true feelings plainly, they would cut as the edge of a sword cuts."

"A sword, sir?"

"Yes; have you one at home, sir?"

"No."

"Ah! I had forgotten—you do not wear this description of weapon."

His adversary's face flushed, and forgetting all his self-control, he said:

"If I do not wear, I use the sword, sir."

Mr. Effingham's eye flashed.

"Good! good!" he cried; "when shall we meet?"

"Meet, sir?"

"Yes!"

"Do you purpose defying me to mortal combat?"

"Precisely, sir."

"The reason?"

"I am not aware that a gentleman need give another any reason—I wish it. Is not that enough, sir?"

"I asked your reason, because it seemed to me, sir, that if this challenge should be given at all, it should proceed from me."

"From you!"

"Yes, sir."

"And, pray, why, sir," asked Mr. Effingham, haughtily.

"Because I am the aggrieved party."

"You!"

"Yes, sir."

"How, if it please you, sir?"

"I regret that 'tis not possible for me to explain—and this I should have reflected upon before speaking."

"Well, sir," said Mr. Effingham, coldly, but cold only by a violent effort, "it is a matter of little importance from

which party the defiance comes. If from you, I accept; if
you do not send it, I will. There, sir! Is that plain?"

"Perfectly, sir," said his opponent, turning pale with
anger at the disdainful coldness of Mr. Effingham's tone, and
losing. at last, all his self-control.

"Well, your answer? I waive all discussions of rank."
His adversary's brow flushed.

"Yes, yes, sir!" he said, "you are very courteous, and
I trust your lesson in the sword exercise will be more worthy
of attention than the present one you give me in politeness.'

"Politeness, sir!"

"I mean, sir, that you adopt towards me a tone which
is most insulting and unworthy."

"Sir!"

"Yes, most unworthy. You will waive all discussions
of rank! By heaven, sir! I think the waiver should be on
my side. Yes, sir, you have overcome my self-control—by
pure force of continued insult driven me to anger. Well,
sir, you shall hear my thoughts now. You have thrown to the
winds all courtesy, you throw my station in society in my
teeth, you think me a peasant—a mere boor—who should
be whipped back to his place when he attempts to make his
breast the barrier between a strong, passionate man, and a
weak, feeble girl! For that is your real cause of quarrel,
sir; you hate me because I stand between yourself and that
young girl, yonder! Yes, sir, you hate me, and you imagine that I will yield to you—that your sword will pass
through my heart, and that you will be left free to persecute
that child, as you have done already, without hindrance.
Undeceive yourself! I am no child! I promise you something more than a weak struggle—the struggle of a girl endeavoring to escape your approaches. Yes, sir! you shall
have a fair field, and my heart's blood if you can take it!
But guard well your own!"

Mr. Effingham was carried away by his rage—his eyes
filled with blood—and, grinding his teeth, he drew his sword.

Furious, blind, mad with passion, no one knows what he
might have done, when, suddenly, a loud "*Diable!*" was
heard, and Mr. Effingham found his sword knocked up by
the scabbard of another perfectly similar to it.

It was the ghost, who, coming out of his room, had heard
the altercation, and arrived just in time.

CHAPTER XLVII.

THE GHOST EXPLAINS WHAT HAD TAKEN PLACE AT THE BACON ARMS.

MR. EFFINGHAM turned abruptly, and saw his counterpart—the exact fac-simile of himself,—as far as dress went, be it understood.

"Ah, it is you, is it, sir?" he said, coldly, as he sheathed his sword.

"Yes, and *parbleu!* you are my friend of the *Bacon Arms!* Why, *bon jour, mon ami!*"

"Good day, sir; you came just in time. I was on the point of committing a very foolish and unworthy action, which, no doubt, would have displeased this gentleman."

"Morbleu! quite likely!" cried the stranger, twirling his moustache. "I do not consider the circumstance by any means extraordinary. Displease him? I believe you. It is calculated to displease a man to have a good short sword run through his midriff without even the satisfaction of making his own sword say click! against the invading weapon!"

And, without a moment's hesitation, the stranger turned to Charles Waters, and, bowing to him, drew the sword from the scabbard he held in his hand, took it by the point, and presented the hilt to the unarmed man.

"If we must have fighting—and I regard it as the natural state of human things—at least, let us have fair play my friends," he said.

But Charles Waters drew back.

"Thanks, sir," he replied, "but we will settle our differences elsewhere."

"A duel?" said the stranger. "Well, I am not fond of duels—it is a villanous mode of settling the said differences. Hilf himmel! could any thing be more unreasonable than such a cold-blooded proceeding! Strike, strike, companion, while the blood is warm; strike, and so fall: or, if you stand, shake hands and go away with a quiet conscience! Drink, and be friends! I abominate your duels, though I have fought many."

"Well, sir," said Mr. Effingham, with his reckless smile "come to-morrow and see another."

"Why, with pleasure!" returned the stranger; "are the arrangements made?"

"Not quite, the cause of strife having just arisen."

"Ah, ah! a pretty girl is in the affair! Morbleu, comrade, I'll see you in your sword exercise with pleasure, though you were going on contrary to the rules just now. A pretty girl, my life on it! Perhaps that charming little comedienne, Miss Hallam, whom I have seen in London, and who is here?"

"Yes, sir."

The stranger shook his head.

"Never fight about a woman," he said, sagely; "one always regrets it—always, comrade."

"Permit me to say that I consider nothing more appropriate."

"Appropriate! See how opinions differ. Perpend, *compagnon:* if you fight about the turn of a card, the rattle of a dice-box there is some philosophy in it—they are worth it—it is rational. But about a pair of eyes—a woman!—never!"

"Well, sir, I still hold to my opinion."

"And are going to fight?"

"Yes."

"Have you a friend?"

"Not yet."

"Let me act for you; and don't think I bear you any ill-will for the affair out yonder. We can easily cross swords on that, if necessary, afterwards," said the stranger, with the utmost calmness and good-humor.

"Thanks, sir," said Mr Effingham; "your offer relieves me from much trouble, and I accept it."

"Who is my principal? in other words, comrade, let me have your name—Effingham, is it not?"

"Yes."

"My own is—hum—well, I am called La Rivière—sometimes Captain La Rivière—not unfrequently the Chevalier La Rivière. Now for your opponent," added the stranger, looking keenly at Charles Waters.

" My name is Waters, sir," he said, " but I really do not see the necessity of—"

"Waters!" cried the stranger; "*tonnere!* is it possible!"

And dropping his hand to his sword hilt, he looked long and fixedly, with a strange expression, at the silent man.

"What surprises you, sir?" asked Waters.

The stranger made no reply; he seemed to have suddenly grown dumb; then he murmured,

"Waters!—Waters!—did you say Waters?"

"Yes, sir; Charles Waters."

The stranger, with his eyes still fixed with the same curious expression on the other, said to Mr. Effingham:

"I regret that I shall have to withdraw my offer to offi ciate as your second."

"Why, sir?" said Mr. Effingham, abruptly, and with some irritation.

"Come, come, comrade; because it pleases me. I can't give a reason at the sword's point," said the stranger, coolly

"Pardon my abruptness, sir."

"Certainly, certainly," returned the stranger, with great good-nature; "and I will state that I think I was well acquainted with a relative of Mr. Waters, in the Seven Years' War."

"With my brother, sir!"

"Was he your brother, *mon ami?* A certain Captain Ralph; was that his name?"

"Yes, yes; did you—"

"Know him? Oh, perfectly well. Morbleu, we were inseparable! Excellent friends—devoted to each other— eating out of the same platter—drinking out of the same glass—loving the same damsels—marching together—sleeping together—defending each other—really inseparable, on the honor of a soldier!"

And the captain laughed, until his moustaches curled up to his eyes.

"I never can think of that man without laughing," he said; "he was such a ridiculous character—had been through so many odd adventures, which he was eternally relating—"

"Yes, yes; I recognize the portrait," said Charles Waters, hanging on the stranger's words.

"Faith, do you?" said the captain; "well, I should recognize him in the dark. You know, now, sir," he added, turning to Mr. Effingham, "why it is not proper that I should act as your second in a duel with the brother of my dearest friend."

"Well, sir, as you choose," said Mr. Effingham; "you are at liberty to act as pleases you, of course."

"Of course; and, therefore, I transfer my offer to Mr. Waters, here."

"Very well, sir."

"You are very kind, sir," said Charles Waters, calmly.

"Not at all, not at all; I owe that much to Ralph; but *parbleu*, I can't go on the field a perfect counterpart of your opponent," said the stranger, laughing.

"I have been wondering, sir, at the perfect similarity."

The stranger laughed heartily.

"The plainest thing in the world," he said; "a real case of highway robbery at an inn, and to this moment I myself am as completely in the dark as to what it means."

"It means that I wanted your soldier's dress," said Mr. Effingham, coolly, "and took it."

"Leaving your own. Good! good!" laughed the stranger. "Don't think I am going to quarrel, or find fault. Nothing astonishes me in this world, and few things make me angry. Faith! I admired your strategy. Figure to yourself, as the French say," continued the stranger, turning to Charles Waters, and curling his black moustache; "imagine me stopping at the tavern called the 'Bacon Arms,' half way between this place and York, the port at which I landed. I am seated in the ordinary, amusing myself by tracing figures on the sanded floor, with my sword's point; I wait for the end of the storm and rain, knowing the value of a good hostelry, when, suddenly, my friend here enters, having outrun the wind, and desirous, like myself, of saving himself a wetting. He looks at me—he admires my costume, and faith! he had reason, for the great Frederic himself always regarded it with a smile of approbation. We drink—there I am never at a loss, morbleu—we converse—we abuse the storm—we become excellent friends. Now mark the sequel. At eleven at night the storm still rages; we agree to retire. Mine host has but one bed-room vacant, with two beds. We go to sleep—I wake up in the morning—and when I come to look for my proper habiliments, diable! they are gone. My good friend, too, has vanished, leaving, however, his own dress! What a comedy! Better than Closter Zeven! I take up the coat—I regard the breeches—I put them on, and turn myself in admiring them.   But faith, they were too tight !   My shoulders ached—my breast felt as if I was cased in armor—faith, it feels so now ! "

And the soldier drew a long breath, which sent flying from the rich waistcoat the two remaining buttons; at which amusing circumstance he laughed again.

" And now, *mon ami*," he said, to Mr. Effingham, " take pity on a poor defeated comrade, who has got the worst of it, who came along groaning over his defeat, who, in conclusion, will cheerfully debate the right of property in the said costume, at the sword's point !   Come now, be magnanimous; let us have a bout ! "

" That is not necessary, sir," said Mr. Effingham, who had listened to the stranger with haughty indifference; " I have no need of the dress at present, as the occasion for which I took it in exchange for my own is deferred some days."

" Oh, you are welcome then, to it, comrade," replied the stranger, who, still looking abstractedly at Charles Waters, had not noticed the cold accent of Mr. Effingham's voice ; " when you wish me to unshell myself, you have but to speak, and I will cheerfully do so.   I will even place my whole travelling wardrobe, at York yonder, at your disposal."

" Thanks, sir : will you come now and resume your dress ? "

" Yes, yes, at once—for these elegant velvets worry me."

" First, however, let me restore to you this bundle of Bank of England notes," said Mr. Effingham, taking from his purse the money, " I found them in the pocket of your. coat—ten notes of ten pounds each."

" Good—good—I had forgotten them completely," said the soldier, thrusting them into his pocket without looking at them; " and now let us proceed to your apartment, *mon compagnon*.   It is understood that this little affair takes place—"

" Day after to-morrow, if that is agreeable to Mr. Waters," said Mr. Effingham, with his disdainful coldness; " I have indispensable engagements."

" What say you, sir ? " the soldier said to the other, ' I act for you."

AT THE BACON ARMS.

" When you please, sir," was the calm reply.

" Well, well now : that is arranged. We shall ta k over matters in the course of the day."

And leaving Charles Waters, the two copies of each other entered Mr. Effingham's apartment—the one aughing, joyous, talking loudly; the other cold, silent, and with a weary, reckless look, which made the contrast perfect.

CHAPTER XLVIII.

HOW HIS EXCELLENCY, GOVERNOR FAUQUIER, GAVE A GREAT BALL, AND WHO WERE PRESENT.

THE day for the meeting of the House of Burgesses had arrived :—indeed, the scene which we have just related took place on the afternoon preceding it.

We have already expended some words upon the appearance of the town for days before this important occasion, and can now only add, that the bustle was vastly greater, the laughter louder, the crowd larger, and the general excitement a thousand-fold increased on this, the long-expected morning. We have no space to enter into a full description of the appearance which the borough presented :—indeed, this narrative is not the proper place for such historic disquisitions, dealing as it does with the fortunes of a few personages, who pursued their various careers, and laughed and wept, and loved and hated, almost wholly without the " aid of government." It was scarcely very important to Beatrice, for instance, that his Excellency Governor Fauquier set out from the palace to the sound of cannon, and drawn slowly in his splendid chariot with its six glossy snow-white horses, and its body-guard of cavalry, went to the capitol, and so delivered there his gracious and vice-regal greeting to the Burgesses, listening in respectful, thoughtful silence. The crowd could not drive away the poor girl's various disquieting thoughts ;—the smile which his Excellency threw towards the Raleigh, and its throng of lookers-on, scarcely shed any light upon her anxious and fearful heart :—she only felt that to-night the crowd at the theatre would be noisier, and more

dense; her duty only more repulsive to her—finally, that all
this bustle and confusion was to terminate in a ball, at
which she was to pass through a fiery ordeal of frowns and
comments; even through worse, perhaps—more dreadful
trials. She had not dared, that morning, when her father
told her he should expect her to *keep her promise*, and accompany the young man, after the theatre, to the ball—the
poor girl had not dared to speak of her secret, or to resist.
Then she had *promised*—that was the terrible truth; and
so she had only entreated, and cried, and besought her
father to have mercy on her : and these entreaties, prayers,
and sobs, having had no effect, had yielded; and gone into
her bed-chamber, and upon her knees, with Kate's little
Bible open before her, asked the great heavenly Father to
take care of her.

All this splendid pageant—all this roar of cannon, blare
of trumpets, rumbling thunder of the incessant drums, could
not make her heart any lighter; her face was still dark.
And the spectacle had as little effect upon the other personages of the narrative. Mr. Effingham, seated in his room,
smiled scornfully, as the music and the people's shouts came
to him. He felt that all that noisy and joyous world was
alien to him—cared nothing for him—was perfectly indifferent whether he suffered or was happy. He despised the
empty fools in his heart, without reflecting that the jar and
discord was not in the music and the voices—but in himself.
And this was the audience he would have to see him play
Benedick !—these plebeian voices would have liberty to applaud or hiss him !—the thought nearly opened his eyes to
the true character of the step he was about to take. What
was he about to do ? that night he was going to the palace
of the Governor with an actress leaning on his arm—there
to defy the whole Colony of Virginia, in effect to say to
them—" Look ! you laugh at me—I show you that I
scorn you ! "—then in a day or two his name would be pub-
lished in a placard, " The part of Benedick, by Champ
Effingham, Esq."—to be made the subject of satirical and
insulting comment by the very boors and overseers. These
two things he was about to do, and he drew back for a moment—for an instant hesitated. But suddenly, the interview
he had with Hamilton came back to him, and his lip was

wreathed with his reckless sneer again. They would not permit him, forsooth!—his appearance at the ball with Miss Hallam, would be regarded as a general insult, and a dozen duels spring out of it!—he would do well to avoid the place!—to sneak, to skulk, to swallow all his fine promises and boasts!

"No!" he said, aloud, with his teeth clenched; "by heaven! I go there, and I act! I love her and I hate her more than ever, and, if necessary, will fight a hundred duels for her, with these chivalric gentlemen!"

So the day passed, and evening drew on slowly, and the night came. Let us leave the bustling crowd hurrying toward the theatre—leave the taverns overflowing with revellors—let us traverse Gloucester-street, and enter the grounds, through which a fine white gravelled walk leads to the palace. On each side of this walk a row of linden trees are ornamented with variegated lanterns, and ere long these lanterns light up lovely figures of fair dames and gallant gentlemen, walking daintily from the carriage portal to the palace. Let us enter. Before us have passed many guests, and the large apartments, with their globe lamps and chandeliers, and portraits of the king and queen, and Chelsea figures, and red damask chairs, and numerous card-tables, are already filling with the beauty and grace of that former brilliant and imposing society.

See this group of lovely young girls, with powdered hair brushed back from their tender temples, and snowy necks and shoulders glittering with diamond necklaces; see the queer patches on their chins close by the dimples; see their large falling sleeves, and yellow lace, and bodices with their silken network; see their gowns, looped back from the satin underskirt, ornamented with flowers in golden thread; their trains and fans, and high red-heeled shoes, and all their puffs and furbelows, and flounces; see, above all, their gracious smiles, as they flirt their fans and dart their fatal glances at the magnificently-clad gentlemen in huge ruffles and silk stockings, and long, broad-flapped waistcoats and embroidered coats, with sleeves turned back to the elbow and profusely laced; see how they ogle, and speak with dainty softness under their breath, and sigh and smile, and ever continue playing on the hapless cavaliers the dangerous artillery of their brilliant eyes.

Or, see this group of young country gentlemen, followers of the fox, with their ruddy faces and laughing voices; their queues secured by plain black ribbon; their strong hands, accustomed to heavy buckskin riding-gloves; their talk of hunting, crops, the breed of sheep and cattle, and the blood of horses.

Or, pause a moment near that group of dignified gentlemen, with dresses plain though rich; and lordly brows and clear bright eyes, strong enough to look upon the sun of royalty, and, undazzled, see the spots disfiguring it. Hear them converse calmly, simply, like giants knowing their strength; how slow and clear and courteous their tones; how plain their manners !

Lastly, see the motley throng of the humbler planters, some of the tradesmen, factors as they were called, mingled with the yeomen; see their wives and daughters, fair and attractive, but so wholly outshone by the little powdered damsels; last of all, though not least, see his bland Excellency Governor Fauquier gliding among the various groups, and smiling on every body.

Let us endeavor to catch some of the words uttered by these various personages, now so long withdrawn from us in the far past—that silent, stern, inexorable past, which swallows up so many noble forms, and golden voices, and high deeds; and which in turn will obliterate us and our little or great actions, as it has effaced—though Heaven be thanked, not wholly !—what illustrated and adorned those times which we are now trying to depict. And first let us listen to this group of quiet, calm-looking men—fame has spoken loudly of them all.

" Your reverend opponent really got the better of you, I think, sir," says a quiet, plain, simple gentleman, with a fine face and eye. " ' The Twopenny-Act' made out too clear a case, in mere point of law, to need the after-clap."

" True, sir," his friend replies, smiling so pleasantly, that his very name seemed to indicate his character, " but I would willingly be unhorsed again by the Reverend Mr. Camm, in a cause so good. Every thing concerning Virginia, you know, is dear to me. I believe some of my friends consider me demented on the subject—or at least call me the ' Virginia Antiquary.' "

"I consider it a very worthy designation, sir; and in spite of my opinion, that 'The Colonel's Dismounted' is an appropriate title—I cannot be otherwise than frank ever—I am fully convinced that equity was with you. But here comes our noble Roman."

As he speaks, a tall, fine-looking gentleman approaches, with an eagle eye, a statuesque head, inclined forward as though listening courteously, a smile upon his lips, his right hand covered with a black bandage.

"What news from Westmoreland, pray, seigneur of Chantilly?" asks the opponent of the Reverend Mr. Camm. "Do they think of testing the Twopenny-Act by suits for damages?"

"No, sir," says the newcomer, very courteously; "I believe, however, that in Hanover county the Reverend Mr. Maury has brought suit against the collector."

"Ah, then we shall get some information from our friend from Caroline! See, here he is. Good day, sir!"

He who now approaches has the same calm, benignant expression as the rest—an expression, indeed, which seems to have dwelt always on those serene noble faces of that period, so full of stirring events and strong natures. The face was not unlike that which we fancy Joseph Addison's must have been—a quiet, serene smile, full of courtesy and sweetness, illuminated it, attracting people of all ages and conditions. When he speaks, it is in the *vox argentea* of Cicero, a gentle stream of sound, rippling in the sunlight.

"What from Caroline, pray?" asks the 'dismounted Colonel,' pressing the hand held out to him with great warmth. "Do the clergy speak of bringing suit to recover damages at once, for the acts of '55 and '58?"

"I believe not," the gentleman from Caroline replies, courteously, in his soft voice; "but have you not heard the news from Hanover?"

"No, sir; pray let us hear—"

"In the action brought by the Reverend Mr. Maury against the collector, a young man of that county has procured a triumphant verdict for the collector."

"For the collector?"

"Yes!"

"Against the clergy?"

" Yes !"

" You said a triumphant verdict ? "

" One penny damages."

An expression of extreme delight diffuses itself over the face of the gentleman receiving this reply.

" And what is the name of the young man who has worked this wonder ? "

" Mr. Patrick Henry."

" I have no acquaintance with him."

" I think you will have, however, sir. His speech is said to have been something wonderful ; the people carried him on their shoulders, the parsons fled from the bench—I found the county, as I passed through, completely crazy with delight. But what is that small volume, peeping from your pocket, sir ? " adds the speaker, with a smile at the abstracted and delighted expression of his interlocutor.

" An Anacreon, from Glasgow, sir," says the other, al- most forgetting his delight at the issue of the parsons' cause, as he takes the book from his pocket and opens it. It is a small thin volume, with an embossed back, covered with odd gilt figures ; and the Greek type is of great size, and very black and heavy.

" Greek ? " says the gentleman from Caroline, smiling serenely. " Ah, I fear it is Hebrew to me ! I may say, however, that from what I have heard, this young Mr. Henry is a fair match for a former orator of that language—De- mosthenes ! "

" Well, sir," says the Roman, " if he is Demosthenes, yonder is our valiant Alexander ! "

" Who is he ? "

" Is that fine face not familiar ? "

" Ah, Col. Washington ! I know him but slightly ; yet, assuredly, his countenance gives promise of a noble nature ; he has certainly already done great service to the govern- ment, and I wonder his Majesty has not promoted him. His promotion will, however, await further services, I fancy."

" Ah, gentlemen, you are welcome ! " says a courteous voice ; " Mr. Wythe, Colonel Bland, Mr. Lee, Mr. Pendle- ton, I rejoice to see you all : welcome, welcome ! " And his Excellency Governor Fauquier, with courtly urbanity presses the hands of his guests.

" You will find card-tables in the next room, should you fancy joining in the fascinating amusements of tictac and spadille," he adds, blandly smiling as he passes on.

The next group which we approach is quite large, and all talk at once, with hearty laughter and rough frankness; and this talk concerns itself with plantation matters—the blood of horses, breeds of cattle, and the chase. Let us listen, even if, in the uproar, we can catch nothing very connected, and at the risk of finding ourselves puzzled by the jumble of questions and replies.

" The three field system, I think, sir, has the advantage over all others of—"

" Oh, excellent, sir! I never saw a finer leaf, and when we cut it—"

" Suddenly the blood rushed over his frill, and we found he had broken his collar bone!"

" The finest pack, I think, in all Prince George—"

" By George!—"

" He's a fine fellow, and has, I think, cause to congratulate himself on his luck. His wife is the loveliest girl I ever saw, and—"

" Trots like lightning!"

" Well, well, nothing astonishes me! The world must be coming to an end—"

" On Monday forenoon—"

" On the night before—"

" They say the races near Jamestown will be more crowded this year than ever. I announced—"

" The devil!—"

" Good evening, sir; I hope your mare will be in good condition for the race—"

" To destruction, sir—I tell you such a black act would ruin the ministry—even Granville—"

" Loves his pipe—"

" The races—"

" Hedges—"

" Distanced—"

" I know his pedigree; you are mistaken—by Sir Archy dam—"

" The odds? I close with you. Indeed, I think I could afford—"

12

"Ah, gentlemen!" a courteous voice interposes, amid the uproar, "talking of races? Mr. Hamilton, Mr. Lane, welcome to my poor house! You will find card-tables in the adjoining room." And his bland Excellency passes on.

Space fails us or we might set down for the reader's amusement some of the quiet and pleasant talk of the well-to-do factors and humbler planters, and their beautiful wives and daughters. We must pass on; but let us pause a moment yet, to hear what this group of magnificently-dressed young dames, and their gay gallants, are saying.

"Really, Mr. Alston, your compliments surpass any which I have received for a very long time," says a fascinating little beauty, in a multiplicity of furbelows, and with a small snow storm on her head,—flirting her fan, all covered with Corydons and Chloes, as she speaks; "what verses did you allude to, when you said that 'Laura was the very image of myself?' I am dying with curiosity to know!"

"Those written by our new poet yonder: have you not heard them?"

"No, sir, upon my word! But the author is—"

"The Earl of Dorset, yonder."

"The Earl of Dorset!"

"Ah, charming Miss Laura! permit the muse to decorate herself with a coronet, and promenade, in powdered wig and ruffles, without questioning her pedigree."

A little laugh greets these petit maître words.

"Well, sir, the verses," says Laura, with a fatal glance.

The gallant bows low, and draws from his pocket a MS., secured with blue ribbon, and elegantly written in the round, honest-looking characters of the day.

"Here it is," he says.

And all the beautiful girls who have listened to the colloquy gather around the reader, to drink in the fascinating rhymes of the muse, in an earl's coronet and powder.

"First comes the prologue, as I may say," the reader commences; "it is an address to his pen:

> "Wilt thou, advent'rous pen, describe
> The gay, delightful silken tribe,
>   That maddens all our city;
> Nor dread lest while you foolish claim
> A near approach to beauty's flame,
>   Icarus' fate may hit ye!"

The speaker pauses, and a great fluttering of fans ensues, with many admiring comments on the magnificent simile of Icarus.

The reader continues, daintily arranging his snowy frill " Mark the fate of the bard," he says, and reads :

> "With singéd pinions tumbling down,
> The scorn and laughter of the town
>   Thoul't rue thy daring flight.
> While every Miss, with cool contempt,
> Affronted by the bold attempt,
>   Will, tittering, view thy plight."

" Tittering—observe the expressive phrase," says the reader.

They all cry out at this.

" Tittering ! "

" Ladies do not titter ! "

" Really ! "

" Tittering ! "

The serene reader raises his hand, and, adjusting his wig, says :

" Mere poetic license, ladies ; merely imagination ; not fact. True, very true ! ladies never *titter*—an abominable imputation. But, listen."

And he continues :

> "Myrtilla's beauties who can paint,
> The well-turned form, the glowing teint,
>   May deck a common creature ;
> But who can make th' expressive soul,
> With lively sense inform the whole,
>   And light up every feature !"

" A bad rhyme ' teint,' and a somewhat aristocratic allusion to ' common creatures,' " says the reader.

" Oh, it is beautiful ! " says a pretty little damsel, enthusiastically.

" I am glad you like your portrait, my dear madam," says the gallant, " I assure you that Myrtilla was designed for you."

" Oh ! " murmurs Myrtilla, covering her face with her fan.

The reader continues :

> "See Laura, sprightly nymph, advance,
> Through all the mazes of the dance,
>   With light fantastic toe;
> See laughter sparkle in her eyes—
> At her approach new joys arise.
>   New fires within us glow!

> "Such sweetness in her look is seen,
> Such brilliant elegance of mien,
>   So jauntie and so airy:
> Her image in our fancy reigns,
> All night she gallops through our veins,
>   Like little Mab the fairy!"

Laura covers her face to hide her delight, in the midst of universal applause.

The reader helps himself daintily to a pinch of snuff from a golden box, and continues:

> "Shall sprightly Isadora yield
> To Laura the distinguished field
>   Amidst the vernal throng;
> Or shall Aspasia's frolic lays
> From Leonella snatch the bays,
>   The tribute of the song!"

And as the gallant gentleman reads, he pauses at "Isadora," "Aspasia," and "Leonella," and, raising his head, reveals the hidden meaning of the verse by gazing at those beauties, who utter little cries of delight, and go into raptures.

He continues:

> "Like hers I ween, the blushing rose
> On Sylvia's polished cheek that glows;
>   And hers the velvet lip
> To which the cherry yields its hue,
> Its plumpness and ambrosial dew,
>   Which even gods might sip!"

Isadora and Sylvia cover their faces, and feel conscious of having made a host of enemies.

The reader reads on:

> "What giddy raptures fill the brain,
> When tripping o'er the verdant plain,
>   Florella joins the throng,
> Her looks each throbbing pain beguiles,
> Beneath her footsteps nature smiles,
>   And joins the poet's song."

Then there is a pause.

" Who is Florella ? " they ask.

" Florella, ladies, I regret to say, is not present," the reader replies, embracing the brilliant and undulating throng with a glance.

" But who is it ? "

" Are you really desirous of knowing ? "

" Yes, yes.'

" I have been told that curiosity was not one of the foibles of the divine sex—"

" Come—come, Mr. Alston," says Laura, " on pain of my displeasure !"

" That is far too dreadful to endure," says the gallant, smoothing his frill with a jewelled hand, and bowing low, " Florella, ladies, is Miss Henrietta Lee."

" Exactly like her—excellent," comes from all sides.

Some more verses are read, and they are received with a variety of comment.

" Listen now, to the last," says the engaging reader.

> "With pensive look and head reclined,
> Sweet emblem of the purest mind,
>   Lo! where Cordelia sits!
> On Dion's image dwells the fair—
> Dion, the thunderbolt of war—
>   The prince of modern wits!

> "At length fatigued with beauty's blaze,
> The feeble muse no more essays,
>   Her picture to complete.
> The promised charms of younger girls,
> When nature the gay scene unfurls,
>   Some happier bard shall treat!"

There is a silence for some moments after these words— the MS. having passed from the gallant's hands to another group.

" Who is Cordelia? let me think," says Laura, knitting her brows, and raising to her lips a fairy hand covered with diamonds, absently.

" And Dion—who can he be?" says Isodora, twisting her satin sleeve between her fingers abstractedly.

" It is !—no, it is not !"

" I know, now !—but that don't suit !"

" Permit me to end your perplexity, ladies," says the

oracle, " Cordelia, is Miss Clare Lee, and Dion, is Mr. Champ
Effingham ! "

A general exclamation of surprise, from all the ladies.
They say :

" It suits him, possibly, but—"

" He may be the prince of wits; still it does not follow—"

" Certainly not, that—"

" Clare is not such a little saint ! "

" Let me defend her," says a gentleman, smiling; " I grant
you that 'tis extravagant to call Mr. Effingham a thunderbolt—"

" Laughable."

" Amusing," say the gentlemen.

" Or the prince of modern wits," continues the counsel
for the defence.

" Preposterous ! "

" Unjust ! " they add.

" But I must be permitted to say," goes on the chivalric
defender of the absent, " that Miss Clare Lee fully deserves
her character :—the comparison of that lovely girl, ladies, to
Cordelia,—Cordelia, the sweetest of all Shakespeare's characters—seems to me nothing more than justice."

The gentlemen greet this with enthusiastic applause, for
our little, long-lost sight of—heroine, had subdued all hearts.

" As regards Mr. Effingham," adds Clare's knight, " I
shall be pardoned for not saying any thing, since he is not
present."

" Then I will say something " here interposes a small
gentleman, with a waistcoat reaching to his knees, and profusely laced, like all the rest of his clothes—indeed, the
richness of his costume was distressing—" but I will say, sir,
that Mr. Effingham's treatment of that divine creature, Miss
Clare Lee, is shameful."

" How ? " ask the ladies, agitating their fans, and
scenting a delicious bit of scandal.

" Why," says the gentleman in the long waistcoat, squar-
ing himself, so to speak, and greatly delighted at the sudden
accession to his importance—the general opinion being that
he was somewhat insignificant, " why, ladies, he has been
running after that little jade, Miss Hallam ! "

" Miss Hallam ! " cry the ladies, in virtuous ignorance though nothing was more notorious than the goings-on of our friend Mr. Effingham, " Miss Hallam ! "

" Precisely, ladies."

" The actress ? "

" Yes."

" A playing girl ! " exclaims a lady, of say thirty, and covering her face as she spoke.

" Falling in love with her ! "

" Possible ? "

" Haven't you heard all about it ? "

This home question causes a flutter and a silence.

" I'll tell you, then," continues the gentleman in the long waistcoat, " I'll tell you all about the doings of ' Dion, the thunderbolt of war, and prince of modern wits.' *He*, the thunderbolt of war ?—preposterous ! *He*, the prince of wits ?—ludicrous ! He may be the king of coxcombs, the coryphæus of dandies—but that is all."

The gentlemen standing around listen to these words, with some amusement and more disgust. It is plain that some secret spite actuates the gentleman in the long waist-coat.

" Well, let us hear Mr. Effingham's crimes," says Laura.

" By all means," adds Isadora.

" Of course," says Myrtilla.

" He has been making himself ridiculous about that actress," continues the chronicler, " and I have even heard, designs to marry her."

The ladies make a movement, to express surprise and indignation, but after a moment's reflection, suppress this somewhat ambiguous exhibition of their feelings.

" He's been at the ' Raleigh Tavern,' making love to her for a month," continues the narrator.

" At the tavern ? "

" Yes, in town here."

" Did any one ever ! " says the lady of uncertain age.

" Never ! never ! " chime in the virtuous little damsels, shaking their heads solemnly.

" He has left his family," the gentleman in the long waistcoat goes on, indignantly, " and they are dying of grief "

" Oh, can it be !"

" Certainly, madam. Why are they not here to-night ?"

" Very true."

" Why is Clare Lee, the victim of his insincerity, away, pray tell me ! They are not here—they are not coming, madam."

At the same moment, the usher announces the squire, Miss Alethea, and Miss Clare Lee—Master Willie and Kate being too small to be seen, which the squire had warned them of. The squire is as bluff as ever, and makes his salutation to his Excellency with great cordiality—Clare is pale and absent, presenting thus a singular contrast to Henrietta, who enters a moment afterwards, brilliant, imposing, and smiling, like a queen receiving the homage of the nobility around her throne. She sweeps on, leaning on the arm of honest Jack Hamilton, and the party are swallowed in the crowd.

Let us return to the group, whose conversation the new arrivals had interrupted.

" Well, I was mistaken," says the gentleman in the long waistcoat, " but any one may see that Clare Lee is dying slowly ! "

At which affecting observation, the young ladies sigh and shake their heads.

" And just think what that man has thrown this divine creature away for," continues the censor morùm, " for a common actress !—an ordinary playing girl—tolerably pretty she may be, but vastly overrated—a mere thing of stage paint and pearl powder, strutting through her parts and ranting like an Amazon ! "

" I think her quite pretty," says Laura, " but it is too bad."

" Dreadful ! "

" Awful ! "

" Horrible ! "

" Shocking ! "

These are some of the comments on Mr. Effingham's conduct, from the elegant little dames.

" He is ashamed to show himself any where," continues the gentleman in the long waistcoat, " and only yesterday met me on the street, and in passing, turned away his head, plainly afraid that I would not speak in return, had he addressed me!"

At which words the gentlemen are observed to smile—knowing as they do, something of Mr. Champ Effingham's personal character and habits.

"He actually was afraid to look at me," says the censor, "and I am told keeps his room all day, or passes his time in the society of that Circe, yes, that siren who is only too fond of him, I am afraid—and I predict will make him marry her at last."

The ladies sigh, and agitate their fans with diamond-sparkling hands. They feel themselves very far above this shameless creature attempting to catch—as we now say—Mr. Effingham: they pity her, for such a thing never has occurred to them—no gentleman has ever been attractive enough for them to have designs upon his heart. And so they pity and despise Beatrice, for wishing to run away with her admirer.

"He is heartily ashamed of his infatuation, and I saw him last night in the theatre, positively afraid to look at the audience—but staring all the time at her," continues the small gentleman.

"But that is easy to understand, as he is in love," says Myrtilla, with a strong inclination to take the part of the reprobate against his enemy.

"No, no, madam," exclaims the censor, "he was really ashamed to look at the people, and took not the least notice of their frowns: he does not visit any where:—he knows he would not be received—he is afraid to show his face."

It seemed that the gentleman in the long waistcoat was doomed to have all his prophecies falsified; for at that moment, the usher announced in a loud voice, which attracted the attention of the whole company:

"Mr. Effingham and Miss Hallam!"

\

CHAPTER XLIX.

HOW MR. EFFINGHAM AND BEATRICE DANCED A MINUET AT THE
BALL.

Mr. Effingham entered under the full light of the central
chandelier, with Beatrice on his arm.   He carried his head
proudly erect, his eye was clear and steady, his lip calm and
only slightly sarcastic:—his whole carriage displayed perfect and unaffected self-possession.   The thousand eyes bent
on him vainly sought in his eyes, or lips, any thing going to
show that he felt conscious of the dreadful, the awful social
enormity, which he was committing.

Mr. Effingham was dressed with extraordinary richness.
He was always elegant in his costume, on that night he was
splendid.   His coat of rich cut velvet, was covered with
embroidery, and sparkled with a myriad of chased gold buttons; his lace ruffles at breast and wrist were point-de-venise,
his fingers were brilliant with rings, and his powdered hair
waved from his clear pale temples like a stream of silver
dust.   He looked like a courtier of the days of Louis XIV.,
dressed for a royal reception.

And how did Beatrice compare with this brilliant star
of fashion—this thunderbolt of war, and prince of modern
wits, as the muse in powdered hair and ruffles had characterized him.   Poor Beatrice was quite eclipsed by her cavalier.   Her simple, unassuming dress, of pearl color, looped
back with plain ribbon, and without a single flower, or any
ornament whatever, looked strangely out of place, thrown in
contrast with the brilliant silks, and velvets, and gold buttons, and diamonds of her companion: her modest, tender
face, and drooping head, with its unpretending coiffure,
looked quite insignificant beside the bold, defiant countenance of Mr. Effingham, which returned look for look, and
gaze for gaze, with an insulting nonchalance and easy hauteur.   We know how reluctantly Beatrice had come thither
—rather how bitter a trial it was to her, and we may understand why she looked pale and troubled, and—spite of the
fact that she had just encountered the gaze of a curious and
laughing audience, without any emotion—now felt her spirit

die within her. It was not because she shrunk from com
ment, half so much, as from the fact that each moment she
expected to see opposite to her the cold, pale face, and sick,
reproachful eyes of Clare Lee—of Clare, who had thrown
aside the prejudices of class, even forgot the jealousy of a
wronged and wretched rival, to press in her arms the rival
who had made all her woe, and that rival a common actress
It was the dread of her eye which made poor Beatrice trem
ble—this alone made her lip quiver and her brow droop.

His excellency Governor Fauquier came forward to wel
come his guests, but started at the sight of Beatrice, and
almost uttered an exclamation. For a moment he was staggered, and said nothing. This soon passed, however, and
by the time Mr. Effingham had accomplished his easy bow,
the governor was himself again, and like the elegant gentleman he was, made a low inclination before Beatrice. Then
he made a pleasant allusion to the weather—that much
abused subject, which has extricated so many perishing con
versations—and so, smiling agreeably, passed on.

Mr. Effingham advanced through the opening, on each
side of which extended a row of brilliant forms, sparkling
with lace and jewels, without any apparent consciousness
that he and his companion were the observed of all observers
—without being conscious, one would have said, of those
murmured comments which greeted, on every side, the
strange and novel scene. His manner to Beatrice, as he
bent down to speak to her, was full of respectful and chivalric feeling; his eye was soft, his lip smiling; the highest
lady of the land might well have felt an emotion of pleasure
in so elegant and noble an exhibition of regard. And this
was not affected by Mr. Effingham. By no means. We
have failed to convey a truthful impression of this young
gentleman's character, if the reader has not, before this
time, perceived that, with all his woful faults and failings,
Mr. Champ Effingham had much in his character of the
bold gentleman—the ancient knight. With those thousand
satirical or scornful eyes bent on her, Beatrice was dearer to
him than she had ever been before. Those elegant ladies
and gallant gentlemen were saying, with disdain, " a common
actress!" Well, he would espouse the cause of that girl
they scorned against them all, and treat her like a queen!

Never had she had more complete possession of his heart—never had his heart thrilled so deliciously at the contact of her hand, resting upon his arm.

As we have said, all drew back from the new comers, and they entered through an open space, like a king leading in his queen. Mr. Effingham looked round, with a cool and easy smile, and led the young girl to a seat, near some elderly dowagers, in turbans and diamonds, who had enthroned themselves in state, to watch their daughters, and see that those inexperienced creatures did not give too much encouragement to ineligible personages. As Beatrice sank into one of the red damask chairs, the surrounding chairs suddenly retreated on their rollers, and the turbans agitated themselves indignantly. Mr. Effingham smiled, with his easy, mocking expression, and observing that one of the diamond-decorated dowagers had dropped her fan, picked it up, and presented it to her, with a bow. The indignant lady turned away her head, with a frown.

"Ah," said Mr. Effingham, politely, "I was mistaken."

And fanning himself for a moment negligently, he placed the richly feathered instrument in the hand of Beatrice.

"My fan, if you please, sir," said the owner, suddenly flushing with indignant fire.

"Your fan, madam?" asked Mr. Effingham, with polite surprise.

"Yes, sir! you picked it up, sir!"

"A thousand pardons!" returned the young gentleman, with a courteous smile; "did I?"

"Yes, sir! that is it, sir! In the hands of that—"

"Oh, I understand," returned Mr. Effingham; and with a low inclination to Beatrice, he said, holding out his hand, "Will you permit me?"

The fan was restored by the young girl, just as she had taken it—unconsciously; and the dowager received it with the tips of her fingers, as if it had been contaminated. At the same moment, the band struck up a minuet, and two couples began to dance.

"How graceful the costume of our young ladies is becoming," said Mr. Effingham, bending down courteously to Beatrice, on the back of whose chair he leaned.

Beatrice murmured, "Yes."

"Much prettier, I think, than that of fifty years ago," continued Mr. Effingham, smiling, and glancing respectfully at the elderly and indignant ladies, who were listening.

The fans waved furiously.

"There is a fitness about the fresh, new style," he continued, "and it suits youth. I do not quarrel, however, with the former costume—turbans, and all that—it is also suitable—for elderly ladies."

And Mr. Effingham, smiling meekly, seemed perfectly unconscious of the storm muttering around him. As he spoke, honest Jack Hamilton, who had left the Riverhead and Effingham party in the other room, approached, and with a movement of his head, asked to be presented to Beatrice.

The young girl could hardly return his bow; she felt such anxiety, that the power of movement seemed almost gone from her.

"Mr. Hamilton is one of my best friends, Miss Hallam," said the young man, who had rewarded honest Jack with a bright smile; "but I shall claim your hand for the first minuet."

"Oh no," murmured Beatrice; "I do not wish to dance. Oh, sir! do not ask me to dance!"

And she stopped, overcome by her emotion.

"Oh, I insist upon it!" said Mr. Effingham, smiling; "it seems to me that that minuet there is abominably performed, and the music is shockingly fast."

"Hallo, Brother Champ!" here said a voice, at his elbow; "ain't I glad to see you!"

And turning round, Mr. Effingham found himself in front of Master Will; but Master Will was so metamorphosed that he scarcely recognized him. Willie had carried out his threat to Kate, and had donned a complete cavalier's costume. His hair was powdered, and gallantly tied into a queue behind; his coat was embroidered and heavy cuffed; his waistcoat nearly down to his knees; his frill irreproachable; his stockings of most approved scarlet silk; and his shoes rosetted with ribbon, and with such high red heels, that the young gentleman walked as it were on tiptoe. Altogether, with his long queue, and quick-moving little feet, Will resembled a large rat, decked out with ribbons, and

—conscious of his frill and the good society he moved in,—on his best behavior.

"I'm delighted to see you," added Will, holding out his hand.

Mr. Effingham shook hands.

"'Say," whispered Will, "is that the girl you're in love with?"

Will started back before the tremendous frown of his brother; for Beatrice heard the words, and turned away her head. Mr. Effingham raised his finger, and was about to say something that would have annihilated the youthful cavalier, when suddenly he felt a soft, warm, little hand take his own, and turning round, he saw little Kate's bright, smiling face.

"Oh! I wanted to come before, but couldn't," she said, leaning her bright little head against his side; "I'm so glad to see you."

And she pressed the hand she held harder.

Mr. Effingham's cynical smile became soft, his head drooped toward the child; but suddenly Kate recognized Beatrice, who had been concealed from her by Jack Hamilton, motionless, coughing, trying to converse;—there was the lady of the tavern—the actress—the person who had caused them so much grief. She drew back sorrowfully, and her little face was covered with a shadow. Mr. Effingham saw it—divined the reason—and his face too was overshadowed. He was about to speak, when—the first dance having terminated some moments before—a second minuet was commenced by the band.

"Come!" said he to Beatrice; and taking her hand, he raised her, and led her forward.

"Not so fast," he said, with a gesture of his hand, to the musicians; "I cannot dance a minuet to a gavotte tune."

And he entered into the broad, open space with Beatrice the mark of a thousand eyes.

The group which we have paid some attention to already —that group which had expressed such delight at the verses of the accomplished (colonial) Earl of Dorset, and who had uttered such a variety of comment on Dion, Cordelia, and Beatrice—the group of which Myrtilla, Isadora, and the

Long waistcoat, were the shining stars—now gazed in horror at the presumption and effrontery of Mr. Effingham.

"Just look!" said Sylvia; "he is positively going to dance the second minuet!"

"With that actress!" said Isadora.

"The playing girl!" echoed Leonella, horrified.

"While we must wait!" added Myrtilla, with some show of reason.

"It is presumptuous!"

"It is shocking!"

"It is insulting!"

"It is outrageous!"

"I will not stand it!" here interposed the gentleman in the long waistcoat, boiling with indignation.

"Just look!" said Sylvia; "did anybody ever see such ridiculous respect and ceremony in a gentleman before?"

"You would think that she was a queen, and he a subject!"

"What a bow!"

"See how he takes her hand, bending to her waist!"

"Ridiculous!"

"But he is very graceful," hazarded Myrtilla, who, as we know, defended faintly Mr. Effingham's character, when it had been attacked by the censor.

"Well, suppose he does bow elegantly," said Isadora, spitefully, envying Beatrice her cavalier.

"True: we do not wish to have him for a partner," said Myrtilla, who was something of a wit.

"There, look at her!"

"Theatrical!"

"Affected!"

"Stiff!"

"Frightened!"

"She looks as if she was going to cry."

"Poor thing!" said Myrtilla; "I think she does not want to dance."

"Does not want to?"

"Pshaw!"

"She is too artful for that!"

"But look! her eyes are moist, as she courtseys, and they seem to beseech him for something," said Myrtilla.

" What odious artfulness ! " cried Sylvia ; " she pretends to look as if she was not dying for joy at being the partner of the fascinating Mr. Effingham."

" I suppose she would not ally herself with his family; they are too low," said Isadora, spitefully ; " may be she has refused his hand."

" Quite probable ! "

" Oh, of course ! "

" Doubtless ! "

And the pretty little damsels curled their handsome little lips ironically.

' She is an odious-looking creature," said Leonella ; " did any one ever see such evidences of low birth ? "

" Oh, I am sure you are wrong ! " cried Myrtilla, too generous to keep silent ; " I think she is very sweet."

" Well, she is not so bad, but—"

" Tolerable, but—"

" A pretty arm, but—"

" Fine eyes, still—"

" Graceful, yet—"

" I think she is an odious, artful, designing creature, but not at all too bad for her partner," here interposed the gentleman in the long waistcoat ; and so the colloquy went on.

Almost every group in the room was uttering something similar to that which we have just listened to. The entrance of Mr. Effingham into the open space, to dance the second minuet of the evening, had caused an awful sensation As he glided through the stately dance to the slow rolling music, bowing profoundly, with his tender, lordly smile, touching the young girl's hand with chivalric respect, pressing his cocked hat to his heart at each inclination of his handsome and brilliant head, all eyes had been bent upon him, all tongues busy with him. And these eyes and tongues had taken equal note of Beatrice. The young girl moved through the old stately dance with that exquisite grace and ease with which she performed every evolution, and her tender, agitated face, as we have seen, tempered the wrath of many an indignant damsel. After the first burst of surprise and anger, the gentlemen, too, began to take the part—as Virginia gentlemen always have done, and always will do—of the lonely girl environed by so many hostile eyes and slighting comments. They forgot the prepossessions of rank, the prejudices of class—no longer remembered that the young actress occupied upon the floor a position to which she was not entitled;—they only saw a woman who had all the rest against her; and their sympathy was nearly powerful enough to make them lose sight of Mr. Effingham's defiance.

A murmur rose as the music stopped, and he led her to a seat; and then a species of undulation in the crowd, near the entrance into the next room, attracted attention. Mr. Effingham had his back turned, however, and did not observe this incident. He was talking to Beatrice in a low tone.

" You see," he said, with his calm, nonchalant voice—" you see, Beatrice, that this superb society, which you fancied you would find yourself so much out of place in, is not so very extraordinary after all. I think that I hazard nothing in saying that the second minuet was better than the first; you are, indeed, far more beautiful than that little dame, whose ancestors, I believe, came over with the conqueror—Captain Smith."

And his cynical smile grew soft, as he gazed on the tender, anxious face.

" It was not so dreadful an ordeal," he added, " though I must say we were the subject of much curiosity. I observed a group, criticising me, which pleased me. There was a fiery young gentleman in a long waistcoat, whom I offended by not returning his bow some months since—and I believe he was the orator of the occasion."

With which words, Mr. Effingham's lip curled.

" See! the very same group—every body, in fact, is gazing at us. Let them! you are lovelier than them all."

And Mr. Effingham raised his head proudly and looked around like an emperor. But Beatrice felt her heart die within her: that minuet had exhausted her strength; each moment she expected to see the pale cold face of Clare looking at her. Mr. Effingham observed how faint she was, and leaning over took a smelling-bottle from the hand of the old dowager, who had dropped the fan—bowing and smiling.

He presented it to Beatrice, but she put it away with the back of her hand: whereupon Mr. Effingham, with a second bow, restored it to the dowager, who, aghast at his impudence, beaten by his superior coolness, and overwhelmed with rage, took it without knowing what she did. Mr. Effingham thereupon turned, smiling, to Beatrice again :

"There seems to be something going on yonder," he said, leaning on her chair, and directing the young girl's attention to the flashing waves of the crowd, which moved to and fro like foaming billows, in the light of the brilliant chandeliers. Beatrice felt an indefinable and vague fear take possession of her heart. At the same moment, Master Willie came pushing and elbowing through the crowd.

"Cousin Clare is sick!" he said, "you'd better go and see her, brother Champ. She liked to fainted just now!"

Beatrice understood all.

"Oh, sir! let me go!" she cried, "go out with me! I shall die here!—oh, I cannot—that dance nearly killed me —and now!—Oh, sir, have pity, give me your arm!"

And rising with a hurried movement, she placed her hand on Mr. Effingham's arm. That gentleman smiled bitterly.

"Yes," he said, "this is the tragedy after the comedy! I understand this fainting."

"Oh, sir, have pity—I must go!" cried Beatrice, "I will go alone!"

Mr. Effingham held her back, and hesitated. At last he said :

"Well, madam—as you please—I have had a pleasant minuet—I will go."

And with the same cold, defiant ease, he led the young girl across the room, and issued forth into the open air.

Without speaking they traversed the walk, with its lindens and variegated lanterns, passed through the crowd of grooms and coachmen, who made way respectfully, and entered the carriage which had brought them. In ten minutes it stopped at the Raleigh, and Mr. Effingham, with a strange throbbing of the heart, handed the young girl out. At that moment he loved her so madly, so defiantly, that he would have given the universe to clasp her to his bosom.

He knew how such a proceeding would be received, however, and led her in silence to her room, where Mr. Manager Hallam was sitting by the fire, toasting his enormous feet.

Then with a bow he closed the door, and returned to the governor's palace.

CHAPTER L.

MR. EFFINGHAM RETURNS TO THE BALL AND DISCOURSES ON THE SUBJECT OF WAISTCOATS.

MR. EFFINGHAM made his re-entrance into the ball-room, with the same disdainful calmness which had characterized him at first. If as many eyes were not turned toward him, that was because he was no longer accompanied by the young actress—was a single cavalier.

Near the door he encountered that group, which we have twice listened to ; and he approached with his satirical and careless smile.

" Ah, really, " he said, to Sylvia, " I am charmed to see you ! Why, how adorably you are looking ! "

And turning round before Miss Sylvia could reply, he added to Leonella,

" Your coiffure is charming ! "

The expression upon the faces of Miss Sylvia and Leonella was so ludicrous, that Myrtilla burst out laughing.

" Ah ! " said Mr. Effingham, in his most petit maître tones, " how could I have so long neglected to place my homage at the feet of the queen of beauty ! "

Myrtilla laughed at this languid and elegant address to her.

" I cannot pardon myself," continued Mr. Effingham, arranging his drop curls; " if Phillis scorns her Corydon, and beats him with her crook, he cannot complain ; his humbled eyes dare not rise higher than the ribbons fluttering on the bodice of his pastoral princess."

The fashion of the time, must plead Mr. Effingham's excuse for this extraordinary speech. Our lovely fore-mothers relished' these rural allusions, and started with delight at the mention of Chloes, Phillises and crooks. And so Myrtilla made a laughing courtesey : and Mr. Effingham turned away. He found himself face to face with the small gentleman who had criticised him so pleasantly, and whose criticism his quick eye had seen reflected in his face, as the young man had danced opposite to Beatrice.

" Oh ! really a great pleasure ! " said he, now, to this gentleman, " are you here too ? "

"Yes, sir," said the small gentleman, sullenly.

"And with as long a waistcoat as ever," continued Mr Effingham, smiling.

"Sir!"

"Yes, a pleasant ball—but the society is somewhat mixed," said Mr. Effingham, with courteous smiles, "things are becoming changed. Is it not so, ladies? Gay, adorable shepherdesses, clad in the bloom and freshness of the spring —am I not right?"

"Yes, you are right, sir," said Sylvia, tossing her little head : a manœuver which Mr. Effingham rightly attributed to the fact that the damsel meant to allude to Beatrice.

"Why, nothing could be plainer," he continued.

"Nothing, sir!" here interposed the small gentleman, with a frown. Mr. Effingham slightly turned round, as much as to say "did you presume to reply to me, sir?" and went on superciliously.

"Very mixed—shockingly," he said; "every body is beginning to mingle in society, and we now see all descriptions of costume. I do not complain of the simple dress of the lower class, yonder—I like it. What I allude to is different. I refer to those individuals who endeavor to make up by splendor what they lack in good-breeding, and who load their dress with all manner of remarkable and extraordinary ornament—"

Myrtilla began to laugh, mischievously glancing at the small gentleman, who winced.

"Shocking taste, and shows their condition," added Mr. Effingham ; "they even persist in wearing those abominable waistcoats, as brilliant as the rainbow, and nearly as long— invariable indication of the parvenu."

And Mr. Effingham smiled amiably at the gentleman in the long waistcoat, who was furious—raised his hand with an air inexpressibly foppish, to the ladies, and moved on.

He encountered Jack Hamilton, who, in the midst of a group of foxhunters like himself, was laughing and talking at the top of his voice.

"Oh, here is Effingham!" said Hamilton, "where is Miss Hallam?"

Mr. Effingham replied, calmly:

"She got tired, and I returned with her. You see,

however, that I have made my appearance again—my friends, I fear, had not an opportunity to speak to me."

And his cold eye told Hamilton very plainly what he meant. Honest Jack laughed.

" By George ! I believe they are all your very excellent friends by this time," he said ; " they calculated without their Virginia blood, when they spoke of resenting Miss Hallam's appearance. They forgot that they were a dozen men matched against one woman."

" And a sword, Hamilton."

" Come, come," said Hamilton, "forget that, and don't let the fellows here, who are jolly boys, as you know, into our little secrets. They are waiting to be recognized by Monseigneur."

This was true ; and when Mr. Effingham held out his hand to the party, who were all slightly acquainted with him, it was taken with hearty warmth, and not a few rough and sincere compliments paid to Beatrice, though they did not scruple to say as plainly that there " was no use in bringing her."

In consideration of their good feeling, our hero pardoned this : and then leaning on Hamilton's arm, passed on. Ten steps brought him in front of his Excellency—and that gentleman, no longer checkmated by the presence of Beatrice, turned away with great hauteur. Mr. Effingham only smiled, and passed on, leaving Jack Hamilton behind.

He went through the room with his cold, disdainful smile, seeking his adversaries :—strange to say, however, they seemed to be far from those ferocious personages described by Mr. Hamilton. He could find nothing to take umbrage at, and so he returned towards the door. The simple fact was, that, proud and disdainful as Mr. Effingham was, he feared to encounter the eye of his father, or of Henrietta, or Alethea, or Clare. He had understood the cause of the young girl's sudden faintness perfectly well. She had entered from the second room, and seen him dancing a minuet with that rival, whom she had so generously forgiven, and clasped to her pure, tender heart—and though Mr. Effingham was ignorant of the fact of the interview, he was at no loss to understand Clare's emotion.

This was the reason why he feared to meet her—and yet

with that dread was mingled a strange desire; as if he wished to stand before her and give her look for look, and break her heart and his own.   Mr. Effingham began to feel a diseased craving for excitement—he had become accustomed to acute and painful emotions; he fed on them as his daily bread.

Fortunately this insane desire was doomed to disappointment.   Clare had left the ball almost at the same moment with himself and Beatrice : had entered the Effingham chariot with the squire and his party just as his own carriage drove off.

Once, as Mr. Effingham drew near the door, he encountered the gaze of Henrietta, who had chosen to remain with Hamilton : and with rage in his heart he made her a low and exaggerated bow.   Then passing by the gentleman in the long waistcoat, with a meaning look full of disdain and menace, he struck his hat upon his head, and rushed, almost, from the room.

His infatuation for Beatrice had never so closely approached madness as at that moment.

CHAPTER LI.

BEATRICE AND THE MANAGER.

HAVING thus briefly related the manner in which Mr. Effingham returned to the ball, and sought for adventures there like a second Don Quixote, though without the good fortune of the noble gentleman of La Mancha, we shall now go back to the moment when Beatrice re-entered her room, after the trying ordeal she had passed through.

As we have said, Mr. Manager Hallam was sitting placidly by the fire, which was far from uncomfortable at that advanced season of the autumn. Upon Beatrice's entrance he turned round, smiling.   Beatrice was in tears, and sobbing.

"What in heaven's name is all this crying about?" asked the manager, who, having emptied his nightly two bottles, was in a most contented state of mind; "you are always crying, Beatrice!"

" Oh, father ! " she said, and then stopped.

" Well, well," he said, impatiently, " speak."

" I am not well."

" How ? "

" It was killing to me."

" Bah ! every thing kills you, but you always continue alive, as I recollect hearing the great Congreve say, once on a time."

" I am really sick, sir.".

" Was the ball brilliant ? "

" Yes, sir."

" Was Mr. Effingham attentive ? "

" Yes, sir."

" Did the set-up women treat you badly ? "

" No, sir."

" You were treated politely ? "

" Yes, sir."

" And danced ? "

" Yes, sir."

" The governor bowed to you ? "

" Very politely, sir."

" Then in the name of all the fiends what are you crying about, daughter ?   You are really a very extraordinary girl You go to a brilliant ball, with a handsome and attentive cavalier ; you are not treated badly by the fine ladies, but very kindly ; you danced among the best, the governor of Virginia made you a polite bow, and after all this, which would turn the head of any common girl with joy, you come back crying, instead of laughing, sorrowful instead of happy. Basta ! as the great Congreve was wont to say, you are foolish ! "

Beatrice sat down, wiping her eyes, and murmuring the words she had read in Kate's Bible, before going—" Oh, Lord, my strength and my Redeemer ! "

" What is that you say ? " asked Hallam, stretching his feet luxuriously on the fender, and looking with muddy eyes at the ceiling.

" Nothing, sir," said the young girl, trying to command her voice.

" Beatrice," said Hallam, " you are perfectly ridiculous · you are throwing away, by your folly and obstinacy, the most excellent offer—I say it without hesitation—which was ever made to an actress. . One would really think that you were a duchess, with your rent-roll and estates, instead of the daughter of an actor, like myself."

Beatrice listened with a strange feeling to these words. Again that martial face rose for her from the far southern land ; again she saw the soldier dying, and her tears flowed afresh.

"Instead of acting as you should do," continued Hallam, working himself into anger, "instead of being to this young man the brilliant and fascinating woman which you are—instead of managing him, and spurring him on, and attracting him—instead of giving him hope, and you know his intentions are perfectly honorable—instead of this, what are you doing? You are making your eyes and face thin with weeping, you are growing ugly from grief at having a splendid position in society thrust on you—you are defying my wishes, madam! You know I wish you to marry this young fellow. Answer; are you not disobedient?" and the manager pushed back his chair, angrily.

"Oh, father, father!" she cried, carried away by her feelings, "I do not wish to be disobedient. I will do all you wish me to do, but that! I will work day and night, and never complain—but do not, do not ask me to marry, or encourage this man! I do not like him, I shudder when he approaches; all my good traits of character—and, indeed, I have some—become changed to bad in his presence. He repels me ; something tells me that he will be my curse yet! Oh, I cannot do as you command—I cannot smile and make myself attractive, and show him that I like him—for I do not! I should be the most miserable person living, were I his wife!"

"Really!" cried the manager. "Truly, madam, the countess is in her tantrums! You would be the most miserable creature alive, as his wife?"

"Oh, miserable, sir!"

"He repels your ladyship!"

"I tremble when he comes near me!" she cried, weeping.

"You would not marry him?"

"Oh, no ; for it would break the heart of a pure girl, who loves him, and would have been his wife, if I had never seen him!"

" Really, you are very magnanimous ! Pray, who is **that**
girl ? "

" Miss Lee, his cousin."

" What does her fate concern you, pray, madam ? "

" She forgave me, and took me in her arms, and kissed
me. Oh, God is my witness, that I would rather cut off my
right hand than make her suffer again ! "

" Where the devil did you enact that fine drama ? " said
the manager, frowning.

" I went to see her."

" You ? "

" Yes, sir ; at her home, near Mr. Effingham's."

" And, no doubt, told her how much you hated him ;
that you were not to blame if her lover was infatuated about
you ; that you had repulsed him, insulted him, asked him
to leave you, exhausted every means to make him abandon
his unworthy project, of marrying you—"

" Yes, sir—I did—"

" You did—' Yes, sir—I did !' sneered the manager ;
" you had the boldness to go and say that to a person, who
will tell him every thing—"

" Oh, no, sir ! for—"

" In future, madam," said Hallam, angrily, " you do
not ride out without an escort. You might be guilty of
worse things than this audacious proceeding."

At this unworthy insinuation, Beatrice felt the blood
rush to her face, and her heart begin to throb with bitter
and rebellious thoughts.

" Oh, father ! " she cried, bursting into tears, " how can
you be so cruel ? "

" Well," he said, " I was wrong ; but your conduct is
bad enough, madam. I suppose this child was at the ball—
his sweetheart ? "

" Yes, sir. Miss Lee was present "

" How did he treat her ? "

" He did not see her."

" Where is he now ? "

" He went back, I believe."

" To see her ! " cried the manager ; " your prospects are
ruined ! Beatrice, from this moment—if it is not too late—
you act just as I bid you ! I will have none of your dis-

13 •

obedience in future, madam ! You shall not beard me with
your cryings, and entreaties, and childish tears. You shall
not ruin your own and my fortune in life. I command you,
madam, to behave yourself in future, better. Take care ! "

Beatrice felt her rebellious heart grow more bitter; she
no longer thought of little Kate's Bible.

" I will have no nonsense, madam ! " continued her father,
in a rage. " I will not have a child like you, setting at
naught all my wishes, and overturning all my plans in life,
by your ridiculous folly. In future, you take no more rides
to meet your lovers, or your lovers' sweethearts. Understand me—I will not be dictated to by my own child ! As
your father, I command you, in future, to give encouragement to this young man. Don't frown and look rebellious
at me—I will not submit to any folly ! If you choose to
act as you have done, I choose to tell you the truth. You
have ridden, Heaven knows where, to see, Heaven knows
who. You have nearly ruined your prospects; he is now
gone back, and if what you say about your interview with
her is true, she will tell him all, and he will never look at
you again ! Madam ! " cried the manager in a fury, " I
shall not endure this ! As your father, I command you to
obey me ! Take care—you have some silly religious feeling, and that feeling will tell you, that if you dare to dis-
obey your father, God will take his account of you. I am
that father—see that you obey me ! "

The young girl's feelings were worked up to the avowal,
her heart was agitated by rebellious and obstinate anger,
but she could not throw off, all at once, her habit of affection and obedience. Still she could not remain silent, and
she cried, with passionate tears : " Oh, you are not my
father ! God has revealed to me my real father. Mr.
Effingham brought here this frock ! " And with a quick
movement, she drew from a drawer the child's garment.
" That God, you speak of, revealed my birth to me ! " she
continued ; " this letter has told me all. My father was
Ralph Waters ; my name is Beatrice Waters ! " And overwhelmed with her emotion, the young girl sunk into a seat,
almost fainting.

The manager snatched the frock and the letter from her
in a violent rage   The truth all at once flashed on him—he

had no one to blame but himself, and with a furious hand he
tore his hair.

" Yes ! " he cried, in a violent rage, " yes ! you have
dared to read that letter ! you have dared to pry into what
was my secret ! "

" Oh, it was mine ! " murmured Beatrice, bitterly.

" You have dared ! "

And Mr. Manager Hallam again tore his hair.

" I could not help it, father ! " cried Beatrice, calling on
God to calm her wicked feeling of rebellion, as she spoke ;
" I felt compelled to read that letter ! I did not mean— "

And she stopped, choked by her sobs. The manager
sank into the chair from which he had risen in the excess of
his rage.

" Oh, do not be angry with me, father ! " cried Beatrice,
burying her head in his bosom. " I did not mean to do
wrong ! I am your daughter still. Do not frown at me."

The manager slowly became calmer.

" I love you as much as ever," said Beatrice. " I felt
wrong just now, when you spoke such harsh words—so unjust !—but now I am calm again ! "

The manager began to cry—doubtless, like the great Congreve.

" Oh, father ! I am so wretched ! " exclaimed Beatrice.
" I did not mean to make you suffer ! "

" To be defied by one whom I have always loved ! " ejacu-
lated Hallam, half seriously, half from policy, giving way
afresh to his emotion ; " whom I raised from infancy, trying
to find her family—defied by her ! "

" Oh, I did not mean to defy you ! indeed I did not !—
forgive me, father ! I am your daughter still ! "

" I am a poor, childless old man ! " muttered the manager,
with his favorite choking cry.

" I will be your child ! " cried Beatrice, weeping passionately. " I will love you as dearly as I always have done,
you know, father—you have been so good to me ! What
matter if I am not your daughter in reality. What matter if I am the daughter of Ralph Waters—the brother of
Charles's father." He started, but not with surprise ; he
had felt that John Waters must be Beatrice's uncle, for
some days. " Why should I leave you, who have been so

kind to me, because I was born in Malta, where my father
died, and am not your daughter? You are my real father—
God sent you! My real name is Beatrice Waters; but I will
be Beatrice Hallam still. Oh, do not cry—you break my
heart!"

She again buried her face in his bosom; but, hearing a
noise, raised it again. Mr. Effingham stood before her, and
had plainly heard the words she had just uttered.

The scene which followed was one of those which are best
left to the reader's imagination. The pen can only describe
passions, or trace utterances to a certain point—beyond that
it yields the field to the painter, who alone can make the
highest passions, the most conflicting emotions, eloquent.
We may imagine the feelings of Mr. Effingham, on hearing
from the gloomy and agitated manager, that his own act had
revealed to Beatrice the secret of her birth; we may com-
prehend the rage of the young man on finding that, by his
own agency, Beatrice had come to know that Charles Waters
was her cousin, his uncle her father; we may further understand the despair of Hallam, the terrible agitation of Beatrice—we cannot describe them.

When Mr. Effingham went away to his room that night,
he was a prey to one of his silent and sombre rages; he had
raised this new barrier himself. The instrument of fate, and
unknown to himself, his hand had opened that sealed book;
and what the young girl had read had for ever separated her
from him. That rival—bitterly hated before, now far more
bitterly—would be her lawful protector; and whether in
their duel he fell or conquered, nothing would be gained. A
thousand tumultuous thoughts like these chased themselves
through his mind—we cannot trace them—it is a repulsive
subject, and we pass on.

CHAPTER LII.

TWO WATER-DOGS.

MR. EFFINGHAM spent a sleepless night, and rose more agitated than ever. With a mind supernaturally active from

feverous emotion, he embraced at a glance all his latter life.
He followed the history of his infatuation for Beatrice from
his first meeting with her in the forest, near Effingham Hall,
through the scenes at the theatre, at her apartment, in the
street, at the ball, to this last final denouement, which had
came like the blast of the trumpet and the roar of the drum,
to finish all before the curtain fell upon the drama.

He surveyed with a lightning-like glance his present position—the state of his mind and life. He felt more than ever
that he must conquer that diabolical angel who had scorned
him, or die. She must yield to him, or he would yield to
her, and pass from the earth. He raved and tore his hair,
and revolved in his gloomy and agitated mind a thousand
plans. All were rejected after a moment's reflection, if
that word could be applied to the operations of the young
man's mind.

He rose in despair, and the room seemed too close to
breathe in. He went out, gloomy, and breathing heavily.
Suddenly, as he entered the passage, a loud, hearty voice
made the windows jar, and, turning round, he found himself
opposite to the stranger.

"Good day, comrade," cried the soldier. "What!
gloomy on such a morning?"

"I am not well, sir," said Mr. Effingham, coldly.

"Come, drink a cup of this abominable Rhenish they
vend at this hostelry," said the soldier, laughing. "You see
me in excellent spirits. I am myself again!"

Indeed, the soldier was no longer cabined, cribbed, and
confined in the tight, foppish suit he had originally worn, but
was clad in the elegant military suit which we have seen
Mr. Effingham return in, on the night he left Williamsburg
for York. The costume seemed infinitely more appropriate
for the stranger's vigorous and martial figure; the heavily-
laced but dark uniform set of his person to great advantage,
and his fine face, with its keen, dark eye and long black
moustache, appeared to far more advantage beneath the rich
Flanders hat. The stranger, in his present proper costume,
was the model of a soldier.

To his merry observation, that he felt in excellent spirits,
Mr. Effingham made no reply.

"Why, see now, you are moody, comrade! That is not

the philosophic state of a *bon soldat*, whether in the ranks, or in life, which, *parbleu!* seems to me as much a battle as Lissa, Glatz, or Minden.   Come! hold your head up!   I have good news for you!"

"What news, sir?" said Mr. Effingham, still cold and gloomy.

"Why, I am just about to go and arrange the details of our little affair:—that is to say, I am going to see Mr. Waters—brother of Ralph: an honest straightforward fellow was Ralph, though I say it, *parbleu!*"

"Well, sir!" said Mr. Effingham, already tired of his companion.

"*Arrange*, is not precisely the word, companion," continued the soldier, caressing the black fringe on his lip; "I believe the day after to-morrow is fixed upon—though the time, as all else, should have been left to us, the wheel-horses —the seconds.   Your friend is Mr.——, you omitted to tell me, comrade, in the multitude of affairs we had to arrange : —you will recollect that you omitted it."

"Say at once, sir, that having a duel forced on me, I had not fixed every thing.   Well, sir, I now say further, that I must defer the whole affair for a day or two longer.   Circumstances," and Mr. Effingham's lip curled, "render me somewhat cooler in the quarrel."

The soldier looked keenly at the young man—but a single glance convinced him, that this delay did not spring from backwardness to match himself in combat against an adversary.   There was the unmistakable fire in the eye; and fighting was a satisfaction to such a man, he felt.

"Perhaps you object to your antagonist," said the soldier, coolly.

"No, sir! I do not!"

"Come," said the stranger, "suppose we have a little bout here on the staircase.   You really seem desirous of trying my ferrara, comrade."

"I have no such desire, sir," replied Mr. Effingham coldly, "and if my tone is harsh, it is because I am in no humor to answer questions, or converse.   I am not well, sir—arrange this matter as you choose.   Mr. John Hamilton will act for me—but I repeat, that I will not meet Mr. Waters for three days or more."

" Well, well, companion, I can arrange that. By heaven
you must have something on your mind, but that is not my
affair. I'll empty a cup of Jamaica—I'm done with the
Rhenish—and get into my saddle. *Bon jour—au revoir.*"

And the soldier, curling his moustache, and humming a
rude song, took his way down the staircase, his huge sword
rattling against the banisters, and making with the jingle
of his heavily-rowelled spurs, a martial sort of music elo
quent of camps.

Mr. Effingham, gazing moodily after him, observed tha.
he stopped suddenly at the foot of the stairs. A gentleman
dressed in black had struck against him, owing to the fact
that the said gentleman refused to yield one inch of the
way. Then Mr. Effingham heard the important and pom
pously-uttered words :

" You should have more respect for the clergy, sir."

And no less a personage than Parson Tag came up, and
with a cold bow passed into the apartment, next to his own
—that one in which we have heard the man in the red cloak
play his violin. The young man gazed after him moodily,
and with a bitter smile ; and hesitated whether he should return to his room, or descend. A glance at the bright sunshine of the clear cold autumn day decided him, and to
escape its brilliance, he went into his apartment again, with
a mocking and gloomy face painful to behold.

Then he sat down, as he had done on that day when
little Kate had come to see him, and again embraced at a
single glance, the sad and gloomy horizon of his life, where
no sun shone, no birds sang. Again he went over the path
which he had trodden—revived those bitter joys, those delicious agonies he had suffered. Full of gloomy wonder, he
weighed all that had taken place in his acquaintance with
Beatrice, and as before, that fatal, unavoidable question came
to him, where would all this end ? He had now defied society for her, and he was convinced that he stood lower in
her regard than ever—he had given up all for her, she dis-
dained him the more for his sacrifice. As his love increased,
she grew colder—he was rushing toward the abyss ! And
that revelation which he had been the instrument of !
Charles Waters was her cousin, and she loved him, perhaps !
He had given that man the right to watch over her, to defend

her. Thenceforward there was a new and more irritating
obstacle.

"Woe to him, if he crosses my path before we stand
face to face, sword in hand!" he muttered, with a sombre
and threatening flash of his proud eyes.

As he spoke, a tap came at his door, and a servant entered.

"Well?" said the young man, raising his head with a
movement which frightened the negro nearly out of his
wits, "what now?"

"Two boatmen, Mas' Effnum—say they want to see
you."

"To the devil with them!" he said: but suddenly he
paused—a light shone from his eyes. Already his mind
had conceived the outline of a strange, desperate, and audacious project.

"About my sail-boat? Yes; go and bring them here
—go!"

And he motioned the negro feverishly toward the door.
In two minutes the door opened again, and the rough-looking
watermen entered, and with their caps in their hands, louted
to the young man, standing respectfully on the threshold.

"Close the door and come in!" he said, gloomily: the
door was shut, and obedient to a sign from Mr. Effingham,
the watermen approached.

"About my sail-boat, I suppose?" he said, curtly.

"Yes, your honor," replied the water-dog, who seemed to
be spokesman.

"Where is she?"

"Down at the landing, by Townes', your honor."

"You got up to-day?"

"Jest so, your honor—and she's as tight a little craft,
as ever walked the water—swifter'n a waterfowl."

Mr. Effingham looked strangely at the rough watermen,
who turned their tarpaulins in their hands, and coughed respectfully behind them.

"Is she fully equipped?" he said.

"Out and out, your honor. I never see a jollier craft;
and she carries sail enough for a merchantman. I was a
sayin' to mate here only jest now, 'at I never hearn o' such
a thing afore."

"And she is down there?"

"At Townes', your honor."

"All ready?"

"Ready as a squall, when the rags are taut."

Mr. Effingham looked at the water-dogs again with the same strange expression.

"Your name is Junks, is it not?" he said, motioning to the man to approach.

"Yes, your honor, and mate's name is Jackson."

"Very well—you are poor?"

"Poor as a lean cat, sir."

"Would you like to make fifty pistoles?"

The water-dogs opened their eyes.

"I'd sell myself to the devil for it," said the spokesman, laughing.

"No; I wish you to sell yourself to me," said Mr. Effingham, with haughty coldness. "Is this weather too cold for a night run down the river?"

"Your honor is jokin'—it ain't warm, but ta'int nothin' to the likes o' us."

"Whoever I brought, then, you are willing to shut your eyes?"

"Oh, your honor's got a frolic on hand? That suits me to a circumstance."

"And me, too, your honor," said mate, in a mumbling voice from behind his thick woollen comfort.

Mr. Effingham, looking keenly at these men, saw that they were such as could be bought for much less than fifty pistoles. Then he was silent. A struggle seemed to be going on in his mind—his brow flushed, then grew pale, and his cheeks were covered with a cold sweat. The water-dogs looked at him wonderingly, for his eyes were not a pleasant sight—they were like lurid lightning.

"Wait here," he said, suddenly, as he heard a door open and close without. "Don't stir until I return."

And hastily putting on his hat, he went out, closed the door, and crossing the passage, entered the room of Beatrice.

CHAPTER LIII.

THE LAST INTERVIEW BETWEEN BEATRICE AND MR. EFFINGHAM.

BEATRICE had just come in, and was sitting in front of the fire, gazing sadly and thoughtfully into the blaze, when Mr. Effingham's entrance caused her to turn round. For a moment these two persons who sustained toward each other such strange and anomalous relations, maintained perfect silence.

At last Mr. Effingham, pale and gloomy, yet gazing at the young girl with passionate love, said abruptly, and in a low tone—

"We meet again; I trust you are well after the ball."

"Yes, sir," said Beatrice, in a tone of quiet, uncomplaining sorrow; "I do not think I feel worse than usual."

"You do not ask me how I am," he said, with painful earnestness.

"Pardon me, sir," she said, in the same low, sad tones. "I hope you are well."

"No; I am far from it—I feel as if my brain was bursting."

"I am sorry, sir—sincerely."

"You are so cold," he said, leaning on the mantelpiece, and gazing at her with fixed, stony eyes. "You have no pity on me."

"*I* pity *you*, Mr. Effingham!"

"Oh, you know what I mean," he said. "We know each other now. I mean that you meet all my love with coldness—a freezing coldness; or, if not, with cold indifference—with contempt! I mean that you do not cast your proud eyes down on the man who suffers, kneeling at your feet, because you despise him and his love. I mean that you have nothing but scorn for me, when I have nothing but passionate, devouring love for you. I mean that I love you —love you with all the power of my soul, with all my strength, with my whole being, and that you disdain to speak to me!"

"Indeed I do not, sir—oh, no! If I have been harsh or cruel, or unwomanly, I beg you to pardon it. I believe that I have spoken harsh words to you sometimes—I regret them. I have no right to scorn any human being, sir. God does not approve of such feelings. Pardon me!"

The earnest, low-toned voice went to his poor, bruised heart—her soft, sorrowful face took away all his anger.

"Oh, why will you not love me?" he said, with painful earnestness. "Why does your heart still remain closed to me? See me here at your feet, Beatrice, with my pride broken, my wilfulness all gone, seeing you only in the uni verse! You are to me the sole light which shines on the dark waters of my life—you know it, why so indifferent to me? Oh, I love you so passionately! so purely! I follow you with yearning eyes—I live in you and through you! Why still despise me?"

"I do not, sir—I must not feel so toward any human being."

"I have been criminally harsh—I have repented of it in the long hours of the gloomy night—repented bitterly."

"I have forgotten it, sir," said Beatrice.

"Then, for pity's sake, do not look at me so coldly!"

"I am not well to-day, sir."

He looked at her with inexpressible love, and said:

"Did you only know how much I suffer when you suffer!"

"I do not complain, sir.

"You must have had a trying ordeal last night"

"Yes; very trying."

"You were the queenliest of them all," he said, gazing on her with passionate love and pride. "Why should you not give me the right to lead you forth in the eyes of the world, as I did before that assembly?"

"Mr. Effingham, I cannot be your wife," she said. "We have said much upon this subject. It only distresses me."

"Why, Beatrice? Give me some reason for my wretch-edness."

A deep flush covered the young girl's sad pale brow, a she thought of Charles Waters.

"We are not suited to each other," she said.

He saw the blush, and his own brow flushed. His super-naturally active mind discerned the hidden reason—left un-expressed—and a pang shot through his heart.

"That is not the real reason," he said a shadow passing over his face.

"I can give no other," she said, with a deeper blush than before.

Anger began to invade the young man's heart like a bitter and poisonous vapor.

"The true reason is, that you love another," he said, with a cruel groan.

"Mr. Effingham!"

"Yes, yes; my rudeness is insulting—my plainness repulsive, I know it!" he said, bitterly. "But how can I feel my heart breaking, and not speak? You love that man!"

"Mr. Effingham, you must know "—she murmured, suffering painfully—"this is obtrusive, sir—I—"

"Oh, do not deny it, madam!" he said, giving way to his bitter and feverish emotion. "You scorn me and my love—you refuse my hand, because your heart could not go with it!"

"You agitate me, sir!" she said, "I am not well! These conversations can lead to nothing!"

"You mistake, madam!" he replied, with his old, gloomy bitterness, "they lead to despair, for I love you."

"I cannot prevent your suffering, sir—I cannot command you to leave me—if I could—"

"You would," he interposed, "you need not assure me of that, madam. You hate me—you scorn me—because you love that man who insulted me in your presence, here. Wo to him!"

And Mr. Effingham's brows grew darker, his eyes flashed with hatred.

"Remember he is my relative, sir," said Beatrice, flushing crimson.

"And your lover!"

"Mr. Effingham!"

"Oh, madam, do not cry out according to your wont. I have ruined myself for you, and naturally feel some objection to being robbed of you by a common boor."

"Sir!"

"Yes, I offend you!—make you hate me more bitterly: but for that same reason that I am lost from seeing your

fatal beauty, and have defied all the powers of this society,
I should be allowed to speak plainly, to throw aside the con-
ventional rules which I have trampled on for your sake."

" I did not wish to go to that ball—it was a cruel trial,"
she said, coldly, and pressing her hand upon her heart as she
spoke, " my father exacted it."

" You did not like your escort, I know," he replied, bitterly ; " you were too good for him, as the vulgar expression
goes."

" Mr. Effingham, this is unworthy ! "

" Yes, madam ! it is ! I know it ! But I cannot feel the
poisoned arrow in my side, like St. Sebastian, and be silent—
not cry out—not utter a groan ! Oh, may you never know
what it is to love, and that hopelessly !—to turn and toss on
your sleepless couch through the long, weary hours of the
gloomy night—to rave and curse and weep—to utter prayers
and blessings, maledictions and blasphemies ! may you never
suffer this cruel agony, which leaves the heart torn, the cheek
pale, the eyes heavy, the brain oppressed with a bitter and
poisonous mist ! may you never love, and feel that love is
hopeless ! "

And, overwhelmed with sour and gloomy emotion, he
turned away. His words went to her heart, but it was
almost her own situation which he painted, and this made
her flush and tremble. But by a great effort she became
calm again.

" You know not what you say," she murmured, " you
know your own sufferings, not mine, sir."

" Yours ! you have suffered this—"

" I have suffered much, sir."

" You have felt those pangs of despised love ? "

" Mr. Effingham, you agitate me ! you have no right to
intrude upon my privacy thus : I am not well, sir—my sufferings do not concern yourself : pray leave me."

" Whom do they concern, then, madam ? "

" Mr. Effingham ! "

" Perhaps your chivalric cousin, Mr. Waters ! "

" You make me unwell, sir ! " said the young girl, flushing. The young man understood what this exhibition of
emotion sprung from, and gnawed his lip until it bled.

" You might pardon that, if you had a little charity," he

said, bitterly; "I believe that I was the instrument in revealing your secret."

"Yes, sir—unconsciously."

"By which you mean, that no thanks are due me.'

"I mean nothing, sir."

"Well, you are right, madam. I would have cut off my right hand before I would have had any agency in revealing that."

"You are truly very friendly."

"I do not pretend to be, where my love and despair are concerned," he said, gloomily; "I had some claim upon Beatrice Hallam, the actress—I have much less on Miss Waters."

"Mr. Effingham—I cannot bear this much longer!"

"You will leave the stage?" he went on, pitilessly.

"I do not know, sir."

"You hope to?"

"I do, sir."

"What a delightful time you will have with that noble gentleman, your cavalier!" he said, with sombre irony. "In future, I see that I shall not be allowed to kiss your hand, or approach you, even."

"Oh, leave me, sir!—"

"In future, my days must be without even your frowns and insults."

"Mr. Effingham, I am suffering!"

"*You* suffering!"

"Yes, sir."

"I, thought, madam, that I monopolized the despair and agony of the whole world."

"You do not, sir."

"And because you suffer, you consider that you have the right to tear my heart. I am despised, because you suffer! I admire your logic, madam!"

"No, sir," she said, growing indignant at his insulting tone, "though much of that suffering has been caused by you."

"Because I have told you my love."

"No, sir—not that only."

"What have I done?"

"Every thing to persecute me: but I say again, that I

do not wish to remember that. I had forgotten it. Pray leave me—I am not well, and cannot bear any more agitation."

He gazed at her long and fixedly, with eyes burning yet stony, cold yet fiery.

"Beatrice," he said, in a gloomy and sombre voice, " this is the crisis of my life. This moment makes or mars me. I have given up all for you—left behind all that makes life happy to follow the ignis-fatuus of your love. If you cast me off, I am ruined—reflect."

"You make me suffer cruelly," said poor Beatrice, turning away, " but—oh, I cannot, will not marry you, sir ! —I cannot ! "

"For the last time ! " he said, taking a step toward her, with clenched hands, and grinding his teeth; "you refuse ? "

" Mr. Effingham, I—"

" You spurn my love—despise me and every thing connected with me—still scorn me ? Reflect, madam ! "

" I cannot marry you, sir. This interview is killing me My breast is—"

" For the last time—yes or no ? "

"No ! then, sir : no ! " cried Beatrice, rising, with her hand upon her heart; " I cannot, will not ! "

With one hand he tore his breast, until his nails were stained with blood—the other opened and clenched, as though in his fury he was grasping some deadly weapon. He looked at her for a moment, with rage, despair, and menace, shook from head to foot, and muttering, " Breast to breast, then ! force against force ! " rushed wildly from the room, and passed into his own, the door of which closed with a crash. A quarter of an hour afterwards the boatmen came out and went away ; and in ten minutes Mr. Effingham made his appearance, pale, and covered with perspiration.

He held in his moist and nervous hand a Bank of England note of large value ; and muttering, " That, too, can be arranged ! " went toward the room occupied by the parson.

CHAPTER LIV.

ÆGRI SOMNIA.

EVENTS hurry on. As the passions and complicated movements of the drama develope themselves, the task of the
chronicler becomes more and more difficult. We must proceed, however, to narrate, as clearly as possible, what fol
lowed the final outburst of the young man's fiery passion—
rejected finally, as we have seen, by the object of his love.

Night drew on, cold and stormy. It was one of those
evenings which succeed late autumn days, when the sun
seems to set in blood, and the vast clouds reposing on the
far horizon are tinged with that lurid light which resembles
the glare of a great conflagration. The wind rose, and
moaned, and died away, and came again, ever becoming
chiller and more mournful. The moon rose like a great
wheel of fire rolled up the sky, over which dark clouds
drifted, driven by the wind ; and the almost leafless forests
seemed to be murmuring to themselves, and whispering
some mysterious secret. The tall, gloomy pines waved like
solemn giants, in the fitful moonlight, and the oaks ground
their boughs together, or parted with their last rattling
leaves, in the stormy gusts, which ever and anon swept over
them, clattering their dry, hard branches.

In the town, every living thing soon housed itself from
the chill wind and the gloomy, fitfully-illuminated night—
and not the cold, cheerless air alone drove them to their
firesides. Those were the times when men believed in
witchcraft and every species of diablerie ; and many persons in the town could make oath that they had seen horrible, uncouth figures, celebrating awful and mysterious rites
on the wild, lonely common, near; where the pine bushes
waved like deformed spectres, throwing long shadows over
the dangerous ground. It was a night for fiends to be
abroad in, holding their wild revels beneath the frosty light
of the great solemn moon; and none cared to brave it,
when a good fire and a cup of foaming ale awaited them.
They looked round fearfully when the gust moaned by the
gables ; and told tales which dealt in terrible mysteries—in

hidden treasure—in fiends, and black dogs guarding it—and how the witches, who had tormented honest Christians, had been burned, not long before, for an example to all evil doers. It was a night to believe in such things, and they trembled at every sound — at the very grating of the branches against the window.

All that day Beatrice had been in a state of agitation and nervous fear. The interview with her father on the night before, had succeeded the trying ordeal of the ball, and then the interview with Mr. Effingham had crowned all. That interview had affected her cruelly—never had she seen the young man so torn by passion, so completely overwhelmed with emotion—never had she known him to utter such despairing cries of agony and torture. It had made her suffer deeply, and shocked her nervous system dreadfully. In addition, she had not slept for more than forty-eight hours, and nothing so prostrates the nerves as this. We cannot wonder, therefore, that the young girl was exhausted in mind and body, by these various and complicated moral and physical trials—subject to a nervous trepidation, which made her start at every noise.

She went through the duties of the day, walking as in a dream, with fixed eyes, and heaving bosom ; her agitation was so striking, that every body observed it, and questioned her about it. She made no reply to these questions—she seemed not to have heard them. Her mind was laboring with its burden of fear and agitation.

As the night drew on, she felt an indefinable dread. Seated in her room, alone, she started at every gust which sobbed around the inn, and trembled at every noise. The moonlight now streamed through the window like a flood of dark, fiery gold, then disappeared, swallowed up in the gloomy and threatening clouds, which swept over the sky toward the far, freezing ocean.

As the night passed on, and midnight approached, she fell into a sort of trance of thought. With a dreamy eye she ran over her whole life, since she had arrived in Virginia— she thought of those persecutions, of the adventure on the river, of her rescue, of that noble face, of those persecutions again, of the ball, of the strange revelation which had so changed her life.

As she thought of that strange conjunction of circum stances, her eye fell upon the volume of Shakespeare, open, from habit, on her lap. She read:

> "And pity, like a naked, new-born babe,
> Striding the blast, or heaven's cherubim, hors'd
> Upon the sightless couriers of the air,
> Shall blow the horrid deed in every eye,
> That tears shall drown the wind!"

The words seemed to apply strangely to her own case. Truly, that deed had been blown in every eye, by an acci·dent which was plainly from heaven. With dreamy eyes, she read on, and came to the passage where the usurper sees the air-drawn dagger, and feels the cold sweat of horror bathe his brow, as he attempts to clutch it. She saw him, with his stealthy tread, gliding slowly, the murderous weapon in his hand, toward the apartment where the murder was to be committed—she heard his low breathing—saw his fiery eyes—almost thought that his awful invocation to the firm earth not to hear his stealthy steps, was really uttered—that she saw the tiger stealing toward his victim with deadly caution. The scene was so clear in her marvellously vivid imagination, that she trembled; and when a bird flew against the window, started up in an agony of fright.

She sat down again, endeavoring to calm herself; the fire was burning fitfully, and she tried to make it brighter. The last sticks, however, were burning out, and the trembling blue flame licked, and struggled, and clung to the whitening embers, and went out. She did not observe it, however she was again buried in thought; and those thoughts fled to the far southern land, enveloped in such mysterious and dreamy interest. It seemed to her that the life she now embraced, with a drowsy and unsteady eye, must have been in another world—a strange, far world, which she could never go to any more forever!

Gradually her eyes closed, her head drooped on her breast, then she would start up, trembling at some noise; and then her head would droop again, the wild stormy gust would lull her, and the fitful weird light of the great, sol·emn moon, would envelope her gentle Madonna-like head in a flood of glory. At last, all her thoughts flowed into each other, merged their outlines, lost themselves in dreams, and overcome by exhaustion, the young girl slept; her head drooping on one shoulder, her long dusky lashes lying on her cheeks, her hair waving in profuse curls round the still agitated countenance.

She had a strange dream. She thought, as the second or third hour after midnight struck, or rather murmured through the silent inn—she thought that her window opened, and a man, enveloped in a cloak, stepped into the room through the opening. The dream was so real, that she thought she felt a gust of chill air blow on her. Then, this man approached her slowly, enveloped as before, in his long cloak and wide drooping hat; took her languid form in his strong arms, raising her without effort;—and passing through the window, bore her, she knew not how, to the ground. A horse stood waiting, and the man mounted, holding her still in his arms. Then they set off like the wind; and shaken by the quick movement, uttering a scream, as the chill air raised by the horse's gallop struck her person, she awoke, and found her dream a reality! What she had regarded as the mere conjuration of her excited fancy, was a terrible fact! what she had considered a mere freak of the imagination, was real, as the gloomy night through which the furious and neighing animal darted, obedient to the spur of his desperate rider! She was in the arms of a man, who wrapped her in his cloak with one hand, while he clasped her waist with the other—the bridle lying on the neck of his flying animal. In five minutes they had left the town and entered the gloomy forest.

CHAPTER LV.

THE FLIGHT AND PURSUIT.

THROUGH the gloom as through the moonlight, under the drooping boughs of the dark pine forest, as across the lonely tracts of bare, waste ground—the furious animal, driven pitilessly by his rider's spur, fled on.

Clouds of foam flew from his reeking jaws, his glossy

coat became as wet as though he had just issued from a river ; still he went on, his speed unabated.

The trees flew by—the moon came out and flooded the flying animal and his burden with its chill light, then swept beneath the clouds again ; the cold wind moaned and sobbed, —still on !

The silent cavalier only drew his hat further over his eyes, clasped the young girl's waist more' securely, wrapped more carefully in the thick cloak the tender body, which shuddered with cold in its thin dress.

That shudder passed over his own person, too, as if they were but one—had all feelings in common—but the horseman betrayed no other evidences of emotion, of life.

Once, his dark fiery eyes, glowing like coals, under his slouched hat, met her own ; once his warm breath, almost his kiss, touched her cheek ; but he did not kiss the cheek. It was only to see if her arm was rubbed against the pistols in his girdle, or the hilt of his sword.

Still on ! The blast blew chiller, the wind seemed to sob, and moan, and laugh in cruel glee at her ; the stars soaring out, looked at her with their pitiless and sorrowfully twinkling eyes, then were obscured again—still on !

She seemed still to be in a dream ; the whole affair had occurred so suddenly, that the young girl could scarcely collect her senses. When she attempted to reason calmly, the dreadful position she occupied deadened her brain, and her mind wandered. Was this not all a mere dream still ? Could it be real ? Was it not the mere fancy of her excited and agitated mind ? Could she not wake from such a horrible nightmare, and sit up ?

As the thought passed through her mind, she felt the arm around her waist cling tighter, and suddenly the animal reared, made a desperate leap, fell upon his knees, sprung up again, trembling, and fled onward faster than before. She looked back, and saw a stream, with high banks ; the current, of great width, glittered in the moon. It was a desperate leap, even for a phantom.

But she began now to collect her thoughts ; and suddenly finding her voice, said, in trembling and agitated tones : " You frighten me ! you hurt me ! Is this a dream or a dreadful reality ? You are killing me ! "

The cavalier made no reply. Beatrice burst into tears, and struggled to release herself from his arms—those arms only held her tighter. She said, moaning, that her position hurt her; the cavalier dropped the bridle on his horse's neck, and with both arms raised her, laid her, so to speak, on his breast; and thus carrying her, like a child, again plunged his spurs into the quivering sides of the flying animal, and fled faster.

The ocean breeze grew colder, the odor of water began to fill the wild, wandering air; the night grew darker and more dismal.

Nothing was heard but the quick smiting of the horse's hoofs—the far, mournful cry of a whippoorwill, and the low sighing of the wind through the solemn pines, under whose boughs the animal passed, like some phantom steed of the German mythology.

She shrunk as the boughs bent down toward her—for they seemed to be gigantic hands of fiends, stretched out to grasp and carry her away; she sobbed, and wept, and entreated, but in vain—still on !

The flying animal issued from the forest, and entered upon a wild waste, from which the James River was visible in the distance, glittering like a silver mirror in the fitful moonlight.

As the young girl caught the flash of the far waters, she suddenly felt the animal arrested by an obstacle, which threw him to one side; a loud voice came to her ears—a voice which sent a thrill through her brain—the cavalier only wrapped her closer in his cloak, and with a muttered curse, fled on. The animal seemed to scent the water, to know that it was his bourne, and with incredible speed darted on, and disappeared in a hollow, thick with pines.

That obstacle which had arrested the animal, was the body of a man; and this man had grasped the bridle, been rolled on the ground by the chest of the flying horse, and then rising, seen the whole disappear like a phantom. It was Charles Waters, and spite of the cloak, the disguise, he had recognized Beatrice and Mr. Effingham.

For a moment the young man stood motionless in the moonlight, overwhelmed with horror; then clenching his hands, he fled after them with the rapidity of a race-horse.

He now felt the advantage of his country training---his days and nights spent in hunting; his speed was scarcely less than that of the flying horse.

As he fled onward, a thousand mad thoughts passed through his mind; curses were on his lips, fire was in his heart.

He blessed God for that strange feeling he had experienced all day, that Beatrice was in danger—a feeling which had accompanied him in sleep, had waked him while night still lay upon the earth: which had driven him forth toward the town—which had led him there to rescue her!

But could he? That animal was going faster than any mortal man could. He would be too late!

Whither were they flying?

That sail-boat he had seen coming up the river, on the day before!

He clenched his hands, and his eyes glared. Still he sped on.

Yes! that was the base scheme of that coward! Yes! he had kidknapped a defenceless girl! She was in his power!

A flame seemed to pass before his eyes; he felt his brain totter: no matter—on!

The river suddenly burst upon his view:—he ran on with staggering steps, heaving bosom:—he saw figures moving on the shore in the moonlight, heard the faint neigh of a horse. He felt the eyes filling with blood—his heart throbbed with the desperate exertion, like an engine—still on!

The moon shone suddenly on the white sails of a boat, as she veered round—the water danced in the moon, and against the silver mirror; he plainly saw the figures of three men, who carried by main force, some object in their arms toward the boat.

With fiery eyes, eyes which saw nothing clearly, but through a flame, it seemed, he still sped on. His strength was exhausted—he tottered as he ran:—he staggered, still on!

They reach the boat—they embark—she is gone! He tore his hair, and uttered a sob of rage and despair.

Suddenly a dark object interposed itself between the worn-out, exhausted, overwhelmed pursuer, and the bright water illuminated by the moon. This object was the hut of Townes the boatman, and a despairing hope flashed through his breast.

He staggered toward it—seeing flame—breathing fire, he thought. A light was burning in the window—a shadow passed to and fro.

He tottered, gasping, to the door—fell against it—burst it open—caught the boatman by the shoulder, and said, almost inarticulately:

"Come!—you must!—I must have!—look there!—they are carrying her off—Miss Hallam, who sailed in your boat! —she is my cousin!—mercy!"

And staggering he would have fallen, had not the boatman caught him in his arms.

CHAPTER LVI.

ON THE RIVER.

THE boatman Townes was one of those men who understand perfectly at a single word, and act quickly. The broken exclamations of Charles Waters, told him plainly all that had occurred—he understood in an instant.

"Blast my eyes!" he cried, cramming his tarpaulin on his head, "I knowed somethin' was a-goin' on! But I didn't dream o' this! I heard them horse's hoofs, but the devil himself couldn't a' dreamed this! I'll have the craft ready in a minute! Stay here, and catch your breath, Charley, and we'll live or die together!"

With which words the boatman grasped a heavy stick, threw down another before Waters, who was nearly fainting, and rushed from the hut.

With two bounds he was at his boat, and slung off the chain which held the bark to the shore. Then with a rapid and experienced hand he caught, and tore open the sail— tied it to the gunwale, and seized his oars. Charles Waters was at his side panting, his eyes on fire, his looks fixed upon the other boat.

Obedient to oar and sail, the "Nancy" darted from the

shore, and plunged her cutwater into the silver expanse raising clouds of cold spray.

The other boat was much of the same description :—her size was greater—she was more ornate—that was all.

On fire with his terrible emotion, his eyes burning, his body trembling, Charles Waters bent to his oar like a giant : it was as much as the boatman could do to keep the craft from whirling round, so tremendous were these strokes. The boat flew.

"Look!" cried the boatman, "I can see him! It is young Mr. Effingham!"

"Yes!—don't stop!"

"Him!" cried the boatman, wonderingly.

"Yes! 'you would live and die with me!' row!"

"That will I!"

And plunging his oar into the water, the powerful boat-man sent the craft twenty feet.

The men in the other boat, plainly saw that they were pursued, and bent to their oars.

The bark groaned with its enormous mass of sail, and careened dangerously. Standing in the bow, with one arm around Beatrice, Mr. Effingham looked on gloomily. He knew very well that a deadly encounter was imminent—this encounter he both desired and dreaded :—dreaded because Charles Waters was her cousin.

The young girl tried to shrink from him.

"Oh, for pity's sake, do not carry me away!" she cried.

He only gazed bitterly at her.

"Oh, it is cruel!" she cried.

"You were cruel to me!" he muttered, hoarsely.

"They are pursuing us—they will rescue me!"

"Yes, when I am dead."

"Oh, it is Charles!" she cried.

"Yes, your excellent cousin: we shall meet soon—I see they are gaining on us!"

And Mr. Effingham drew a pistol.

"Oh, for mercy's sake!—mercy! do not fire!" exclaimed Beatrice, clinging to his arm.

"Be easy, madam," said Mr. Effingham, gloomily, "I only meant to try the lock: the sword will settle it. Row, there, row!"

And seizing an oar himself, he bent to his task with desperate energy. He dreaded the encounter more than he would acknowledge.

Beatrice kneeling and watching the boat which was pursuing them, could only pray.

That boat fled toward them like a seagull. It seemed to dart rather than move. Every stroke of the large oars whirled it onward through the foamy surges, and the mast groaned.

"We are gaining!' cried the boatman, "look!"

And he raised his hand, to indicate the position of the two vessels.

"Row! row!" cried Waters, hoarsely.

The boatman bent to his oar again. The little bark flew over the water, leaving a long track of foam, which glittered in the moonlight. Her triangular sail bent in the wind—her mast groaned—she bore on like a living thing.

The excitement of Charles Waters was terrible. His brain was on fire, his heart felt as if ice were pressed to it. That woman whom he loved more than all the world, was being torn from him by his insolent rival—who had plainly compassed her abduction by some skilful trick!—she was being borne away before his eyes! And uttering a groan of rage, he threw in a strength in his oar-strokes which seemed almost supernatural.

The boats neared—but the greater surface of sail on the foremost still made escape probable. The strength of the rowers must soon wear out at the rate they were going—then the foremost boat would leave her pursuers behind. She was already flying before the wind, and, as we have said, careening perilously.

"Oh, they will escape!—I am wearing out!" cried Waters, with a despairing groan.

"Cheerly, cheerly!" answered the boatman, "we'll give em a whack yet."

And he rowed more powerfully.

"I will throw myself into the water and die there, but I will overtake them!"

"Look!" shouted the boatman, "her mast's snapped! hurrah!"

It was true—the boat could not carry the press of sail,

14

and too well built to capsize easily, the frail mast had oroken under the press, and fallen over the side with all its mass of canvas.

The craft was no longer any thing but a wreck :—like a wounded sea-bird, whose wing has been broken by the hunts-man, she paused in her course, verred round and threatened to go down with every wave.

The pursuers darted toward her like lightning—they were now not ten yards off.

Again the foiled and infuriated young man drew his pis-tol, and this time it seemed with deadly intentions.

The barrel glittered in the moonlight as he levelled it. Then again he replaced it with a curse, and with one arm round Beatrice, as though he would die with her, awaited the approach of his pursuers.

They were but two men—yet he knew they were desper-ate.

The boat darted toward him—the sides of the small ves-sels crushed together : Charles Waters and the boatman, armed with their heavy clubs, threw themselves from their own into Mr. Effingham's craft.

"You come to your death !" cried the furious young man, rushing toward Charles Waters, "woe to you !"

His foot caught in the sail which cumbered the gunwale, and he half fell.

Beatrice rushed toward her cousin, and he caught her in his arms. At the same moment Townes levelled the fore-most waterman with his club : the other grappled with him, and endeavored to plunge a knife into his side.

Mr. Effingham rose overwhelmed with fury. His blood boiled with rage—he was in one of his madnesses of passion.

He saw only that one sight before him—Beatrice clasped in the arms of his hated, abhorred rival. He only under-stood that that rival had defeated him, despised him.

The blood rushed to his head—he staggered, and draw-ing his pistol, levelled it at Charles Waters' breast, and fired.

A sudden careening of the boat deranged his aim, and the ball, drawing blood from Beatrice's shoulder, struck the waterman Junks, just as he had nearly strangled Townes, and had lifted his knife to stab him.

That sudden careening of the boat, saved the .ife of Charles Waters and his friend.

" Oh ! you've got it ! blast you ! " cried Townes, as his adversary fell.

Mr. Effingham saw all : he saw his two companions dis abled—he saw himself left alone to contend against his enemies—he saw that all was lost.

One thing remained—revenge ! And as Charles Waters seeing him rise sword in hand, raised his arm, protecting Beatrice with the other, the infuriated young man plunged the weapon into his breast.

Waters fell backward, dragging down Beatrice who had fainted. The sword snapped off in his body within six inches of the hilt—only the hilt and the stump remained in Mr. Effingham's hand.

With a wild cry the boatman, Townes, threw himself on his knees beside his friend, and, crying like a child, sought to stanch the blood.

" No—do not—mind me ! " said Charles Waters, faintly, and turning deadly pale as he spoke, " attend to —— Beatrice ! "

And drawing the blade from his breast with a desperate effort he fell back.

The boatman tore his hair with both hands, and wept until he was worn out. Suddenly he started up—woe ! to that man ! He was alone on the boat, with the wounded and dying.

A hundred yards from the boat, he saw the young man swimming desperately toward the shore. Exhausted, overwhelmed with horror, the boatman sunk back and fell, his head striking heavily against the side of the boat.

CHAPTER LVII.

THE FATHER AND SON.

MR. EFFINGHAM, uttering a wild ourse, had thrown himself into the water as Charles Waters fell, and still holding the stump of the bloody sword, had struck out toward the shore.

At one moment he determined to make no effort to reach the shore, to let the dark waves ingulf him—but nature prevailed. Still grasping madly the weapon, he swam toward the bank, and issued from the water near the point from which he had started.

His horse was grazing where he had left him, and came whinnying to him.

He mounted, and plunging the broken sword into the scabbard, looked over his shoulder.

There was the bark upon which the mortal encounter had just taken place—a dark object upon the silvery expanse.

He turned from it gloomily.

Where should he go?

He looked around him from side to side, and shook his head. That was a hard question. But one thing he knew —that he would not stay there to be devoured with rage and despair.

Motion! motion! and striking his spur into the animal's side so cruelly, that it neighed with pain, he set forward furiously, his hair streaming in the wind—his lips writhing —his eyes glaring with despair.

All was thenceforth lost to him—he was lost!—his infatuation for that diabolical angel had ended, as he predicted, in a terrible crash, which shook the props of his whole life! But at least he had no longer that rival.

Every noise startled him—he trembled at the moaning of the wind—shook at the fitful shadows:—the moon seemed to grow pale, the stars to fade. Still the wild animal fled on—the bridle on his neck—his sides reeking with sweat.

The young man knew nothing of the road he was taking:—he did not see that the animal, with a strange instinct, had followed the road to the hall, avoiding the town.

Still on! more desperately, still he urged the flying horse with his spur—he tried to outrun his thoughts in vain. They pursued him like ferocious bloodhounds, and caught him with their sharp teeth, and tore him!

The sobbing, panting animal bounded onward wildly— passed mile after mile, and entered the forest stretching around the hall, just as the first streak of dawn reddened in the east.

The young man raised his head and looked around.

"This place is familiar to me," he muttered, "it is home!"

And he groaned.

The poor moaning animal halted in front of the great portico; and, panting, covered with sweat, foaming at the mouth, stood still. Mr. Effingham dismounted and passed his hand over his neck—the affection of that animal was grateful.

Suddenly a voice startled him and he turned round. It was a negro just risen, and his face expressed the greatest delight at seeing his master back. Mr. Effingham gave him his hand—ordered him to attend to his horse—and then, scarcely knowing what he did, entered the hall, sombre, and moving slowly.

He sat down in the library, where a fire had just been kindled, for the squire was accustomed to rise very early: and looking round, took note of all the familiar household objects, which he had not seen for so long—years, it seemed to him.

There was the squire's writing-table covered with papers, and ears of corn, and specimen apples, and large heads of wheat. There was the plain leather-bottomed chair with the marks of powder on the carved back, where the old gentleman's head had rested. There was the book-case half open—the "Gazette" lay on a chair—Willie's new whip was on the floor. There was his mother's portrait over the fire-place:—he turned from it with a groan. There was little Kate's embroidery now finished, and converted into a screen:—he looked away from that too. And the shadow on his brow grew deeper:—his pale lips writhed.

A step behind him, startled him, and he rose. The squire stood before him.

The old gentleman's pride was all broken in his heart, by the sight of his long lost son; and he would have grasped his hand hard: but Mr. Effingham drew back.

"No sir," he said, hoarsely, "do not touch that hand: there is blood on it!"

"Blood!" echoed the horrified squire, with wide distended eyes.

"Blood!—the blood of a man: perhaps that of a woman too."

And the shadow in the dark eyes grew deeper.

The squire fell into a chair overwhelmed with this an
nouncement: he could not speak at first. At last he re
gained his voice, and said, with a gasp:

"Blood? whose blood?"

"A rival's."

"Who?"

"Mr. Charles Waters."

The old man groaned.

"That woman!—that woman!" he said, in a low voice,
which trembled piteously.

"Yes, sir, that woman!" replied his son, with eyes which
resembled nothing human, "you were right in warning me
against her. She has ruined me—I am lost!"

The squire could not reply:

"I have committed a murder, sir," continued Mr. Effing.
ham,—"see, my sword is still bloody, I believe—"

And drawing from the scabbard the stump of the weapon, on which some drops of clotted blood still hung, he
threw it on the floor before the old man.

"A murder?" cried the squire, turning deadly pale.

"Well, sir—no: not an assassination, for his arm was
raised to strike me, and he was not alone—"

"Thank God!—I am spared that'" groaned the old
man.

"But it is scarcely better," said the young man, in the
same tone of gloomy calmness, "I carried off a woman, sir:
that woman, whom you rightly dreaded so:—yes, she has
been my evil genius—my fate! I loved and hated her—I
was mad! But this is from the purpose. I carried her off
—was pursued—first on land—then on the water—we were
attacked—my associates in the diabolical affair were both dis-
abled, one of them by myself, one by his adversary—then I
plunged my sword into my enemy's heart, having first tried
to kill him with my pistol. thinking, from a stumble I made,
that he would strike me unprepared. That is it, sir."

And looking at the squire with lurid eyes, the young
man paused.

"I believe the ball wounded the woman," he added,
hoarsely.

"But thank God, you did not kill in cold blood!" cried

his father, "it was while your blood was hot, and in a strug-gle. My poor son! how fatally this has ended!"

And the squire covered his face.

"Yes, sir—ruin has been the end for me :—henceforth, I am lost. As I shall probably be wanted by the officers of the law some time to-day, I think that we had better decide upon something."

"Yes—yes!" cried the squire, starting up, "you are right! The officers of the law arrest you!—my son!"

And the old man, with some of his youthful heat, flushed to the temples.

"The middle age is past," said Mr. Effingham, with the same sombre calmness; "we cannot drop the portcullis, and from our castle bid defiance to all foes."

The squire fell into his seat again.

"There is one way which ends all, and well ends it," continued the young man, with the calmness of incipient madness; "I have another pistol—if the water has not wet-ted the powder."

And he drew it from his belt. The squire wrested it, with a groan, from his hand.

"Well, sir—you are right. I feel that this is the act of a coward. I have no intention of committing suicide :— what remains?"

"To the continent!—Oh, you can go to Europe."

"I'm tired of it, sir."

"But Virginia—you cannot remain in Virginia."

"True."

"The paper, there!—see what vessel sails, and when Perhaps one goes from York, or Norfolk, this very week."

And the squire seized the paper: the first words he read, were:

"On Saturday, the 21st, will sail from the port of York, for Amsterdam, *via* Liverpool, the bark CHARMING SALLY, Capt. Fellowes—"

"That is to-morrow! Oh, go in this vessel!" cried the agitated squire, losing all his pride, and melting at the sight of the pale and disfigured features of his son.

"Well, sir—that will suit me as well as any thing else."

"I will send off a servant to engage your passage in the

ship, instantly—Cato will understand :—he is as secret as
night : instantly !"

And the squire hastened out.

Mr. Effingham sat down again with the same stony calmness :—that calmness would not have pleased a physician.
He was in that state of despair which deadens the nerves.

Suddenly a light step came down the stairs—Kate entered—saw him—ran to him, and with a face radiant with
joy, threw her arms round his neck, and pressed her cheek
to his own.   Then, as a sequel to all this, she burst out crying, from pure delight.

Mr. Effingham removed the arms, and rose :—she shrunk
back, frightened at his expression—it was terrible.

" Oh, cousin, Champ !" she cried, " you won't drive me
from you !"

He was silent.

" Oh ! you are not angry at me, for ——, oh ! you make
me feel so badly !"

And she sobbed.

"I cannot talk to you now—I cannot kiss you—I am
not angry with you—" he said.

And muttering to himself, he went his way to the chamber, which he had occupied before leaving the hall, and disappeared at the turn of the great staircase from Kate's eyes.
The child sat down, and wept piteously.

The day drew on, and still the young man remained in
his chamber.   Miss Alethea passed in and out, making pre-
parations for him, and her face was observed to be bathed
in tears.   The squire shut himself up in his library, and
only once came out to ascend to Mr. Effingham's chamber.

About noon a visitor in a military dress, and with a countenance convulsed with passion, came to the Hall, and was
closeted for an hour with the old man in the library, from
which were heard high voices, " parbleus !" and exclamations.   Finally the voices moderated, and the visitor, still
much moved, but more calm, came out and rode away.

The squire went to the young man's room, and told him
that the brother of Charles Waters—Captain Ralph Waters,
had just come and informed him, that his brother was not
dead—though he was despaired of—and the young woman
scarcely at all injured.   A flush greeted this information
then a sombre frown.

" Was there no challenge left for me," he asked.

" By Captain Waters ? "

" Yes, sir."

" None."

And the squire, to avoid further embarrassing questions, went out. The Captain had come to take Mr. Effingham's life in return for his brother's—simply and purely—and he would have " left a challenge," had the squire not made him change his mind. How this was effected must remain a mystery.

The night drew on cold and gloomy, and Mr. Effingham was to set out for York soon after midnight. He and the squire sat up talking, for neither could sleep. No persons were present but themselves, and we know nothing of that conversation.

About two o'clock, when a chill wind had arisen and moaned round the gables, Cato came and reported the horses ready, and took his master's baggage.

Mr. Effingham then wrapped himself in his cloak; buckled on a new sword, calmly, and went out.

As he entered the passage he was approached by a small figure clad in white. This was Kate, who was in her night-clothes, and who pressed with her bare feet the chill polished oak of the floor.

" Oh, cousin Champ ! " she sobbed, " please don't go without kissing me ! They made me go to bed, but I couldn't sleep, for you were going. Oh, don't go away feeling angry with me. Please kiss me ! "

The hard heart was overcome : he stooped down and took the child in his arms, and pressing her to his breast, two large bitter tears rolled down his pale thin cheeks. Then hastily kissing her, he again wrapped his cloak around him and passed on.

In fifteen minutes he was in the saddle.

The wild wandering wind sobbed mournfully around the lofty gables and through the pines.

This was the sound which greeted Mr. Effingham as he turned his back upon the Hall, and rode forth into the cold, gloomy night.

CHAPTER LVIII

THE AUTHOR OF THE MS. SPEAKS.

" HERE let us pause," says the author of the manuscript from which these scenes are taken, " and looking back on the current of events which we have seen flow on through light and shadow, endeavor to extract briefly their significance.

" In the history of my respected ancestor, Champ Effingham, Esq., I think I discern something which reminds me of an Eastern fable I have met with. The enemy of Humanity, the tale relates, came and found the first man sleeping calmly under the palms of paradise : and gazing long at him, endeavoured to find some weak point of attack. But the lordly face of the sleeper made him groan with rage and disappointment. He saw the brows made to conceive pure and noble thoughts—the chiselled lips shaped to express those thoughts, and utter prayer. He saw the strong arm, with its iron muscles, moulded wondrously to strike and overthrow wrong, should wrong trench upon the fair fields it cultivated :—all repelled the enemy. At last he observed the movement of the sleeper's heart, and kneeling down, tapped upon it with his finger. It sounded hollow, and the enemy smiled, as only fiends smile.

" ' Here is a cavity ! ' he muttered ; ' I will fill it with passions ! '

" And, leaving the sleeper writhing in his slumbers, the enemy of souls disappeared.

" My worthy ancestor, Mr. Effingham, seems to have afforded proof that this fable is not wholly fanciful. His passions were so strong that he was led by them to the commission of actions which he often regarded with wondering disgust in after years :—that infatuated young man whose acts he recollected, scarcely seemed to be himself. His mad passion for the young girl had changed his whole character. Chivalrous and noble, it made him persecute a woman, and exhaust the depths of bitterness and weakness. Sweet-tempered and affectionate, under all his languid and satirical indifference, if the phrase may be used, his character was changed by that infatuation into one of sour and bitter scoffing and mocking sarcasm. Careless of the prejudices of rank, and disposed to treat all men with cordiality and kindness, it made him taunt with low birth the rival who supplanted him. Venerating his father, it led him to write to that father a letter of cold defiance—and lastly, it made him commit an action which madness alone excuses—the forcible abduction of an unoffending girl :—and his wild, turbulent, mad career, was wound up by an attempt to take th life of a man whose only crime was love for that woman who had driven him mad.

" Mr. Effingham was a true descendant of the man tempted by the fiend, and filled with passion.

" But then we may observe in this career equal proof of what Mr. Charles Waters had said to the man in the red cloak—that the human heart is not radically false and hateful, but suffers for the crimes it is led by passion to commit, cruelly; and ever strives to disentangle itself from the meshes of that fiery net which is bound around it by fate.

" In the midst of all his delinquency—when he was persecuting the young woman—defying society and his family, uttering unworthy and insulting words to his rival—carrying off Beatrice—striking at the heart of her defender :—all this time, remorse and sombre rage with himself burned in his agitated heart like fire. We have traced some of the scenes in his lonely chamber, in which these stormy emotions were bared to his own consciousness, even in words—and we have seen on one occasion, that the fury of his suffering and remorse nearly led him to self-destruction. We have seen how on that occasion he caught the child to his heart, and called her his guardian angel and blessed her :—at that moment his good impulses were strong, and had not the words of his friend revived the slumbering passion in his heart, many of the events herein narrated would never have occurred.

" Even in the midst of his most furious rages—when he tried to persuade himself that he was the victim of cruel injustice and unjustifiable scorn, his heart still whispered to him that he was the wrong-doer ; and in that night and day after the river-fight, his remorse grew to a climax. We have seen how he was touched by the affection of an animal, how he mingled his tears with those of the child when she bade him farewell. Those tears were not unmanly ones, and are pleasanter to think of now, to me at least, than all his fearless acts, his scornful defiances cast in the teeth of the universe.

"I have not space to speak further of those other personages who were grouped around my ancestor, the central figure of them all, and attracting to his splendid and fiery graces, his wild passions, every eye : Beatrice—pure and lovely creature ! whose portrait I have vainly striven to delineate, must be passed by : and Charles Waters, too ; the pure thinker. In after pages of this history I shall endeavour to develop further those feelings which, so much more than mere events, enter into the lives of my personages."

CHAPTER LIX.

TWO SCENES ON A WINTER NIGHT.

THE writer, after these moral reflections, which we have transcribed for the benefit of our readers, goes on to narrate how, after the fight upon the river, the two watermen leaped into the "Nancy," and without exchanging compliments, excuses, or regrets, ran off with that craft ; even Junks with a bad wound in his arm, rowing as if the officers of the law were already on his track :—further, he goes on to tell how Charles Waters, by his own request, was borne to his father's : —how Beatrice, stanching her bleeding arm, would not leave him :—how the old man wept and sobbed as he met his dying son :—how the Chevalier La Rivière, otherwise Captain Ralph Waters, uttered furious " morbleus !" and threats, and tore his moustache :—and how, day by day, nursed by the tender hand of Beatrice, the young man's wound in the shoulder-blade grew gradually better, and his deadly pallor changed more and more to the hue of health : —all this is related by the worthy writer of the MS., at considerable length.

It is not necessary to dwell upon these scenes : the reader, no doubt, will be able to understand all that is necessary

without the aid of the chronicler. Let us pass over a
month, and on a winter night enter the plain and simple, but
cheerful and comfortable mansion of the old fisherman, and
see what the inmates are engaged in.

The apartment is the one which we have already entered
several times, and a cheerful fire is burning in the wide,
rude fireplace. Two stones serve the purpose of andirons,
and a hook stands out prominently from the great cross-
beam. The light of the fire fills the room, bathing in its
full rich flood of warmth and brightness the nets, the fishing rods, the brown rafters overhead with their strings of
onions and bacon flitches ; and these humble objects take a
glory from the brilliant light, and seem to laugh and move
about as the flame rises and falls, in a sort of ecstasy.

In one corner of the great chimney sits old John Waters with his venerable gray head bent down, his face bright
with its habitual smile of simple good-nature and kindliness.
The old man occupies the chair of state, which is woven
into a species of basket-work and softly cushioned—the work
of Charles. He wears his ordinary dress of fustian; his
stockings are of woollen, and his huge shoes are decorated
with huge buckles. His gray hair is tied in a queue behind,
and in his hard, bony hand the old man holds a corn-cob
pipe, which he replenishes from time to time by inserting
his fingers into the ample pocket of his long waistcoat, and
then thrusting the bowl into the ashes, from which it re
appears crowned with a burning coal, and sending up clouds
of fragrant smoke.

Opposite, and crouching on his stool, sits Lanky, the cart-
boy, who seems to be eternally protesting against something.
for he shakes his head from north-east to south-west inces
santly, and gazes into the fire with a profundity which would
have delighted Newton. Lanky is clad in a pair of orna-
mental woollen stockings, and has enormous feet, which oc-
casionally are stretched out toward the blaze, then withdrawn, as the warmth penetrates too feelingly into his shins :
—his short clothes are of leather, and are much soiled—his
waistcoat is tattered and torn, and the pockets are stuffed
with whip-lashes, nails, and iron rings, apparently the debris
of some defunct harness;—his coat has lost a portion of
the skirt. Lanky has been working all day—has been with

the cart of fish and vegetables to Williamsburg; and now
like an honest fellow with an excellent conscience takes his
ease on his stool, and munches when the hunger fit seizes
him, his bread and bacon, and, as we have said, carries on
that silent protest against something or somebody, with his
head, which closely resembles a pine knot.

Immediately in front of the cheerful fire, and seated
close to the rude pine table, Townes, the boatman, and the
Chevalier La Rivière—or, dropping this nom-de-guerre, Captain Ralph Waters—occupying themselves with a sheet of
paper, lying on the rough board, on which the Captain has
traced a diagram, the lines of which are something less than
an inch in breadth. Townes is clad in his usual dress, half
sailor, half farmer, whole boatman. The Captain is resplendent in the fine military suit which we have seen Mr.
Effingham dressed in, and his long sword lies by him on a
settee. His moustaches are longer and blacker than ever;
his eye more laughing, his voice louder, his "parbleus!"
more emphatic, as he explains the diagram of the battle of
Rosbach to the boatman.

"Faith! there it is!" says the Captain, twirling his
moustache, and making a dig at the paper with his broad-
nibbed goosequill, "there is the river Saal—these dots here
represent Marshal Soubise's forces, opposite the head-quar-
ters of the great Frederic; and here, at this line, Prince
Hildbourghausen had posted himself."

"Hill—who?" asks Townes, scratching his head, "talk
it out plainer, Captain."

"Hildbourghausen!" says the soldier, laughing; "faith!
that is nothing to some of the jaw-breakers I have been
compelled, for my sins, to pronounce, *mon ami!*"

"Hell—bug—housen," says the boatman, in a low, med-
itative tone, "now I've got it!"

"Well, here was the river—we crossed on the 5th of
November, all colors flying—a glorious day, and a glorious
set of devils to fight it out—though I say it. I can't go
over the battle—but fifty thousand mounseers bit the dust,
or were taken:—see, here was my share."

And opening his coat, the soldier showed a deep scar on
his breast.

"A bayonet did it—but I ran the fellow through for it,

and the great Frederic made me a captain. What a beast
he was !—And morbleu ! what a leader !"

"Well, now, seems to me," says Townes, "them things
don't pay. Is scars all you get in the wars, Captain
Ralph ?"

"No, I'm indifferent rich."

"Really, now."

"Yes."

"How did you get the pistoles together ?"

"They were not pistoles, *mon ami*—they were florins and
guilders," says the Captain, with a strange, wistful smile
which is a pleasant sight to look upon.

"Guilders ?—I have seen some of that coin," says old
John Waters, cheerfully, "come tell us, my son, something
more of your doin's than you have done."

The Captain pauses for a moment, and passes his hand
over his eyes dreamily: then he raises his fine head, and
says, manfully :

"Very well, *bon père* : ten words, more or less, will do
that. You know that when I was eighteen, and had an indifferent smooth face, I ran away—half with your knowledge,
half without—"

"You were not a bad son," says the old man, pleasantly.

"No, I believe not. Well, I got to Europe, found that
I must starve or enlist, and having a natural turn for eating
heartily, and an intense aversion to starving, at once accepted
his gracious and serene majesty's shilling. We were shipped
at once to the Continent, and under the Great Frederic, the
Protestant champion, as we called him, fought like a parcel
of honest English dogs, every time we could meet with the
mounseers, who were equally the enemies of Prussia and
England.

"Very well, I knocked about—got a wound at Rosbach,
also my Captaincy—had a public compliment paid me after
Lissa—a devil of a fight, comrade !—and at Glatz had the
misfortune to be taken prisoner, as I was about to run my
hanger through a fellow all bedizened with lace—a Colonel,
at the very least. I mention the great pitched battles—the
skirmishes, countermarches, night-encounters, here, there,
every where, are understood. Well, I was taken after Glatz
—Glatz was in '59, mark you—to a little town in the inte-

rior, where a fort was held by the troops of his Gracious
Majesty, the King of France—in the Rhine-land.   There I
became no longer a bachelor."

With which words, the wistful expression again passed
over the soldier's face.

" She was a soft, bright-eyed girl—I don't know how I
ever came to love her," he murmured; " she was a good wife
to me, and having sold my commission at her earnest request,
I lived in that little town for two whole years—or there-
abouts.   She was a tender heart—my poor Katrina."

And the Captain frowns, to conceal his emotion.

" Married, my son—you ain't a-tellin' me you were married ? " says the old man.

" Yes, yes," says the soldier, raising his martial face
with a sigh.   " I married and lost my wife—all within two
short years."

There is a silence.

" Poor thing: she loved me devotedly, and left her whole
fortune to me.   What did I want with it, when she was
gone ?—well, well, the money amounted to some fifteen or
twenty thousand pounds English coin, and that is what I
have."

" Twenty thousand pounds ! " ejaculates Townes, with
astonishment.

" Yes, yes," adds the soldier, " but in spite of the fine
fortune—a great fortune for a poor soldier, her death nearly
unmanned me !   She was a good girl ! "

And with dreamy eyes the Captain twirls his moustache,
and sighs.   His auditors are silent.

" After that," he continues, " I found myself no longer
fit for peace—the void in my heart, friends, called for war.
How could I live there, looking on all those objects she had
looked at with me ?· No, no !   I could not, and I buckled on
my sword again.   Ah, *mon ami !* ah, *bon père! vous ne
savez*—bah ! English is the best !   Well, well ! I went back
again to the camp, did my duty, they said—got some more
wounds—and slowly my good spirits came back to me !—She
was a good wife !—she is in heaven !—"

" And you came away when the war ended, Captain ? "
says Townes, " for I hearn tell somethin' 'bout the peace o
Fontybull ! "

" Fontainbleau, *mon ami*—yes, I threw up my commission then—turned my back on camps, and as my heart began to grow strong again, it turned toward old Virginia here. I got into the first ship, leaving my gold in London there—and came over. The sea voyage set me up again—that, with the fighting, and here I am as fresh and hearty as a lion."

With which words the Captain looks with great affection at old Waters, and seeing that Lanky is nodding, stirs that gentleman up with his foot. Lanky starts and looks around in utter and profound astonishment—at which comical expression the boatman laughs, and Captain Ralph goes on with his adventures.

Let us now pass through the door directly in the rear of the astonished Lanky, and look around us. The apartment is wholly different from the one which we have just left: it is smaller and neater. The fireplace is surmounted by a tall mantel-piece, upon which are ranged a number of old volumes, and in the recess to the right, some neatly-constructed shelves are covered with more books, and a great number of papers—chiefly old copies of the " Virginia Gazette." Immediately beneath this bookcase, if we may call it such, stands a small table covered with sheets of paper, some of which have been written upon, while others contain geometrical diagrams. A little window, with very small panes of thick, bluish glass, opens on the river, sleeping in the chill winter moon. In one corner of the room, a low narrow bed is seen—in the corner opposite, a partition juts out, indicating that a narrow staircase leads from without, to the two small rooms above.

Before the fire, which sings and murmurs cheerfully, are seated Charles Waters, and on another, but lower chair, Beatrice. He is very pale, and his cheeks are thinner than their wont; but his clear eye is as full as ever of frank truth; his sad smile as sweet.

Beatrice is radiant with that tender and childlike beauty which characterizes her; and as she sews and talks in a low tone, when he is not reading to her, she raises her large melting eyes to his face, with a look exquisitely soft and loving. Both are clad very simply.

There is for a time silence in the small cheerful room, which, with its homespun carpet, and rude shelves and ruder rafters, is yet extremely neat and cheerful, and home-like. The voices of the interlocutors in the next room come to them indistinctly.

The words, " She was a good wife ! " however, are heard plainly : and Beatrice raises her tender eyes.

He smiles faintly.

"Ralph is telling some of his adventures," he says, " but they cannot be more singular than those which we have passed through."

And his eye dwells with great tenderness on the gentle, girlish face.

" Oh ! how strange—yes, how very strange ! "—she murmurs, gazing into the fire : " it seems to me almost like a dream."

"It is a bright reality, which has restored you to us," he replies, taking the little hand.

" Yes—yes."

And her head droops, quietly. The round rosy neck is half illuminated, half shadowed, by the fitful firelight; and the curls seem to nestle closer : the face is plain, and a dewy glance trembles from the eyes.

" After so many wanderings, so many singular experiences, such rude contact with the world, and all sorts of people—ah ! to see you here at last, it is strange indeed."

" Yes—yes—but he was very kind to me : " she murmurs.

" He was a kind-hearted man, and loved you, Beatrice : I do not know whether he made any exertion or not to find us and restore you—and I do not attach very great blame to him. Ah ! had I found you, I should have hesitated long before parting with you."

And the thin hand plays gently with her own.

" He was very kind to me," she repeats, in a low tone, " and that last interview with him in this room was very trying. You remember, Charles, how bitterly he complained, at first, that I would not return to Europe with him—"

" You could not."

" No, I could not ! and yet I felt very deeply the sepa-

ration : I told him so, you know, and thanked him for all
his fondness and kindness, to poor Beatrice Hallam, his
daughter for so long:—and so you know he relented, and
shed some tears, and took me in his arms, and said he did not
blame me—that I was right—that blood was the strongest,
after all :—and so he blessed me and kissed me, and now
he is far away on the sea, sailing for the old world."

With which words Beatrice droops lower, her hair covers
her face, she weeps in silence.

He looks at her with inexpressible affection, and caresses
with his pale hand the tender head. She raises her face,
and he sees the tears.

" Weeping, dear ! " he says.

" I cannot help crying a little, thinking of him," she
murmurs.

" But, they are not bitter tears."

" Oh, no ! "

" You do not regret your determination ? "

" Oh, no—no ! "

And she looks at him with so much love, that his heart
throbs, and his pale cheek is for a moment reddened, as if
the flush of some golden autumn sunset bathed it.

" You do not complain of having to leave all that brilliant life ? " he says.

" I thank God, that I was permitted to abandon it."

" For our poor house, here—ah, it is very poor."

" But I have you—and uncle—and— "

The weak voice gives way.

" And we have you—" he murmurs, holding out his
arms with an expression of pride and joy, which illuminates
his countenance like a glory.

In a moment she is in his arms—pressed to his breast,
sobbing and weeping, and nestling close to his bosom. She
will be his dear wife, she says—she has promised that she
will forget all for him in future—never grieve—she is not
grieving now, her tears are tears of joy, she feels that God
has been very good to her, and she is happy.

And the red firelight lingers lovingly upon them, heart
to heart, cheek pressed to cheek : the moonlight struggles
to come in and share their joy :—the room is still and holy.
And from the adjoining room, come cheerful voices soon,

and merry laughter, and the loud camp-expletives of Captain Ralph. Then the voices moderate, the soldier's tone is lower, he has gone back to his happy days : and as they listen, the gentle head resting confidingly on his bosom, those low words are heard again, and echo in their hearts :

"**Yes,** comrade—a good wife !"

www.ingramcontent.com/pod-product-compliance
Lightning Source LLC
Chambersburg PA
CBHW060531030726
47498CB00004B/1151